kiss the bride

Also available from
Lucy Kevin
and Harlequin HQN

SAY I DO

LUCY KEVIN

kiss the bride

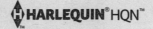
HARLEQUIN® HQN™

ISBN-13: 978-0-373-77902-4

KISS THE BRIDE

Copyright © 2014 by Harlequin Books S.A.

The publisher acknowledges the copyright holder of the individual works as follows:

THE WEDDING DRESS
Copyright © 2012 by Oak Press, LLC.

THE WEDDING KISS
Copyright © 2012 by Oak Press, LLC.

SPARKS FLY
Copyright © 2011 by Oak Press, LLC.

Recycling programs for this product may not exist in your area.

Printed in U.S.A.

CONTENTS

Dear Reader,

I've always found weddings to be incredibly romantic. The dresses, the decorations … and, of course, the bride and groom's first kiss after saying "I do."

Anne, Rose and Angelina each have a special connection to The Rose Chalet, a fictional one-stop wedding venue in the San Francisco Bay Area. With romance surrounding them all on a daily basis, it's easy to get swept up in the magic of falling in love. Of course, true love often appears in the most unexpected ways and the most unexpected times. …

I hope you are able to find a quiet corner to curl up in to enjoy reading the three love stories in *Kiss the Bride*. I would love to hear from you! Please contact me at www.lucykevin.com.

Happy ever after,

Lucy Kevin

THE WEDDING DRESS

CHAPTER ONE

DESPITE THE DOWNPOUR, Anne Farleigh looked like an angel as she hurried up the walk to her front door.

A very wet angel.

But even soaked to the skin, with her long hair and dress both utterly drenched, she was beautiful.

Gareth Cavendish had been waiting in the rain in front of her house for the past hour—enough time to make some calculated guesses about the woman who lived in the old-fashioned but obviously well-cared-for home. For starters, there was a white picket fence running around it. Gareth didn't know many people who actually had white picket fences, but it spoke to him of a family that had lived there happily for a long time.

Of course looks could be deceiving, as the contents of the envelope in his jacket pocket proved.

The case was straightforward. Jasmine Turner, a twenty-one-year-old woman from Oregon, wanted to track down the father who had abandoned her and her mother. She'd hired Richard Wells's law firm to represent her.

Since leaving the police force six months earlier and starting Cavendish Investigations, Gareth had worked several private cases for Richard. Most, unfortunately, involved cheating spouses. The Farleigh case, however, came with a large potential bonus: if Jasmine won her case and was awarded half of her biological father's estate, Gareth would end up with an additional payday—enough to keep his new private practice comfortably afloat.

As Anne moved closer to the front of the house, Gareth saw that she was smiling. How, he wondered, could someone be that happy about being caught in the rain?

Even more peculiar was the fact that when she finally spotted him standing in the rain by her front porch she didn't seem at all suspicious. Instead, she smiled directly at him, stunning him for a moment.

"Hello," she called out. "Are you looking for someone?"

Quickly regrouping, he asked, "Are you Anne Farleigh?"

She nodded and sent another of those pretty smiles his way. He moved up onto her covered porch and was about to reach into his jacket for the envelope when he looked into her eyes and stopped cold.

Her eyes were the most incredible shade of blue, like the ocean on a perfectly sunny day. Even in the middle of a rainstorm, the way she was looking at him warmed him through.

Gareth needed to serve her and get out of there. Yet, in spite of the rain and the situation, he wasn't in a hurry to leave.

Not with such a lovely woman standing in front of him.

He pushed the thought away as he finally grabbed the envelope and held it out to her. "This is for you."

She took the envelope, opening it with the obvious excitement of someone expecting a pleasant surprise.

While she took out the legal papers, he realized she was close enough for him to smell the sweet floral scent of her perfume.

She finished reading and held out the envelope to him. "You've made a mistake. You have the wrong person."

"Your parents were Edward and Chloe Farleigh?"

Anne nodded. "Yes, but—"

"Then I'm afraid there hasn't been any mistake. I'm here to serve you with papers relating to your father's other daughter."

Anne shook her head sharply. "No, I'm sorry. You've got this all horribly wrong. My father didn't have another daughter. It's just me."

"He did have another daughter, Ms. Farleigh. Her name is Jasmine Turner. She is his biological daughter as a result of a relationship he had with Deirdre Turner twenty-two years ago." Even though Gareth couldn't help but feel bad for blindsiding her with the news, he had to do his job. "This is official legal notice that you're being sued for a share of your father's estate."

People never reacted well to being told that they were being sued, and he knew what to expect. Anger, disbelief, shock, dismay and then resentment.

What he wasn't expecting was that Anne would simply push the envelope back into his hand, letting go so that he had to either catch it or let it fall into the puddle gathering on the porch at his feet.

"I'm sorry, Mr.—"

"Cavendish. Gareth Cavendish. And you can't just give me back these papers. You've been legally served with them now."

"While I don't understand how a mix-up like this

could happen, I do know that you've served these papers to the wrong person, because my father would never have done something like this."

She said it perfectly pleasantly, even a bit apologetically, as if she was sorry Gareth had wasted his time. Underlying her every word was a certainty that told him she wasn't going to budge from her position. With that, she put her key in the lock of her front door.

"Ms. Farleigh," he said again, "I'm certain there hasn't been a mistake."

"And I'm certain there has been. Good night."

She stepped through the door and shut it behind her.

CHAPTER TWO

ANNE'S HOME WAS full of happy memories—from the knickknacks collected by her mother, to the old photographs on the walls. She had made a few changes over the years since her parents' deaths, but had kept it bright and happy, with hints of its classic past. Most of the furniture in her bedroom, for example, consisted of antique pieces she'd inherited, such as the large four-poster bed that had been her parents', and the old chest of drawers with the scuff marks at the bottom from where her tiny feet had kicked it when she'd been a toddler.

She took off her wet clothes and stepped into the warm shower, smiling as she thought about how lovely Tyce's concert at The Rose Chalet had been…and how sweet it was that he and Whitney had finally declared their love for each other. She'd much rather think about her friends than the man—albeit a very handsome man—who had come to deliver those legal papers to her a few minutes ago.

She appreciated good-looking men just as much as the next woman, but her reaction to this one had been out of the ordinary. Probably, she decided as she dried off and dressed, because he seemed to be the perfect combination of rugged and gentle. His dark hair had curled a little too long over his collar, and every part of him had been big and strong, from his shoulders to his hands. She'd felt as if she could stare into his dark eyes for hours.

Anne headed downstairs a few minutes later, wearing a favorite long-sleeved dress of her mother's to which she'd made a few small alterations to fit her slightly smaller figure. A few half-finished dress designs were strewn across the dining room table. As a dress designer, working at The Rose Chalet kept her very busy, not just with wedding dresses but also with designs for the bridesmaids and flower girls.

She went to the sink to fill her kettle with water to make a cup of tea but ended up stopping with her hand halfway to the faucet. Gareth Cavendish was still standing out in front of her house in the pouring rain.

Had he been there all this time that she'd been getting dry and warm? Why was he still here? She'd made it perfectly clear that he had targeted the wrong person with his legal papers.

A faint twinge of pity flashed through her. No doubt, he had some monster of a boss who would shout at him or maybe even fire him for making this mistake. Anne knew how lucky she was to be working with Rose at the chalet. Best friends since childhood, they were always there for one another.

Gareth looked utterly miserable. So miserable, in fact, that she pulled a clean dish towel out of a kitchen drawer, then walked back to her front door and poked her head out into the damp night air.

"Would you like to come in for tea, Mr. Cavendish?"

From under his umbrella, he looked at her as if she'd just asked him if he'd like to take up juggling. "Excuse me?"

"Would you like to come in and have some tea?"

Anne repeated. "You must be very wet and cold by now."

He hurried over and left his soaking-wet umbrella on the porch. As Anne stepped aside to let him in, he said, "You really shouldn't let strangers into your home like this."

Anne raised her eyebrows. "You've already told me who you are and what you want," she pointed out. "I don't think many criminals do that."

"But how do you know I am who I say I am?" Gareth countered. "You haven't even asked me for any ID."

Sensing it would make him feel better, she held out a hand. "Well, then, you'd better show me some ID, hadn't you?" After he showed her his license, she said, "Come dry off and sit down." She handed him the wildly colored dish towel. "You've been standing out there forever."

After rubbing the towel over his hair and face, he carefully folded it and put it on a nearby marble tabletop. Then he sat down on the large couch covered in plush deep red velvet. The room was filled with mementos, sketches of designs, piles of books and all the other comfortable clutter of her life. While she poured his tea, his eyes skimmed over the old-fashioned Singer sewing machine she kept on a small table in the corner.

She passed him the cup and saucer, and his hand brushed hers as he took it. His skin was surprisingly warm despite the cold rain he'd been standing in. He took a sip of the tea, then put it down and took out the envelope again, laying it next to the teapot.

Anne worked to fight back a slight tightening in her chest. "Honestly, there must be more than one Anne Farleigh in the world. Or," she supposed out loud, "perhaps you've got the wrong name altogether of the person you're looking for."

"You sound very certain, Ms. Farleigh."

"Call me Anne," she said with a smile, ignoring the envelope that Gareth was pushing closer toward her.

"Okay, then, Anne, can I ask why you're so convinced this has nothing to do with you?"

"Because my mother and father loved one another. I don't just mean that the way that people sometimes say it automatically. They truly, deeply loved one another. They even died in one another's arms. When the car crashed—" she had to pause for a moment to push away the brutal image "—they reached out for each other's hands and held on through to the end. Would they have done that if they weren't so deeply in love?"

"I'm so sorry about the way they died—" Gareth began, but Anne kept going.

"I've never been deeply in love with anyone, but I know that if I *were,* I would never cheat on them. That person would be enough to fill my heart and my life. They'd be *everything.* There would be no reason to cheat. So, you see, this person you're talking about— who cheated on his wife and had a daughter no one knew about—can't be *my* father."

Gareth nodded as though he understood, and she was glad to have finally gotten through to him. But her relief was short-lived as he asked, "Your father was an author who traveled to Oregon many times on book tours, wasn't he?"

When she nodded, he said, "Then I'm sorry, I really am, but you *are* the Anne Farleigh I'm looking for. This isn't easy, I know, but your father, Edward Farleigh, had a lover in Ashland. She had a daughter twenty-one years ago named Jasmine Turner. Jasmine feels that your father unfairly left her out of his last will and testament. She wants what she believes to be her rightful share of the inheritance."

"But this is silly," Anne insisted in a calm voice even though it would be so easy to let herself get angry with this woman, Jasmine, and at Gareth for being so insistent that his client was right. The thing was, the only reason she'd be angry with either of them was if they were right. Which they weren't. "I don't know how you've come to this conclusion or what your client has told you, but she isn't my father's daughter. I've told you, my mother and father loved each other too much for something like that to have happened."

She started to push the papers back across the table, but Gareth held up a hand to stop her. "Anne, it doesn't work like that. You've been served with legal papers now, and you can't just give them back. If the two of you can't resolve things in mediation, then I'm afraid this will have to go to court."

Court? She looked at Gareth for several seconds, reality finally dawning. "I'm really being sued?"

"Yes," he said with a grave nod tinged with obvious regret, "you're really being sued."

CHAPTER THREE

ANNE LOOKED as stunned as any of the victims he'd seen in his years on the force, as if she couldn't believe that the world could actually throw something so awful her way.

It was understandable, of course, given that he'd just shown up at her door to tell her she had a sister she'd never heard of. He wanted to reach out and tell her that everything would be fine, but they were on opposite sides of the case. His job was to represent Richard Wells's law firm as they worked with Jasmine Turner to get her what she felt was her due.

Still, he found himself saying in a gentler voice than he usually used with the people he served, "Sometimes we don't know the people closest to us as well as we think we do." As he said this he was reminded of his closest friend, Brian, who had betrayed both him and the law.

"That must be a hard way to look at the world," she murmured.

Gareth shrugged. "It's just the way the world is. Things aren't perfect. People aren't perfect. The best you can hope for is that if you stick to the rules, you'll at least end up doing what's right." He tried—and failed—to stop himself from saying, "Get yourself a good lawyer, Ms.

Farleigh. If you're planning to fight this, you're going to need one."

"Fight it?"

"The alternative is that you agree to Jasmine's request and give her the share of your father's estate that she believes she is entitled to. But whatever you eventually decide, you need to attend the mediation. All of the details are in the papers I gave you." Gareth had explained it simply and calmly, but Anne still looked shocked.

"But that's just—" She stood, picking up the teapot to take it into the kitchen. "I'm sorry. You'll have to excuse me. I have work to prepare for tomorrow."

Gareth understood this was her way of closing down the discussion. He should go, should never have been drinking tea with her in the first place.

Instead, he said, "I take it you design dresses?" He gestured to her sketches and sewing machine.

He welcomed the shift in Anne's face from wary to passionate as she nodded. "I create wedding dresses for brides at The Rose Chalet."

He'd heard of the wedding venue through friends on the force who had planned their weddings over the years, and knew it was top-notch.

"From what I can see, it looks like you're very good at it."

"I love what I do." She beamed at him, and it felt as if his heart actually stopped beating as she said, "I've always tried to capture the love that the bride and groom feel for one another. It helps that I saw how deeply in love my parents were."

He'd been hoping to segue back onto the topic of

the legal proceedings more gently than that, but Anne clearly wasn't going to give him that chance.

"That's why you don't want to accept that these proceedings are real, isn't it?"

"Do you have any idea what it's like to have someone come into your home and accuse your father of—" Her flash of anger left as soon as it had come. "I'm sorry," she said, changing gears. "I imagine you're really a very nice man. In fact, I'm *sure* you are. It's just… Excuse me a moment."

She left the room and came back in with something wrapped up in waxed paper.

"There's always too much wedding cake, and it's too good to throw away. There was some left over from the wedding at The Rose Chalet and I thought you might like it. I've wrapped it up so it won't get wet on the way out to your car."

Gareth had been thrown out of plenty of places over the years, had even left a biker bar headfirst when one of his clients didn't like being shown proof that his wife was cheating on him. But he'd never had someone throw him out quite like this before.

He took the cake and was heading for the door when he was strangely compelled to put out his hand and say, "Despite the circumstances, it was good meeting you, Anne."

"You, too."

Her hug took him by surprise, so that for a moment or two he could only stand there. He hadn't run into many people who hugged rather than shook hands— especially in a situation like this. And as her delicate curves pressed against him, it was all he could do to hang on to his professionalism, standing perfectly still until she pulled back.

"Goodbye, Gareth," she said softly but firmly.

He walked out to his car and climbed in, trying to make sense of everything that had just happened. He didn't think he'd met anyone with quite such a positive outlook on life before—almost determinedly so—but could anyone really believe there wasn't even the slightest chance that one of their parents had cheated at some point?

Gareth returned to his apartment, a luxurious space with views out over the bay. His modern furniture had been picked out for him by an interior designer, because the thought of picking it out by himself hadn't seemed at all appealing. While he was on the force, he'd had a steady paycheck that could easily cover his monthly payments. Now, however, his income was dependent on the quality and frequency of the cases he was able to take on.

He'd thought the Farleigh case would give him and his assistant, Margaret, some breathing room. But it hadn't turned out to be nearly as straightforward as he'd hoped.

Not now that he'd met Anne Farleigh.

Gareth was taking off his jacket when he realized there was something in one of the outside pockets. He unfolded the envelope full of legal papers from his pocket with as much wonder as if it had been a rabbit pulled from a hat.

How had she—

The hug.

Despite himself, Gareth smiled.

CHAPTER FOUR

ANNE ARRIVED at The Rose Chalet early the next day
with her sketchbook, fabric samples and a beautifully
organized photo album of wedding dresses she'd designed over the past five years. She was very much
looking forward to working with Felicity Andrews from
San Francisco magazine to help create the perfect wedding for her.

Rose and RJ were in the chalet's main room, cleaning up the mess left from Tyce's concert. RJ was working to take down the lighting rig, while Rose mopped
the dance floor. The chalet's regular cleaning crew had
already mopped, but Rose was never satisfied until everything gleamed.

Always elegant, this morning the chalet's owner had
tossed her suit jacket over a chair and rolled up her shirtsleeves. She'd tied her auburn hair back, which Anne
thought showed off her friend's beautiful cheekbones
and deep green eyes perfectly.

Anne had always been impressed with how well Rose
and RJ worked together, as if they'd synchronized their
movements. Not only did they care about one another as
friends and coworkers...Anne had always thought that
attraction simmered between them, as well.

Only, Rose had a fiancé. And, presumably, she wouldn't
be marrying Donovan if she didn't love him. Perhaps

whatever she felt for The Rose Chalet's handyman was just a passing thing—a friendship that had become a little too close?

Anne had tried to ask Rose that question late one night, but when her friend had turned white and pressed her lips firmly together, Anne had immediately laughed off her question as if it were a joke, and then changed the subject.

"Need a hand?"

Rose looked up from her mop and smiled. "Hi, Anne, perfect timing. With Phoebe and Tyce's hours shifting a bit lately, we could use the extra help."

As Anne picked up a garbage bag, she was struck not by the fact that their little family at The Rose Chalet was getting smaller day by day, but by the wonderful relationships that had developed over the past few months. First Julie had fallen in love with Andrew, then Phoebe and Patrick had found a love match, and now Tyce and Whitney were together.

Anne had never had that kind of luck when it came to love. She'd dated, of course, and most of the men had been perfectly nice, but romance should be a lot more than just *nice,* shouldn't it?

One day, she told herself, she'd find a love as pure and wonderful as her parents had had.

"Will the whole crew be working on Felicity Andrews's wedding, Rose?"

Her friend stopped mopping for a moment. "Phoebe will be back from Chicago just in time to come in and do the flowers. Julie and Andrew have agreed to handle the catering. And Tyce has arranged for another band director to take over temporarily while he's on vacation in Colorado with Whitney." She sighed. "I'm sure it will go well, but I do wish we had everyone here for the event."

"We'll find a way to make it work," RJ assured her.

"I hope you're right," Rose said. "*San Francisco* magazine is *big*. If Felicity doesn't like what we do for her wedding, then it could really hurt the business. But if she likes it—"

"She'll love it," RJ insisted. "Right, Anne?"

"Of course she will." Anne smiled reassuringly at her friend, even though it was harder than usual to stay positive and cheerful, given what had happened last night with Gareth and those papers he'd tried to give her. "We're going to knock Felicity's Jimmy Choo heels off!"

Thirty minutes later, when RJ had finished with the lighting rig and had left the sparkling-clean building, Rose asked, "Are you okay, Anne? You don't seem quite like yourself this morning."

"Oh, I'm fine," Anne said quickly, but her accompanying smile didn't quite reach her eyes.

"Anne, it's me," Rose said gently. "I've known you since we were kids."

"Since Mrs. McKlusky's class at school," Anne reminisced. "Do you remember that boy who always used to—"

Rose shook her head. "Don't change the subject. I know when there's something going on with you. Do you want to talk about it?"

No. She definitely didn't want to talk about it, or give the whole crazy story any credence at all.

But she also knew that Rose wouldn't let it go until she came as clean as the shining floors. Because that was what best friends did for each other.

"Last night, when I got home, there was a man waiting outside my house in the rain."

Rose's eyes widened with alarm. "Are you okay? Did you call the police?"

"Don't worry," Anne quickly reassured her, "he practically is the police. And besides, he was a perfect gentleman. Cute, too."

"I'm confused," Rose said, her expression mirroring her words. "What did he want?"

"He's a private detective, and he had some silly story about... Well, you wouldn't believe me if I told you."

"Try me."

Anne forced herself to keep smiling in an attempt to treat last night's situation like the absurd mistake that it was. "He says my father had a secret daughter from an affair he had over twenty years ago and that she's going to sue me for her share of what my parents left me."

When Rose's eyes widened, Anne said, "I told you that you wouldn't believe it. He tried to serve me with court papers, and when I told him he'd obviously made a mistake, he just kept standing outside in the rain." She paused before adding, "I felt so sorry for him that I invited him in."

Rose still looked more than a little alarmed as she asked, "What happened then?"

"I poured him tea, he tried to serve me the papers again, and then he left with a piece of cake."

"Cake?" Rose asked with the same worried frown she'd been wearing since they'd started talking. "He served you with papers?"

"Oh, no, I put them in his jacket pocket when he left."

"You did *what?*"

By now, Rose looked a lot more than worried. In fact,

Anne hadn't seen her looking like this since the time she'd found those three Australian backpackers sleeping in her garden shed.

"Anne, you can't do that."

"But I did."

"But you *can't*."

This time, Anne was the one frowning. "That's exactly what Gareth said."

"Gareth?"

"The detective. Gareth Cavendish." Despite his reasons for showing up at her front door last night, Anne smiled at the thought of him. "He really was pretty cute."

Rose had pulled out her phone by then and was scrolling through her contacts. "I don't care how cute he is. Not when he's acting for someone who's suing you. We need to find you a lawyer."

Anne put her hand on her friend's arm. "This is a mistake, Rose. My father didn't do this. He *couldn't* have."

Rose momentarily looked up from her phone to put an arm around her friend. "I know how hard this is, but do you think someone would go to the trouble and expense of suing you if they didn't think they had a reasonable case?"

"But that's…"

Anne could feel the abyss opening up in the pit of her stomach, but she forced herself to keep smiling. All her life, her smile had been her armor. As long as she kept smiling, nothing could really be that bad.

"I'm on your side," Rose assured her. "But you really need to—" She was interrupted by the bell at the front door.

"That must be Felicity Andrews," Anne said, a wave

of relief flooding through her. She hadn't ever been quite so grateful for the arrival of a client. "We shouldn't keep her waiting."

Rose had never left a client waiting a day in her life. But, for once, she looked conflicted. Finally, she said, "Okay, let's go give the publisher of San Francisco's biggest magazine the wedding she deserves."

CHAPTER FIVE

"TELL ME what happened again," Gareth's assistant, Margaret, requested. The slightly water-stained envelope of legal papers sat on her desk between her computer and the picture of her four children. "I want to be sure I've got it straight."

For fifteen years, they had worked together at the precinct. When he'd left, she'd had enough faith in his ability to succeed as a private investigator to come with him. He couldn't let her down.

"Why do I get the feeling that you're enjoying this?"

"Enjoying it?" Margaret shook her head. But she did smile, just a little. "I'm just trying to work out how it is that Gareth Cavendish, the toughest P.I. this side of anywhere, managed to get himself thrown out of a house by a woman who designs wedding dresses for a living."

"It wasn't like that," Gareth insisted.

"Come on, there has to be some kind of reason why the papers you needed to serve Anne Farleigh are on my desk rather than with her."

"That part's easy. She slipped them into my jacket pocket when I left."

He didn't think it was wise to mention the fact that Anne Farleigh had been hugging him at the time.

Nor did he plan on admitting just how much time

he'd spent thinking about her since first meeting her last night.

"Why didn't you drive straight back over there to make her take them?" Margaret looked concerned. "Gareth, this isn't like you."

"There's something—" he wasn't exactly sure how to put it "—different about Anne."

Margaret raised one eyebrow into a high arch. "Anne?"

He quickly backpedaled. "Ms. Farleigh."

On a sigh, his assistant asked, "Different how?"

How could he tell her what it had been like watching Anne walking through the rain, smiling as she enjoyed every moment of it? And how could he possibly explain that for the first time since coming to terms with his ex-partner's lies, something had pushed through the shields Gareth had put up around himself?

Finally he said, "She's a nice woman."

"Nice." Margaret's echo came at the same time that she tapped her pencil on the desk in the way she did when she was thinking about how to solve a problem. "Well, regardless of how nice she is, we need to deal with this before Richard Wells hears about it. He could decide you aren't the man for the job to deal with little Miss Reverse-Pickpocket."

"Don't call her that, Margaret." He felt strangely protective of the woman he'd met less than twenty-four hours ago. "It's clear that this situation comes as a complete surprise to her. It can't be easy to find out that the father she loved and trusted wasn't so trustworthy and lovable, after all."

"This is a legal case," Margaret pointed out. "You know what you have to do, even if it isn't what you'd like to do. I know the papers have been served whether or not she keeps them. But I can guarantee that Richard won't be at all happy if he learns about her sticking them back in your pocket. You need to give them back to her. And make sure she keeps them this time!" When he didn't immediately agree, her expression softened. "You know I love you like a son, don't you? And that I left the precinct with you because I believe you're the best detective in this city?"

"I know." And he did. He also knew her well enough to brace for what was about to come next.

"I want you to succeed. I want *us* to succeed. And I know we will. But this case is a big part of building the foundation for our success, so you need to think about how bad you want it, and what you're willing to do about it." She paused before adding, "I will accept and go along with whatever decision you make. Just promise me you'll actually think this situation through."

Gareth knew Margaret was right. Only, at the same time, he knew how much this would hurt Anne…. And just the thought of her hurting was enough to make his chest squeeze tight.

And yet, if he didn't get her to take this seriously and attend the mediation, the case would end up in court. He barely knew her but he imagined the last thing Anne would want was a public discussion of her father's infidelities.

Margaret waited until he was almost at the door to his office before saying, "One other thing. Brian called. I told him that you weren't in, and he said he'd try to call your cell number later."

Gareth fought against the twisting in his gut at the mention of his old partner and closest friend. "Thanks for warning me."

Was Brian finally calling to apologize? And did he really think that an apology would fix things? He'd deliberately falsified reports so that his girlfriend's kid wouldn't be part of a drug-possession case. As soon as Gareth had found out, he'd insisted that Brian come clean. Rules were rules, after all, especially for a police officer. But Brian held firm, claiming that the kid deserved another chance in life without a record and that he was going to give it to him.

Deciding whether or not to turn in his friend had been the most difficult decision of Gareth's career. But, in the end, he hadn't been able to do it. He couldn't ruin his friend's life like that. All he could hope was that his old friend would do the right thing…or leave the job of his own free will.

When Brian did neither of those things, Gareth knew he was the one who had to go.

And that was why he had to go serve these papers to Anne Farleigh again and make sure she attended the mediation. Because however beautiful and sweet Anne was, he owed his best to his client, to Margaret and to himself, too.

And in a strange kind of way, he owed it to Anne. Because if he could get her into mediation, maybe he could help keep the case from becoming even uglier.

Heading back into Margaret's office, he picked the water-stained envelope off her desk and said, "I need the address for The Rose Chalet."

THE ROSE CHALET WAS, he had to admit twenty minutes later, a very nice spot by the bay, surrounded by beautiful gardens. Walking through the main gate, he quickly found an elegant redhead talking to a handyman.

"You're really telling me that you don't think you should have worn overalls to mop the floor this morning?" the man asked.

The woman looked slightly shocked. "And have Felicity arrive early and see me like that?"

"I don't think she'd have minded. She didn't mind how I'm dressed, did she?"

"You and I both know that's because she was checking you out…even though she's getting married here soon. I don't think I'd get the same reaction."

"I don't know," the man replied. "I think you look good no matter what you wear."

Just then, the woman saw Gareth. She looked a little flushed, and no wonder, the way the two of them were flirting.

"Hello," she said. "I'm Rose. Can I help you?"

He quickly put two and two together and realized this was Rose from The Rose Chalet.

"I'm looking for Anne Farleigh. Is she here?"

"What's this about?" Rose asked him, a heavy note of suspicion in her voice.

Clearly, she was very protective of her colleague. Gareth was glad. Even from the short time he'd spent with Anne, he knew she deserved good friends who would look out for her.

Hopefully, her friends would prove more loyal than his had.

Rather than explain the situation to her, he simply said, "I was just hoping to catch her here."

Rose gazed at him for a long while, and he felt as if she was assessing him top to bottom, inside and out. Finally, she said, "Sorry, you've missed her. I believe she headed home a half hour ago."

Gareth nodded his thanks, then headed back toward his car. Odds were, he was going to spend quite a bit of time standing outside Anne's house until she finally emerged again.

Good thing it had finally stopped raining.

CHAPTER SIX

ANNE LOOKED AT the boxes spread out on the floor in front of her, trying to remember which one held the bolt of fabric her parents had brought back from a trip to India many, many years ago. It would be perfect for Felicity Andrews's wedding dress.

Assuming, of course, that she could find anything at all in the huge stack of boxes.

There were mementos from her father's book-signing trips, books that they hadn't had enough shelves for, newspaper cuttings, even old clothes that still had some wear in them. Too many happy memories for Anne to have thrown away.

Fortunately, the meeting with Felicity Andrews at The Rose Chalet had gone perfectly, Anne thought as she rooted through yet another box and found a collection of porcelain dolls she'd completely forgotten about. She set the box aside with plans to study the Victorian-era dresses worn by the dolls more closely in the following weeks.

Anne always asked her brides to talk about their fiancés because it was the best way for her to understand the tone of the dress they were looking for, whether sweet or gentle or, in Felicity Andrews's case, fiercely passionate.

Sitting with Felicity that afternoon and hearing her

talk about how deeply her passion—and love—ran for her fiancé had immediately sent Anne's mind drifting to the man she couldn't seem to get out of her head… and wondering just how deep Gareth Cavendish's passions ran.

But as nice as it was to think about the handsome private investigator, she needed to focus on The Rose Chalet's most important client to date. Especially given that Felicity had been, in large part, responsible for helping Anne regain her usual happy equilibrium that morning. She'd confirmed that her magazine was going to do a special wedding issue, with Anne's creations having a starring role. Even better, upon hearing that Anne still had her mother's wedding dress, Felicity had suggested it would make the perfect centerpiece for the shoot.

If only she could find the fabric to make Felicity's dress. If Rose had been there, Anne had no doubt her friend would have systematically inventoried each box and found the fabric within fifteen minutes. But every time Anne opened a box, she couldn't help but think back to where the contents had come from. The tiny teddy bear her mother had given her as a baby. The costume jewelry she and her mother had collected at yard sales when she was a little girl and would wear when they pretended to have tea with the queen.

Nothing, however, affected her quite as much as the collection of love poems her father had written for her mother.

As Anne read the poems one by one, she imagined her father's deep voice reading them to her mother as she sat beside him on the love seat. They'd been so perfect together. So happy.

Inevitably, her thoughts returned to Gareth—to what

he'd claimed was true about her father—and a brief flash of anger flowed through her before she pushed it away.

The doorbell rang, and when she went to answer it and saw Gareth standing on the front porch, she felt as if she'd conjured him up out of thin air, simply by thinking of him again and again throughout the day.

"We need to talk," he said in that low voice that sent thrill bumps moving across the surface of her arms. "Can I come in?"

A part of her had known he'd come back, hadn't she? Especially when she'd slipped the envelope into his pocket as he was leaving. And while she wasn't looking forward to dealing with a legal case, she couldn't deny that, on a purely female level, it was very nice to see him again.

She'd been attracted to him from the moment she saw him, but she still couldn't quite work out why. Obviously, the "incredibly good-looking" part helped, but it was more than that. Gareth was nothing like the creative novelist her father had been. Instead, there was something stable about him. Dependable.

He promised, "This won't take too long" as she stepped aside to let him in. As he headed through to the living room, he couldn't miss the boxes strewn all over the floor. He raised a questioning eyebrow. "What's all this?"

"I'm looking for some fabric," Anne said. "I'm sure it's in one of these boxes." She smiled up at him. "I imagine your office is perfectly neat?"

"Mostly." He gave her a small smile that made her feel tingly all over. "Thanks to Margaret."

"Margaret?" Anne felt a twinge of something other

than tingles flicker through her. It took her a moment to identify it.

She was jealous. Of Margaret…whoever Margaret was.

"She's my office manager," he explained, "though there are days when she can feel like my boss if I'm not keeping up with my schedule."

Anne smiled. "It can be like that for me sometimes. So many dresses, so little time, and they have to be perfect, don't they? I mean, I couldn't let someone get married in a dress that wasn't perfect."

Still, even as she spoke, she was reeling from the emotions another woman's name out of Gareth's mouth had brought up in her. Because she could only be jealous if…

"This sewing machine must have quite a few years on it," Gareth said as he put one strong hand on her Singer.

Anne was struck by the contrast between his tanned, masculine fingers and the dainty faded olive-green machine. "My mother had it when I was a child. I can picture her sitting here every time I use it."

Gareth nodded, then said, "With all these boxes, I thought for a minute…"

She couldn't resist moving closer to him as she asked, "What did you think?"

"That you were taking the case seriously enough to look for proof that your father didn't—"

"Why would I need to do that?" Yet again, she had to fight like crazy to push away the new rush of anger and frustration. She picked up the love poems. "Would my father have written these if he didn't love my mother?

So please, don't start up again with how I have a secret half sister."

"Believe it or not," he said gently, "I really don't want to do anything to hurt your memories of your parents."

"Then don't. Would you like some tea?" Anne asked it automatically, but she was almost grateful when Gareth shook his head. "My friend Rose seems to think that I should take all this a lot more seriously."

Gareth looked at her, staring straight into her eyes. His gaze was so *intense*. "I met her earlier today when I went by The Rose Chalet. She seems like a good friend."

"She is. In fact, Rose is the closest thing I have to a sister," she added pointedly. "Which is why I'd really appreciate it if you'd please tell this woman to withdraw her case."

But Gareth only shook his head. "If you really believe Jasmine Turner isn't your sister, then you should prove it before this case gets out of hand."

"Gets out of hand how?" Anne asked. She had visions of bailiffs showing up at the front door to take everything away from her.

They couldn't do that. Could they? The world had to be fairer than that.

Gareth reached out as if he would take her hand, but then, at the last second, he put his hand in his pocket instead. "Do you want all of this in the public eye? Because if you don't come to the mediation, that's what will happen."

Anne froze at that thought. The idea of someone dragging her parents' names through the press like that was almost too much to bear.

"Are you saying you'd tell reporters?" Anne asked

incredulously. "You wouldn't really do something like that, would you?"

"No, I wouldn't do that to you, but if this goes to trial, people will find out. Edward Farleigh wasn't the biggest author in the world, but he was big enough that people will be interested, and we won't be able to stop that."

As he spoke, Anne tried desperately to make sense of the way her life had turned upside down in the past twenty-four hours.

"Even though you're certain that your father couldn't have done this, you should still go to the mediation—preferably with your own lawyer. I'll be right outside, Anne, I promise. It will just be you, your lawyer, Jasmine, her lawyer and a professional mediator. Go there and prove your case. Show Jasmine and the mediator that you're right. Please at least talk to them. It's the best thing to do."

Part of her knew that Gareth was right. Going to this meeting would be the only way to deal with the situation before it ruined her father's reputation. Yet it seemed so unfair that someone could just show up and start questioning his marriage and behavior.

Just as unfair as her parents' sudden deaths had been. They shouldn't have been snatched away like that. And now, she thought as her eyes filled up with tears, someone was trying to take away her memories of them, too.

CHAPTER SEVEN

GARETH'S GUT SQUEEZED tight as Anne started crying. Another investigator might have tried to ignore the pain of this sweet, funny, beautiful woman, but he couldn't do it. Instead, he reached out to try to soothe her by putting a comforting arm around her.

He honestly expected her to flinch at his touch. He was the enemy, after all. So when she surprised him, yet again, by putting her head on his shoulder and sinking down onto the couch with him while she cried, he couldn't stop himself thinking about how perfect it felt to hold her like this.

"It's going to be all right," he promised.

She turned her face to his so that he was looking into the depths of those perfectly blue eyes…close enough that their lips were just a few inches apart.

"Gareth," she said, his name barely more than a whisper.

He had dated plenty of beautiful, intelligent, talented women. Yet not *one* of them had made him feel the way Anne was making him feel right now. What was more, not one of them had made him want to open up to them—to let them into the parts of himself that he kept hidden.

Maybe it was because, even after having known her

only a day, he sensed that Anne would never take advantage of him in any way.

So when she started to close the rest of the distance between them, her lips moving closer slowly, almost imperceptibly, Gareth wanted to pretend that he couldn't see it coming so that he could stay there and let this wonderful woman kiss him.

But he couldn't.

Not when she was on the other side of a case from him.

The rules for a situation like this were clear. And he'd always lived his life strictly by the rules.

Pulling back, taking his arms from around her and standing up was one of the most difficult things he'd ever done. But he did it anyway.

"I need to give you these again." He took the envelope of legal papers out of his pocket and handed them to her.

Gareth's gut twisted yet again at the clear disappointment—and hurt—on Anne's face as she stood. He wished he could confess that he'd been drawn to her from the moment he first saw her. And that he wanted her more than he'd ever wanted any other woman.

Only, actually saying either one of those things would be completely unprofessional.

And totally against the rules.

Helping her navigate the legal case as cleanly as possible was all he could do.

"Gareth, did I do something wrong?"

"No, of course you didn't," he said softly. "Please promise me that I'll see you at the mediation tomorrow."

Anne stared at him for a long moment before finally nodding. "All right, I'll go. But I'm not going to bring a lawyer. I'm sure I can explain everything myself. Are you sure you won't stay, though? For tea, or...?"

It would have been so easy to say yes. So easy and, with Anne, so perfect. But he couldn't break the rules like that.

Not even for her.

"I have to get back to the office."

It was hard keeping things flat and professional and heading for her front door as if nothing was wrong. He managed to walk all the way out to his car without looking back, but he risked a glance in the rearview mirror, and saw Anne wave goodbye. As if she'd had a friendly visit from an old acquaintance.

Of course, they'd almost become a lot more than that.

He couldn't stop thinking of what it might have been like to close that distance between them and taste the sweet softness of her lips rather than pulling away.

"Stop it," he told himself aloud. "It's not going to happen. It *can't* happen."

Gareth put his Jaguar in gear and got out of there, because every moment he spent looking at her meant another one he had to fight not to go back into the house and finish what they'd nearly started on the sofa.

"DID YOU DO IT?" Margaret asked when he walked back into his office.

Gareth nodded, even as his gut twisted at the memory of Anne's tears.

"I'm proud of you," she said, and then, "There's a visitor waiting in your office, but I need to talk to you about that first, because—"

Gareth wasn't in the mood to wait. Dealing with a new client was exactly what he needed. It was the only way he'd manage to get thoughts of Anne out of his head.

He pushed his office door open and stepped inside. "I'm sorry to have kept you waiting, Ms.... Kyra, what are you doing here?"

Brian's girlfriend stood up and smiled at him. "Gareth, it's good to see you again." Her voice was warm despite all that had happened six months ago. "Brian said you wouldn't want to see me, and that you would be angry with me."

"It's not you I'm angry with."

"Your secretary was very protective. She didn't want to let me wait for you." Kyra shook her head. "All this anger. Can't we get past it? You and Brian used to be inseparable."

"That was before he broke the rules," Gareth said.

"Yes," she admitted, "he broke a few rules. But he loves me and my son, Bobby, and he only wants what's best for us. In my experience, as long as no one gets hurt, doesn't love matter the most?"

"Rules matter," Gareth insisted. "If they don't, there's chaos, and everything breaks down."

Brian's girlfriend stepped back from him. "I'm not here to argue with you. I'm here to give you an invitation."

Gareth was instantly wary. "What kind of invitation?"

"Brian and I are getting married. We're having an engagement party later this week, and we want you to be there. Brian hasn't said it, but I know it's what he wants. And that he's hoping the two of you will be able to put the past behind you. Please say you'll at least think about it."

She put the invitation on his desk and walked out of his office. Gareth stared at the thick cream paper, wondering how Kyra could possibly think that he'd want to go to their engagement party or that he'd be okay with spending time with Brian again when his friend couldn't be trusted to tell the truth anymore.

And did he and his girlfriend really think that Gareth could put aside everything he stood for, all of his convictions, just like that, for *love?*

CHAPTER EIGHT

As Anne picked out her outfit for work the next day, she caught herself sighing for what had to be the dozenth time.

What was wrong with her?

Moping around was so *negative,* and that wasn't the kind of person she wanted to be. Yet there was something about the thought of what had happened with Gareth yesterday—the almost-kiss that had kept her up half the night replaying it over and over—that was profoundly frustrating. So much so that yet another sigh slipped by her normally optimistic defenses.

In the past few months, she'd seen her friend Phoebe become far less cynical about the world thanks to her relationship with Patrick Knight. Anne really hoped that kind of thing didn't work in reverse, too.

It was just…that moment yesterday, when Gareth's mouth had been only inches from hers and his arms had been around her, had been so good. More than that, it had felt *right*.

She'd spent so many years looking around for Mr. Right, even letting Phoebe and Tyce talk her into occasionally dating one of their friends. But, with everything Anne had seen of her parents' marriage, it had just seemed so obvious that she would know when the

right person came along. Unfortunately, none of the
men she'd dated had ever come close.

Heading downstairs to get breakfast, she put a pot on
for tea. While the water boiled, she got a box of cereal
out of the pantry and reflected that when she'd been in
Gareth's arms on her couch, she could have sworn there
was something special between them—an impossible,
perfect connection that she'd felt nothing could break.

Until he had broken it by pulling back from her.

If they had that kind of connection, then surely he
should have felt it, too? Surely the thing about perfect
love was that it should be perfect, not something that
people got confused over, or pulled back from, or…

She looked down and saw that she was pouring tea
into her cereal bowl.

"Damn it!"

Anne paused, more than a little horrified with herself
for the way she was behaving this morning.

Which brought her to something else she couldn't
make sense of. Her parents had been such perfect, happy,
loving counterparts to each other. Whereas Gareth was
at the heart of a legal process that was slowly tearing
Anne apart.

Didn't that mean he couldn't possibly be right for
her?

And yet, Anne still wished he had closed that gap
between them and kissed her yesterday.

Abandoning her breakfast, she walked back over to
the pile of boxes still spread out all over her living room
floor. On top of one of the boxes was a picture of her
mother and father on their wedding day.

Her mother looked radiant in her wedding dress,

like a princess. Her father was incredibly handsome in his suit.

Felicity Andrews and *San Francisco* magazine were expecting to use her mother's wedding dress for the photo shoot. Fortunately, it hadn't taken Anne long to find the dress. She'd gotten it out of its box many times over the years to stare at while she waited for inspiration to hit. Just thinking of the love her parents had had was always enough to fuel her creative juices.

Anne held the gown up to the light with a critical eye, looking at it the way she would a dress ready to be fitted to a bride. It was beautiful, but there was still a lot of work to do. The beading around the edges had faded over time, and some of the stitching had come loose. It would all need to be redone by hand. She ran the silk of the dress through her fingers, feeling the beading as she went.

Remembering her mother saying the beads had been a special gift from her father for the dress, she wondered if they had picked out the beads together. Or had her father brought them home from one of his book tours? He *had* gone on a lot of trips without her and her mother, hadn't he…

On impulse, she pulled out her cell phone and dialed Rose.

"Hi, Anne," Rose said, picking up the phone after the first ring. "How are you today?"

"Wonderful," Anne said automatically, because… well, why wouldn't she say it? "I'm just starting to work on my mother's dress for the photo shoot."

"The magazine feature is going to be a big deal," Rose said. "It should attract a lot of attention, for you especially."

"That would be nice," Anne said. "Plus, it means I get a chance to go through all of my parents' old things."

"Ah," Rose said, "the boxes."

"The boxes," Anne agreed, because Rose liked to tease her about the number of them taking up odd corners and closets. Keeping the phone pressed to her ear, she got out the sewing box Rose had given her one year as a birthday present, and started carefully using a needle to unpick the thread of the beading where it was worn. As she worked she said, "My mother was always sewing, wasn't she?"

Anne thought back to her mother greeting the two friends after school with milk and cookies and then sitting with them to gossip about the goings-on at school while she deftly worked at beading with her nimble fingers.

"Yes, I got the sense she loved it, but it was also a way for her to keep busy," Rose said. "Especially when your father wasn't there."

That was true. Her father had often been away, and it would be so quiet with just the two of them there together.

"Lots of people spend time apart, though," Anne pointed out. "Look at Tyce and Whitney."

"Yes, but as soon as Whitney graduates from vet school, they're planning to live together full-time."

"What about Phoebe and Patrick?"

"They go back and forth between San Francisco and Chicago so often I never know if I'm going to have a florist or not from one day to the next," Rose said.

"But they're deeply in love, aren't they? Just like you and Donovan. I mean, you don't always see him every day, because he's so busy with work, but you're committed to spending the rest of your lives together."

"That's the plan," Rose said lightly; then her voice turned a little more serious. "Is this a roundabout way of talking about what happened yesterday with the investigator?"

"No, I'm just saying that even if my father wasn't at home all the time, it didn't mean there was anything *wrong.*"

"No, of course not," Rose replied. "Your father had to tour the country for his work."

"Exactly."

Anne was suddenly hit with a vivid picture of the way her mother would stand looking out the window after the taxi had left to take her father to the airport again. She'd tried to keep such a brave face on, but her sorrow had been palpable.

"I know Mom seemed so *lonely* sometimes, but that just shows how much they loved one another, doesn't it? That they cared about each other so much it hurt every time they were apart. Is it like that with you and Donovan?"

"I see him practically every day. In fact, I'm going to see him in a minute."

"Darn it, you should have told me I wasn't calling at a good time."

"Anne, I have all the time in the world for you. And if you need to talk—"

"Say hello to Donovan for me. I'd better get back to work," she said as she put down the phone and looked back at her mother's dress.

It was actually romantic, when she thought about it,

the way her mother had all but counted the moments until the man she loved returned from the road.

Thinking about it any other way…well, that idea just hurt too much, so Anne threaded a needle instead, getting to work on the beading. It was one of those jobs that wasn't technically difficult but it did require concentration and patience.

All the images she had of her parents' wedding came from photographs and her vivid imagination, but that didn't stop her from feeling their love for each other every time she touched the dress. All she needed to do now was—

"Ow!"

She sucked her finger until it stopped hurting, and when she was sure she wasn't going to bleed all over the dress, she told herself to concentrate as she got back to work on the beading. It was proving trickier than expected, because too much force would tear the silk, while not enough wouldn't get the job done.

Anne squinted closely at the fabric as she worked, trying not to think about Gareth, or the case, or…

A snag.

Somehow, she'd snagged some of the delicate fabric on the dress. If she wasn't more careful, it could turn into a full-fledged tear.

Finally accepting that she was all thumbs today—right when she couldn't afford to be—she carefully put aside her mother's dress, determined not to do any more damage.

What was wrong with her?

But as she glanced at her watch, the answer was painfully obvious. The mediation was due to start in fifteen minutes.

She'd been trying to ignore it all morning, thinking about her parents, the dress, talking to Rose…anything but the thought of sitting opposite a woman claiming to be her sister and trying to be polite while a stranger made *accusations* about her father.

Yet Gareth had been clear that he thought this was the only way to get the whole crazy mess straightened out before it went any further. And she'd promised him that she would go.

Anne found her first real smile of the day as she thought about seeing Gareth again. He'd said that he wouldn't go inside the meeting room itself, but she could imagine him standing outside, waiting for them to sort this whole mess out.

He did look so good standing outside places, after all.

And afterward, when the nonsense about her father was resolved…well, Anne could easily imagine laughing with him over it all, and then maybe, just maybe, they could revisit the moment they'd had yesterday. Only without the pulling-away-at-the-last-minute part, of course. And then, once everything was neatly back in place in her life, she would come home and restore her mother's wedding dress to its original glory.

CHAPTER NINE

ANNE HAD EXPECTED a courtroom, or at least a judge presiding over it, not a small conference room in the courthouse, with Gareth standing outside. He looked wonderful in another of those oh-so-formal suits of his that made her want to greet him with a hug just to rumple him up a little bit.

A young woman stood beside him, presumably Jasmine Turner. She was blonde with blue eyes, but as far as Anne was concerned their similarities stopped there. Especially when she looked into Jasmine's eyes, which had a hard glint to them that Anne had never seen before—not in her father's eyes or her own.

Still, Anne was going to do her best to look for the good in Jasmine Turner. After all, disliking someone at first sight just wasn't in her DNA. People almost always turned out to be nicer than you might think when you gave them a chance.

"Hello, Anne," Gareth said. "This is Jasmine Turner and Richard Wells, Jasmine's lawyer."

"She's late," Jasmine snapped. "The mediator is inside already."

"Actually, I'm in the middle of a very important project and I've come here on very short notice. I'd like to know how long this will take," Anne said. "I have to rework the beading on an entire dress and—"

"It will go quicker if you stop talking about dresses," Jasmine snapped.

The gray-haired lawyer opened the door to the mediation room. "Why don't we get started?" he said, trying to defuse the situation.

Anne nodded. The sooner they did this, the sooner she could show everyone just how delusional they all were. "Whenever you're ready."

"That would have been about five minutes ago," Jasmine replied, rolling her eyes.

Gareth interrupted in a conciliatory tone. "Remember, the idea here today is to talk things through to see if we can come to an amicable agreement about what should happen next."

Anne wanted to kiss Gareth for reminding them all to remain calm and reasonable. The three of them went into the conference room, leaving Gareth behind. Seated at the head of a large conference table was a woman wearing a gray business suit. She peered at them over the rims of her glasses. Jasmine and Richard headed for one side of the table, while Anne went to the opposite side automatically. She did her best to maintain her usual happy demeanor, smiling at the mediator as she sat down.

"You must be Jasmine Turner and Anne Farleigh," the mediator said, addressing them rather than the lawyer. "I'm Rebecca Williams, and I'll be mediating this discussion. The aim here today is to see if we can't prevent the case between the two of you from going to court. I'd like this to be an open and polite discussion. I know that can be challenging in difficult circumstances, but I won't allow this meeting to degenerate into an argument. You'll each have the chance to say everything you need to say, but the price of that is that you have to let the other person speak, too." She turned to focus on Jasmine. "Now, I understand that Ms. Turner is asking for half the estate of Edward Farleigh?"

"I am," Jasmine said. "It's what I should have received years ago. I'm only asking for what I deserve."

The mediator turned to Anne. "And you, Ms. Farleigh, are resisting this claim because—"

"Because this is nonsense," Anne said. "I'm sorry, but my father would never have cheated on my mother. So there's no way he could have had an entire other family."

"Yes, there is!" Jasmine insisted.

The mediator held up her hand. "Ms. Turner, it would be best if you could please tell us why you believe Edward Farleigh to be your father."

Richard Wells opened the file folder he'd brought in and slid it in front of his client.

"While my mother raised me by herself, there was a man who came to the house sometimes when I was a little girl. I didn't know who he was, but when I got older I started asking about my father. I couldn't help wondering if that man was him. Finally, a few months ago, my mother gave me the name of my biological father. His name is Edward Farleigh."

"Maybe," Anne said, trying to be reasonable, "your mother made up a name to get you to stop asking."

"My mother wouldn't do that."

"And my father wouldn't have had a relationship with someone other than my mother," Anne countered. "He loved her too much."

"We're here to discuss the facts of a case," Ms. Williams reminded them, "not to speculate about motive."

Jasmine nodded. "All right. It's a fact that I saw Edward Farleigh's photograph in a newspaper. It's a fact that I recognized him as the man who used to come to the house when I was a little girl. And it's a fact that when I confronted my mother, she ended up admitting that he is my father."

"Is your mother here so that we can confirm that?" Ms. Williams asked.

Jasmine looked slightly uncomfortable, shifting in her chair. "She said...she didn't want to be part of all this."

Anne smiled to herself. If this woman's own mother didn't want anything to do with her case, then why would anyone else believe what she said?

"Clearly, if your mother isn't prepared to go along with this," Anne said, "you must have made a mistake. Maybe there's someone who could actually help you find your real father? Someone like Gareth?"

Jasmine rolled her eyes. "He's the one who helped us put together the rest of the story."

"You saw this man you think might have been your father, what—a couple of times?"

"Closer to a dozen. We've pieced together the dates he visited with the dates of the affair he had with my mother. They coincide with dates Edward Farleigh was on book-signing tours."

"Are you sure you didn't take a bunch of dates my father was on tour and fit your memories around them?" Anne asked. "Because if you really *wanted* him to be your father—"

"He *is* my father!" Jasmine practically spat at her.

"Why don't we hear about the dates?" Ms. Williams interrupted. "Then we can go from there."

Jasmine gripped her papers tightly as she started to read from her list.

Anne wasn't sure what reading the dates would do to help their situation. After all, she had been just a girl at the time, so she hadn't kept track of the exact dates of her father's tours.

Until, suddenly, one leapt out at her.

"Did you just say May seventeenth?" She laughed out loud, because she simply couldn't help it.

It was over. It was finally over.

"What's so funny?" Jasmine demanded. "Do you think this is a joke?"

Ms. Williams intervened. "Ms. Farleigh, why don't you tell us what's so important about May seventeenth?"

Anne smiled. "It's my birthday. Do you really think that my father, that *anyone's* father, would spend his daughter's birthday with some other family? This is ridiculous."

Jasmine stood, and her lawyer spoke up. "It seems that we made a mistake in trying to resolve this situation with mediation. Thank you for your time, Ms. Williams." Jasmine didn't so much as acknowledge Anne as she stalked from the room. Richard Wells hurried out after his client.

Anne didn't care about either of them as she thanked the mediator and practically bounced her way out of the room to where Gareth was still standing by the door.

He looked at her carefully. "How did it go?"

Anne beamed at him. "I'm glad you talked me into coming today."

"You are?" Gareth sounded more than a little surprised.

"Yes, I am." Anne reached out to hug him. "Thank you. If I hadn't come, then it wouldn't be over."

Gareth raised an eyebrow. "Over? You and Jasmine agreed to a settlement that quickly? I'm surprised Richard didn't say something about it when he left…and he didn't look particularly happy, either."

"No, we didn't agree to a settlement. I simply explained to her why she couldn't possibly be my sister. Even her own mother wasn't prepared to stand up for her, so what does that tell you?"

"Anne," he said slowly, "I'm not sure this case will be quite so easy to wrap up. Why don't you tell me everything that happened?"

"Must I?" Anne asked. "I just want to take this whole stupid mess and put it behind me so that I can get on with my life."

"I'd feel a lot happier if you did tell me."

Anne thought for a second or two. Strictly speaking, she should probably be getting home to work on Felicity Andrews's dress, not to mention her mother's dress. On the other hand, when the alternative was spending more time with Gareth, it wasn't exactly a difficult choice.

Especially when she remembered that moment yesterday when they'd been so close to one another.

"Okay," she agreed. "I'll tell you everything. But only if you let me tell you over lunch."

CHAPTER TEN

GARETH SHOULD HAVE said no, of course. Private detectives didn't go to lunch with the people on the other side of the case they were handling. Not unless they were trying to talk them into accepting a settlement. And certainly not because the woman happened to be beautiful and wonderful and impossible to get through to.

So how did he come to be sitting across from Anne in a small restaurant with views out toward the Golden Gate Bridge, looking into her eyes?

Yes, he needed to find out what had happened in the mediation...but the real reason he was here was that he'd been so swept up in Anne from the first moment he'd set eyes on her walking in the rain that it had been impossible to say no.

Still, he had to try to keep some measure of professionalism. "Now will you tell me how things went in the mediation?"

Anne made a little face. "For just a few more moments, could we pretend we're simply out enjoying a nice lunch together?"

Gareth didn't need to pretend to enjoy himself around Anne. And, surprisingly, he found he wasn't quite ready to ruin the moment by pressing her for more details about the case. "So, you've lived in San Francisco all your life?"

Strictly speaking, he knew the answer because he'd done his research for this case, but he just wanted to hear Anne talk. She had a beautiful voice, so full of hope and optimism. He could listen to her talk all day.

Besides, there was something very different about listening to Anne tell her story rather than studying a list of facts he'd compiled about her. Lists of facts didn't have her infectious enthusiasm, for one. And a list couldn't include all the little details and subtle nuances that made a stranger into a real person.

"Yes, I've lived here all my life in the same house I live in now. What about you?"

"I have a place not that far from here. I moved to the city because there was a good job available with the police here, before…before I went solo."

She paused as if to digest that new piece of information, before saying, "So you must know all the interesting spots in the city."

How, he wondered, had she innately known that he didn't want to talk about his reasons for leaving the force?

"Actually, apart from traveling around for my cases, I pretty much stay in my neighborhood."

"You've really never gone looking for all the neat little areas in the city?" Anne asked, sounding surprised, as if she couldn't believe that everybody didn't spend their days wandering around San Francisco.

"I've been busy building my own business," he said, but even he could hear it as the lame excuse it was.

Anne shook her head with a smile, reached out across the table to take his hands in hers. "There are so many wonderful things in this city. Anywhere, if you just look. Come with me."

She stood up, still holding on to his hands. Her hands were small and should have felt delicate, but there was an unexpected strength to them.

"Where are we going?" Gareth asked. "Don't you want to eat lunch?"

"Yes, we'll do that later." She grinned at him. "Right now, I'm going to show you what you've been missing out on." He couldn't miss the sweet challenge in her sparkling eyes as she pulled him toward the door with obvious enthusiasm. "What do you have to lose?"

Possibly quite a bit, considering he shouldn't even be here with her in the first place.

And yet, it was strangely easy to ignore that thought and let Anne pull him from the restaurant.

"Anne, we've just walked past my car."

"The place I'm taking you is close by, and besides, it's a lovely day."

He hadn't really given the quality of the day much thought. He'd been too busy thinking about the mediation, about the case…about Anne. Now, though, he had to admit, it really was a nice day.

"Sure, let's walk."

She threaded her arm through his as they headed down the street. "It's amazing the things you see if you just take the time to look for them. Things you never thought you might see."

"Are you taking me to see the Painted Ladies?" Gareth asked. He'd driven by the seven historic, colorful houses several times. Maybe Anne thought he hadn't really looked at them properly before.

"Oh, no, I'm sure you've seen those," Anne said. The secretive hint to her smile indicated she wasn't about to spoil the surprise by telling him where they were going.

She led him into a small park, along garden paths hemmed in by greenery on both sides so that it felt like a space cut off from the rest of the world, even though they were still just a little way from the restaurant.

"Have you spotted them yet?" she asked.

"Spotted what?"

Gareth looked around, glancing over flowers and shrubs, a tree or two and not much else. What did Anne want him to look at? He tried looking again, more carefully this time, slowing down as his eyes scanned the space around him.

Finally, he saw something unexpected.

Plants were flowing up out of old sneakers, high heels, men's dress shoes, even a few tall boots. They were bedding plants, mostly, but a few larger specimens poked up out of open-backed shoes, allowing the roots to spread.

"It's beautiful, isn't it?" Anne said.

It should have looked like random littering. It should have looked too odd to be beautiful. It should have been pure chaos.

Yet, Gareth had to admit that the flowers made the shoe garden a riot of colors, while the shoes in between blended with those colors. It was strange but also very beautiful indeed. He found himself smiling as he looked around the place and considered the thought that someone could have done this.

"Who put all this together?"

"People just come along and plant shoes."

"But it should be chaotic," he told her when he couldn't make sense of it.

Anne smiled. "I suppose so, but fortunately, it seems to work anyway."

She led the way around another bend in the path to a spot where there were trays of bedding plants along with soil. Gareth could guess what she intended.

"Oh, no. No way."

"Everyone should do it at least once." She took off her own shoes without hesitating. They were beautiful heels that matched the dress she was wearing. Gareth guessed that she'd either customized them herself or made the dress to fit the shoes.

"You're really going to plant a flower in those shoes?"

"Of course. Come on. Try it. You won't regret it."

He had a moment's hesitation, given how much the shoes he was wearing had cost, yet Gareth found himself bending down to untie them.

Together, they chose plants for each of their shoes and then got down to work.

Anne planted hers beside his. "There," she said. "Doesn't that feel good?"

It did. Better than he'd have thought. And as they padded out of the park together, Anne in her bare feet and Gareth in his black dress socks, in that moment he felt as if he could tell her anything.

But he really didn't want to talk about the case just then. Which really left only one other thing…

"Do you remember before, when I mentioned leaving the precinct?"

"Yes. From your tone of voice, I was wondering if something happened to make you want to leave."

"My partner, Brian, met a woman. He fell in love with her."

"That doesn't sound like a reason to leave your job."

"It wasn't." Gareth kept walking. "Except she had a kid, and the kid was in trouble. He'd made the kind of friends who didn't think twice about having him transport drugs for them. Brian looked the other way." No, Gareth thought, he had to tell her the full truth. "Actually, it was worse than that. He 'lost' some of the evidence."

"He did that just because he loved someone?"

"Yes, but what he did was also illegal. In the end, even though I knew the right thing to do was to turn him in, I couldn't. So I left the force instead."

Anne paused, looking up into his eyes. "Why are you telling me this?"

"I need you to know how important the law is to me. How I can't just ignore it, even if I want to."

"Because you want to do the right thing," Anne said, reaching up to touch his face.

"Because I *have* to do the right thing. It isn't just my job—it's who I am."

"And what's the right thing to do now?" she whispered.

"I should go," he whispered back, "but I can't."

And then he kissed her.

CHAPTER ELEVEN

ANNE MELTED INTO Gareth's arms, and when they finally pulled apart, she stared at him breathlessly. She knew Gareth was a man who believed in doing things the "right" way, but who'd have thought that extended to his kissing abilities?

Because his kiss had been more than right.

It had been *perfect*.

"You realize it's going to be a long walk back to my car without any shoes?" Gareth said. Even though he was clearly conflicted over his feelings for her, he said it with a smile.

Anne's heart leapt at his grin. He usually seemed so very serious, as if the world wasn't something to be enjoyed.

"We're not in a hurry, are we?" she asked.

"No," Gareth said slowly, "I guess we're not."

Anne liked the fact that he was making time for her.

She liked the fact that he held her hand as they walked, while rubbing the pad of his thumb against the inside of her palm in unconsciously sensuous circles. And she liked the way he looked at the city around them as if he was seeing it for the first time, but he still kept looking back at her. Oh, yes, she most definitely liked *him*.

She might even, she thought with a giddy little inner twirl of her heart, be starting to fall in love with him.

"When we get back to the restaurant, how about we go back in for some food?" she suggested. "I don't know about you, but I'm hungry."

"That's because we never got around to ordering or eating lunch."

"I couldn't wait another second to show you around," she pointed out, laughing. "I think it was worth it, don't you?"

"Absolutely."

When they got back to the restaurant and finally ordered, she was so incredibly tempted to reach over the table, pull Gareth forward and kiss him again.

Only, she wanted to savor the moment. And build up slowly to what she hoped would come next.

Their physical attraction was key, of course, but she wanted to get to know everything about him so that they could build a connection that was deeply emotional, as well.

"Did you always want to be a detective?"

"Actually, I wanted to be a football player when I was a little kid," Gareth replied with a laugh. "But after the second time I broke my nose, I nixed that idea."

"And that's when you decided to become a cop?"

He shook his head, his expression serious again. "My father was an honest man. He's the one who taught me how important it is to obey the rules. He was strict, but he was a good man. Always." Gareth's mouth tightened. "One day, his employer claimed that he'd been stealing from them. My father didn't do it, and there was never any real proof, but they went ahead and fired him anyway. That made life hard for us for a while."

"Oh, Gareth, I'm sorry. That sounds horrible."

"It was," he agreed, "until a police detective who was

on the case started digging deeper. He said the facts didn't quite seem to line up, and he couldn't sleep at night if an innocent man with a young family had been penalized for something he hadn't done."

"Did the detective prove your father was innocent?"

Gareth nodded, finally smiling again. "He did. Now it's your turn. Tell me about your favorite dress you've designed over the years."

He listened with surprisingly strong interest while she talked about the differences between velvet and silk, what it was like working with different clients and how it felt to look at a bride on her wedding day and feel the pride and wonder of being a part of one of the most important days of the woman's life.

"Do we want to stay for dessert?"

The only thing Anne wanted for dessert right then was him, but she didn't say that. She couldn't say that. Not when she didn't want to rush things.

"I should probably be getting back home. Did I tell you I have an upcoming photo shoot with *San Francisco* magazine for my wedding dresses?"

"You have something that important to get ready for and you still spent half the day planting shoes with me in the shoe garden?"

"Anything to keep you from having to wear a black trench coat and hover in dark alleyways following bad guys," she teased.

Gareth laughed. "I think we can safely say that going to the shoe garden with you was more fun than that. A *lot* more fun."

After he drove her home, when he was walking with her to her door, Anne knew how easy—and how wonderful—

it would be if he came inside with her. She could pretend that she was just inviting Gareth in for coffee.

Or…she could be far more direct than that by just grabbing him and kissing him.

Except, as she stood on her doorstep, the pulsing attraction between them stronger than ever, she instinctively knew it would be better to take things slower. To let them build naturally.

Yes, she could invite Gareth in and have a wonderful night with him…but she wanted so much more than one wonderful night.

It was the same with the dresses she designed and sewed. She could throw some fabric together and produce something wearable in an afternoon, but it wouldn't be right. It wouldn't be perfect.

And it certainly wouldn't be enough to represent what lay between two people on the most important day of their lives.

"Thank you for today," she said. "I had a really good time."

Gareth leaned forward, and for a moment she thought that he might kiss her again. She wondered how long her resolve would last if he did. Probably not that long.

He simply touched his lips gently to her cheek. "Goodbye, Anne."

How many other men, she thought as she watched him drive away, had she known who were capable of being such perfect gentlemen?

How many men had she met who were capable of being so perfect in any way?

Anne half closed her eyes, smiling to herself, wondering if things could possibly get any better.

It turned out that they could, because when Anne

headed inside and picked her mother's wedding dress up again, what had seemed so tricky earlier in the day flew beneath her fingers, her needle moving deftly to restitch the decorative edging of the gown.

Anne had always known that you couldn't rush making things the way they were meant to be. It was just a question of giving them the care and attention they needed until they were ready.

She flashed back to the kiss she and Gareth had shared in the park, and then to how easy he was to talk to, how wonderful it was just to be near him, and what a perfect gentleman he'd been.

Yes, she thought with a smile as she worked, it had ended up being a very good day.

Practically perfect.

CHAPTER TWELVE

GARETH ARRIVED at the office early the next morning. His afternoon with Anne had invigorated him—her passion for life made him want to be a better man. She'd also gotten him thinking about his business…specifically *why* he was working as a private investigator. His reasons for becoming a cop had been so clear and he wanted that kind of clarity again.

Margaret was at a dentist appointment with her youngest child, so when the phone rang in her office, he picked up. "Cavendish Investigations."

"Gareth." He recognized Richard Wells's voice immediately. "We need to talk."

"What can I do for you, Richard?"

"Can you get some of the DNA of that Farleigh woman?"

Gareth had known this was coming, hadn't he? Still, he carefully confirmed, "Jasmine wants to get a DNA test to prove shared paternity?"

"Exactly, and the easiest way to do that is to persuade the Farleigh woman to provide DNA. It's simple, conclusive and should put a stop to the nonsense that went on at the mediation."

Gareth took several slow deep breaths to deal with the quick rise of anger that came from hearing the disdain in Richard's voice when he spoke about Anne.

"You do realize it won't be easy to get her to go along with this test, don't you?"

"From what we could see between the two of you outside the mediation room, it looks like you've gotten to know her pretty well." Gareth's fists curled at the suggestive sneer in the lawyer's voice. "That should help when it comes to persuading her."

"You want *me* to talk her into doing the test?"

"It's what I'm paying you for."

"And if Anne won't agree to do it?"

"You talked her into going to the mediation, didn't you?" Richard snapped. "I'm sure if you point out to her that the alternative is having her father's body exhumed so that we can take a DNA sample from that, she'll be more amenable to giving you one."

Gareth had seen and heard some unpleasant things in his time as a cop, but this was pretty damn high up the list. "You'd actually do that?"

"In a heartbeat. Though it would be easier if you could just 'find' a sample. I don't care how you do it," Richard said. "Just get it done."

He hung up, leaving Gareth standing there holding the phone.

"You look like you've just seen a ghost," Margaret said as she came in through the front door. "What's wrong?" When he didn't answer right away, she said, "Don't make me guess like I do with my teenagers."

"Richard wants me to force Anne into giving a DNA sample."

She frowned. "DNA evidence is not uncommon in a case like this. What's the problem, Gareth?"

The problem was that people didn't go in for DNA

tests in legal cases unless they were already pretty certain of the outcome.

"This will destroy her, Margaret."

Margaret reached out to put a hand on his arm. "And that won't be your fault."

"You honestly don't think it will be my fault if I push Anne into the test that proves her father cheated on her mother and destroys everything she ever thought about her family?"

"No," Margaret insisted. "It won't. It will be her father's fault for cheating. You have a job to do. All you can do is try to make it as easy as possible. So far, I'd say you've been a lot kinder to Anne Farleigh than anyone else would have been."

Gareth shook his head. "The point is that it's *me* dragging her into it."

Margaret sighed theatrically. "Working for a P.I. with a conscience is tough going. At this rate, my kids are never going to get their way paid through college." She paused and gave him a small smile. "But I knew exactly who you were when I went with you, Gareth. You're one of the best men I've ever known. And you need to do what's *right*."

Gareth didn't pause before picking up the phone again.

"Gareth?" Richard Wells said. "That was quick. You've managed to set things up already?"

"No," Gareth said.

"So you've come to me with more problems? I don't have the time to sit and hold your hand while you do your job."

"Actually, this is about my job." Gareth didn't hesitate. "I quit, Richard."

"What?"

"I'm not doing any more work for you on this case."

There was silence on the other end of the line for a second or two. "This is a joke, right? You made the mistake of getting too close to Anne Farleigh, and now you can't do your job anymore."

"Then it's just as well that I'm quitting, isn't it?" Gareth said. "I'm done, Richard."

"You're done, all right," Richard replied. "Don't think you're getting any more work from my firm. Or from any of our clients. Oh, and you'd better not go running to Anne Farleigh to blab what you know."

"I don't work for you anymore, Richard," Gareth pointed out.

"You signed a nondisclosure agreement when you agreed to do this job, or did you forget that part? Look it over, and you'll see what it will cost you if you breathe one *word* of this to Anne Farleigh."

"A minute ago, you wanted me to talk her into the DNA test."

"And it will still get done," Richard said. "But now I'm thinking that if we time it right, she might just fold completely."

"You can't—"

"Oh, yes, I can," Richard said. "It's you who can't save her. You can talk to her all you like, but if you tell her anything you were told in confidence—"

Gareth hung up the phone with a loud bang.

"Looks like I'll have to put off buying that private island for a while, won't I?" Margaret said softly. And yet, her expression told him just how proud she was of him, despite the fact that they were going to have to find several new cases, and fast.

"Sorry," Gareth said. "But I need to go—"

Margaret put a hand on his arm. "I know exactly what you're going to do. Just promise me you won't do anything that will get you thrown out of that nice apartment of yours. With all of my kids taking up space all over the house, I don't have room for you to move in, too."

Gareth headed first for Anne's house, but when she wasn't there, he knew where he'd find her. She was in The Rose Chalet's main hall, talking to a woman Gareth didn't recognize, and there was a recording device sitting on the table between them.

For the briefest of moments, Gareth feared that Richard had somehow managed to get someone down there to force a deposition out of Anne, and he started forward. Then he realized they were talking about dresses. Thank God.

"I don't pay too much attention to what the trends are," Anne was saying. "Instead, I try to figure out exactly what's right for the individual client and her wedding. Too often, people wear dresses that are beautiful, and they're the right style for the season, but they aren't right for them."

"And do you only use specific materials?" the reporter asked. "Some designers are very careful about where they source things these days."

"I use whatever looks right, wherever I can find it," Anne said with a smile. "For Felicity's dress, for example, I had the *perfect* fabric in a storage box at home."

Gareth's chest squeezed tight as he stood there watching her. He had to tell her about the upcoming DNA test. He had to warn her, had to inform her of the kinds of things Richard and Jasmine might come out with when this case went to court...

And then what?

Gareth had no doubt that Richard would make good on his threat to sue Cavendish Investigations. He'd likely win, and then both Margaret and Gareth would have to start over.

And yet, fear of having a lawsuit brought against him wasn't what stopped Gareth from just walking up to Anne and saying it straight-out. If it had just been that, he would have done it in a heartbeat.

No, what stopped him was the sure knowledge that leaking information to Anne would be breaking the rules. And whatever Gareth thought of Richard Wells— and it wasn't very much at this point—Gareth had given his word. He'd signed a contract. He'd made a legal commitment.

Could he go back on that? Even for Anne?

A few minutes later, when her interview was winding down, she looked up and spotted him. "Gareth! What are you doing here?" She hurried over to hug him hello. "Are you here to take me out to lunch again? It's a bit early, but I think we're almost done here, aren't we, Tessa?"

The female reporter looked Gareth up and down. "Sure, have fun. I think I have everything I need, and I'll email you if any other questions come up."

"So," Anne said, slipping her hand into Gareth's, "where are we heading for lunch?"

He knew he ought to say *nowhere.* Or that he ought to warn her about the DNA test, rules be damned.

But right at that moment, with her lips so close to

his, Gareth couldn't think about anything other than how wonderful it had been to kiss her and how much he'd like to do it again.

CHAPTER THIRTEEN

"How DID YOU find this place?"

The tiny diner looked as if it had been transplanted straight out of the 1950s, and it seemed to be run by about twenty assorted members of the same boisterous family, all of whom bustled about.

"I was walking past one day," Anne replied, "and everyone inside looked so happy. I knew that it had to be a good place to eat if it made people that happy."

Would anyone else have decided to try the food in a diner for a reason like that?

Only Anne.

And, he had to admit as he took a bite of his hamburger, the food was pretty good…though it didn't even come close to being as good as his present company.

All through lunch, Gareth was mesmerized by every movement Anne made, every elegant gesture, every beautiful smile.

And there were so many smiles….

He shouldn't be taking this day off, especially when he needed to line up more clients in the wake of quitting Jasmine and Richard's case. So what was it about Anne that made playing hooky seem perfectly all right? And what was it about her that made him smile just watching her talk with the waitress?

Unfortunately, his smile didn't last long. Not when he still had to tell her about the DNA test.

Because all it took was a half dozen of her smiles for him to realize that the nondisclosure agreement didn't matter. She did.

Now, the tricky part was finding the right way—and time—to tell her.

ANNE LAUGHED as they checked on their shoes in the shoe garden, remembering that wonderful day. Then Gareth told her the story of the first time he'd chased a criminal as a cop, and how they'd both ended up so out of breath he'd barely been able to read the man his rights.

"You must have been very determined to go after him like that. What had he done?"

"Actually, he was a shoplifter," he admitted with a wry twist of his lips. "But he'd broken the law, and I wasn't about to let him get away."

They both laughed then. Gareth was so easy to talk to. They started to walk back to his car and ended up on a park bench beside a small pond. They bought a loaf of bread from a nearby bakery so they could throw bread crumbs to the small flotilla of ducks that bobbed on the water expectantly.

The best part was that he always listened so intently. When she started to tell him about different kinds of lace and this lovely little place nearby where she liked to buy it, only to realize that a big, tough private detective probably wouldn't be interested, he actually suggested that they drop into the store, rather than trying to change the subject as most men would have.

"I think I'd rather sit here awhile longer," Anne suggested, sliding her hand into his.

A LITTLE WHILE LATER, sitting on Pier 39, they watched the sun start to set. It was one of those things Gareth had heard of doing, but who actually did it?

Anne did.

She looked as beautiful as ever as she tilted her face up to the sky to soak up the rays of the setting sun. He couldn't imagine standing and watching a sunset alone, but with her, it actually made sense.

It was such a small thing, but Anne took small things and looked at them until she found the beauty in them, and when she did, he could see the beauty, too, for the very first time.

It was almost enough to drive thoughts of the DNA test from his mind.

ANNE FELT AS IF she was living a fairy tale as she walked along the sandy beach in the moonlight, hand in hand with Gareth.

It wasn't just how strong or how steady he was. No, those things were wonderful, but the best part, the part that made it special, was the fact that he seemed to feel the same way. He was content to walk with her in comfortable silence until she noticed a particularly beautiful shell, or until she wanted to tell him about the time she'd been to the beach with Rose back when they were kids.

And yet, Anne could tell Gareth was thinking about something as they walked. Something important.

She hoped he would feel comfortable enough to talk to her about it soon.

GARETH WHIRLED ROUND in a circle with Anne in his arms. He still wasn't sure how she'd talked him into dancing barefoot on the beach with no music. It wasn't the kind of thing he did.

Except that here, now, with her, dancing in the sand made perfect sense.

"That's it," Anne said breathlessly. "You just have to listen for the music in the waves."

A few minutes later, their legs tangled up, they tumbled down together on the sand. They were so close now that it was easy to kiss one another. Easy and amazing at the same time.

They held each other like that for long minutes, looking out over the waves, Gareth's arms wrapped around Anne as they did so.

It was perfect. Too perfect to ruin by saying the wrong thing.

He'd tell her about the DNA test when he took her home. That would be better, anyway, because then he could comfort her in private if the news hit her hard.

"Would you like to come back to my place for a late-night dinner?" Anne asked out of nowhere.

"Your place?"

Anne nodded. "I haven't planned anything, but—"

Gareth cut her off with a kiss. "I'd love to."

ANNE DIDN'T HAVE anything in her fridge that could be remotely considered as ingredients for a romantic dinner, yet she did her best with what she could find, throwing together chicken, rice and a sauce packet she didn't remember buying.

"This is great," Gareth assured her when he tasted it. He was always so kind. As they ate, they talked about their childhoods and tried to outdo each other with silly stories of adventures they'd had as kids.

All the while, Anne felt as if Gareth was circling around something. She tried to be patient and let him tell her in his own time.

Was there any chance that he was going to say that he was in love with her?

He had to tell her.

Gareth had been putting it off all day, but Anne deserved to know about the DNA test.

He'd do anything to spare her pain. He'd seen how upset she'd been when he'd first come to her house, and how happy she'd been after the mediation when she'd thought it had all gone away, yet he couldn't *not* tell her.

Not when it meant that Richard Wells could spring the news on her at any time.

Gareth put his fork down, trying to find the words. "Anne, all day there's something that I've been trying to figure out how to tell you."

"I know you have, Gareth," Anne said with a wide smile on her beautiful mouth.

And then she kissed him.

Anne kissed Gareth as passionately as she'd ever kissed anyone, and then she slid her hand into his and pulled him through the living room and up the stairs.

When she turned back to face him at the threshold of her bedroom, he was looking at her with such hunger that a shiver of need took her over, body and soul.

She reached up on tiptoe to kiss him again, a kiss that was sweet and tender and wonderful.

When they pulled back, Gareth looked as if he might say something, but Anne beat him to it.

"I love you, too."

CHAPTER FOURTEEN

ANNE WOKE UP to the sun coming through the window of her bedroom, spilling in and over her. Through the window, the sky was a perfect blue, the birds were singing to each other, and the bright green leaves on the trees were dancing in the light breeze.

Everything was *perfect*.

She could hear Gareth downstairs in the kitchen. He'd obviously tried hard not to wake her, but Anne's eyes had flickered open the moment he'd moved from beside her, giving her a fabulous view of his toned body as he dressed.

Anne went into the bathroom and showered, enjoying the feel of the water on her skin. The way the warmth caressed her skin reminded her of Gareth. Although, she thought with a laugh, the truth was, everything reminded her of him right then.

Last night had been everything she had always dreamed it might be. Not just physically satisfying but emotionally satisfying, as well. There hadn't been any barriers between them, just so many sweet yet sinful moments where she wasn't sure where she stopped and he began.

She dried off, then put on a sky-blue T-shirt she'd customized with silver stitching around the edges, and a pair of jeans with extra decorative patches. Every small thing leapt out at her this morning, from just how much she appreciated the old pictures on the wall to how stunning her mother's wedding dress looked on one of her dressmaking stands in the living room.

And then there was Gareth. He stood in the kitchen with his back to her, cooking scrambled eggs on the stove. He turned as Anne entered the room, and she was on the way to give him a good-morning kiss when they were interrupted by a knock at the door.

She was surprised when he quickly moved past her. "Why don't you go ahead and start on breakfast?"

Since he had just gone to the trouble of making her breakfast, Anne took her plate of eggs and toast to the kitchen table by the window. They tasted great—just the way she would have made them herself. She was on her second or third mouthful when the sound of Gareth's raised voice drew her attention.

"I don't care who you say you are. You aren't coming in."

"You think you can help her hide from this?" another man's voice demanded in a hard tone. "I was told to deliver this to Anne Farleigh, and you aren't going to stop me from doing my job."

"Wanna bet?"

Anne shot up from the table, spilling her scrambled eggs as she hurried through to the hall.

The man at the door was big and tough-looking, dressed in a dark suit and holding an envelope.

"What's going on?"

He started to step past Gareth, but Gareth wouldn't let him pass.

"Anne Farleigh?"

"Yes," Anne said, "that's me. Who are you?"

"My name is Terrence Blithe. I work for Richard Wells, Jasmine Turner's lawyer. He's asked me to inform you that Ms. Turner intends to submit to a DNA test proving that she's Edward Farleigh's daughter."

He threw the envelope to her, and she caught it out of sheer reflex.

"Those are the details. He's also told me to let you know that if you don't agree to take part in this DNA test, he will ask the judge to consider your noncooperation when it comes to deciding how much to award. And that he'll press for the exhumation of Edward Farleigh to get the DNA evidence he needs."

"Wait a minute," Anne said, staring down at the envelope. She looked back at the man at the door. "I don't understand."

"That's your problem, lady. Have a nice day."

He walked off, leaving Anne standing there, trying to make sense of what had just happened.

Have a nice day? She'd been having a nice day. The best day ever, and now...

Her eyes were starting to blur with tears as Gareth put his arms around her and took her into the living room. His voice was gentle. "I'm sorry. I should have warned you, but—"

"You should have warned me?" Suddenly, Anne felt as if the hardwood floor beneath her was falling away. "You *knew?*"

Anne tried to ignore the negative feelings that suddenly sprang up the way she had done so many times before. But this time it was like trying to plug the Hoover Dam with her finger.

She pushed back from Gareth and stared at him as

if she didn't even know him. Because, right then, she wasn't sure she did.

Especially when he said, "Yes, Anne, I knew."

"You knew and you didn't say anything?" Each word felt brittle as it fell from her lips. "How could you let them blindside me like this?"

"At first, I didn't say anything about it because I couldn't. I had a legal obligation not to."

"And rules are rules," Anne said, half turning away from him as she felt the tears starting to well up in her eyes.

Years' worth of tears began to fall, tears she'd managed to hold back through her sheer determination to be happy.

"I tried to tell you," he insisted.

"When? When did you try?"

"I needed to find a way to tell you that wouldn't hurt so much, but it was so hard, and I couldn't figure out how to do it last night. I hoped it would be easier this morning, and that I could find a way to explain it without hurting you."

Anne whirled back toward him, her hands balling into fists. "You think that *this* doesn't hurt?"

Oh, God, it hurt.

It hurt so much. It was as if her parents had died all over again. For years, Anne had worked hard to press that pain down. The depths of hurt drowned her every time she tried to breathe. She'd only managed it by remembering how much her parents had loved one another. By clinging to that knowledge as tightly as she could.

But it had been a lie.

All of it.

Jasmine and her lawyer wouldn't ask for a DNA test if they thought there was even the remotest possibility that Edward Farleigh wasn't Jasmine's father. Which meant that all time her father had claimed to love her mother so much, all time their marriage had seemed so perfect, he'd been having an affair with some other woman.

And had been the father of another little girl.

"Anne," Gareth began, reaching out to touch her shoulder.

"Leave me alone!"

Anne had wanted to believe that she and Gareth had found the same magical love as her parents. But now she knew that the two of them were just as big a lie as her parents had been. Because the whole time she'd been in Gareth's arms, kissing and sharing her bed with him, he'd known what was going to happen.

In her rush to get away from him, she crashed into her mother's wedding gown on the dress stand.

Wedding dresses were a symbol of two people promising to love one another. Promising to be *faithful* to one another. Anne had made her living stitching together a symbol of perfect love, but now she knew that love was the biggest lie of all.

"I hate this stupid thing!"

She tore the dress from the stand, wanting to tear it into rags, then burn those rags like the meaningless scraps of fabric they were. Her fingers ripped at it, pulling apart seams and opening up lines of stitching like wounds.

And yet, none of it, *none* of the mess she'd just made of the once-beautiful dress, looked as bad as she felt right then.

"Anne! What are you doing?"

He caught her arms and pulled her back from the dress, holding her against his chest.

Anne fought to break free from him. She wasn't going to let herself cry in his arms the way she had before. And she definitely wasn't going to let him promise her that everything would be all right.

Nothing was all right…and wouldn't ever be again.

"Let. Me. Go."

"I know how upset you are right now," Gareth said as she pushed away from him, "but don't keep destroying your mother's dress. Not when I know how much it means to you."

"You don't know anything about me," Anne snapped back, letting herself lash out for the first time in her life. "I was stupid enough to think I loved you, but love is just a word, isn't it? Just something people say to try to feel better about their pointless lives."

"That's not what love is," Gareth insisted.

"No, you're right," Anne said. "Love isn't even that, because it *doesn't* make you feel better. It just tears you up inside."

Gareth reached out to put his hands on her waist and wouldn't let her evade his touch no matter how she tried. "You have to keep believing in love."

"Why should I, when it's just another lie?"

"Because love is real."

"And how could you possibly know that?"

He didn't hesitate. "Because I love you."

A part of Anne wanted so desperately to believe him. Because if she could believe in his love, then maybe…

No, she wasn't going to put her faith in any more fairy tales. She couldn't.

She broke free of his grip. "Get out, Gareth. Just…
get out."

"Anne—"

"Get *out!*"

A few seconds later, when the door closed behind
him with a soft click, Anne collapsed on the pile of
ripped and ruined fabric from her mother's wedding
dress and cried every last one of the tears she'd held
back since she was a little girl standing at the window
with her mother, watching the taxi take her father away
one more time.

CHAPTER FIFTEEN

GARETH WAITED in his car outside Richard Wells's office until he saw the lawyer leave. Gareth had set up a meeting for him using a false name. What he was about to do would only work if the lawyer wasn't here in his office. Even then, Gareth would be breaking so many laws he could barely believe he was really about to do this.

Breaking and entering, burglary, possibly even industrial espionage. If he was caught, he could not only get his P.I. license revoked but maybe even end up in jail.

But if it helped Anne, he didn't care.

All those years of sticking to the letter of the law were gone in a flash. For Anne, he'd gladly break the rules if it would take away her look of betrayal when she'd realized that he knew about the DNA test. If what he was doing would restore her faith in him, it would be worth it.

Was this what Brian had felt when he'd found out his girlfriend's son was caught up with a bad group?

Gareth had spent so long hanging on to his certainty that things were black-and-white, and that Brian had done the wrong thing. And yet, with Anne's happiness on the line, he could suddenly see so clearly why someone would break the rules for someone they loved.

Just as Brian's fiancée had said, love changed everything.

Absolutely everything.

Gareth got out of his car and strode across to the law offices, making sure he looked confident as he said hello to the receptionist, then headed to the office area. No one tried to stop him. After all, he'd been here enough times to be recognizable, and he obviously knew where he was going.

He headed straight up to Richard Wells's office and a young woman came over. "Can I help you?" She asked the question rather flirtatiously, while clearly admiring the way he looked in his dark suit.

Gareth, fortunately, had always been good with names. "Nikki, it's good to see you again. I'm here for my meeting with Richard."

"Oh, no," she said with a small pout, "there must have been a mix-up. Richard just left the office for a meeting downtown."

"I really don't have much time," he grumbled in a tone that indicated he in no way blamed her for the mix-up but that he was frustrated by the inconvenience just the same.

"Would you like a cup of coffee while you wait in his office?"

She was already pouring him one, and after he thanked her for it, he said, "I suppose I could give him a few minutes."

Luck was on his side when the lights on her phone suddenly lit up.

"Please let me know if you need anything else while you're waiting," she said before rushing back to her desk to deal with the flurry of calls.

It had been that easy to get into Richard's office. For the next few minutes, he was all alone to look out over the city's skyline, admire the mementos the lawyer had picked up from around the globe, enjoy his cup of coffee…and steal a look at the file relating to Anne's case.

Fortunately, it was at the top of the pile of files on Richard's desk.

Making sure he could still hear Nikki's voice as she dealt with the callers, he slipped on gloves so he wouldn't leave fingerprints, then reached for the security camera over the door and slipped a piece of black tape over it. If he found anything in Richard's file, he'd photograph it on his phone. He wouldn't risk taking documents.

Ten minutes later, he pulled the tape from the security camera and then informed Nikki that he'd have to reschedule his meeting with Richard. He hadn't taken a single picture because there wasn't anything in the files but cold, clinical facts.

The only new information he'd learned was that Anne had given a DNA sample and the results would be back soon.

When had she agreed to do that?

And, really, what had he been expecting to find in Richard's case file? Because nothing could change the fact that Edward Farleigh was Jasmine's father. So what was he actually trying to do? Win the case for Anne? Deal with Jasmine Turner? Beat Richard Wells?

All he really wanted to do was make Anne happy. In fact, he'd give anything to do that.

But how?

Fortunately, by the time he left the building, he had an idea. A good one, he hoped.

Realizing just how much ground he had to cover before the DNA results were revealed at the follow-up mediation, he pushed the gas pedal to the floor as he called his office on his cell.

"Gareth?" Margaret said on the other end of the line. "Where have you been this morning? We've had several inquiries for new clients, and I'd like to schedule their consultation visits with you as soon as possible."

"That's great," he said, "but there's something else I need to do first. I need the address for Jasmine Turner's mother in Oregon."

FIVE HOURS LATER, he drove through the pretty town of Ashland, Oregon, until he found the house he was looking for. The sun had set, and small garden lights lit his way up the front path. He'd barely knocked on the door when Deirdre Turner opened it.

She looked a lot like her daughter, even though she must be in her late forties. Gareth was struck by how close her blond hair, blue eyes and elegant good looks resembled Anne's mother in the photos he'd seen of the Farleigh family.

"Deirdre Turner? My name's Gareth Cavendish—"

"Yes, you're the detective who was helping Jasmine go after Edward's daughter."

"It's actually quite a bit more complicated than that. Which is why I need to talk to you."

"I'm sorry, Mr. Cavendish, but I've already told Jasmine I won't help her with this."

She started to shut the door, but Gareth jammed his foot in it before she could lock it on him. He'd already broken the law so many times already today. Did one little piece of trespassing matter?

Except, of course, for the part where it felt as if he might have a couple of broken toes.

"Ms. Turner, please. I'm not here because Jasmine sent me. I'm here because I'm in love with Anne Farleigh, and I don't want to see her hurt."

"You're in love with her?" Deirdre opened the door slightly, and he barely held back a wince as the bones in his foot began to ache. "Even though you've been working for Jasmine and her lawyer?"

"I'm not working for them anymore," he said. "I love Anne too much to stay on the case. But I can't let her deal with this on her own, either. Not when everything is about to spiral out of control."

Jasmine's mother stared at him for a long moment before stepping back. "Why don't you come in, and we'll see if we can find some ice for that foot."

She took him through to her living room full of pictures of Jasmine growing up. It reminded Gareth of the family photos in Anne's home.

Deirdre handed him an ice pack for his foot and set a cup of coffee onto the table beside him before finally sitting down, her own cup cradled in her hands.

"I love my daughter," she told him, "even if I don't agree with what she's doing."

"Why don't you agree with it?"

"It isn't what Edward would have wanted. Jasmine is so angry about it all that she won't listen to anything I say about how it all played out between me and her father."

"Can you tell me what happened?" Gareth asked.

For a moment, he thought Deirdre wouldn't do it, but

then she nodded. "I met him when he came to Ashland on a book tour. I'd read all of his books, and I think I'd kind of fallen in love with the *idea* of him, if that makes any sense. Anyway, after the book signing, when everyone else had gone, he looked so lonely that I invited him to come to a party with some friends of mine. We talked for hours, and I must have reminded him of his wife. I was young enough not to know better, and when one thing led to another, I didn't think to stop it, even though it was clear he'd never had an affair in his life… nor did he really intend to. Had it not been for Jasmine, I very much doubt I ever would have seen him again."

"So Edward Farleigh is definitely Jasmine's father?" Gareth asked.

Deirdre nodded. "When I told him I was pregnant, it was clear that he didn't want to leave me to deal with raising a baby all on my own. He sent me money to help out, and he used to visit from time to time to see Jasmine." She made sure to clarify, "He and I only slept together that once, you see, and it was clear just how horrible he felt about what he'd done to his wife."

"How often did he visit?"

Deirdre sighed. "I guess that's where all these problems started. You see, I wouldn't let Edward visit too often, because I knew how confusing it would be for Jasmine to have a father who was there and gone again. I thought it was better if he was simply a 'family friend,' because I knew Edward would never leave his family for us. He loved Chloe and Anne too much and missed them every minute he was apart from them. But he loved Jasmine, too. I'm sure of it. He would have liked to have spent so much more time with her, but knowing that we'd never have him completely, and that it would only end up breaking Jasmine's heart, I cut off contact with him when she was just a little girl." Her eyes were bleak. "I honestly believed this way was better. Only, when she got older she wouldn't stop asking about him, and then she found his picture…."

"I understand," Gareth said. "You had a terribly difficult choice to make. And you made the best one you could at the time."

"I wish my daughter understood things the way you do. All this time, she grew up wondering who her father was and what she'd done to make him go away, even though I told her it wasn't her fault. The whole court case…I don't even think it's about the money. I think it's more that she just wants something that was Edward's, because she never got to have *him*."

"Whereas Anne did," Gareth said softly. "Ms. Turner, I know you don't know me and that you don't owe me anything, but there's something I'm really hoping you will do…."

CHAPTER SIXTEEN

"I NEVER NOTICED BEFORE," Anne declared, "just how nice the ceiling is in here."

Lying next to her on the dance floor of The Rose Chalet that evening, Rose turned her head toward her friend. "You're drunk."

"So are you."

And they were. Completely smashed.

"Well, what else are best friends for?" Rose asked.

"You're totally my best friend—" Anne's words slurred slightly "—but this isn't just sympathy drinking, is it?"

"Yes. It is!"

"No," Anne insisted. "RJ went off to go on a date with some other woman, and now you're all—"

Rose made a sound that was a cross between a growl and a hiccup, and Anne quickly shut her mouth. Well, as quickly as she could, given how numb her lips felt.

They lapsed into a brief silence punctuated by more gulps from the bottles close at hand.

The fizzy, sweet champagne helped Anne admit, "Did I tell you that I tore up my mother's dress?"

"No! What a horrible idea, Anne. Why'd you do that?"

Unfortunately, getting drunk hadn't helped her forget one single thing that had happened. She could still remember the hurt, the despair she'd felt when she'd yelled at Gareth to leave.

And how it had been even worse when he'd actually left.

"Because it was a lie!" Anne declared.

"Hold on. That doesn't make sense."

Rose rolled over so that they could talk face-to-face. Her friend's features blurred slightly when Anne did the same thing.

"It's a dress. Not a lie. Can't be both." Rose held up a hand in front of her face as if she was counting her fingers to make sure they were all there. "No, it definitely can't be both."

"Not the dress," Anne said.

"You just said it *was* the dress."

Rose looked more than a little perplexed. Though frankly, given the amount they'd both had to drink, even the painted design on the ceiling was looking pretty confusing.

"Everything," Anne insisted. "Everything's a lie."

"Oh, God," Rose said. "This is like being back in Mrs. Findler's philosophy class. Do you remember her?"

"I remember all kinds of things," Anne assured her. The alcohol didn't help her forget. Instead, it seemed to clear away the walls she'd put up around her memories.

All those times her father hadn't been home. The way her mother would always be so down but utterly determined that everything would be normal. And, especially, the way Anne felt she had to pretend along with her. With happier smiles. Bigger hugs.

"My dad had an affair," she said softly, before repeating it in a louder, angrier voice. "My dad had an affair, and I think my mom knew about it. And now his *secret* daughter wants half of everything, and Gareth didn't tell me what they were going to do, even though we slept together and he *knew the whole time,* and the next mediation is tomorrow morning before the wedding to go over the DNA samples, and they died, Rose. *They died.*"

Rose put an arm around her as they lay together on the floor in a messy drunken heap. "I know, honey. I know. But you have to try to be positive."

"Why?" Anne demanded. "I'm so sick of being positive. My parents die, and I have to be positive, like nothing has happened. Gareth lies to me, and I have to be *positive.* When has being positive ever made things hurt any less?"

Not now, that was for sure.

"It feels…it feels like there isn't anything good left now from when I was a kid," Anne said. She paused to drink more of the champagne. "It's like I made all that up. Like the only parts that were real are the parts that hurt."

Rose made a fierce—but blurry—face at her. "There were good parts. Do you remember my mom taking us fishing down in the bay, and we all stood up in the boat and fell into the green, slimy muck?"

Anne supposed that *had* been kind of fun.

"And there was the time you made us dresses for the high school dance," Rose continued. "Do you remember? I went with Billy Stevens, and you were with…"

"Nerdy Neil," Anne said with a small smile this time.

"Do you remember those glasses he wore? They must have been an inch thick. And as I recall, he was the only guy in school who thought coming over to 'help with math homework' actually involved math homework."

"We passed math, though," Anne pointed out.

"And there was the time you decided that cheerleading was mostly about being bright and positive, so you joined the squad. That lasted, what, a week?"

"It's not my fault they didn't want me to redesign their team uniform. I thought it was a nice gesture."

Rose kept on like that, with more good, fun, happy memories, and slowly Anne had to admit that her childhood hadn't been all bad.

"Did you really destroy your mother's dress?" Rose asked, the idea obviously having taken a while to sink in through the champagne.

"Ripped it up into tiny pieces," Anne confirmed.

Rose's eyes suddenly grew big. "Wait a minute. You didn't cut up Felicity's dress, too, did you?"

"Of course not. That would have been *wrong.* Her dress is so beautiful…"

"Your mom's dress was beautiful, too," Rose pointed out.

Anne lay there for a second or two, her eyes half-closed to try to keep her tears from falling.

"Yes," she said, "it was. And then it wasn't."

"I don't think I'm drunk enough to understand that one," Rose said.

"I don't know if I can make wedding dresses anymore," Anne said. "Not when they're supposed to be about love and happiness and forever."

"Well," Rose said slowly, "you know I hope you'll change your mind when we sober up. Especially because you've got one wedding dress you absolutely *have* to make."

"I already told you," Anne said, "Felicity's dress is done."

"Not hers," Rose said. "Mine."

Yikes! Apparently, there *were* some things alcohol could help you forget.

How had she managed to forget her best friend's wedding? Especially when it was coming up so soon?

"It's just," Anne said a bit defensively, "that there are all these people who come through here getting married, and you're getting married, and Julie has Andrew, and Phoebe has Patrick…even Tyce got Whitney. What about me?"

Rose squeezed her tighter. "Your turn will come."

Anne shook her head. "I used to think that one day, *the one* would show up, I'd get married and have this perfect life."

"I don't think people get perfect lives," Rose said, philosophical now. "I think we mostly just get lives."

"It shouldn't work like that," Anne insisted.

"But it does."

"But it *shouldn't*." Anne made herself stop before they began a back-and-forth that could go on for hours. "Have you ever had a man kiss you and, all at once, it felt perfect? Like all of your dreams had just come true?"

Rose didn't answer for a second or two, until, very softly, she murmured, "Yes."

"Oh, of course you have," Anne said. "You're marrying Donovan. He's your knight in shining armor."

"Did someone call for a knight in shining armor?"

RJ unexpectedly walked into the room, dressed up in a shirt and slacks.

"Aren't you supposed to be out on a date?" Anne asked him without getting up off the floor.

"My plans got canceled at the last second, so I thought

I'd come back here and check that everything was ready for tomorrow."

"We already checked," Rose said as she worked at trying to sit up.

RJ raised an eyebrow at her slightly slurred explanation. "Then what are you two doing here so late?"

Anne had an answer for that one. "Getting drunk. You could, too, except I'm pretty sure we drank all the champagne."

"There's a little left in your bottle," RJ said, "but we should probably be getting the two of you home, don't you think?"

Anne smiled at that, especially when RJ bent down and more or less picked Rose up. He was always so sweet. Not to mention good-looking and kind. A short while later, he came back, lifting Anne to her feet. "Come on," he coaxed in a gentle voice, "let's see if those legs of yours work."

They did, just barely, and she appreciated the help RJ gave her even as she wished that it was Gareth's arms around her instead.

CHAPTER SEVENTEEN

GARETH'S JAGUAR LEFT skid marks on the pavement outside Anne's house the following morning as he slammed on the brakes and leapt from the car. He'd driven for hours with no sleep, but the envelope in his jacket pocket—and his love for Anne—made the all-nighter worth it…as long as he could get it into her hands in time.

He knocked at her door, and when there was no answer, he said, "Anne, are you in there? It's me." Knowing the odds were extremely high that she didn't want to see him, he called out again, "Please, Anne, just open the door."

Was she sitting in her house, so wrapped up in the misery he'd helped to bring into her life that she couldn't even come to the door? Just the thought of that made something tighten painfully in Gareth's chest. He tried calling her on her cell phone, but it went straight to voice mail.

He couldn't take the chance that she was in there, all alone. After all the rules he'd broken for her already, what was one more?

He rammed his shoulder against the front door, and the lock gave on the first attempt. There were still shreds of wedding dress on the living room floor, but there was no sign of her. After a quick check of the upstairs, he pulled out his phone again.

He quickly dialed the number for the courthouse. "I need to know the time of the Turner versus Farleigh mediation," he said to the harassed-sounding man who answered. "It was supposed to be scheduled for 3:00 p.m. today."

"I'm afraid I can't divulge that information, sir."

Fortunately, Gareth thought he recognized the man's gravelly voice. "Jerry? It's Gareth. How have you been? I haven't seen you in quite a while."

"Gareth, it's good to hear from you! I was out in New York visiting my grandkids for a while. Listen, I didn't know it was you on the phone. Give me a minute and I'll check the schedule." There was a pause while he flipped through his papers. "Actually, they've moved things around today. It's just about to begin."

After Gareth promised to come by to look at pictures of Jerry's grandkids, he ran back out to his car. He sped toward the courthouse, praying he could get there in time, not caring even the slightest bit about rules and laws as he nearly ran two red lights and swerved between lanes.

The only thing that mattered was Anne.

Five minutes later—record time, considering Anne lived ten minutes away—Gareth jumped out of his car and rushed inside the building.

Relief swept over him when he saw Richard Wells's new investigator standing by the door of the conference room where the previous mediation had been held.

Terrence stepped out into Gareth's path as he got close, holding up a hand. "Where do you think you're going?"

"Into the mediation."

All those years of chasing the bad guys down had

made him pretty darn quick on his feet, and it wasn't hard for him to get past Terrence and into the room.

Richard was there with Jasmine, and the mediator from before, Ms. Williams, was there, too, but Gareth barely spared them a second glance. He had eyes for only Anne.

She looked…well, frankly, she looked more than a little hungover. Worse than that, she looked so *serious,* wearing a plain dark suit.

Yet, despite all that, she was still the most beautiful woman he'd ever seen.

Still his angel.

She was also clearly shocked to see him.

"Gareth? What are you doing here?"

Richard butted in before he could reply. "You have zero business being in this room, Cavendish. I fired you, remember?"

Gareth ignored the lawyer and said, "Anne, I have something I need you to see. It's urgent."

"He can't just come in here like this, can he?" Jasmine asked. "We were just getting to the results of the DNA test."

Gareth ignored Jasmine, too, as he took the envelope out of his pocket. "Please, Anne."

She looked at the envelope and then back at him before saying, "The way I remember it, the last time you came to me with an envelope, it wasn't such good news."

"This one…" Gareth paused. "I don't know if it's better, but I think it will help."

"Help?" Richard Wells's face reddened with anger. "Ms. Williams, this is going too far. He can't just introduce new evidence like this. He shouldn't even be in here. He has no legal right—"

Anne stood up and asked the mediator, "Could we please have a recess?"

"We're just about to get to the important part," Jasmine insisted. "She can't just walk out because this isn't going well for her. Richard, I demand that you stop them!"

But Ms. Williams had clearly had enough. "Everybody be quiet right now!" She glared at Gareth. "You've barged into the middle of my mediation session, you're in some kind of complex relationship with the parties involved, and you seem to be determined to introduce some kind of new evidence into the proceedings. May I ask why you're doing all this, when you know it might lead to you being thrown out of here by security?"

There was only one answer to that. An answer that he would happily tell the world.

"Because I love Anne Farleigh."

"Oh, very nice," Richard sneered. "Very sweet. We're in the middle of a serious legal process, and you come barging in to declare your undying love. Honestly, what kind of—"

"Mr. Wells," Ms. Williams said, her expression much softer now, "I don't think it would hurt to have a short break at this point. Not when I think we could all do with some time to calm down. I'll see you all back here in fifteen minutes."

"Thank you," Gareth said as he reached for Anne's hand and pulled her out of the room and into a quiet corner.

"I…" Anne shook her head. "I want to believe what you just said in front of everyone, Gareth. I want to believe you so much, but people lie. They cheat. Things go so wrong."

"They go right, too," Gareth assured her. He gently cupped her chin with his hands so he could look directly into her eyes. "Can you honestly tell me that you don't feel the same way?"

Anne shook her head. "I do love you. So much. But I'm just not sure love is enough anymore." She paused and looked at the envelope in Gareth's hand. "What's so important that you had to burst into the middle of the mediation?"

"It's a letter," Gareth said. "From Jasmine's mother."

Anne looked up, shock in her eyes. "From…from *her?* I don't understand. Why would you bring me something like that?"

"I wanted to try to find something that would win this case for you. Something that would make all this go away. I even broke into Richard Wells's office to look for evidence."

"You did that for me?" Anne said. "But that's breaking the rules."

"I know it is. And I didn't find anything, because there was nothing to find. I want to keep you safe, Anne. I want to make you happy. But I finally realized I can't just patch things up for you and pretend something is false when it isn't." He held out the letter to her. "Jasmine is your half sister, and nothing I can do will change that. But hopefully this will help make things a little better. Last night, I went to see Deirdre Turner, Jasmine's mother. We had a long talk about Jasmine. About your father. About you and your mother. And she wrote this for you." Gareth handed Anne the envelope.

Anne finally took the letter out of his hands, staring at it with as much fear as he'd ever seen on a person's face. Gareth thought back to the eager way she'd opened that first envelope he'd given to her at the start of all this; to the excitement she'd had at the thought of a stranger giving her something.

He wished that he could give her back that joy, but maybe that was the price of seeing the world the way it was.

He knew how she'd helped him to see things differently. He wanted to do the same for her.

"Do you know what it says?" Anne asked.

"No," Gareth replied. "But I do know what Deirdre told me. Read it, Anne. Trust me, I wouldn't have brought this to you if I thought it would hurt you more."

With a sharp motion, Anne ripped open the envelope, took out the letter folded inside and began to read.

CHAPTER EIGHTEEN

DEAR ANNE, she read,

I know that I must be the last person you want to receive a letter from. I can't imagine how hard it must have been for you, finding out about all this.

That was almost enough to make Anne stop reading. She didn't want sympathy from Jasmine's mother, of all people. Yet with Gareth looking at her expectantly, she kept going.

None of us can change what happened, and since I have a daughter I love, I wouldn't change anything even if I could. But I can try to explain.

That was enough to catch Anne's interest. She shut her eyes for a moment. There had been so many times in the past few days when nothing had seemed to make sense, and everything had seemed to be falling apart. Maybe an explanation would help.

You're probably very angry with your father for having an affair. I'm not sure there's anything I can say to make that right, but I am sorry for the pain it has brought you. Please remember that

he and I were both a lot younger then, and your
father was so terribly lonely when he was apart
from your mother.

Anne had never seen that loneliness in her father,
but she could remember it in her mother all too easily. She could remember the way her mother had tried
to keep them both so busy while her father was gone,
trying to fill up the days so there wouldn't be time to
think about him. Yet it had never worked. Thinking
back now, Anne could remember the pauses and the si-
lences, the wistful looks when her mother had thought
she wasn't watching.

We only shared one night, and I know both of us
regretted what we'd done soon afterward. But then
I couldn't regret it anymore, because he gave me
Jasmine. Edward was a good man, and if he had a
fault, it was that he tried to love too much. He loved
your mother, he loved you and he loved Jasmine,
too, even though she doesn't see that right now.

Anne's eyes stung with fresh tears, but she forced
herself to keep going.

When we love people, we want to protect them,
even when that turns out to be the wrong thing to
do. Edward wanted to protect you and your mother
from the pain of finding out about the mistake he'd
made with me. Your mother may have wanted to
do the same, because I suspect she knew, toward
the end. I know that I wanted to protect my daughter when I kept her father's identity from her.

As she read it, Anne knew this was all true. Her mother *had* tried to protect her. Wouldn't her father have tried to do the same and more?

I'm not asking for your forgiveness. I'm asking you to understand. As parents, as people, we try to do our best. We try to be perfect for the people we love, because we know better than anyone just how much they deserve that perfection. Yet we aren't perfect. We make mistakes, and then we make more mistakes trying to protect the people we love. None of that changes how much we love the people we care about.

I won't claim to have known Edward Farleigh the way your mother knew him, but I knew him enough to know that he did his best for the people he loved. And he loved you and your mother very, very much.

Deirdre Turner

Anne folded the letter up carefully.

Her father had done so much that was wrong. He'd betrayed her mother. He'd betrayed her. He'd had a whole other side to his life that she'd known nothing about.

Yet even as she let herself be angry, even as she finally faced the pain of accepting the truth about what her father had done, she also found another emotion pushing in alongside it.

Understanding.

Yes, she hated that her father had cheated on her mother. Of course she hated that he'd had a daughter he'd never told them about. But, for the first time in her life, Anne could see her mother and father for who they really were.

She was no longer wrapped up in a fantasy she'd created about her idea of *true love*. She was no longer tied to her image of them holding on to each other in the car crash, or how perfect they'd looked on their wedding day.

Instead, while they were still the wonderful parents that she'd loved so dearly, they were also, like anyone else, full of flaws and problems and mistakes.

It was so hard for her to see them like that. To think that her mother had known about her father's affair… and that the two of them had simply tried to do their best to make things work despite it.

But was that what love truly was? Anne wondered. Accepting the flaws rather than the easy perfection she'd always dreamed about? And was it only when things went wrong or were difficult that two people *had* to love one another to keep going?

Only, she already knew the answer.

Because he was standing right in front of her.

She reached for Gareth and wrapped her arms around him. "Thank you for doing this for me."

"I'd do anything for you."

Ms. Williams poked her head around the meeting-room door. "It's time to come back inside."

Anne went back in with Gareth beside her. Jasmine and Richard Wells were sitting together on the other side of the table with matching stern expressions. Yet when Anne looked at the other woman now, all she could see was the pain Jasmine must have felt growing up, thinking that her own father didn't care enough about her to want anything to do with her.

On impulse, Anne pushed the letter across the table.

"What's this?" Jasmine demanded, looking at Anne with suspicion.

"Something I think you should read."

Richard Wells quickly interjected, "My client isn't going to read anything until I have looked it over."

But Anne wasn't the least bit intimidated by the lawyer. "If Jasmine wants you to read it, you can, but she should read it first. Her mother wrote it."

"My mother?"

Jasmine opened up the paper and started to read. Anne watched the swirl of conflicting emotions move across her pretty face as she read.

Anne knew exactly how she felt. When she was done, Jasmine looked up.

"I need some time to think." She spoke to Ms. Williams. "I need to talk to my mother. Could we postpone this mediation?"

"Jasmine," Richard said, "we have her right where we want her. What are you doing?"

"Thinking. And, as I said, I'd like to postpone this mediation."

"If that's what everyone wants," Ms. Williams said with a look toward Anne, who nodded.

"Let me see that," Richard said, grabbing the letter and quickly reading through it. "This is nothing, Jasmine. Nothing." He snarled at Gareth, "Where did you even get this? Approaching the client's family like this is a flagrant breach of your nondisclosure agreement."

"How, exactly?" Anne asked, before Gareth could ask the question himself.

"Well, he obviously used the address in the file—"

"As opposed to just looking it up?" Anne smiled across at him. "Deirdre's address is easy to find, Mr. Wells."

Richard Wells stood up, pointing a finger at Gareth. "I'll find a way to make it stick, and if that doesn't, there's still the question of you breaking into my office. Did you think I wouldn't find out about that?"

Anne put a hand on Gareth's arm to let him know she had this. She had his back the way he'd had hers.

"Gareth went to your office to meet with you. You weren't there, so he left."

The lawyer looked from Gareth to her. "Hiding behind your girlfriend now, Cavendish? Well, don't worry, I'll find something that will get your P.I. license revoked. You'll never work in this town again."

"I didn't know people actually said that," Anne said, enjoying the expression on the lawyer's face as she took the letter back out of his hand. She put her arm through Gareth's. "Let's get out of here."

She managed to wait until they got out of the room and around to a quiet corner before kissing him. He kissed her back, gently. Tenderly.

"You're amazing, you know that?" Gareth said.

"I love you."

"I love you, too," Gareth replied. "And I'm going to do everything I can to make life perfect for us."

Anne shook her head. "It won't be perfect. It will be messy, and complicated…but that's how life is, isn't it?"

When Richard Wells pushed past them and set off for the exit, she had to ask, "Can he really do all those things he threatened to do?"

Gareth shrugged. "Maybe. At this point, I've done quite a few things I shouldn't have. But I'm not too worried about it." She loved seeing him smile, especially knowing just how much love was behind it. "Now, how about I get you home so I can help you stitch a wedding dress back together?"

CHAPTER NINETEEN

GARETH STOOD at the doors to The Rose Chalet's main reception room, watching the photography session before the wedding. Felicity Andrews not only looked stunning in the dress Anne had designed, but she was clearly radiant with joy at the knowledge that she was going to be married in a matter of hours.

After the bride headed off to join her bridesmaids and Anne brought out her mother's wedding dress, the eyes of the photographer from *San Francisco* magazine grew wide.

"Are you *sure* this is right, Anne? After seeing Felicity's dress, I had assumed you were more about the classic look."

Anne ran a hand over the dress. She had patched and sewn frantically in her living room, working away on that small Singer that had belonged to her mother. In the final hour, Gareth had helped hold the dress steady so that she could do the finish work quickly with a needle and thread.

Even so, the results didn't look anywhere close to perfect. Anne had repaired most of the rips, but she'd also widened a few so that they showed off flashes of the lining beneath. She had created a sophisticated patchwork effect by sewing pieces of fabric from old dresses of her mother's, and she hadn't repaired the torn beading around the edges at all. There was even some yellowing, so that the once-pristine white dress was now closer to ivory.

"This is exactly right," Anne assured the photographer.

"You're sure? I could always shoot this segment after the wedding if you wanted another hour or two."

"This wedding dress," Anne said softly, "*is* my parents' marriage. Not just the first perfect day, but the whole thing. It has rips and tears. Some have been patched up, some have had other memories sewn in, but it's still beautiful because it's *real*. It's not some fairy-tale ideal of what it should be."

"Okay," the photographer said. "If you're sure."

"I'm sure." Her eyes flicked across to find Gareth's. "I'm sure about a lot of things now."

As the photographer started taking pictures, Gareth walked outside and took out his cell phone, looking through his history of incoming calls until he found the number he was looking for.

A woman answered. "Hello?"

"Kyra, it's Gareth."

"Gareth?" Brian's fiancée sounded almost as surprised to hear from him as he was to be making this call after all this time. "Is everything all right?"

He thought about Anne in the next room and the way she'd smiled, not for the camera but for him. "It's better than that. Is Brian there?"

"Sure, I'll get him. Just hold on."

He wasn't exactly sure what he was going to say to his former partner. He only knew that he had to say something.

"Gareth?" Brian's voice still sounded the same as it

always had—warm and ready to laugh as if they'd only just been speaking to one another an hour ago, rather than six months ago.

"Hi, Brian."

There were so many memories to sort through. Memories of working together as partners, along with memories of what Brian had done to protect his soon-to-be stepson. Those memories hadn't gone away. It was just that Gareth thought he understood them a little better now.

"I'm phoning about your wedding," Gareth said. Brian hadn't just been his partner. He'd been his closest friend. "I know I didn't make the engagement party, but I was hoping I wouldn't miss your wedding, too."

He could practically see his ex-partner grinning. "I wouldn't want that, either," Brian replied, and then, "What changed your mind?"

"Plenty of things." Gareth looked over at Anne through the windows. "Is it okay if I bring someone?"

"That would be Anne Farleigh?"

He tried to work out how his former partner might know that. One answer immediately sprang to mind.

"You've heard from Richard Wells."

"He called into the station with some crazy story about you both breaking into his office." His friend laughed at the thought of Gareth breaking and entering.

"Listen, Brian," he said. "What I did, I did, and I'll deal with the consequences. But Anne wasn't a part of anything. She didn't know about any of it. I know I don't have the right to ask, but whatever fallout there is from this, make sure it falls on *me*. Just me."

"Nothing's going to happen," Brian said. "He didn't even have any security footage. Evidently, it went on the blink for a few minutes yesterday afternoon. Too bad technology is so hard to count on."

Gareth had to grin at that. He'd missed bantering with his old partner. But Brian's upcoming wedding wasn't the only reason he'd called. "How's Bobby doing?"

"Good. He's making a lot better choices when it comes to his friends these days. He's even on course to get into a good college."

"You must be proud."

"I am."

"Brian, I wanted to say that I'm sorry. I finally understand why you did what you did."

"I'm sorry, too," his friend said. "I shouldn't have put you in that position."

They talked for a few more minutes, and Gareth felt as if a weight had been lifted from his shoulders by the time he hung up. When he turned his attention back to the photo shoot, Felicity Andrews was back being photographed beside Anne and her mother's wedding dress.

"It's such a different take on the theme," Felicity declared, looking at Anne's handiwork on her mother's wedding gown. "I love it! It's almost as perfect as the one you made for me. You'll see. This time six months from now, *everyone* will want dresses like this with the whole history of a relationship in them. It's such a great idea."

Rose came into the room. "Felicity, I don't want to hurry you, but it's only an hour before the wedding's due to start, so we'd better get you ready."

"It is? Well, it looks like I have to go, then. Come on, Marsha."

She took the photographer with her, and Gareth moved over to take Anne into his arms.

She was smiling, not quite her old smile, where everything in the world seemed to be as perfect as could be, but he thought her new smile was even more beautiful.

It wasn't just armor. And it didn't come out automatically, which only made it more precious...because it meant that it was only there when there was something worth smiling about.

And as he pulled Anne into his arms, he knew there was plenty worth smiling about.

CHAPTER TWENTY

FELICITY ANDREWS'S WEDDING was the event of the year.

Journalists were making notes for magazines, and there were several people in attendance whom Anne recognized from TV, all of them wearing their finest. Clearly, when the publisher of the city's big magazine got married, everybody made an effort.

Making an effort, Anne thought with a smile. Sometimes that was what things were about.

Yes, Felicity looked perfect out there, but Anne knew now that it wasn't about perfection. It was about the moments when things weren't perfect. Life got complicated and messy and sometimes went completely wrong, and all she could hope was that Felicity and her new husband would love each other enough when those times came.

Gareth stood with his arms around her, watching the ceremony until the musicians started to play. "Would you like to dance?"

Anne let him take her in his arms as they whirled their way around The Rose Chalet's dance floor, enjoying the moment.

She didn't know what the future held, but this moment was as perfect as things got. And not knowing exactly what the future might hold was actually quite fun when she thought about it. Sure, not *every* surprise would be wonderful, but if Gareth was there with her, it was a reasonable bet that they would weather them together.

He stretched one arm out, and Anne turned a neat pirouette under it before he pulled her back tight to him and kissed her.

"This is wonderful," Anne said.

"I have a feeling from the conversations I've overheard about Felicity's dress that it's going to get even more wonderful. A lot more people are going to want one of your dresses and a wedding at The Rose Chalet."

"That's nice," Anne admitted, "but I was actually thinking about how wonderful it is to be this close to you."

Given how tightly Gareth held her, Anne guessed that he was thinking the same thing.

"I honestly wish that today would never end."

"Me, too," Anne said, "but when it does, I'm not at all worried about what the future holds. Not if you're around."

"Well, I plan to be around for a very, very long time," Gareth promised her.

"Good." Anne entwined her arms around his neck. "In that case, you should know that I've decided to give Jasmine half of what my father left me."

He didn't look surprised, even as he said, "You realize that it probably isn't going to make Jasmine your best friend overnight, right?"

"I know, but it's the right thing to do, and I don't want to have to fight a long court case where all that happens is that Richard Wells makes more money. Besides…I have a *sister,* Gareth."

"A sister who has been trying to sue you," Gareth

pointed out. He had that slightly worried note in his voice again.

"I understand. I really do. Jasmine's angry, and I guess I can see now that she has a right to be. She looks at me, and she sees the person who got all of her father's attention. And I guess that when I look at her, I'll always see a reminder of what my father did, and that will hurt a little."

"Then why do it?"

"Because it's okay that it hurts," Anne said. "Hurting means that we're facing up to it, and facing up to it means that one day—" She stopped, sighed, then smiled. "You're right. We may not ever be friends, but at least we might have a chance at getting to know each other. And getting past the hurt."

"You know that settling means Richard will get a cut of the money?"

Anne shrugged. "I can't help that, and neither can you. Though I might try holding out until he agrees to leave you alone. I didn't like him threatening you."

"I think you did a good job of letting him know that," Gareth said. "You don't need to worry, though. I spoke with my ex-partner, Brian, before the ceremony."

Anne knew what a big deal that was for him. She lifted his hands up to her lips and pressed a kiss to them before saying, "I'm so proud of you."

"It actually was easier than I thought it would be. And he doesn't think Richard is going to be a problem at all."

"It must be difficult," she said softly, "breaking so many rules in such a short space of time."

"It is. And I don't plan on making it a habit. But it turns out that there are also good reasons to break them sometimes, and I can't think of a better reason than you. What Brian did for Kyra, I understand it now. You will come with me to his wedding, won't you?"

"I *do* love a good wedding." She paused, laughing. "Of course I'll come. Anywhere that you are, I want to be."

Anne could so easily imagine waking up beside him years from now—ten, twenty, forty years from now.

His expression grew serious as he said, "There's something else I wanted to tell you."

"You can tell me anything."

His mouth curved up before he said, "I'm going to change the focus of my business so that I spend my time reuniting families. Finding loved ones who have run away or disappeared. Finding the descendants of people who've died with no will or without leaving details on how to contact their family. It's a whole branch of investigation that really interests me."

She could see Gareth doing it brilliantly. Bringing families together and changing lives for the better.

"I love that you're going to help reunite families."

"That's not all I want to do," he said as he pulled her closer despite the fact that the music had stopped.

"Tell me what you want, Gareth." Because whatever it was, she had a feeling she already wanted it, too.

"I want to start my own family. With you."

"That sounds..." Anne tried to think of the right word, and she realized there really was only one word for it. *"Perfect."*

EPILOGUE

CLEANING UP after a wedding was exhausting, no matter how many people were helping. Even with Gareth joining in and keeping Anne's mind on the job in a way even Rose had never been able to manage. There was still so much to do after an enormous wedding like Felicity Andrews's that it seemed as if they would never get to the end of it all.

Rose watched the two of them, thinking how good they looked together. Anne reached out to touch Gareth from time to time, as if she could still barely believe he was real. Or maybe just because she knew that she could. Rose was happy for her friend. If anyone deserved a happy ending, it was Anne.

Phoebe was there, too, clearing away the flowers, looking so different these days in ways that had nothing to do with her colorful wardrobe, and everything to do with the fact that she spent most of her free time with Patrick.

Tyce was still in Colorado with Whitney, and even though it hadn't been easy to put on this wedding without him, Rose was absolutely thrilled that they'd rediscovered their love after five years apart.

So many friends, made so happy. That was what Rose loved about the wedding business. Even when the details were as overwhelming as they'd been for Felicity's wedding, in the end it was all about love.

And soon, it was going to be her turn to walk down the aisle.

She and Donovan had taken their time, carefully planning out the future. They'd even started to build a house together. Her wedding date was almost here.

So why did she feel as if there was something not quite right? Given the extensive planning they'd done and her expertise, it should be the most beautiful wedding ever.

Frustrated with her train of thought, Rose picked up a heavy garbage bag and headed for the Dumpster at the very edge of her property, but the train just chugged right along with her.

RJ came out of the building and frowned as he caught her standing in the middle of the lawn, gripping the garbage bag for dear life.

"Still feeling the champagne from last night, aren't you?" he teased. "The rest of us have got it covered here. Why don't you sit down with a big bottle of water?"

Normally, she wouldn't have shirked her postwedding duties. But tonight, all she could do was nod and let him take the bag from her.

"You did a great job with this wedding. You should be proud of what you've created at The Rose Chalet. Really proud."

Maybe, she mused as he walked off to throw out the garbage, RJ was right about the postchampagne headache that had been burning around the edges of her brain all day. Best friend or not, she shouldn't have gotten drunk with Anne the night before the biggest wedding of her career. Rose couldn't even remember now how it had all happened.

But she could remember who had helped take her home and, before that, how Anne had asked if she'd ever shared a perfect kiss with someone, one that had made her feel cherished and loved.

She also remembered that she hadn't told Anne the truth last night about the identity of the man who had given her the perfect kiss.

How could she when it hadn't been Donovan?

* * * * *

*Turn the page to read THE WEDDING KISS,
featuring Rose Martin, owner of The Rose Chalet.
Enjoy this next story in the wonderfully romantic
ROSE CHALET series by Lucy Kevin.*

THE WEDDING KISS

CHAPTER ONE

"Are you sure there's nothing I can do to help?" Rose Martin asked Anne Farleigh for the third time, looking around Anne's living room.

"I'm absolutely, positively sure."

Rose and Anne had been close friends since kindergarten. When Rose had opened The Rose Chalet as a San Francisco wedding venue five years ago, she'd immediately hired Anne as her on-staff wedding-dress designer.

"This is *your* bridal shower," Anne reminded Rose, "which means no running around trying to take care of everything like you usually do. For today, you get to sit back and be treated like a princess while everyone else gets things ready." Anne swept an admiring glance over her. "Besides, you look beautiful today and you don't want to get any wrinkles or stains on that gorgeous outfit."

Rose had worn her hair loose over her shoulders, but she'd contrasted that by wearing a slightly formal dress in dark green. Normally, she wouldn't have dressed up quite so much for a wedding shower, but she wanted to make sure she made a good impression with Mrs. McIntyre, her fiancé's mother.

Rose took a deep breath and forced a smile for her friend, before following Anne's directions and taking

a seat on a printed floral chair in the living room. She
clasped her hands together on her lap and watched the
activity bustling all around her.

Julie Delgado was bringing in the food, assisted by
her fiancé, Andrew Kyle. Julie had briefly taken care
of catering for the chalet about a year ago, and that was
when she'd met Andrew, a famous TV chef. The two of
them had been the first couple from among the staff at
The Rose Chalet to find a happy-ever-after.

Phoebe Davis, who had done the flowers for The
Rose Chalet since the day Rose had opened her doors,
was working her usual magic with exquisite flower bouquets. Her boyfriend, Patrick Knight, was helping her
by placing the large vases exactly where Phoebe wanted
them, and then she finalized the arrangements.

Classical music played through the speakers set up
throughout the venue. The music director for the chalet, Tyce Smith, had a knack for knowing just the right
songs to pair with each bride and groom, and today he'd
put together a beautiful selection for Rose. His girlfriend, Whitney Banning, had traveled from Colorado
to attend today's party.

Even Anne's fiancé, Gareth Cavendish, a private investigator, was helping to move furniture around.

Rose never ceased to be amazed by how big a part
the chalet had played in all of her friends' relationships.
After Julie and Andrew had fallen in love, Phoebe and
Patrick had met on the dance floor at one of the weddings. And then, in an even more romantic twist, after
losing touch for five years, Tyce and Whitney had been
unexpectedly reunited when Whitney had been a brides-
maid at her aunt's wedding. Only Anne and Gareth
hadn't met at The Rose Chalet.

Now Anne's beautiful Craftsman house was a hive of activity. A hive in which Rose suspected she was to be the carefully immobile queen bee. Honestly, though, she wasn't sure how much longer she could sit here doing nothing. She was used to not only working long hard hours, but also multitasking. Sitting still while everyone else bustled around her wasn't something she would ever get used to, even though they were clearly doing a great job without her help.

"You know," she said to Anne as her friend brought over a glass of wine, "we could have held this in the chalet just as easily, and then you wouldn't have all this chaos in your home."

"Oh, don't be silly," Anne said. "You know how much I wanted to throw this shower for you. Besides, you're having the wedding at the chalet, and the bachelorette party will probably start there. Plus, we'll all be working there for the next week. Don't you think it's nicer to have at least one event somewhere else?"

Rose nodded as she looked around the large front room of her best friend's house. It was decorated in a retro style that suited Anne perfectly. Most of the furniture was antique, and it really was a beautiful place to hold the shower.

Rose could still hardly believe everything that had happened for Anne over the past few months. From out of the blue, her friend had learned not only that her beloved father had had an affair twenty years ago… but that she also had a half sister named Jasmine. The other woman had been intent on getting half the estate that Anne's deceased parents had left her. She had even taken Anne to court for the money. Fortunately, in the end, Jasmine had decided to behave reasonably.

"I'm so glad Jasmine decided to accept your offer to give her half the worth of the house in cash, rather than insisting that you sell it," Rose said to her friend.

"Me, too," Anne admitted. "Though I'm even more glad that she might actually want to try to meet for coffee one day soon so that we can get to know each other better." Anne looked pensive for a moment, before brushing the thought away with her hand in the air. "But today isn't about me. It's about you. And there's only one week to go until you and Donovan get married!"

One week.

One week until Rose Martin became Mrs. Rose Mc-Intyre, wife of a successful plastic surgeon who came from one of the most important families in California.

She felt as if she'd been waiting for their wedding day for so long. Now that it was almost here…well, it was hard to wrap her head around it. Donovan was off on a hunting trip with his father and a few colleagues, and would be back in a day or two. In the meantime, there were so many final details to sort out—the music, the dress, the flowers and decorating the chalet.

"We are going to get everything done in time, aren't we?" Rose asked Anne.

"Of course we are. You know," her friend said with a grin, "you sound just like one of the brides who come through the chalet. So I'll tell you exactly what I always tell them. We're going to make everything *perfect* for you. It will be your dream wedding."

Anne hugged her, and Rose let the warmth of her friend's arms cut through the chill she hadn't been able to shake all day. As she did, Rose couldn't help quickly looking over her friend's shoulder and checking that everything was ready for the shower. Music? Check.

Food? Julie had said more was on its way, but even now, the buffet table looked great. Flowers? Thanks to Phoebe's flower arrangements, the room both smelled and looked beautiful.

So why did Rose still feel so nervous?

She sighed, knowing exactly why.

Vanessa McIntyre, Donovan's mother, was San Francisco's leading society maven. Her hair was never out of place, her body was kept in perfect shape by a combination of personal trainers and the very discreet attentions of Donovan's plastic-surgery colleagues, she was always immaculately dressed…and of course she had both the refined tastes and the perfect manners of someone who knew *exactly* how wealthy her great-great-grandparents had been.

That kind of perfection was, frankly, a lot to live up to. Rose was only too aware that her own hair often had a mind of its own, and that she tended to freckle far too much in the sun—that was, when her pale skin didn't simply burn first. And while she knew which fork to use at the society dinners she attended, Rose spent almost every one of those meals wondering when people would see through her charade.

Because, instead of growing up in San Francisco's high society, Rose had spent her childhood doing her homework in the back room of the bowling alley where her mother worked.

Just then, Phoebe came over to join Rose and Anne. Her beautiful dress hugged her figure, and her dark hair spilled down her back. Her high cheekbones were slightly flushed from the exertion of arranging the heavy vases of flowers.

For a second or two, Rose found herself wondering

if standing between her two beautiful friends was really
that good an idea.

"What's wrong?" Anne asked her.

"I was just thinking, what if Vanessa McIntyre sees
me standing with the two of you and decides that her
son could do a lot better?" Rose laughed, trying to make
a joke of it. "And what if she decides that I urgently need
the attentions of a couple of plastic surgeons, a team
of beauticians and at least one specialist in deportment
before I'm allowed to marry Donovan?"

"Oh, don't be silly," Phoebe said. "You're gorgeous,
Rose."

But when Rose still looked worried, Anne leaned in
close and joked, "How about this? I'll sneak her phone
out of her purse during the party to see if she has a team
of beauty consultants on speed dial, and to warn you,
I'll wink three times in a row if she does."

That would have been funny if Rose hadn't chosen
that moment to look down and realize that in her worry
about the wedding, she'd started biting her nails. It was
a nasty habit she thought she'd trained herself to stop
doing a long time ago. She hurriedly balled her hands
up into fists so the others wouldn't see them.

"Whitney," Phoebe said as Tyce's girlfriend came into
the room, "you must know Vanessa McIntyre, right?
She's not so bad, is she?"

After several years as vice president of Banning In-
corporated, a large wellness-products company that was
founded by her father, Whitney had decided to make a
career switch and was now training to become a vet-
erinarian. But she had grown up in the same society
circles as the McIntyres.

Whitney looked lovely in a pair of dark slacks and a

light blue blouse as she smiled and nodded. "I've met her at various events. She's always been perfectly polite to me. I'm sure she's a very nice person," Whitney added.

"Rose," Anne assured her, "you're elegant and intelligent and beautiful. I'm sure she adores you, just as Donovan does."

"But," Rose found herself saying, "what about *my* mother?"

"Your mother's lovely," Anne insisted. "*Everybody* likes her. I used to love getting to spend time with her at the bowling alley."

Rose's mother more or less ran the bowling alley where she'd worked for more than two decades. Both Rose and Anne had spent countless hours there as kids, bowling when no one else was around, eating free snacks from the concession booths and doing their homework with the sound of balls knocking down pins in the background.

Rose definitely loved her mother. It was just...what would a highly regarded society queen like Vanessa McIntyre make of Susie Martin?

Half the time, Rose could still smell the disinfectant used for the bowling shoes on her mother whenever they were close. As much as Rose hated to admit it, she'd actually been half hoping that Mr. Philips, who owned the bowling alley, wouldn't give her mother this Saturday off. That way she and her mom could have celebrated Rose's upcoming wedding privately instead.

When the doorbell rang, Rose quickly turned to answer it before anyone else could leap up. She opened the door and saw RJ Knight, The Rose Chalet's handyman and gardener, standing on Anne's front porch.

Oh, my, she thought, *he looks good today.* He was wearing casual jeans and a flannel work shirt with a couple of buttons opened at the neck. As usual, his dark hair had an untamed look to it and his piercing blue eyes gazed out evenly from underneath.

"RJ?" She worked to repress the flutter of awareness from the warmth of his gaze on her as she asked, "What are you doing here?"

CHAPTER TWO

IT ALWAYS TOOK RJ a few seconds to take in Rose's beauty. He remembered the first time he'd met her, when he was interviewing for the position at The Rose Chalet. He'd expected a round, matronly woman to be the owner of the wedding venue...not the young, gorgeous, vibrant redhead who had greeted him with a brisk handshake and a long list of incisive interview questions.

Perhaps it should have made a difference that today was her wedding shower, and that she was marrying someone else. But it didn't.

Because she was still the most beautiful woman he'd ever seen.

The dress she wore today clung to her in a way that RJ could not ignore. The color matched the deep green of her eyes perfectly.

The truth was that she looked just as good wearing jeans and an old shirt when they were working in the chalet's garden on a quiet morning when no clients were around.

"Julie asked me to bring this." He lifted the full tray of food a little higher.

Phoebe quickly came to the door. "Oh, good, RJ, you're here with the rest of the buffet. I'll let Julie and Andrew know."

Rose stepped aside to let him in, but not before he breathed in her clean, fresh scent. RJ walked into the living room, put the tray down on one of the smaller side tables and uncovered it.

"Everyone's so busy, I should probably just take care of laying the canapés out properly," Rose said.

Knowing she always wanted to make sure every last little thing was perfect, without any prompting he mirrored Rose's movements and the two of them laid out the canapés with the rest of the food on the buffet table. Anything he could do to make things easier for her, he would.

"Well," she said when they were finished, "I think that looks pretty good. Hopefully, Donovan's mom won't be able to find fault with the food."

"How could she possibly find fault with anything here today?" RJ asked, turning to her as he asked the question.

Rose shifted nervously. "Well, there's my mom…"

"You're worried about your mother meeting Donovan's mother?"

She sat down on one of the chairs in Anne's living room, looking out the window. "They don't exactly come from the same world. I just don't want either of them to be uncomfortable with one another."

RJ didn't know what to say, even though he knew exactly what he *wanted* to say. Namely, that if Donovan's mother disapproved of Rose or her mom, then it wasn't Rose or Susie's problem. It was Mrs. McIntyre's.

"Maybe they'll both get along famously," he suggested.

Rose looked up at him from the chair. "I can't see that happening somehow. I mean, Vanessa is a wealthy, sophisticated woman, while my mom probably earns half the salary of Vanessa's housekeeper."

There were moments when RJ wanted to shake Rose and remind her that her working-class roots weren't anything to be ashamed of. And she definitely shouldn't be ashamed when it came to being in the same room as a woman whose major contribution to the world was giving birth to Donovan McIntyre. *That* was hardly a major achievement, in RJ's book.

But Rose was his boss, and his friend, and if RJ wanted things to stay that way he knew he would have to add that thought to the ever-growing list of things he didn't allow himself to say to her.

"I can't imagine anyone not being impressed by the way you've made The Rose Chalet such a success. Vanessa McIntyre would have to be crazy to think you aren't good enough for her son."

"Thanks, RJ," Rose said with a small smile that didn't linger nearly long enough. "How is it you always know just what to say to make me feel better?"

Maybe because I know you better than anyone else?

Or maybe because he hadn't meant it as a pep talk, but as the simple truth. Not only was Rose more beautiful than any other woman he'd ever met, but on top of that she'd made the chalet the premier boutique wedding venue in San Francisco.

"It's just a knack, I guess," RJ replied.

"Well, I hope it's a knack you hang on to," she said, "because I get the feeling I'm going to need a few more pep talks before everything is in place for the wedding. You'll do that for me, won't you, RJ?"

Maybe he should say no. Or maybe, just maybe, he should say what he'd wanted to say for so long—that

Rose should abandon the wedding and give him the chance to show her how good they could be together.

The trouble was, he would never break up someone's relationship. He could never be the other guy. Not when he knew how bad that felt. He remembered all too well a part of him dying when he'd found his now ex-wife in bed with another man. A man he'd known from their social circle. A man he'd trusted.

Even though he wanted Rose so much he ached with it, RJ told himself over and over again that he could never get in the middle of her relationship with Donovan.

Still, how could he forget the one perfect kiss he and Rose had shared? When they'd kissed that one unexpected time, it felt as if she understood everything about him, and that they were truly meant for one another.

Yet he'd obviously been wrong, because she'd never so much as mentioned the moment since. And if their kiss—their connection—hadn't meant as much to her as it had to him…well, then he would just have to keep adding to the list of things he wouldn't say to her.

Hating how nervous and worried she looked, he had to assure her, "Your wedding is going to be perfect. Even by *your* crazy standards," he teased.

"My standards are not crazy," Rose insisted. "They're just meticulous."

He grinned. "Meticulous, huh?" It was so easy to fall into this playful banter with her.

Rose glanced around the room with a look that he recognized all too well after working with her for five years. She looked as if she might go around and check everything for the party just one more time.

"Maybe if I—"

RJ put his hand on her forearm. "Everything is going to be fine. Better than fine. The wedding shower is going to be perfect. Anne and Phoebe have got it covered. Trust me."

Rose sighed as she relaxed slightly beneath his fingers. "What would I do without you?"

It was so good seeing her finally relax a little. He could see those small changes as she loosened up slightly—the tension leaving the corners of her mouth and around her eyes.

He wanted so badly to reach out and pull her closer. It wouldn't take much to drag Rose tight against him, his hands going up to soothe the tension from her shoulders while his lips moved down to hers.

Suddenly, Rose seemed to sense how close they were, because her breathing came a little quicker. Or was that RJ's imagination?

But he knew he wasn't imagining the heat in her eyes, nor the slight parting of her lips and the flush in her cheeks as she stood up. He stood up, too, knowing all he needed to do was move an inch closer and then he could—

"*There* you both are," Anne said, sweeping into the room with Julie at her side.

Julie pulled Rose away, asking a question about wedding-cake designs, and Anne took RJ's arm. "It's almost time for this bridal shower to start. Which means no men. Even you. So out you go. We'll see you tomorrow."

As RJ let Anne lead him to the door, he said, "Take care of her today, Anne, will you?"

She gave him a look that spoke volumes. "Of course

I will, RJ. She's my best friend and all I want is for her to be happy."

That was all he wanted, too.

CHAPTER THREE

ROSE WAS TRYING to pay attention to Julie while she talked about cake frosting and decorations, but all she was really doing was watching, out of the corner of her eye, as RJ left Anne's house.

Why did she always find herself watching him like that these days?

And why did she also find herself thinking about him even when he wasn't around?

And why, when Anne had drunkenly asked her whether there was anyone whose kiss had made her feel cherished and loved, had Rose thought of him?

After all, they were just friends.

And they'd had only one little kiss....

THE BAR WAS FULL. Full enough that only two seats remained. Couples and small groups were laughing and enjoying themselves while the music blared from all corners of the room. The atmosphere was just this side of raucous.

Everyone at The Rose Chalet had worked hard to organize and arrange three back-to-back-to-back Valentine's Day weddings for three couples who had been willing to pay nearly twice Rose's usual fee to get married on the most romantic day of the year. They'd all worked late to put on the celebrations, with Tyce pro-

viding the music, Phoebe and Anne helping out at the reception, and RJ dealing with the last-minute problems that always seemed to crop up. By the time the last wedding had wrapped up, it was pretty late.

Rose and RJ had left the chalet at an hour when most people were already celebrating Valentine's Day with the one they loved—out at a restaurant for a romantic meal, or toasting one another in a bar like this one.

"I can't believe Donovan stood you up on Valentine's Day," RJ said, sitting down next to Rose.

He looked good, as usual, wearing a slightly more formal shirt and pants so that he could fit in with the wedding guests as he worked around them during the events. Right then, though, his shirtsleeves were rolled up to show the muscles of his forearms.

Muscles she liked looking at far too much.

"Donovan didn't stand me up," Rose said defensively. "He called to let me know he's going to be late."

Donovan had been planning to take her out for a Valentine's Day meal at a five-star restaurant, but an emergency had come up at his clinic. He'd often had to wait for her to finish up with a wedding, so she told him she could certainly wait another hour or two for their dinner.

"It sure felt like he was standing you up when we were standing out in the rain," RJ pointed out in what Rose felt was a particularly unhelpful way.

Still, she politely said, "Thanks for waiting with me, RJ."

"It is my pleasure," he said.

She looked around the very boisterous bar. "Though I'm not sure we should have gone off to a bar. We could have waited at the chalet."

"We've been cooped up there all day long, working triple-time. And you've been run off your feet today by needy brides and panicking grooms. If anyone deserves a drink tonight, it's you."

Rose couldn't argue with his excellent reasoning. "You're right. He can call my cell phone when he gets to the chalet."

As RJ raised his arm to get the attention of the bartender, Rose decided that this was a good moment to let her hair down a little, literally. She pulled out the clip holding her hair back in a ponytail, then shook her hair out.

"Do that too much," RJ observed after the bartender slid their drinks over, "and you'll have half the guys in here hitting on you."

"I'm pretty sure that if they're here on Valentine's Day, they're already with someone," she pointed out.

He shook his head. "Trust me, there are plenty of single guys in a bar like this, and all of them are waiting for a woman like you."

She laughed, flattered by the admiration in RJ's eyes despite the fact that she had a fiancé. "I don't think that's very likely."

His eyes darkened as he gazed at her across the table. "I think you might be surprised, Rose."

She was trying to pull her gaze away from his when, suddenly, the bartender cut the music and waved his hands for silence.

"All right, everybody. We all know that today's a very special day. Which is why we've decided it's also the day you all get a chance to win five hundred bucks. The rules are simple. Ladies, grab your gentlemen and

give them a big Valentine's Day kiss. The best kiss of the night takes the money. Are we all clear?"

That got a few cheers from the crowd, especially when one bubbly and frankly quite drunk-looking woman grabbed the surprised-looking man next to her and planted a kiss on his lips.

"Well, it looks like we have someone to get us started," the bartender said. "Now, who else do we have? Who wants that five hundred bucks?"

Rose laughed along with the rest of them, but she could see how uncomfortable RJ looked right then. Given that he worked at a wedding venue, he surely couldn't have a problem with seeing people kiss in front of him, so it had to be something else, didn't it?

What, then?

The bartender was walking past couples in the bar, asking them one by one to give it their best shot. If anything, that seemed to make RJ even more uncomfortable.

Was it the money?

RJ was such a talented landscaper that she knew he could have made big bucks with his own business. Instead, he'd chosen to work for her, for a salary that was perfectly fine, but would never make him wealthy.

Was he thinking about everything he could do with that five hundred dollars, if only she could loosen up and help him win it?

"Would you like to take a shot at it?" Rose asked him.

"What?" He looked shocked by her suggestion.

Since she couldn't bring up the money and bruise his pride, she said, "You probably canceled your own

Valentine's Day plans to wait with me. The least I can do is help you win the big prize here tonight."

RJ shook his head. "I didn't have any plans."

Now, that was hard to believe. A great-looking, wonderful guy like RJ didn't have some girl waiting for him on Valentine's Day? There was something very wrong with the world if that was the case.

With tequila buzzing around inside her, on top of the champagne she'd had earlier at the wedding, Rose couldn't help feeling that there ought to be laws against men as good-looking as RJ being left alone on Valentine's Day.

"Why not?" she asked him.

He shrugged. "You know how things get. Everything's booked, and then when you actually decide to make plans, there's nowhere left you want to take someone." He paused. "And no one you really want to take."

To Rose, all of that sounded like a lie. As if RJ wouldn't have been able to book the perfect date ahead of time. As if he wouldn't have been able to make it special for some lucky girl.

Unless...well, everyone knew how much prices went up for Valentine's Day. After all, hadn't they done that at the chalet for the three weddings?

Maybe she'd been right with her first guess, and he simply couldn't afford to take a woman out on a night like this. Considering she was going to be spending the evening in a restaurant with Donovan where the meals cost enough to bankrupt a small country, it didn't seem fair. Not at all.

"Now, then," the bartender said, turning to her and RJ, "on to our next happy couple."

"Sorry, buddy," RJ started to say, but Rose didn't let

him get any further than that. She'd kept him at work late on Valentine's Day; he'd stood in the rain with her until Donovan had called; and working for her was the reason he couldn't afford to take a girl out on a nice date this evening.

She was going to make certain he won that five hundred dollars.

Rose wrapped her arms around RJ's neck, pulled him close and kissed him.

She started out softly, learning the contours of his lips with hers while she closed her eyes. She kept kissing him like that until he dragged her off her barstool, pulled her tight against his muscular body and kissed her back with so much passion that she couldn't help but surrender to him totally.

Rose explored RJ's mouth hungrily. His kiss was perfect, and exciting, and dangerous all at once, even as the feel of his lips against hers made the moment feel so natural and safe that Rose wanted it to last forever.

Finally, they pulled back to cheers and whoops from the rest of the bar. Rose stepped back, red-faced, hardly able to believe what she'd just done.

"Ladies and gentlemen," the bartender said, "I think you'll all agree that we've found tonight's winners!"

ROSE PUSHED THE MEMORY back into the recesses of her mind. Their kiss hadn't meant anything. It had just been a stupid gag to help RJ out. It hadn't been *real*.

She had Donovan. She was *marrying* Donovan.

Donovan, who was just about as perfect a man as any woman could wish for. In fact, if she sat down and designed her perfect man, he'd be everything her fiancé was. Great-looking. Successful. Hardworking. Confident. Sophisticated. Stable.

So why did she keep thinking about that darn Valentine's Day kiss with RJ?

Why did thoughts of that kiss keep popping into her head regardless of what she was doing, so that she had to beat them back by reminding herself just how perfect her fiancé was?

Rose was only too grateful when the doorbell rang and the first shower guests arrived.

CHAPTER FOUR

ANNE'S HOUSE WAS packed with women. Everyone who worked at The Rose Chalet was there, along with old school friends and people Rose had met either through their weddings, or *their* friends' weddings…and this was just the bridal shower.

Rose couldn't help thinking what it would be like at her actual wedding, with just about everyone she and Donovan had ever met showing up. At least, it had seemed that way when they'd been putting together the invitations. She noticed the pile of shower gifts on one of the side tables; she was amazed to see how thoughtful her friends were.

"You look so beautiful," Marge Banning said, having arrived a short while after her niece, Whitney. As The Rose Chalet's most regular client, not to mention being distantly connected to Donovan's family through one of those complicated networks that involved the very rich, of *course* she had been sent an invitation to Rose's wedding shower.

"Thank you," Rose said. "Can I get you a fresh drink or a bite to eat from the buffet?"

Marge gave her a warm smile. "This day is about you. Just like your big day is going to be. Somehow you're going to have to figure out how to sit back and enjoy it, aren't you?"

Rose tried hard to smile at the thought of letting everyone else take care of the details. Anne took her arm a moment later and brought her over to a couple of school friends who were reminiscing about old times.

"You look so elegant now," one of them said. "I bet you're going to look incredible on your wedding day."

Rose tried to imagine it herself. Anne had been quite coy about the dress designs so far, taking measurements but insisting that Rose had to trust her vision for the design. And she did, of course. How could she not trust her friend?

It wasn't that Rose couldn't envision the dress.... It was more that she was finding it hard to imagine the day itself.

She tried to visualize Donovan standing under the gazebo at The Rose Chalet, waiting as she walked up the aisle in a pristine white dress. But every time she closed her eyes the man she saw standing at the altar wasn't Donovan. It was—

"So, where is my son's bride?"

Rose tensed slightly at that voice, cultured and throaty. Vanessa McIntyre had arrived.

Hurriedly, Rose smoothed down her dress, feeling as if she was back in school, being summoned to the principal's office. She'd met Donovan's mother a half-dozen times, and after each dinner party she'd come away feeling as if she should be trying a lot harder when it came to measuring up to Vanessa's son.

"Vanessa, I'm so glad you're here."

Donovan's mother was tall, and her hair was short and elegantly styled, showing off features that made her look a lot younger than her sixties. If Rose was half as fit and toned at that age, she'd be very grateful.

Vanessa leaned forward to not quite kiss both of her cheeks. She wasn't a woman who was big on physical contact.

"I wouldn't miss out on the chance to spend time with my son's future wife now, would I?"

She pressed a small but tastefully wrapped package into Rose's hands. Even without opening it, Rose knew it would be expensive. Tasteful. And, quite likely, glitteringly useless.

Vanessa looked around the room. "Well, isn't this a quaint little place to hold a party?"

"My friend Anne owns this house," Rose explained as Anne heard her name and came over to say hello. "Anne and I have been best friends since we were children, and she will be my maid of honor at the wedding."

"It's lovely to meet you," Vanessa said as she shook Anne's hand, her rings glittering with jewels, her manicure perfect. "You don't see many houses this old in San Francisco these days. They usually get knocked down to make way for more modern structures." Vanessa didn't say whether she thought that was a good thing or not. "How many bedrooms does it have?"

"Three," Anne replied, fortunately nonplussed by the rather forward question.

"How cozy. Do you have children?"

"No, I've just recently gotten engaged."

"Well," Vanessa said, "that's good. It means there's plenty of time to find someplace big enough to hold a family."

"Would you like a canapé?" Rose offered hastily.

"Oh, no, I couldn't." Vanessa patted her trim waistline. "I have my diet to think about. As do you, I'm sure," she added with a pointed glance at Rose's stomach, "just like every bride who wants to look her very best for her wedding."

With that, Vanessa drifted off to schmooze with the two members of the Banning empire who she'd just realized were in the room. She quickly had Marge and Whitney in a corner, talking to them about a fashion house she'd just invested in.

When the doorbell rang again and Susie Martin walked into the room, Rose was touched to see that her mother had put on a dress rather than wearing the slacks she was most comfortable in. Even so, the contrast with Vanessa McIntyre couldn't be more pronounced.

Susie was a little shorter than Rose, with a body that had long since gone from curvaceous to simply comfortable. She had the same creamy skin and red hair that Rose did, but where Rose carefully controlled her hair with plenty of conditioner and some savage work with the comb each morning, her mother's hair was wildly frizzy.

"Oh, don't you look just *perfect!*" Her mother pulled Rose into a big hug. Fortunately, Rose thought as she let herself sink into her mother's warmth for a few seconds, she didn't smell of disinfectant from the bowling shoes today.

After they pulled apart, her mother greeted Anne with her customary ebullience. "Anne, there you are. Still happy with that gorgeous private detective of yours? I'm so thrilled for you. Of course, my girl has found herself a very handsome man of her own, hasn't she?"

Rose hurried to catch up with her mother, who was hitting the buffet by that point, grabbing a delicately spiced chicken leg and setting to work on it while holding a glass of wine in her other hand.

"I can't wait to meet Donovan's mom. Is that her?" Without waiting for Rose to reply, she strode over to Vanessa, whose smile turned a little glassy when Susie juggled her chicken and wineglass into one hand, thrusting the other out for a handshake.

"Hi, you must be Donovan's mom, Vanessa! I'm Susie, Rose's mother. It's so nice to finally meet you."

Vanessa reached out a hand, just barely making contact with Susie's. "You, too. And what a brightly colored dress," she said as she looked at the flower-printed fabric. "Are you planning on wearing something similar to the wedding?"

"Oh, yes. Anne has already agreed to help me come up with a dress. Where will you get yours?"

"From a couture house," Vanessa said.

"I'm so happy that your boy and my girl are getting together," Rose's mother went on. "I've heard so much about Donovan. You must be so proud of your son."

"Yes, of course," Vanessa agreed. "Donovan has achieved a great deal. He's widely respected in his field. He's had several papers published on improvements in surgical technique, and he does so much for charity. It is hard not to be proud."

"I'm very proud of Rose, too," her mother responded. "In fact, everyone? Could I have your attention for a moment?"

"Mom," Rose said, "please…"

It was too late by then, of course, as her mother's booming voice easily cut through the crowd of women.

"I'm Rose's mom, Susie, and I want to say a few words about my daughter. She's a beautiful, intelligent, wonderful person, and she has done so much with her life, even running her own business. She's worked very hard, and I think she deserves every good thing that happens for her. And now she's getting married! I'm so proud of her and I can't wait to see her and Donovan getting married beneath the gazebo at the chalet."

That got a brief murmur of approval. Anne actually clapped her hands together in delight. "The gazebo is going to be such a romantic place to exchange your vows."

Phoebe agreed, "It's going to be perfect."

"You're getting married under a *gazebo?*" Vanessa said, her lips pinching together. "Donovan didn't tell me that." She drew her lips together again, this time into what was clearly supposed to be a smile. "How precious."

Meaning *how tacky,* Rose thought. *How overdone.*

She noticed that Phoebe and Anne had latched on to her mother now, talking to her and drawing her into a far corner of the party, but the damage was done. Rose could practically feel the disapproval radiating off Vanessa. And why not? She'd said herself what a great catch Donovan was. A man who could have had any woman he wanted.

Yet he'd picked a girl who wanted to get married under a "precious" gazebo.

Rose wanted to curl up and die right there and then.

If only RJ were there, she found herself thinking, he'd find a way to make her laugh about it instead.

That errant thought was all it took for her to realize that RJ was, in fact, the answer to her prayers. If anyone could help her out with this, he could.

She turned to Vanessa. "Actually, I haven't had the heart to tell my mother that Donovan and I have made the decision not to use the gazebo in the wedding."

"What a relief it is to hear you say that," Vanessa said. "I simply couldn't imagine Donovan agreeing to something like that. Not when it isn't his style at all."

"Of course it isn't," Rose agreed, knowing it was true and that Donovan had likely only agreed to it because he knew how much she'd always dreamed of being married beneath the chalet's gazebo. "Would you excuse me for a minute?"

Whitney looked over at her as she made a dash for the back of the house, shooting her an obvious *are you okay?* look.

Rose nodded and smiled, because what else could she do? When she got to the back door, she dug out her phone. The text to RJ didn't take long to put together. Urgent. Meet me at the chalet tomorrow morning. Change of plans for the wedding. I need your help.

CHAPTER FIVE

WHAT KIND OF GUY was happy to come into work on a
Sunday morning when the rest of the city was still in
bed?

RJ was, at least when it was Rose asking for his help.
He could no more keep away from her when she needed
him than he could stop himself from thinking about her
when he wasn't near her. There was something about
the way she tilted her head when things were bothering
her, and the way she occasionally bit down on a strand
of her hair without thinking about it. Tiny things. Personal things that RJ was sure hardly anyone else noticed, but that had captivated him from that first day
he'd spent with Rose at the chalet.

He'd walked over this morning rather than driving
the truck. His house wasn't too far from the chalet, and
he guessed that whatever Rose needed, he'd already
have the tools on-site. Idly, he wondered if the rest of
the crew would be there this morning to help her out
with whatever the emergency was. As much as he liked
his coworkers and friends, part of him hoped that they
wouldn't be there. The Rose Chalet always felt so different when it was only him and Rose.

Of course, there probably weren't going to be too
many quiet moments this coming week. The buildup to

any wedding was busy, but Rose's wedding was, obviously, so much more than that of a valued client.

His chest squeezed at the thought of the part he was going to play in putting the finishing touches on Rose's wedding that week. Especially when it meant watching her give herself to a man who simply wasn't right for her.

He shook these thoughts from his mind as he walked through the chalet's gardens, down past the gazebo that stood in the middle of the rose garden. He slipped in through one of the side doors and into the main hall. It was empty of furniture at the moment, except for a single table on which RJ could see a pile of wedding magazines.

Rose was standing in the middle of the floor, looking around as if she was trying to imagine something. She was wearing dark jeans and a soft cream sweater, her hair tied back with a ribbon. She'd taken her heels off to go barefoot, the way she sometimes did when there wasn't anyone else around. RJ knew, without having to hear it, that she would be humming a show tune to herself. For all that Rose pretended to like classical music, songs from musicals were always what she ended up humming.

Sure enough, when RJ got closer, he could hear the strains of an old Rodgers and Hammerstein number.

He loved knowing so many little things about her. Like the fact that for all she pretended not to like sugar in her coffee, claiming it ruined the full complexity of the flavor, he knew Rose actually preferred it heaped with the stuff. Or the way she would draw little maps of wedding setups on Post-it Notes while she was on the phone, but insist on making a properly drawn-out plan before they got to work.

What irritated RJ—no, what made genuine anger flare up just thinking about it—was his near certainty that Donovan didn't know any of those little things about her.

The plastic surgeon looked at this wonderful, individual woman, and what did he see? Some cookie-cutter image that probably had more to do with his own imagination than with reality.

And if her fiancé never really *saw* her, RJ was convinced the other man didn't really want *her*. Donovan McIntyre just wanted someone who was willing to fit into the carefully labeled space he had in his existence, marked *wife*. Which, as far as RJ could see, had everything to do with making him look good at champagne parties and absolutely *nothing* to do with Rose.

Yet, bizarrely, there was a part of RJ that couldn't help being a little pleased about it. Because it meant that all those small special things about Rose were his and not Donovan's. They were things that he shared with Rose and no one else. To RJ, Donovan McIntyre had no right to those parts of her. In fact, he had no right to *any* of her.

Yet somehow, a week from now, Donovan would have all of Rose, while RJ would have nothing.

Why couldn't Rose see how wrong her fiancé was for her? RJ thought as he stepped forward into the room.

"Good morning, Rose. What's the emergency?"

Rose hurried over to the table with the bridal magazines. Most of them had sticky notes on the pages, often in two or three different colors. She opened the one closest to her.

"What do you think about a wedding setup lined

with fountains and arranged so that it looks like the bride and groom are standing in the middle of a big pool of water?"

"It sounds like you'd get very wet," RJ said, moving to stand beside her. This close, he was intensely aware of every movement she made, her scent, the flecks of gold in her green eyes.

"Well, how about if we put up enough mirrors so that it looks like there's an infinite number of weddings going on while Donovan and I—"

"Rose," RJ asked, "what's going on? I thought your wedding was settled. You're going to get married beneath the gazebo. It's all planned."

She shook her head rapidly, several strands of hair flying out from her ponytail. "I can't get married underneath a gazebo. *No one* gets married underneath a gazebo these days."

He frowned. "Of course they do. At least half our weddings use the gazebo."

"That's exactly why I can't use it for my own wedding."

She turned to look at the gazebo through the windows of the main hall, and that was when RJ saw the faint smudges beneath her eyes.

"What's going on, Rose?" RJ asked again in a gentle voice, hoping that he'd get a better answer this time. "The gazebo was one of the first things that you settled on for the wedding."

"Well, maybe that's what's wrong, then," Rose countered. "Maybe it was just a stupid decision that I made far too early."

"Tell me why you've changed your mind. I know you wouldn't change your whole wedding over nothing."

"It's…it's Donovan's mother. She was at my bridal shower, and she doesn't much care for gazebos. So it has to come down, and we need to think of something else."

"She told you this?"

He wasn't sure which part he had a harder time believing—that Donovan's mother would try to change the whole wedding around at the last minute, or that Rose would go along with it. Although, actually, if Donovan's mother was anything like her son, it wasn't too hard to believe that she would try to interfere with what Rose wanted.

"She didn't *say* it, exactly," Rose said. "But it was pretty clear. She was telling me about how old-fashioned it was, and—" She cut herself off with a sigh. "None of those details matter, RJ. What matters is that I'm not having my wedding under it. I mean, I'm a wedding planner. What will it look like if *I* do something so out-of-date? So quaint and *precious?* I need you to get rid of it."

RJ normally didn't like to refuse Rose anything. Before now, he'd helped her switch around details of entire weddings. He'd helped her clear up after weddings when almost none of the others had stuck around; he'd put together impossible wedding setups, like the *Gone with the Wind* theme for the multiple Banning weddings. He had taken over flower-arranging duties when Phoebe had been trying to figure out her relationship with Patrick, and he'd even made sure Rose had gotten home after a rare night of overimbibing with Anne.

But this?

He wasn't sure he could do this, not when he knew how much pain it would cause her to give up her dream wedding.

"Why do you care what Donovan's hoity-toity mother thinks?" he asked. "This is your wedding, and it should be exactly how you want it to be, rather than how she wants it. What did your mother think about you changing your wedding plans?"

"I haven't told her yet." Rose lifted her chin as she faced him. "But it doesn't matter what she thinks, because I don't want the gazebo anymore."

"I don't believe you."

She whirled then, going for the small toolbox that he always kept in the storage closet. "If you won't do it, I'll do it myself."

She came out with a hammer, heading for the door. He stepped in her way.

"What are you doing?"

"Get out of my way." When he didn't move, she reiterated every word with increasing volume...and desperation. "Get. Out. Of. My. Way!"

RJ reached out to catch hold of her wrists. He wasn't going to let her destroy the gazebo just like that.

He held her there, their torsos brushing close to one another, their lips with just the briefest space between them.

Closing that gap was all he'd wanted to do ever since their Valentine's Day kiss. If only he'd asked Rose out before Donovan had, things would have been so different. He was sure of it.

He'd spent so much time trying not to get in the way, trying to do the right thing. But none of that changed how much he wanted her right now.

And it never would.

"Donovan doesn't deserve you." Those words were out before he could stop them. He wasn't even sure that he wanted to stop them anymore. "Rose, from the moment I first saw you, I—"

His words fell away as she stepped back from him while shaking her head.

A TORRENT OF FEELINGS boiling away inside Rose threatened to rise to the surface.

Why did RJ keep questioning her decision not to use the gazebo?

Why wouldn't he just help her make new wedding plans like she'd asked him to?

And why, oh, why, had he stopped short of actually kissing her again?

Hold on, what was she *thinking?*

That was the problem. She couldn't think straight anymore. There were too many emotions running riotous inside her. The same emotions that sprang up inside her every time RJ was near…and, lately, even when he wasn't.

She was engaged to Donovan. But he never walked into a room and made her feel as though everything around her might be about to spiral out of control. He had everything going for him. Everything. Being with him was like being in a fairy tale. One where the handsome prince hadn't decided to love a princess, but had somehow *opted* for *her* instead, and was now slowly showing her that she could be a princess, if she only tried hard enough to fit into his world.

With Donovan there were clear lines. Good and bad, high-class and cheap, proper and improper.

With RJ, everything seemed to be jumbled together in one big exhilarating and unexpected mess.

But she couldn't afford any messes right now, because she was about to get *married* to Donovan McIntyre!

Rose carefully put down the hammer then looked back at RJ. "I'm marrying a good man in a few days, a man who trusts me as much as I trust him. I need this to be perfect…and I can't afford to have things complicated."

"I'm not trying to make things complicated for you, Rose," RJ promised her.

But that was exactly what he was doing—couldn't he see that?

"You've helped me so much the past few years. You've been truly indispensable. But I need to know that I can rely on you to help me with my own wedding. Because if you can't…"

Actually, she didn't know what she'd do if he wouldn't help her. Everyone else at The Rose Chalet, they were her friends, and they did great work, but with RJ, he was always *there*. Whenever she needed him.

He seemed to think about her question for a while before stepping back from her and nodding.

"Of course you can rely on me. Whatever you need, I'm here for you, Rose."

CHAPTER SIX

"You HAVE TO hold still," Anne cautioned Rose on Monday morning while she continued to pin her wedding dress in place.

This was the first time her best friend had let her see the dress she'd designed, and it was absolutely beautiful. Anne had used layers of everything from white silk to pale ivory cotton, so that what looked at first glance like a plain white wedding dress became a subtle collection of different shades every time Rose moved.

Which she was apparently doing far too much of, given the way Anne kept catching her skin with the pins she was using to tack the dress in place.

It was hard not to move, though, because around them The Rose Chalet was a hive of activity and noise. Phoebe had a couple of sample floral arrangements ready, and was talking hurriedly on the phone. Tyce was doing the same, making amendments to a musical score at the same time, apparently finalizing the arrangements of the pieces the string quartet would be playing. Julie was away in the kitchen, putting together samples from the menu.

"I know you have a great metabolism, but you mustn't eat too much when Julie gets here," Anne said in the muffled tones of someone with half a dozen pins sticking out of her mouth. "I don't want to have to do all this again on the morning of the wedding."

"It's not Julie's delicious food we have to watch out for," Rose assured her. "It's all these parties Donovan has me going to."

Anne smiled. "It sounds like fun. All those people, all that champagne."

Rose nodded, even if the truth was that she was overwhelmed by all of the champagne toasts and formal dinner parties. It seemed as though every single one of Donovan's friends wanted to celebrate his impending wedding. Or maybe it was just what they thought they were supposed to do.

Either way, Rose had spent plenty of time sitting in rooms where she didn't really know anyone, trying to make conversation with friends of Donovan who were mostly interested in how each other's business was going, or what exotic location they'd just come back from. They also liked to talk about golf…a lot. Unfortunately, Rose didn't have a lot of conversational options when it came to golf.

At some of these gatherings she'd find herself at one end of a room with the wives and girlfriends of Donovan's friends, while her fiancé was at the other. Rose enjoyed discussing fashion, or shoes, but after the first dozen conversations about the latest TV star or the newest boutique, she'd grown more than a little bored with the whole thing.

"There," Anne said, "it's ready."

Rather than head to a mirror, Rose simply stepped over to one of the large windows and looked at her reflection.

"It's the most beautiful wedding dress I've ever seen,

Anne. Thank you." Truly, it was the dress she'd always dreamed about getting married in.

That thought had her looking beyond the glass, to the chalet's garden. RJ wasn't there at the moment, but he'd been outside working for most of the morning.

He hadn't started on the new setup yet, but the gazebo was now gone. For a moment, the garden didn't look quite right to Rose's eyes.

"Are you sure about changing your wedding plans this late in the game?" Anne asked, moving to stand beside her.

"It just wasn't right anymore," Rose said.

She'd spent so long imagining her perfect wedding over the years—long before she'd known Donovan. Every so often, she would just shut her eyes and picture herself on her wedding day, with the gazebo behind her, wearing a wedding dress that had looked in her mind's eye so much like the one Anne had designed for her. She'd have all her friends around her, and her perfect man would be standing beside her, ready for that perfect kiss of true love when—

Rose started as she realized the features of the man in her imagination were more rugged, unshaven and square-jawed than those of her fiancé.

The features belonged to someone she could imagine coming close to kiss her, because he'd nearly done just that the day before.

Rose's eyes shot open as she realized that she was imagining RJ.

Why did she keep doing this to herself?

Why did her brain—and her heart—keep spinning back to what had almost happened yesterday...and to what *had actually* happened last Valentine's Day?

She was going to be marrying a handsome, intelligent, successful man, so why wasn't Donovan the one she was daydreaming about? Shouldn't she *want* to spend every second with him?

"Rose, are you okay?" Anne asked.

Before she could reply, Phoebe stepped into the room. "Rose, I don't want you to panic, but I think there might be a small problem." She frowned. "Actually, quite a large problem."

"What's wrong?" Rose asked.

"It's the orchids for the wedding arrangements." Phoebe gestured to the samples she'd put together. The elegant white orchids had such delicacy and class that they were perfect for the sophisticated wedding Rose was trying to put together.

"What's wrong with the orchids?" Rose asked. "They look perfect."

"They would be," Phoebe agreed, "if I could get enough of them for the wedding."

"You've never had a problem sourcing the right flowers before."

"I know, and I'm sorry, but evidently there's a mite that's spreading through the local orchid suppliers. Until they get it cleared up, they can't provide me with enough white orchids for another dozen bouquets, let alone a whole wedding."

Rose forced herself to take a mental step back and think about what she'd do if it was a client's wedding that was being affected like this.

"Can we try someone who isn't local? I know it would be a long drive in from Southern California, but I'd be willing to pay the extra transportation fee."

"I've already called around quite a bit," Phoebe said.

"I was hoping that I could figure it out without having to bother you, but I can't find anyone who can guarantee enough flowers of the right quality. At least, not anyone close enough to drive them over. If we tried flying them in we could run into problems with the effects of un-pressurized holds on the plants, and packaging, and—"

"I get the idea," Rose said.

"I'm going to have to come up with an alternative be-fore the wedding," Phoebe explained in a regretful voice. "Which means we're going to have to sit down and talk about arrangements again. I'm so sorry about this, Rose."

"It sounds like you've tried everything you can," Rose reassured her friend. "I really appreciate it, Phoebe. And really, if it's just the flowers that are a problem, then we're not in bad shape at all."

Tyce walked in just as she was finishing her sen-tence, a grimace on his face. He ruffled his already fairly messy hair further as he said, "You know how Donovan wanted a particular string quartet to play the wedding?"

"Yes, I saw the paperwork. They're booked for next Saturday."

"That was before they performed for a guy who books string quartets for tours of Europe," Tyce said. "They've just found out they're going to tour around Germany, shoot over into Austria and then do a week-long residency in the Vienna Concert Hall. I tried tell-ing them that we had a contract, but they don't care. It's just too big a gig. They're getting on the plane tonight."

"Okay," Rose said slowly, "so we'll just have to hire a new quartet."

"It might be a bit more complicated than that," Tyce explained. "Most of the established quartets are booked within a week of the event. At this point, the best I can do is to hit some of the local music colleges and try to put one together. Which means auditions, and rehearsals, and maybe changing the set list just so that we've got pieces everyone can play up to concert standard." Tyce repeated the words Phoebe had said moments earlier. "I'm so sorry about this, Rose."

"No, no, you're doing the best you can in a difficult situation, Tyce. I appreciate it. At least the food isn't a problem—"

Of course, that was right when Julie walked in. "Rose, can we chat for a minute? My seafood supplier just told me the crab fishermen have gone on strike, and I'm afraid I won't be able to get in enough for the first course, so—"

Rose put her head in her hands, which stopped Julie midsentence. When she lifted her head up, she said, "Whatever you need to do to the menu, however you need to change it, I trust you, Julie."

And, honestly, the worst part wasn't that her dream wedding was blowing up piece by piece.

No, Rose thought, the very worst part about all of this was that none of this was distracting her from thinking about RJ for even one second.

Instead, Rose found herself thinking about the ways he'd be trying to make her relax if he were here, probably telling her a joke, or even throwing out solutions one after the other, rapid-fire. In situations like this, he was so reliable, so safe.

Yet, whenever she thought back to his mouth on hers in the bar on Valentine's Day, there had been nothing safe about it.

It had been dangerous and wild.

Which wasn't what she wanted.

Or was it?

"Rose?" Anne said as the others went off to try to fix the various issues that had just cropped up. "What's wrong?"

She managed a halfhearted smile. "Only you could be in the middle of a situation where practically every detail of my wedding has just collapsed and still manage to ask what the problem is."

"True," Anne said. "But that's because I'm the only one who knows you well enough to guess that whatever is bothering you has nothing to do with any of those things, does it?"

No, Rose thought, Anne wasn't the only one sensitive to her feelings. RJ would have spotted it pretty quickly, too.

Of course, that thought didn't make her feel any better.

"There it is again," Anne insisted, "the frown that hasn't quit since your wedding shower. What's going on? I want to help."

"Have you been taking investigating lessons from Gareth? How is he, anyway?"

"He's great. But changing the subject won't work today."

Rose didn't know what to tell her best friend. "It… it's crazy."

Anne put a hand on her shoulder. "Whatever it is, it's not crazy if it's upsetting you."

Finally, Rose gave in and admitted, "It's RJ."

Anne didn't say anything for a long moment. "What about him?"

Oh, God, Rose couldn't believe what she was about

to say…but she had to tell someone or else she was going to burst.

"I almost kissed him yesterday. And last Valentine's Day, I *did* kiss him. And it was good. Really good. I… I've been thinking about him a lot." She paused for a moment before admitting, "I can't seem to stop thinking about him, actually."

"Well, obviously."

Rose paused at that. "What do you mean, 'obviously'?"

Anne gave her a knowing smile that had Rose wondering if she and RJ had been fooling anyone.

"Sparks have always lit between the two of you. And he obviously cares a great deal for you."

"I care for him, too," Rose said, "but I'm marrying Donovan. I can't keep thinking about another man."

Anne was quiet for a few seconds, as if she was trying to work out whether to say something. "Can I ask you a question without you getting angry?"

"You're my best friend. Of course you can."

"Why are you marrying Donovan?"

Rose's brain felt as if it emptied out and then filled back up again too fast. "Why wouldn't I marry him? He's a great guy. He works hard in a business that helps people. He's handsome. And he makes me feel safe. With Donovan, I'm never going to end up with the life my mother has."

"But do you love him?" Anne asked her.

"Of course I do," Rose shot back. Maybe just a little too quickly.

Anne looked out the window to see that RJ was back, measuring up the ground outside the chalet. "It seems to me that a lot of the qualities Donovan has also apply to other people."

"No," Rose disagreed. "Every time I'm in the same room with RJ lately it feels like the world is disappearing out from under me. The last thing I feel is safe with him." She looked around at the hall, turning her back on where RJ was working, because she couldn't look at him without the knot twisting tighter in her stomach. "I can't feel like this right before my wedding, Anne. Please, just tell me that it's all going to be okay."

If there was one thing that she could rely on the world's biggest optimist for, it ought to be that.

"It *will* be okay," Anne promised her. "Of course it will. Because if you really love Donovan, and if he's the one your heart aches for every time he's not there, then when you marry him everything will be fine."

And as Anne gave her one more hug before heading back to the dress, Rose tried desperately to pretend that her stomach hadn't sunk further with each word her friend had said.

CHAPTER SEVEN

RJ FINISHED TAKING measurements out in the garden, watching Rose through the windows as he worked. She looked incredibly lovely in the wedding dress Anne had created.

By the time he went back inside, she was in her skirt and blouse again. With her hair tied back, her whole ensemble looked just a little too formal, the way so many of Rose's clothes did these days when he couldn't persuade her to work with him in the garden. With her sleeves rolled up or dirt-stained overalls on, she always looked so beautifully natural.

Today, however, she looked so tense that he immediately tried to ease her mind by saying, "I've been working on the new setup and it's going well."

"That's great, RJ," Rose replied. "It's nice to know that one thing is going right."

He frowned. "Are there problems with the rest of the wedding plans?"

"Let's put it this way—anything that can go wrong *is* going wrong."

"Not your dress," he said. "It's beautiful, Rose."

Their eyes held for a long moment before she said, "Thank you," and then, "Unfortunately the food, the flowers and the music all have to be practically redesigned from scratch for one reason or another." She laughed, but there wasn't much humor in the sound. "I never thought I'd see the day when Anne was the one person I didn't have to worry about being ready by the wedding day."

"She's not the only one," RJ assured her. "I'll get this new setup finished in time."

"I know you will, and it's good to have someone I can rely on. Although at this rate," she continued, "we'll probably find that the dress has gone missing right before I need to walk down the aisle."

"You're worrying too much." RJ didn't step closer to put an arm around her shoulders, even though he badly wanted to. "How about if we get some lunch and I'll go through some of the details for what I have in mind for the new setup. I know a place that does great chili fries."

"Chili fries?" He could see the hungry gleam in her eyes before she said, "Actually, I need to watch my weight so that Anne doesn't have to readjust the dress."

"Don't worry," RJ said with a grin, "one plate of fries won't hurt anything." Before she could protest again, he put his hand on the small of her back, gently but firmly. "Come on, a change of scenery will do you good."

He managed to keep her moving all the way out to his truck, then drove quickly to the place he had in mind, a small diner he'd come across on the way to the local lumberyard. It was a place workingmen went in the middle of the day, and definitely not somewhere Rose would go with Donovan. If the plastic surgeon ever found himself touching something in a place like this, he'd probably spend the next day or so scrubbing up.

Apparently, Rose thought pretty much the same thing when they pulled into the diner's gravel parking lot.

"*This* is the place you're taking me?"

"You're going to love it," RJ said with a smile. It

was time to remind Rose who she really was, not who Donovan wanted her to be.

"But there are plenty of other places we could go."

"None that serve chili fries like these."

"But this looks like a total dive."

He turned off the engine and got out of the truck to make it clear that they were staying. Rose seemed to get the message, or maybe she was just finally able to admit to herself that she wanted the chili fries more than she wanted to avoid the diner. He helped her carefully climb down from the truck and they headed inside together.

One basket of chili fries later, and Rose had taken off her jacket and was no longer sitting bolt upright in the booth.

"You're right—these are really good fries," she admitted. "They remind me of when I was working at the bowling alley to save money for college—only with maybe just a bit more grease," she said with a grin that he loved seeing.

"You never told me you worked at the bowling alley."

She flushed. "It's not exactly something I like admitting to, working the same dead-end job as my mom."

"I don't see what's wrong with doing the same job as your family. And you've accomplished a lot since then."

"Not compared with the people I meet at Donovan's parties. The ones who aren't doctors are lawyers, and the ones who aren't lawyers are in politics."

RJ wished Rose could see how important she was to the clients she worked with at The Rose Chalet, and to her employees and friends.

Most of all, he wished she could see how important she was to him.

"Why don't you tell me your new idea for the wedding setup?"

Rose was obviously trying to change the subject, and RJ decided to let her. He didn't want to make things harder for her. He didn't ever want to do that.

"And thank you, RJ, for doing all this at such short notice."

"I'll do whatever you need me to do," he said with feeling. "Knowing how much you like roses got me thinking about the traditional rose ceremony." The standard version was simple: an exchange of roses between the mothers of the bride and groom during the ceremony. "Just two people exchanging roses might be nicely symbolic," he explained, "but it feels like it isn't big enough. So why not have everyone at the wedding exchanging roses? All the guests on your side and everyone on Donovan's."

He watched her face light up at the idea, before she quickly stamped out her obvious pleasure. "Thank you for the idea, RJ, but I don't think it will work. Not when Donovan will have so many more guests than I will. His family, his colleagues, his most important clients."

"We can figure it out," RJ insisted, even though it annoyed him that Donovan should have more guests than Rose at their wedding, as if Rose's friends and family didn't matter the same way his did. "I was thinking of rigging up a topiary runner over the seating area. If I put it together with latticework, I can make it look like it's raining rose petals as you walk along the aisle, and then as you walk past each couple in the wedding party, they can step in and exchange roses."

For one brief moment, RJ thought Rose might go for it. Her eyes certainly seemed eager, maybe even a little dreamy, yet he could see the instant when she reconsidered…and made her final decision.

She shook her head. "No, we can't do that. It's too messy. Too showy. And the rose ceremony has been done too many times before. It has all the problems that getting married under the gazebo had."

Which, as far as RJ could see, mostly consisted of Donovan's mother not thinking it was up to her standards.

Was Rose really going to try to design her entire wedding to live up to what she thought Vanessa McIntyre would like?

"It's not elegant enough," Rose continued. "I want my wedding to have style. I want it to be absolutely perfect, with nothing going wrong."

Rose, of all people, should have known that weddings were big, messy, *fun* events. Yes, there was space for style and elegance, but even then, most couples tended to let their hair down a little during one of the most important days of their lives.

But to RJ it sounded as if Rose wanted her big day to be like a catwalk show. Beautiful to look at, but without any fun or spontaneity.

He felt as if there were two Rose Martins these days. There was the woman she thought she ought to be—the person Donovan wanted her to be. This was the woman who seemed to be too willing to put aside her wedding arrangements because of what people thought.

Then there was the *real* Rose. The woman who rolled up her sleeves and helped him pound in nails and dig in the garden. The woman who devoured chili fries in diners.

The woman who had kissed him.

Yet he knew if he said any of that, Rose would simply deny it and pull away from him.

So instead of *saying* it, he needed to *show* her the difference. Chili fries in the diner had been a start, but he needed to do more…and fast.

"Are you sure you don't want to try the rose ceremony?" he asked one more time. "It seems to me that it would be perfect for you, Rose. It would say who you really are."

"Maybe that's the problem. Maybe you don't know me as well as you think you do."

A flare of anger at just how wrong she was had him quickly coming back with "Well, then, tomorrow we should do some research. You know, so that I can actually be a help to you, rather than just guessing about what it is you want."

"Research?" Rose asked. She sounded suspicious now, but RJ wasn't going to let it go that easily.

"We both agree that it's vitally important for a bride's wedding to reflect her true self, and you don't think I've got it so far.

"So tomorrow," RJ continued, "why don't you take me somewhere that does show who you really are? Somewhere that will give me plenty of inspiration for your wedding day."

Rose paused. "I don't know, RJ. I have so much to do now with helping Phoebe, Julie and Tyce."

"They're total pros and you know they can deal with any problems they run into. But I might not be able to produce the perfect wedding setup for you without your help. I mean, look at my first two attempts."

"I guess," Rose said slowly, "that makes sense."

Tomorrow morning, he'd let Rose hold the reins, but

in the afternoon, RJ vowed that he was going to finally get a chance to show Rose who *he* thought she was.

And maybe, just maybe, that version would include her loving him the way he'd always loved her.

CHAPTER EIGHT

ROSE WAS IN the chalet the next morning, looking at a drawing for a new flower arrangement, when RJ walked in and she completely lost track of her train of thought.

"Are you ready to go, Rose?"

There was part of her that wanted to find an excuse not to do this. It wasn't as if they could afford the time away from the wedding preparations, and the thought of spending the day with RJ was…well, actually, it felt pretty good.

Which was exactly the problem. Being with RJ shouldn't be so good all the time.

Even so, she'd given him her word. And she never went back on her word.

When they went out to his truck, he asked, "So, where are we headed so I can learn who the real Rose Martin is?"

She gave him directions and he drove without asking any other questions. Apparently, he was willing to be surprised, and she was happy to sit with him in comfortable silence.

With Donovan, she'd have found something to discuss, even if it was getting him to talk about the internal politics of the plastic-surgery world. But *comfortable* wasn't a word she'd ever use to describe Donovan. *Dangerous* wasn't it, either.

How, she found herself wondering, could RJ be both comforting and dangerous at the same time?

It was another five minutes before they reached their destination—an art gallery. RJ found a parking spot out on the street, looking up at the building as he did so. "This is the place that reflects the real you?" he asked with more than a little skepticism.

"Absolutely," Rose replied. "Donovan took me here about a month ago. He knows the owner of the gallery. It's very beautiful. Very refined. I'm sure we'll be able to find lots of inspiration for the wedding inside."

"Okay," he said in an easy voice, "but I was hoping you'd take me somewhere that's personal to you."

"This *is* personal to me," Rose insisted. "Well, for both Donovan and myself. It's a place that we've spent time together."

She could remember the first time she'd come to the gallery with Donovan—it had been a private showing. Both the art and the customers had seemed so pristine and perfect, and at first she hadn't felt as if she fit in at all. It had seemed as if everyone was speaking their own private language. Yet Donovan had slowly begun to introduce her to people—the gallery owner had seemed nice, and Rose had gradually found herself feeling more and more at home.

If only she could make RJ understand....

Hold on. Why was it important that he understand? He just needed enough inspiration to be able to produce a workable wedding setup, she reminded herself. That was all.

They went inside, and RJ took a long look around at the pieces on display. Turning to her, he said, "So, which piece do you want to show me first?"

The artwork displayed was comprised of many different styles and mediums, from jagged sculptures constructed from pieces of found metal, to paintings that were little more than blocks of color. There was even a few fabric pieces that were as much simple design pieces as they were art. Rose waved RJ over to one of the sculptures, purely as a place to start.

"So," he said, "why this one?"

"Well…" She tried to think of something she liked about this particular sculpture. "I like the way the artist has taken ordinary objects and reused them, turning mundane objects into something special."

"Funny," RJ said in a considering voice, "over all the years we've worked together and have been friends, I've never seen you drawn to anything so cold and sharp." Before she could interrupt him, he said, "You've always appreciated beauty, and softness, and things that make you laugh."

Warmth at his words warred with the frustrated realization that he wasn't giving her a chance to show him how she'd changed. But before she could explain herself any better, the gallery owner, Millicent Richards, moved to their side.

She was easy to recognize, thanks to a wardrobe that was as much an art installation as clothing. Her features had the tight, symmetrical perfection that kept Donovan and the other plastic surgeons in his office booked solid.

"Hello, Millicent." They air-kissed each other on both cheeks as if they were in Europe rather than in San Francisco. "I'd love for you to meet RJ. We work together at the chalet. RJ, Millicent owns this gallery."

"It's so nice to meet you, RJ," Millicent said with an appreciative gleam in her eye for the good-looking

man standing before her. A look bright enough that
Rose felt a wave of possessiveness rush through her
before she could stop it. "Can I help either of you find
something today?"

Rose forced herself to smile at the other woman. "Actually, we're here to get some last-minute inspiration
for the wedding. RJ is helping me put it all together."

Millicent nodded as if it made perfect sense that they
would have come to her gallery for inspiration. "Do let
me know if I can help in any way. I'm very much looking forward to the wedding. You're really very lucky to
have captured Donovan McIntyre's eye. All of the other
girls in our circle are jealous beyond belief that he's
taken. Then again, you and Donovan really do make
the perfect couple, with the way your coloring perfectly
complements his. Well done, Rose."

A potential customer caught Millicent's eyes and
she hurried off before Rose could insist that jealousy,
"capturing" and complementary coloring had nothing
to do with her upcoming marriage to Donovan. She
and Donovan were marrying one another because they
wanted to spend the rest of their lives together. Why
else would they build such a lovely home together, or
make such an effort to ensure that their wedding was
going to be absolutely perfect?

She tried to turn her focus back to looking through
the pieces on display with RJ, but it wasn't easy to do so
when he was gazing at her with such intensity. It was almost as if he was trying to see all the way inside of her.

With a hand that she willed not to shake, she pointed
out a delicately painted watercolor of a woman who
looked formal and elegant. "That's what I'm looking

for," she explained. "A sense of refinement and beauty for my big day. Does that make sense?"

"I'm starting to get the picture."

They kept walking around the gallery, stopping in front of each of the pieces. Some were abstract; others were more classical. RJ kept asking her questions about her reactions to each piece.

It was actually a lot of fun, getting a chance to take the morning off from wedding preparations. Even better, she had to think so hard about her reaction to each piece of art that she couldn't spend every second rewinding back to the way they'd almost kissed on Sunday morning.

That kiss had been one crazy impulse, just as the previous kiss on Valentine's Day had been. A temporary infatuation and nothing more.

Knowing it was best if they kept their focus on the wedding, she asked him whether it would be possible to create a Grecian feel for The Rose Chalet in the four days remaining.

"If that's what you really want, I'll find a way to do it."

"That's great," she said. "I'm glad we did this."

RJ smiled at her, and she worked to ignore the warmth that coursed through her as he said, "I am, too. It's made things a lot clearer."

Yes, it definitely had. Rose checked the time. "Why don't we go get some lunch? There are some great little places nearby that Donovan has taken me to. My treat as a thank-you for all this effort."

"If you really want to thank me," RJ suggested, "why don't you spend a little more time with me after lunch? Actually, there's somewhere I'd like to take you."

"Where?"

"That part's a surprise. I think you'll enjoy it, though, and it won't keep you from heading back to the chalet for too much longer."

She hesitated. There wasn't much time left before the wedding, and there was still so much to do. But the only real reason she had for saying no was the thought she wouldn't be able to control herself around RJ.

A couple more hours with him was the perfect way to prove to both of them that she could.

She smiled at him. "You're on."

CHAPTER NINE

Lunch had been everything RJ would have expected after spending the morning at the pretentious gallery. It had been a fancy place where the other customers looked at him strangely for wearing jeans and boots. Clearly, in their world, men didn't have jobs that involved getting their clothes dirty.

The food itself was a long way from the reimagined simplicity that Julie and Andrew had been putting together for wedding clients at the chalet. Even Rose didn't seem to be getting quite as much out of the meal as she wanted to pretend, and RJ was only too glad when they finally got going.

The timing, fortunately, was perfect for his plan. Neither of them spoke as he drove to the other side of the city. He loved the way they didn't always have to talk. He enjoyed joking around with Rose, too, but being comfortable enough with her to share the quiet and stillness for a while was also special.

"Okay," Rose said eventually, "enough mystery. Where are we going?"

RJ pointed to the sports field that was just coming up on the left. "We're here."

He found a spot to park and when they got out of the truck they were immediately surrounded by a small horde of kids who barely came up to their shoulders. They were all wearing identical baseball uniforms.

"Coach RJ!" one of them said. "Billy hit me in the head with a ball!"

"Let's see if you've got a bump on your head." RJ brushed the boy's hair from his forehead. "Looks like you'll live to play another game. I'm sure it was an accident, wasn't it, Billy?"

"It was! His head got in the way of the ball at the last second."

RJ made sure not to laugh, or to even break into a grin, as he said, "Shake hands, both of you, and then we can practice a bit before the other team arrives and the game gets started."

They made their way over to the field and RJ set them off running some quick sprints to warm up.

When he turned to Rose, she was smiling. "So this is your Little League team? I always wondered if I'd ever get to see Coach RJ in action."

He'd come by a couple of years ago to see if they needed some help reseeding the field, and when it turned out that the kids didn't have a regular coach, he'd stepped in. It was why he'd brought her here with him today. He knew the only way he could get Rose to stop stressing out about her wedding was to get her involved in helping other people. After all, it was why she'd built The Rose Chalet: to give people one special, perfect day.

"How about being my official assistant coach for the afternoon?"

"Well," she said with a slow smile that utterly transformed her face from pretty to stunning, "I have always been a bit of a baseball fan."

The kids were done with their sprints by then, so RJ got them practicing throwing and fielding grounders while Rose threw a ball for one of the smallest, shyest boys. She'd always been so good around kids. Yet he knew kids weren't on Donovan's agenda, at least if the original specifications for the house RJ's brother, Patrick, had designed for them were anything to go by.

The more time RJ spent with Rose, the less he could work out what she was doing with her fiancé. Judging from the visit to the art gallery, Donovan seemed to see her more as an ongoing project to hone and refine than simply as someone he loved. Though maybe given what he did for a living, that wasn't so surprising.

RJ could see how happy she was as she declared each of the kids "safe" while they practiced sliding into home plate one after the other. Very quickly, she forgot her reservations and self-consciousness. And it was impossible to be elegant and restrained when running around after a bunch of kids. Even in a nice blouse and skirt. Especially in those, because they showed the dirt far more than dark jeans and a T-shirt would have.

Once the other team arrived, they took their places on a set of old bleachers that held an assortment of parents and elder siblings who had come to watch the game. The field didn't yet have a real dugout—RJ was working on plans with the city to build one soon—so he usually either stood against the fence or sat in the front row of the bleachers to give instructions and encouragement to the kids.

Rose rubbed at a spot of mud on her skirt, and RJ said, "I suppose I should have told you to wear jeans. That way it wouldn't matter if you got them dirty." He gestured to his own clothes, now every bit as muddy as Rose's.

"And you," she said with a wicked little spark in her eyes, "should have worn a baseball uniform."

Hmm…was that her way of saying she would have liked to see him in tight white pants and a short-sleeved shirt?

RJ could see Rose continuing to relax minute by minute, play by play. Pretty soon, she was shouting out encouragement along with everyone else. She even leapt up out of her seat when the parent who had volunteered to umpire called Billy out at first base.

"Out? He was *not* out!"

RJ grinned, then looked around for the ice-cream seller who usually stopped by when the games were going on. He spotted the man and touched Rose lightly on the shoulder.

"Want an ice cream?"

He'd half expected her to say no given that they'd only just had lunch together, but Rose nodded instead. "Why not? I'll get them, though. You need to focus on coaching your team. I want you guys to win."

She was right. Normally he never would have shifted focus from his team, but he had a reason for everything he was doing today. Including this.

"It'll only take a minute, and anyway, I have you to fill in for me, don't I?"

Rose looked a little panicked at that suggestion. "Me? I don't know enough about baseball to coach your team while you're off getting ice cream."

"Maybe not, but you do know about keeping people organized. You'll do fine," RJ assured her. He headed over to the man with the ice-cream cart and ordered two ice creams on a stick, one in the shape of SpongeBob and the other in the shape of Spiderman, both with gumball eyes. All the while, he kept an eye on both his team and Rose.

When he came back to the bleachers, she was busy giving encouragement to the next batter. "You can do this," she assured the small boy. "You're going to hit the ball so far that everyone on base will have time to run to home plate before the other team even gets to the ball."

"But I've never hit a home run before," the boy pointed out.

"Are you arguing with me, Michael?"

"No, Coach Rose."

The boy went out to the plate. The first pitch flew past his bat, and so did the second, but he knocked that third pitch right past the shortstop and into the outfield, where the left fielder let it pass right between his legs.

"Come on, Michael!" Rose yelled. "Run, run, run!"

"See? What did I tell you? You're doing just fine." RJ handed her the ice cream. SpongeBob's face had started to melt a bit, but it was still a big yellow square of ice cream on a stick.

Rose stared at it as if she was about to complain that she didn't eat food like this, but that thought was quickly overruled. She grabbed the ice cream and promptly licked off one of the eyeballs.

"This is really fun. I love how enthusiastic they all are," Rose said, before jumping up out of her seat when another great hit landed in the outfield.

"It looks like they aren't the only ones who are having fun."

She smiled at him. "Honestly, this is the most fun I've had in a very long time."

For RJ, though, the best part about the baseball game was just being next to her, close enough that he could hear everything she called the umpire under her breath when she thought no one could hear.

It would have been so easy to reach out and touch her. If only that wouldn't risk ruining the whole day.

A few seconds later, when the game was tied and the tension on the bleachers had ratcheted up several degrees, Rose reached out and gripped RJ's hand in hers. She held on to it while the last of their batters lined up at the plate. With a runner on third base and two outs, they needed a good clean hit to win the game, but right then, RJ could barely keep his focus on the game, could barely think about anything other than the feeling of Rose's hand in his.

He could remember the kiss they'd shared—every last detail. It was the best kiss he'd ever experienced. It had been the closest he'd ever felt to any woman, including his ex-wife.

Yet right then, just holding hands on the bleachers with Rose was even sweeter.

"Yes!" Rose yelled, dragging him to his feet as the ball sailed into the outfield. "We've won!"

For a moment, he thought that she might hug him, and maybe that would have been even better than the hand-holding, but instead Rose dropped her ice-cream stick into the garbage can and rushed forward to congratulate the kids.

And even when she told him she needed to get back because Donovan would be picking her up soon for a champagne toast one of his colleagues was throwing for the two of them, RJ knew the afternoon had gone better than he could possibly have hoped.

Rose had held his hand. They'd sat on the bleachers during a Little League game, just like a couple would have done. And it had felt so right.

More than that, the afternoon had proved that the real Rose was still in there somewhere, and that she was still a smart, funny woman who would rather eat an ice cream at a children's baseball game than go to an art gallery any day.

CHAPTER TEN

THE PARTY WAS everything Rose had come to expect from Donovan's friends. It was stylish, elegant, refined…and she kept having to hold back a yawn. Of course, she reminded herself, they were all here to celebrate her and Donovan, so she should be enjoying herself.

Rose had barely had time to get home and change before Donovan picked her up. She'd thrown on a sleek navy blue dress and heels, but without the time to put together anything better, she felt severely underdressed next to the collection of plastic surgeons and their model-beautiful wives and girlfriends. Donovan had assured her that she looked lovely, but she'd had a hard time believing he meant it.

Maybe it was because of the way he'd said, "You look lovely tonight, Rose," as calmly as if he'd been telling a client how well her surgery had gone, and with just as little passion.

She knew he had a measured approach to life, but she hadn't wanted to just be told that she was looking good; she'd wanted to *feel* it. She'd wanted his smoldering gaze to silently tell her that what he really wanted was to cut the party short, take her back to his place and get her out of the dress she was wearing.

The trouble was, she'd never seen Donovan give her a look like that. It wasn't exactly the proper thing to do, was it? As for going to bed together…well, they'd hardly seen much of each other recently, and when they had they'd both been busy planning the wedding.

Donovan always told her he believed the key to a successful relationship was clear and open lines of communication. Now, if only they could actually work on that.

Well, this wasn't the moment; that was for sure. They were currently standing beside one of Donovan's friends, who was telling a story about the time they'd both talked a senatorial candidate into a face-lift…and the apparently miraculous results it had produced for his career. She had been introduced to Edward at a champagne reception earlier in the week. He had a different woman by his side tonight, though to Rose's eye they were more or less interchangeable—both were blonde and pretty.

"And now we have at least one friend in high places," Edward said, "thanks to Donovan."

"His eyebrows are in a high place, at least," another surgeon joked. "Permanently now."

That got a laugh from everyone, and Rose remembered to join in at the last second.

"To Donovan and his lovely bride-to-be," Edward finished.

The guests abbreviated the toast to simply "To Donovan!" But Rose was willing to let that go. After all, they were his friends, and she knew she should be making more of an effort. The trouble was that half the things she felt like saying weren't exactly things she suspected the group would think of as witty or funny…or even appropriate.

"It's nice of so many people to want to wish us well, isn't it?" Donovan said a short while later.

"It is," Rose agreed with a smile that felt brittle and

forced. There was no comparison between how she felt right now and how much fun she'd had out at the Little League field earlier that day with RJ and the children.

Thinking of RJ during this party had Rose feeling terribly disloyal. She reached for Donovan's hand, but as she did so her mind immediately flicked back to the feel of RJ's large, callused hand in hers during the game. Reaching for him had been such a simple, natural thing to do.

God, what was wrong with her? She shouldn't be thinking about RJ at all—especially this close to her wedding. Yet thoughts of him kept coming, kept intruding. Like how she could imagine the way he'd liven up this party, for one thing. Even without saying much, he'd make it so easy for her to feel comfortable. With RJ, she'd be able to relax.

Why couldn't she relax on her own? Why should she need RJ around for that? Maybe all she needed right now was to loosen up just a little. Rose resolved to try it with the next couple they talked to, another plastic surgeon with another pretty blonde on his arm.

"Frank," Donovan said, "it's good to see you."

"I wouldn't miss your celebration, now, would I?"

Donovan nodded to the woman with his friend. "Tiffany, you're looking great as always."

"So, what do you do, Tiffany?" Rose asked.

The other woman looked surprised by her question. "I'm a model. Thanks, in large part, to Frank's brilliant work."

The phrase "A little remodeling before the modeling?" popped into Rose's head. But she knew better than to say the words out loud. Instead, she simply forced her smile to remain fixed on her face.

"Frank," Donovan said, "weren't you telling me that you are planning on opening up a new practice?"

"That's right. Not too far from you, as it happens. But don't worry, I won't steal all of your clients," he said with a slap to Donovan's back. "I know you still have a wedding to pay for. Unless, of course, it's on the house, since the wife-to-be owns the wedding venue!"

Wife-to-be? Rose clenched her teeth together behind her smile. She had a name. It was Rose.

"My staff volunteered to work our wedding for free as a gift," she explained, "but I couldn't possibly allow them to do that when they have bills and mortgages to pay."

Donovan gave her just a small shake of his head; not disapproving, exactly, because he was never that, but gently warning her away from continuing to talk about the finances surrounding their wedding.

Rose felt her insides curl up into a tight little ball, knowing she'd made a faux pas by talking about money at all, even though Frank had done just that with his silly joke.

When Donovan was dragged away to talk business, Rose found herself standing in the corner listening to Tiffany talking about a photo shoot she'd just done.

"The photographer had every ounce of his attention focused on me. It made me feel so sexy. But then, you must know exactly what that feels like. After all, you've got Donovan, haven't you?"

Rose barely stopped herself from frowning. "Oh, yes," she made herself say, "you're right. Donovan's wonderful." And he was. He was nice and kind to her and they enjoyed art and opera together. What more could she want?

"You're very fortunate, you know," Tiffany said. "Everyone was wondering which lucky girl would get Donovan, and it's *you*."

It was the same thing Millicent had said to Rose in the gallery that morning. Only, Rose couldn't help but think it made her sound more like a lottery winner than the woman Donovan McIntyre loved with all his heart and couldn't wait to start a new life with.

Rose was still thinking about that while Donovan drove her home a while later, but there were plenty of other things on her mind, too. The party. The baseball game before that. The hundreds of times RJ had made her laugh over the years.

And how wrong it would be to keep what had happened last Valentine's Day from her fiancé.

"RJ and I kissed once," Rose blurted.

Perhaps another man would have crashed the car at hearing her confession, but Donovan didn't do that. He didn't even pull over, either, though he did glance at her when they stopped at a red light.

Why wasn't he reacting?

And why, oh, why, did she want to push him until he did?

"It was last year on Valentine's Day, and we did it for a contest in a bar. But we did it, and I wanted you to know."

Now, Rose could see the tension in Donovan's jaw as he kept driving, but he didn't slow down, and he didn't shout. Instead, she watched him spend the next few seconds thinking it all through.

"Well," he said at last in a very reasonable voice, "I guess that's only to be expected."

"Only to be expected?" Rose repeated. "Is that all you have to say? That it's 'only to be expected'?"

"You're a very beautiful woman, Rose, and it has been obvious for a while now that your gardener likes you."

"But..." Rose wasn't sure what to say. She wasn't sure exactly what reaction she'd been hoping for, but it should be more than this, shouldn't it?

Donovan was the man she was marrying, but he was reacting to the news that she'd kissed another man as if it was nothing. As if it didn't matter to him at all.

"Don't you care?"

"Of course I care," Donovan said. "I just don't see that getting angry about it will help matters. This accidental kiss you had with your gardener is simply something we need to talk through rationally, like the two reasonable adults that we are. Or were you expecting me to drive straight over to his house and punch him in the face?"

"Well, no." Though that might at least have shown her how passionately he felt about her. And she felt a nearly irrepressible urge to correct Donovan when he called RJ a gardener. Because he was so much more than that. The truth was, she couldn't run The Rose Chalet without him.

"Besides, you just told me that it wasn't anything serious, just a contest on Valentine's Day."

"Doesn't it bother you—a contest that involved kissing another man?"

"Perhaps a little," he said, "but I can understand it, too. You wanted to see what it would be like to enjoy a brief forbidden moment. Let's face it, Rose, that's all it was. Perhaps if you had kissed someone else I might be more upset. But it isn't like your gardener is actually a threat to us."

"RJ isn't just a gardener," she finally had to retort. "Not only has he designed and landscaped pretty much the entire Rose Chalet property, he's also helped with the important details in putting hundreds of weddings together."

"Okay, so he's a useful gardener who is also good with a hammer and nails," Donovan said. "It still doesn't mean he'd ever be good enough for you. It was just a silly moment of fun for you, but it was nearly a year ago now, yes? A meaningless kiss from a year ago."

"But that's... Donovan, why are you being so reasonable about this?"

"I love you, and more importantly, I trust you, Rose. I trust you to make the right decisions, and to know just how good we are together. You obviously feel guilty about the kiss, but you don't need to. You really don't."

"But—"

"You've unburdened yourself and I'm not upset. Everything is fine between us. Perfectly fine."

It was all so reasonable and neat, so sealed off and free of emotion. In that moment, Rose felt like screaming... and that just made her feel worse.

Why couldn't Donovan *react*? Why did he have to be so measured about things? Why, for once, couldn't he just go with what he felt, like so many other men would have?

Like RJ would have.

She tried to push the errant thought back, but it could not be ignored. If RJ had heard that she'd kissed another man, he would have reacted passionately and intensely.

Beside her, Donovan just kept driving, his expression as calm and unperturbed as if she'd never admitted to kissing another man at all.

CHAPTER ELEVEN

RJ WENT TO WORK early that next morning. He wasn't going to give Rose anything less than her dream wedding, even if it meant he had to put in extra hours before anyone else was on the property. In fact, it was probably better that way, because then she wouldn't see all the details as he built them. Some surprises he wanted to keep for her big day.

He was using a nail gun to get two-by-four beams into position in the main hall, and wanted to get them in place before Rose could see them. It wasn't exactly an elegant solution, but it would give him a strong core to build the rest of the structure around.

The same strong core that Rose seemed to be so determined to ignore in herself.

"Hey, RJ." He looked up to see his brother approaching.

"Patrick, I thought you'd be busy working on Rose and Donovan's new home. Aren't they planning on moving in after the wedding?" Thinking about the two of them together in the new house had RJ's gut tensing.

"We're actually pretty close to completion," Patrick told him.

"I bet it goes even quicker now that Donovan is willing to spend money on additional contractors."

"Don't look a gift horse in the mouth," his brother told

him. "It means that I can come down here to offer my services. Or was Phoebe wrong when she told me you have to rebuild the entire wedding setup from scratch?"

"No, she wasn't wrong."

"I'm surprised to hear that Rose changed her mind about the whole thing. That isn't like her."

RJ didn't want to go into the details, even with his brother. "The important thing is that it needs to get done by Saturday."

Patrick shrugged and picked up a hammer without asking, starting to nail a crossbeam into position. "We've both done plenty of jobs like that. It starts out one way and ends up as something else entirely."

Just then, Tyce arrived. RJ checked his watch in mock surprise. "Isn't this the earliest you've ever been in to work? All that time around Whitney has changed you, man."

Tyce grinned. "I hope so, but that's not why I'm in early. Since you're working on a new setup, I'm going to need to put up a new lighting rig."

"Are you still having trouble getting enough students for your strings section?" RJ asked with genuine concern. Rose *deserved* the wedding of her dreams.

She also deserved the right groom, of course.

"I've been speaking with a talented quartet, but whether they have enough pieces together to play the whole gig, I'm not sure. I'm going to have sound tracks and speakers ready as insurance."

"I'll tell you what," RJ offered. "If you can help Patrick and me out with this, I'll help you with the lighting rig and the speakers."

They set to work, and soon the three of them were making better progress than RJ had hoped for. After an hour or so, they paused to inspect their handiwork. It was looking good.

"RJ," Patrick said from out of the blue, "I need to talk to you about something important."

RJ's brother pulled a box out of his pocket. Inside was a platinum wedding set, sparkling with small diamonds.

Patrick is going to ask Phoebe to marry him?

RJ had known that his brother was serious about his friend and coworker at the chalet, and that Phoebe was serious about him, too. Yet he'd never thought they'd move this quickly.

Tyce immediately joked, "It's lovely, Patrick, but you know, you just aren't my type."

"I know it might seem a little soon, but I love Phoebe so much, and if she's ready, I'd love to get married."

"Welcome to the club," Tyce said with a grin. "Whitney and I have been talking, and I was going to speak to Rose about setting a date here next year. Apparently, it's going to take that long to arrange for all the Bannings to turn up at once."

RJ stood there, trying to take it all in. Here were two men who previously would have been as likely to discuss their feelings as to run naked down the streets of San Francisco, yet now they were talking about weddings and how in love they were.

Suddenly, RJ couldn't keep from admitting his own feelings.

"I'm in love with Rose."

His words hung in the air for a second or two before Patrick slapped him on the shoulder.

"At last, he confesses the truth. Does she know it yet?" his brother asked.

"Wait a minute. You already knew how I felt about Rose?"

"Of course. We all do," Tyce broke in. "The two of you have always had something special between you. So," he said, echoing Patrick's question, "have you told her?"

"She's getting married to another man," RJ reminded them. "In three days."

"They aren't married yet," Patrick pointed out, before frowning. "I hope you haven't put off going after Rose because of what happened with your ex-wife."

"Of course I have," he told his brother. "I never wanted to break up a relationship that way, by encouraging Rose to cheat on Donovan."

No, he'd simply wanted her to realize that Donovan was all wrong for her and to dump him so that he could cleanly ask her out. But that had never happened.

"Look," Patrick said in a no-nonsense manner, "I'm not sure you and Betsy were ever meant to be. You were both young when you got married, and when she cheated on you, I know it hurt. But I also know that you're happier since leaving her than you ever were in that relationship. My guess is that you both are. Take it from me, RJ—the important thing is whether you're with the person you really love, and that she really loves you, too. How you end up there is not that important."

"Your brother has a point," Tyce agreed.

RJ shook his head. "It isn't that simple, guys. What if it turns out that Rose *would* be happier with Donovan?"

"Then she'll marry Donovan," Patrick said. "It's simple, really. If she loves you, she'll be with you. If she loves Donovan, she'll be with him. But if you don't fight for her, then you'll never know who she really loves."

All this time, RJ had been hanging back, not saying anything, hoping that Rose would somehow notice how much he loved her. But his brother was right; he couldn't keep doing that.

At the same time, he couldn't go behind Donovan's back to steal her away. Because no matter what Patrick said, that would be too much like what his ex-wife had done to him.

"I need the two of you to handle things from here. Here's a rough sketch of the new plans." He shoved the paper into his brother's hand. "There's something I've got to take care of. Immediately."

CHAPTER TWELVE

THE BUILDING WHERE Donovan worked didn't look like any medical clinic RJ had ever seen. It looked more like a spa. Yet this was definitely the place, he thought when he noticed that the brass plaque outside had Donovan's name in gold-tipped letters right at the top.

RJ bet that wasn't an accident. Donovan wouldn't settle for his name being anywhere but at the top.

Inside, the reception area was carpeted, with expensive armchairs and discreet prints around the walls. The receptionist was very pretty in an understated way, a balancing act RJ was sure was deliberate. They'd probably looked at head shots when making a hiring decision, wanting someone good-looking enough to suggest that their plastic-surgery services worked. Then they'd put her in a soft and understated outfit and a conservative hairstyle that would make the patients feel slightly superior.

The young woman looked up as RJ approached. "Hello, can I help you?"

Her smile indicated that she thought he was attractive and not quite like the usual potential clients who came into the practice.

A month ago, RJ might have taken the hint that she was interested. He'd been out with plenty of women since his divorce. But now there was only one woman who would do. In fact, maybe that had been true the whole time. It would certainly go a long way toward explaining why none of his relationships over the past five years had lasted very long.

"I'm here to see Donovan McIntyre. Is he in the building?"

"I believe he's in his office on the fourth floor. If you'd like to take a seat, I'll find out if he's available to see you."

"He'll see me," RJ assured her, and headed toward the elevator door.

"Wait!" the woman called after him when it opened immediately and he stepped inside. "You can't just head up like this."

But the elevator door had already slid closed behind him and he knew better than to wait around until McIntyre decided to invite him up. For all RJ knew, the plastic surgeon would keep him waiting for hours to try to show how superior he was.

He got out on the fourth floor and walked along the hall, looking for the right office. It didn't take more than a few seconds to locate it, because of course Donovan would have the biggest office with the best view.

As RJ approached, a woman came out of Donovan's office. She was clearly pleased with the work the surgeon had done on her face and body.

"I'll look forward to seeing you at our follow-up consultations," Donovan told the woman a beat before he noticed RJ.

He walked into the office without waiting for an invitation.

"Is there something you need help with, RJ? For the wedding perhaps?" Donovan asked in a calm voice.

"I'm here about Rose."

"Of course you are." Donovan's mouth curved up slightly at the corners as he sat back in his large leather chair like a man who didn't have a care in the world. "I bet you want to talk about that nothing little kiss you shared, don't you?"

When RJ didn't mask his surprise quickly enough, Donovan looked even more amused. "Oh, yes, she told me about that. I'm glad that she did, in fact, because now that we've got that piece of nonsense out of the way, she and I can get on with our lives together. Oh, and I'd suggest you start looking for a new job. She was very contrite about the kiss and I know how much easier it would be on her if you simply did the right thing and walked away. After the wedding, of course. The last thing Rose needs right now is for her gardener to leave her in the lurch before her own big wedding. It needs to be her perfect day."

RJ's hands had fisted and he couldn't hold back a snarl. "It won't be her perfect day with you there."

But even that didn't quite get a reaction out of Donovan, who continued as calmly as if he and RJ were having a business meeting. "And who would you have take my place? You? So that you can drag her off to live in a handyman's shack? Rose deserves more than that. She's elegant, and perfect, and—"

"And you want to make her into a lifeless little doll like the woman who just left," RJ cut in. "You aren't interested in the real her, any more than you're interested in the emotions or feelings of any of the women who come here to hire you to remake their bodies. You probably don't know the first thing about Rose. Can you even tell me what her favorite flower is?"

Donovan held back for a few seconds, as if he were going to proclaim himself above this question-and-answer session about his fiancée. Clearly, though, he couldn't help himself from proving just how much he knew about the woman he was about to marry.

"Rose's favorite flower is the red-and-yellow bromeliad," Donovan answered. "I've given them to her on several occasions."

"Then you wasted your money," RJ said, "because her favorite flowers are roses, just like her name. Don't you pay attention to her at all?"

"I pay Rose all the attention she requires," Donovan said.

RJ, his voice heating up, demanded, "Then what's her favorite food?"

"Grilled salmon."

"Wrong. It's a hot dog with all the trimmings. And her favorite place in the world is the chalet, closely followed by her mom's bowling alley, not some pretentious art gallery. And her favorite song isn't some boring classical piece, either. It's—"

"You know," Donovan said, raising his voice for the first time since RJ had barged into his office, "it really is very sad, seeing a grown man behaving like this. Acting out over a crush with behavior better suited to a schoolkid. Not accepting that he hasn't got a chance with a woman who wants so much more than he can offer."

"You still don't get it, do you?" RJ growled. "You don't care about Rose. You don't love her. You just want to live with the *idea* of her that you've created."

"And yet I have so much more than that," Donovan snapped back at him. He leaned over his desk. "You say you know Rose so well and that there's no way I should be with her, but which one of us is Rose marrying? Who is she *choosing* to be with? Not the guy whose life isn't going anywhere. Not the guy who can only offer her exactly the kind of life she's worked so hard to get away from. No, she's choosing to be with me."

"We'll see about that," RJ promised him. "I came here to give you fair warning. Consider yourself warned."

Donovan glared at RJ, obviously angry now. "Should I pretend to be scared? You've barged into my office and basically told me that you're planning to take my fiancée. But you've forgotten the only thing that matters." Donovan put his hands flat on the polished desk. "I'm a better man than you, and no amount of ridiculous posturing on your part will change that. Rose doesn't want you, or anyone like you. She wants me. Now please leave my office. I have another appointment in a few minutes, and then later, I have dinner with Rose at a restaurant that does not have hot dogs on the menu."

"That's where you're wrong," RJ told him. "She doesn't want fancy restaurants or champagne or art galleries. She wants love. And she's going to get it from the only man capable of giving it to her. *Me.*"

CHAPTER THIRTEEN

WHEN ROSE ARRIVED at the chalet, she was surprised to find Patrick and Tyce turning it into a cross between a fairy-tale castle and a rose garden. They were busy rigging up trellises over every available surface. The guests would have a perfect view of the ceremony, yet it would be as if she and her groom were the only two people in the world.

It wasn't what she'd asked for. If RJ had been there, she would probably have pointed out that she'd already said no to this plan.

Which made her a little bit glad that RJ wasn't there right then, because every cell in her body told her this design was *perfect*. Rose could imagine nothing better than standing there in the dress that Anne had created for her, getting ready to say *I do* with—

Well, with Donovan, of course.

"Do you have much more to do?" Rose asked Patrick.

He looked up from piecing together some latticework and smiled. "RJ's plans were very clear, so it's going pretty well. It shouldn't take too much longer."

"This is going to take a lot of orchids," Tyce remarked.

Orchids? Rose shook her head as she remembered that, yes, orchids were what they'd been thinking of for the wedding. That seemed so long ago now.

"Not orchids," she said. "Phoebe couldn't get them. It's going to have to be…"

She almost said *roses,* even though she'd already vetoed that idea because roses weren't "special" enough. Only, all she could see when she looked at this setup were masses of roses in red and white, pink and yellow, blended together to produce something magical and wild all at once.

It wouldn't be remotely what she'd asked RJ for, but it would be perfect. So utterly perfect for her. And exactly the kind of wedding she'd dreamed of her whole life.

"Where is RJ?" Rose finally asked.

Patrick and Tyce glanced at one another, and then shrugged in unison.

"I'm not sure," Patrick said. "He said that there was something urgent he had to do."

She was worried about what could have urgently cropped up for RJ to leave in the middle of things—especially so close to her wedding date. Rose made herself concentrate, heading into her office to keep on top of everything. Even without any clients coming in this week, there was still so much to do—finances to keep on top of and a dozen emails to answer. Plus, after she and Donovan jetted off to Aruba for their honeymoon, there would still be weddings booked at the chalet. Which meant Rose had to make sure that everything was lined up beforehand: lists of suppliers, and schedules, and clients' special requests. All of this detail needed to be carefully outlined for her staff.

Her phone rang, and Rose hurried to answer when she saw Donovan's number on the call display.

"I'm really looking forward to tonight," she told him as soon as she picked up.

She had decided tonight was the night Donovan would finally look at her with that possessive, slightly dangerous gaze she'd been so desperate to see the evening before. Somehow she'd pull it out of him…and she'd make sure she felt the same thing for him, too.

"Actually, that's why I'm calling. Tonight is going to be a bit of a problem. I have a valued client who has come in for some emergency work. She has a photo shoot the week after next, and if I don't get the work done at once, the inflammation won't have faded enough."

Rose could just about understand that, but even so, it wasn't exactly life-threatening. "Oh," she said softly, "I see."

"Of course I'd rather have dinner with you." There was just the tiniest hint of reproach in Donovan's voice. "And I've always supported you when you've had to work late."

"I know you have. We've been at so many parties lately. It's just that I was looking forward to having some time with just the two of us." Time to make sure they had the spark a bride and groom should have.

"And we'll have that," Donovan assured her. "Right after the wedding."

At the moment, it seemed as if the whole world was divided into two parts. There was the world before the wedding, full of chaos, confusion and clients dragging Donovan away from romantic dinners. Then there was the world after it, where they were finally married and everything was supposed to be perfect.

At least, that was the way Rose wanted to imagine it. But the details of what her life would be like after she married Donovan slithered through her mind like slippery fish.

"By the way," Donovan added in a faintly amused tone, "you'll never guess who showed up at my office earlier today."

"Who?" Rose asked. At various points, he'd had movie stars and minor celebrities, business leaders and politicians on his operating table.

"RJ." Donovan paused a moment, obviously to let the shocking news sink in. "He came to tell me that he intended to 'fight for you.'" He laughed. "I practically expected him to challenge me to a duel."

"RJ came to your office?" Rose said, absolutely shocked by what Donovan had just told her.

"He walked straight in and told me that I wasn't good enough for you. And that because he knew all these silly things about you, such as you liking to eat hot dogs and go bowling, that I should just step aside and let him have you. Honestly, the man's a joke."

Rose couldn't stand to hear Donovan talk about RJ like that. But at the same time, how could she defend what he'd gone and said to her fiancé?

"I don't know what to say, Donovan."

"You don't have to say anything," he assured her. "It's too ludicrous for words. A grown man acting like a schoolboy, all because of a kiss that didn't mean anything. I just thought that you should know what kind of man you have working for you."

Even though she couldn't bring herself to agree with that, she felt she had to say, "I'm sorry he bothered you."

"A man like him could never bother me. I know you'd never take him seriously. I think he was confused, to be honest. He seemed to be convinced that I'd jump up and punch him, yet why would I do that?"

Because you love me, Rose thought. *Because you can't stand the idea of anyone else kissing me.*

"He doesn't understand that real relationships aren't wild and crazy and full of upheaval," Donovan continued. "After all, why should I ever feel threatened by him? I really am very sorry about tonight, Rose. I'll make it up to you in Aruba on our honeymoon."

She knew she should be completely mortified at the idea of RJ bursting into Donovan's office, telling her fiancé that he intended to try to win her over. She couldn't imagine Donovan or his friends ever doing anything that impulsive or reckless.

But she couldn't stop herself from relishing the knowledge that RJ had put himself completely on the line and confronted Donovan without worrying about the consequences.

It was an incredibly brave thing to do. How many other men would have done that?

At the same time, she knew RJ's sudden declaration hadn't actually changed anything. Donovan had simply brushed it off, after all.

Yet if things were that simple, why didn't they feel simple?

She needed to find RJ. She needed to explain that he couldn't do something like this three days before her wedding. He'd left all of this too late.

Far too late.

CHAPTER FOURTEEN

RJ's HOUSE WAS close enough to The Rose Chalet that Rose was able to walk to it, even in her heels. When she got there, she stared at it, stunned.

Whatever she'd been expecting his house to look like, it wasn't this beautiful home with classic lines and a fresh clean exterior. Clearly, his brother, Patrick, had been involved in designing it, because Rose recognized a handful of signature elements from the house he'd built for her and Donovan. What was more, the well-tended garden turned what might have been simply a nice place into a truly wonderful property.

She went to knock on the door and found it open a crack. She called out his name, but when he didn't appear she let herself inside. There were family photos on every wall, along with several of the entire crew at the chalet that must have been taken over the years.

This wasn't the home of a man who was planning to walk away at any moment. RJ's home was stable. Strong. And full of warmth. Not to mention that in order to afford a place like this, RJ had to be doing a lot better with his finances than she'd thought.

Calling his name as she walked through the house, she found him in his home office, talking on the phone with a laptop open in front of him. The laptop showed pictures of roses of every color.

"And you can do it for Saturday?" he asked whoever he was speaking with. "Great. Here's Phoebe's number so that you can work out her exact requirements."

He hung up, then noticed Rose standing at the door. "Rose?" he said, looking a little surprised. "I didn't hear you come in."

"Donovan told me what you did," Rose said without preamble, because she knew she had to. They needed to—finally—talk about what was between them, even though it was bound to be difficult and awkward. "He said that you went to his office and told him that he didn't deserve me—that you were going to fight for me."

RJ didn't even hesitate before he nodded. "Yes. That's exactly what I did, and what I said. And I meant it, Rose."

She knew she should chastise him, but how could she? The truth was that the way RJ had put himself on the line for her was absolutely amazing.

He stood and moved to where she was standing. Close enough that it was hard to think straight. Her brain kept getting stuck on how great he looked. How great he smelled. And how great he kissed.

Not to mention how dangerous it would be to actually act on any of the feelings that were running through her mind. One touch, one word, was all it would take for her neat-and-tidy life plans to come crashing down around her.

"You're supposed to be my rock." Tension and conflict boiled away within her. How, she wondered, could anyone deal with these kinds of deep and swirling emotions without exploding? "You've always been there to help make sure that The Rose Chalet succeeded from the start, when it was nothing more than a dream. You've always been there to hold things together when everything is complete chaos."

She took a deep breath and made herself continue as RJ stood and watched her with such beautiful, understanding eyes.

"You've always made things better. *Always.* My wedding's in just three days. Three days," she repeated as if either of them could have possibly forgotten, "and I'm marrying Donovan."

Maybe she no longer had the right to ask RJ for what she needed, but what else could she do? Well, actually, her imagination was providing her with plenty of possible options, ranging from reaching out to kiss RJ, to another vision entirely, which involved both of them sprawled across his desk.

Rose forcefully pushed those thoughts aside. She couldn't give away everything she'd so carefully pieced together just because of an attraction that only burned hotter with every moment the two of them were together.

She just couldn't.

"I'm asking you to help me one more time." She took a shaky breath before repeating, "Just one more time."

RJ COULD SEE how hard this was for Rose, coming to him this afternoon. She looked so torn, as if she didn't know what she wanted anymore and was afraid that no matter what she did it would be the wrong decision.

It hurt him to see her in so much pain.

And it hurt even worse knowing that he was the cause of it.

Normally, if he could do anything to stop her from hurting, he would do it in a heartbeat.

But this time, he couldn't. It would make things so much simpler for Rose if he were to just step away. But he loved her…and he didn't believe for a moment that Rose would be having so much trouble if she didn't love him back at least a little. If she didn't care, then it would have been easy to tell him she loved Donovan, not him.

"You know I'll be there for you no matter what," RJ said, and it was the truth. If Rose genuinely did love Donovan instead of him, then he wasn't going to get in the way of her happiness.

It was just that everything in him screamed that she *didn't* love Donovan. And he was certain that Donovan didn't love her. Not the real her, anyway.

RJ moved closer to her. Even when they were just working with one another out in the chalet's garden, simply being a few inches away from her made it feel as if there was electricity sparking between them.

"But don't you know why I've always been there for you, Rose? Don't you know why I always will be?"

Rose looked as if she was on the verge of tears. He could see the tension in every line of her features, and he hated being the one responsible for it. If he could, he would chase away her worries and her fears with a joke, or stroke them away with the gentlest of touches. But this wasn't the time for jokes, and as much as he wanted to reach out and touch Rose, he knew that he couldn't.

"You're always there for me because you're a good man," Rose finally answered. "One of the best men I've ever known."

There had been so many instances in the past when

RJ had stopped short at times like this, because he'd known that he was pushing Rose into areas where she simply wasn't comfortable. He'd wanted to make things easier for her…only, it turned out that by not forcing them to face what was between them, he'd ended up making everything so much more difficult to deal with.

And now there was no time left. Not when there was so much at stake.

Everything was at stake.

"That isn't the only reason, Rose," RJ said softly. "Tyce, Patrick and Andrew are all good guys, but they don't help you in the same way I do, because they don't feel the way I do about you."

"RJ…" Rose began, but he pressed on before she could tell him to stop. He needed to say this. He needed her to hear this.

"I do all these things because I love you."

There. He'd finally told her how he felt. The words were out there and they couldn't be taken back.

Not that he would ever take them back, even if he could. He'd wanted to say those words to Rose for so long, and now that he finally had, he wouldn't stop there.

"I've loved you from the moment I laid eyes on you, Rose. I loved you when I kissed you back at the bar all those months ago. I've loved you through every wedding we've worked on. I love you now, right this very second. And I always will."

In all the years they'd worked together, he'd never seen her cry. But now tears rained down her cheeks and they didn't look as if they were going to stop anytime soon.

He pulled her to him, holding her tightly against him

while she cried. He couldn't leave her standing crying and not comfort her. He simply couldn't.

Not even when she didn't say *I love you* in return.

CHAPTER FIFTEEN

THE NEXT MORNING, Rose found Vanessa McIntyre standing in the middle of the chalet's main room.

"Ah, there you are, Rose," Vanessa said. "Anne here was just telling me, in great detail, about some of the weddings you've put on. It was—" she paused as if searching for just the right word "—fascinating."

"I knew you'd love it." Anne smiled as she said that, and Rose couldn't make up her mind whether her friend was very gently making fun of Donovan's mother or not. "Well, there are one or two things with the dress I need to sort out. It was lovely meeting you again, Vanessa."

Vanessa managed to get a hand out between them, which was usually the best defense for people who knew how much Anne liked to hug. Anne looked at her hand for a second, glanced at Rose and then shook Vanessa's hand solemnly before walking off.

"She's very…unique."

"She's my best friend."

Vanessa's expression verged briefly on disapproval. "Yes."

After the horrible night Rose had had, not only sobbing in RJ's arms but continuing to cry long after she'd gotten home, taken a bath and crawled under the covers, Rose simply didn't have the energy to deal with Donovan's mother this morning.

Unfortunately, that hadn't stopped Vanessa from showing up unannounced.

"I wasn't expecting to see you today," Rose said in as brisk a voice as she could manage given how tired she was from tossing and turning all night as dreams of being in RJ's arms took over her brain every time she closed her eyes. "I'm sure you must be very busy."

Vanessa gestured to the wedding preparations. "Did you think that I wouldn't take the time to see how my son's wedding preparations were coming along?"

Her son's wedding. Rose thought about reminding Vanessa that it was her wedding, too. Instead, she said, "It's all going well so far. This structure—" the one replacing the gazebo that had been too "precious" for Vanessa to possibly approve of "—will have flowers all over it."

"The orchids we talked about before?" Vanessa looked around at the setup and frowned. "Don't you think those will look a little fussy? Maybe some other flower would be better for the occasion."

Rose very carefully didn't mention the mite that had been going around the local orchid growers' collections. "You're right. We'll have to come up with something else. I'll get my florist on it at once."

"Good," Vanessa said, and for once there was a note of approval, as though the correct responses to any problem were to agree with her, and then to find someone to immediately handle it.

"Did I tell you that Julie Delgado and Andrew Kyle are doing the catering for the reception?"

"Yes, you did," Vanessa said. "Of course, there are those who say that Andrew's cooking isn't quite what it was before he started with this new food-simplicity thing. Not that I'm one of them, you understand."

Rose nodded. She understood better and better with everything Vanessa said. So far, in this conversation, she'd come very close to insulting two of Rose's friends and had tried to change the wedding plans yet again.

Yet what could Rose do? Vanessa was Donovan's mother.

"Oh, that reminds me," Vanessa added as if it was nothing. "A great many of the guests on my side have to be gluten-free. I'm sure you've already made arrangements for that, but I thought perhaps I should mention it just in case you're not prepared. You might as well make sure the entire menu and cake is gluten-free, just in case."

Rose didn't dare look at her own reflection in the window just in case she saw steam flying out of her ears. She couldn't believe Vanessa hadn't mentioned her guests' gluten allergies long before now. Julie and Andrew were going to kill Donovan's mother...that was, if Rose didn't do it first.

Of course, Vanessa didn't seem to notice that anything was amiss as she announced, "Well, dear, let me know if you need help with anything. I'm sure I can make some calls. But now I must leave for a coffee meeting with the board of the San Francisco Philharmonic." Two air-kisses later, one to both of Rose's cheeks, and she was wafting away on a cloud of Chanel No. 5.

As soon as she disappeared, Anne returned to stand beside Rose. "Is she gone?"

"Yes." Rose barely bit back a *thank God*.

"In that case, I thought I should let you know that there's a tiny problem with the dress."

Rose felt every minute of the sleep she hadn't gotten the night before in how slowly her brain managed a response. "What's the problem?"

"You see," Anne explained, "I've been using this wonderful thread I found at a little market—it's for the beading around the edge of the dress. But then it turned out that I didn't have quite enough, and now the little stall I bought it from isn't there anymore. So I'm going to have to unpick all the thread and redo that section, because otherwise it won't look perfect, and it *has* to look perfect, right?"

"Right," Rose agreed resignedly, wondering if there was anything else that could go wrong with her wedding. Well, there was only one way to find out. She braced herself even as she said, "Anne, can you go gather up everybody for a quick meeting?"

While she waited for her friends and employees to come see what she wanted from them, Rose looked out of the window to where RJ was working in the garden. It was still early, but even though she hadn't seen him when she'd come in, it looked as if he'd been working out on the chalet grounds for hours.

Had he even slept last night? Their talk had been so emotional, and then she'd broken down and cried in his arms just because he'd told her that he loved her. She'd been so terribly, horribly confused by her own feelings for him. She couldn't imagine how he was feeling today.

It was so difficult every day, seeing him and wanting to be close to him. And even harder knowing that after she married Donovan she'd not only see RJ here every day, but she'd likely still feel that attraction between them, too.

Because if it hadn't disappeared by now, how could it magically disappear with her wedding?

And there was the fact that RJ had told her that he loved her, that he'd always been in love with her.

She'd never thought that he would actually say it. Instead, she'd thought he'd understand she was going to be with Donovan. That he'd find a way to make their professional relationship, and their *friendship,* continue to work, just as he always had before.

Yet he'd done it—he'd said the three little words that could never be unsaid.

I love you.

Oh, God, how could they possibly work together now when even staring at him in the garden made her heart ache?

She couldn't do this anymore. She just couldn't. Once the wedding was over and she was safely married to Donovan, she wouldn't be able to work with RJ any longer.

And, honestly, wasn't it the best thing for both of them in the long run? She could really focus her full attention on her new husband, and maybe RJ would finally feel free enough to make the most of his landscaping skills…and find a woman who would love him back.

Her gut twisted at the thought of RJ with another woman. Still, she stepped out in the garden and called out, "RJ, could you come inside a minute for a quick meeting with everyone?"

A few moments later, Julie, Phoebe and Tyce followed Anne into the main room.

"I know all of you have been working really hard this week, but I—" Rose paused. "What I wanted to ask is, are all of you still having problems getting everything together for the wedding?"

Perhaps she should have said *my* wedding, but saying *the* wedding helped her feel as if she was simply organizing her crew for one of the hundreds of events they'd successfully pulled off over the years.

She'd been hoping for a chorus along the lines of *Don't worry, everything's fine,* at least from Anne. Yet for once even her extremely optimistic best friend was quiet.

Tyce spoke up first. "I've got a string quartet together, though the harpist has pulled out now. The trouble is finding enough time to rehearse."

"And I'm still having problems finding all the roses we need on such short notice," Phoebe said.

"I'm also hitting a few speed bumps with an alternative menu," Julie said.

That reminded Rose. "Vanessa just told me that everything needs to be gluten-free."

"What?" Julie looked nothing short of horrified. "But I've already started the cake!"

"And you know I still need to find the right thread for the dress," Anne added. "I think I'll be done on time. At least I hope I will…"

Rose sighed, and then risked a glance at RJ.

"The setup is nearly done," he assured her, "and I'll help where I can with the rest of it."

Rose nodded her thanks, because she didn't know what to say to RJ right then. She certainly couldn't tell him that she wasn't going to be able to work with him in the future, not when he was already speaking to the others one by one, presumably about what he could help them with.

She was so stressed-out that she could feel the tension rising up through every muscle. She thought her body just might fold in on itself from the sheer pressure she was putting on herself, and everyone else, to pull things off. They'd all put so much into trying to make her wedding perfect, and yet nothing seemed to be going right.

At this rate, she was going to succeed at nothing other than pushing away her closest friends.

"All right," she said. "Drop everything. I don't know about the rest of you, but right now, I could use a drink."

Her staff of good friends looked at her as if she'd just sprouted an extra head.

"I'm serious," Rose said. "We're all stressing out over this wedding, and I never wanted the chalet to be like that. So I think the best thing we can all do right now is go find a bar somewhere, relax a little and then see if everything makes more sense after that."

One by one, the others nodded. Tyce spoke for the group. "You know I'm always up for *that* kind of workday."

"I know the perfect place," Phoebe volunteered. "It isn't very far from here."

They walked as a group, one big family that swept Rose along as she tried to conduct a conversation with Anne about thread types…while also trying to ignore the way RJ was looking at her.

A look that said she meant absolutely everything to him…and he'd love her forever, just as he'd told her less than twenty-four hours ago.

"So does it make an actual difference which thread you use?" Rose asked her friend in what she hoped was an interested tone.

"Of course it makes a difference," Anne insisted.

"There's how strong it is, and obviously the color and shine, not to mention allowing for certain kinds of stitches. But I'm sure I'll figure out a way to have everything finished on your dress within the next two days."

Rose didn't notice where they were going until she looked up and saw the sign for the bar. It was the very same bar she'd once gone to with RJ when Donovan had been late to pick her up for their Valentine's date.

The very bar where she'd kissed RJ.

CHAPTER SIXTEEN

PHOEBE, TYCE, ANNE and Julie were crammed into a booth while RJ was getting drinks and Rose was in the bathroom.

"Am I the only one who thinks that, at this rate, those two are never going to get it together?" Phoebe asked the rest of the group.

"They *should* be together," Anne said. "You can see how much they love one another. Well, I can, anyway."

"We all can," Julie agreed. "I've known them less time than the rest of you, but it's obvious, isn't it? What I don't get is why they *still* aren't doing anything about it. Especially when she's about to marry the wrong man in two days!"

Tyce shook his head. "We all know how messed up things can get when you're in love. It can be hard to see what's right in front of you."

Phoebe hadn't even believed in the existence of love before Patrick came along. And now…well, it was more than just RJ being Patrick's brother that made her want to see him happy. She wanted her friends to have what she had. A real, true, lasting love.

"Rose and RJ are our friends," she said. "And if there's anything we can do to help them, I think we should do it. Even if it's a risk."

"If I hadn't been working for Rose at the chalet, I wouldn't have found Whitney again," Tyce said.

"And I never would have met Patrick on the dance floor if not for Rose," Phoebe agreed.

"I probably would have found Gareth," Anne said with her customary optimism, "but Rose helped me to deal with a lot of really difficult things with my parents and half sister."

"Me, too," Julie added. "I mean, I know she fired me initially, but she was kind enough to give me a second chance."

"She's done a lot for all of us," Tyce said. "And so has RJ."

"I can't believe how hard he's working to help her this week, considering that it's Donovan's wedding," Phoebe pointed out, though honestly, she knew what the Knight brothers could be like. Selfless to a fault.

"It's *Rose's* wedding. That's why he's doing it," Anne explained, though they all knew that. "And maybe… well, maybe he's been picturing himself as the groom, rather than Donovan."

Tyce gestured toward the far side of the bar. "There's the back exit. Anyone coming with me?"

Phoebe wasn't surprised to see everyone else stand up. She did, too.

"I just hope that with us leaving them alone today, these two will *finally* manage to tell one another what they really feel for each other."

Everyone murmured their agreement as they got the heck out of the bar.

As soon as Rose came back from the bathroom, she saw that the table they'd chosen was deserted. RJ was still there with six full drinks laid across the otherwise-empty table, but the others were gone.

She knew exactly why they'd abandoned her there with RJ, and for a moment, Rose felt a flash of panic.

Maybe, she tried to convince herself, it was actually a good thing. There were so many things she hadn't said to RJ yesterday, and floods of tears definitely weren't the way she wanted to leave things between them. Maybe if they talked, they could get some closure. Rose had to believe that.

"Did they at least say goodbye?" she asked as she sat down.

"No. Clearly, they hoped that if they snuck out, we'd talk."

"They're right," she said in a voice that shook a little on the two words.

"I'm sorry, Rose," he said in a voice raw with emotion. "I know what you want from me. I know you want me to make it easy for you, but doing that is so damned hard."

"I don't think anything about this is easy," Rose said.

She was so nervous suddenly that she grabbed one of the beers. She was surprised by how good it tasted, so much better than all the champagne she'd been forced to sip at the endless parties Donovan's friends and colleagues had been throwing for them.

"I want to be everything you want me to be, Rose. Everything you need me to be. It's just that…I can't do that and fight for you, too. And I *want* to fight for you, Rose. Because I love you."

"Please," Rose begged him. "Please don't say that again."

"Why not?" RJ demanded. "Why can't I tell you I love you when it's the truth?"

Rose put the beer back down on the table with such force that it sloshed over the rim and a drop slid down the side of the glass like a teardrop. "Because it makes things too complicated."

RJ sat on the other side of the table, so handsome, so strong. Yet despite that strength, she could see how much everything she was saying—and everything that she wasn't—was hurting him.

After a few more seconds of silence, he spoke. "The situation wouldn't be complicated if you didn't feel anything for me. If I thought you didn't care about me at all, then I'd walk away. But you do care, Rose. I know you do."

"Of course I do," Rose snapped back, frustration getting the best of her tongue. "But it doesn't change anything, does it? I've had feelings for you for a long time, and you never did anything about it before. Why now?"

"You were always so careful with me. Until Valentine's Day last year, when we were at this very same bar and you grabbed me and kissed me. Then I knew you had feelings for me, too. But you were with Donovan. So I waited for you to realize you wanted to be with me instead of him. But now…there isn't any more time to wait."

"That's right," she said. "There isn't. You've had time, RJ. You should have said something after we kissed." Her hand started to rise to her lips at the still-potent memory of their kiss, and she barely stopped herself in time. "You could have said something a hundred times. Why wait until three days before my wedding?"

When he didn't answer immediately, she started to

get up. Maybe talking to him like this was a bad idea, after all. Maybe their relationship just wasn't destined to end well.

RJ grabbed her arm and caught her, pulling her back into the booth. "You know that I was married?"

"Yes, before you came to work for me."

"What you don't know is that my wife had an affair with my best friend. I found them together, and that hurt worse than anything I'd ever experienced. I swore to myself that I would never *ever* do that to someone."

"So all this time—"

"I know you aren't married to Donovan, but I didn't think I could live with myself if I came between you. I didn't want to hurt anyone, even Donovan McIntyre, the way I got hurt. It wouldn't have been right."

"But it's right to do it now?" Rose asked. "So close to our wedding?"

RJ looked terribly uncomfortable, but he nodded. "I have to."

"Why, RJ?" Rose demanded. "What's changed?"

RJ didn't say anything for a second or two, but then he looked her in the eyes, and Rose could see without having to be told just how much he wanted her.

How much he *needed* her.

From time to time, she'd thought that he was letting too much of what he felt for her show through at work, but now she realized just what an amazing job he had been doing of holding back what he'd felt all this time.

The intensity of what Rose saw in his eyes was almost frightening. Except that it was RJ, and nothing about him could ever frighten her, because if there was one man in the world who would rather die than hurt her, it was RJ.

"What changed?" he repeated softly. "That's simple, Rose. I realized that what hurts a lot worse than anything my ex did to me is not being with you. It hurts like hell to stand there on the sidelines every day while you're with Donovan, while he's trying to turn you into someone you're not."

"Donovan loves me," Rose said, and she believed that he did. Still, Donovan had never looked at her with anywhere near the burning intensity she could see in RJ's eyes. Her fiancé was always so restrained, so controlled.

"Not like I do. And I know you don't want to hear it, but I'm going to keep saying it, Rose. I love you. I want to be with you. And I'm saying it now because it's our last chance."

Oh, my God, Rose thought as she paused to really let his words of love sink in. Was she actually *considering* leaving Donovan and being with RJ?

No, she couldn't.

What kind of woman would back out of her own wedding?

RJ had said he didn't want to be a man who broke up a relationship. Well, Rose couldn't imagine being a woman who walked out with so many people depending on her.

Everything was set. The guests, the venue, even the gluten-free cake that Julie was likely already preparing. Not only did Donovan expect her to say *I do* to him on Saturday, but his family and friends would be horrified if she stood him up.

Walking out not only wouldn't be right, but it would be exactly what people like Vanessa McIntyre would expect from the poor girl from the wrong side of the tracks who didn't know how to behave. Who fled at the first sign of trouble the way her father had, when he'd left Rose and her mother to fend for themselves so many years ago.

Rose had worked her entire life to stop being that girl. She couldn't go back to being her now.

Not even for RJ.

"I can't do it," Rose said. "I can't just throw away my wedding like this. If you'd come to me months ago, then maybe, but now...now it's too late. It's far too late."

He sat there staring at her, obviously trying to work out what to say to make her change her mind. The trouble was, there wasn't anything he could say. Because it wasn't about how she felt now.

It was about what was right. And that wasn't going to change.

"Please don't hate me," Rose asked him, even though she knew she had no right to make that request anymore.

The look on RJ's face would have broken her heart, if it hadn't already been crushed to smithereens.

"I could never hate you. I could never do anything but love you." He closed his eyes for a brief moment before reopening them and saying, "I can't keep working at The Rose Chalet, being near you every day, knowing that there's no chance for us. I'll stay on until you can find someone to replace me, but I can't keep standing in the wings, watching another man live the life I want with you, Rose. I just can't."

She felt as if every part of her would tear apart, one cell at a time, at the thought of not seeing him every day.

"I know," she whispered.

And, just like that, it was done.

CHAPTER SEVENTEEN

SOMEHOW ROSE MADE it through to the following night, when her friends whisked her off in a limousine for her bachelorette party.

"I love limos," Julie said.

"Me, too," Phoebe said, "especially the free treats and drinks. Who wants what?"

Rose sat there quietly. She wasn't in the right mood for partying. Not that they were exactly going out clubbing. Maybe an evening at the exclusive spa they had booked would make her feel better about everything that had happened with RJ. Or not.

On the other hand, it probably would help her look her best for her wedding the next day. That was a good thing, right? Assuming everything *was* in place for the wedding.

"How can we leave the chalet when there's still so much to get done before tomorrow?"

Anne leaned across to touch her arm, her expression one of concern. No one had asked Rose about her conversation with RJ at the bar. Then again, Rose knew it was perfectly clear what had happened, not only from her distraught expression when she'd returned to work, but also because RJ hadn't come back with her.

"Try to relax and enjoy yourself tonight, Rose. Everything will be fine."

"Anne, you'd say that if there were a five-ton weight hurtling toward you." Which was exactly how Rose felt right then.

"We won't let you down, Rose."

"I know you won't," she said softly, even though twenty-four hours ago, it had seemed as though the whole wedding was on the verge of disaster.

Phoebe, Anne and Julie were more than just her employees. More than just friends. They, along with Whitney, had become her family. Even so, it was hard to see how they could have solved her wedding's technical problems in so short a time.

She had to know. "How could you possibly have solved all the problems so quickly?"

"RJ," Phoebe said simply. "He knew a guy who knew a guy who could supply all the roses we needed at short notice."

"He came through on the catering, too," Julie said. "It turns out that he knows someone with a crab boat who goes crabbing as a pretty serious hobby. I didn't have to change the menu too much, which meant I easily had the time to rework the cake to make it gluten-free."

"And I know he found Tyce a rehearsal space," Whitney said, "so that the string quartet will be perfectly in sync with one another by the time they actually play."

Rose looked at Anne. "What about you? Did RJ find you more of that thread you couldn't get?"

"No, where would he have possibly found that?" Anne replied just when Rose was starting to think that RJ could do nothing wrong. "Although," her friend added, "he did point out that if I quickly dyed the same make of thread a different color, I wouldn't have to redo the whole thing. I really should have thought of that myself."

So RJ *had* saved the day there, as well.

He'd done so much, had put so much effort into making her wedding perfect, even though the idea of her marrying Donovan was tearing him up inside. And before that, he'd put everything he had into making The Rose Chalet a success. Whenever things had gone wrong, whenever she was starting to panic, he'd always been there.

How, she wondered helplessly, could he continue to give so much to her when she knew his heart was breaking?

And how could she possibly keep her heart from breaking, too?

Whitney reached out to touch her arm, not saying anything, and Rose was glad she didn't. Because one sweet word would have had her bawling her eyes out in the back of the limo.

They arrived at the spa, just outside the city, situated on a hilltop with beautiful views. Twenty minutes later, while she was in the middle of a massage she couldn't manage to enjoy, her cell phone rang.

"Can't you leave it?" Phoebe suggested.

Rose shook her head. "It's Donovan."

He didn't know about her crying in RJ's arms. He didn't know about what had happened in the bar, and he definitely didn't realize how much RJ had done to pull off the perfect wedding for her.

"Hi, Donovan!" She tried to sound as bright and happy as she could, but failed miserably with the lump in her throat.

"Rose, I just wanted to phone and see how my blushing bride is doing."

Desperately, she tried not to think about RJ kissing her, or declaring his love for her, or taking care of every last detail of her wedding.

"I'm at the spa with the girls" was all she could manage by way of a reply. She couldn't have forced out the lie that she was "fine" if her life had depended on it.

"I wish I could be with you tonight," Donovan said.

In response, Rose couldn't stop herself from saying, "You deserve so much better than me."

Momentarily, her statement seemed to take Donovan aback. Finally, he said, "Rose, you're a wonderful woman. I wouldn't be marrying you otherwise. I know I'm not exactly the most demonstrative of men, but I wanted you to know that I love you."

"I—" Rose didn't know what to say. "That's—"

She knew that she should be saying *I love you, too,* but with the tears that were threatening to overwhelm her, she couldn't get the words out. Her problem was solved by Phoebe taking her phone from her.

"Donovan? This is Rose's bachelorette party, and it's girls only. I'm hanging up now, and then I'm hiding her phone. Bye."

Trust Phoebe to do something like that. Something Rose would never have dared to do, but which she'd desperately needed *someone* to do right then. Because as Phoebe put the phone down, Rose's tears began to fall.

Anne rushed over from her facial, and both Julie and Whitney were quick to join them after waving away the aestheticians.

"Rose?" Anne said. "You need to talk to us. What happened?"

"It's RJ. He told me—" Her voice broke. "He told me he loves me."

"Of course he does," Julie said in a gentle voice. "And it's about time he finally told you."

She wasn't even surprised anymore that everyone knew. Besides, what did it matter if everyone knew how RJ felt about her when she was marrying another man?

"He also told me he'll be leaving the chalet after the wedding."

"I understand why he would need to do that," Phoebe said, "but what I don't understand is why you're still marrying Donovan when RJ told you he loves you."

"Because I accepted Donovan's proposal and we have a house we've built together and…it's all been arranged forever! But now I feel so guilty for thinking about RJ whenever I'm around Donovan, and I feel guilty when I'm with Donovan for not clearing things up with RJ."

"Oh, Rose," Anne said, moving in to wrap her arms around her friend. The others joined in.

"I need to apologize for trying to push you and RJ together," Whitney said. "I was so sure it was what you both wanted."

"Me, too," Phoebe admitted, "but we've just been making things harder for you, haven't we?"

"All I want," Rose told her friends, "is to get through this wedding in one piece."

Anne spoke for the others. "If that's what you want, then we're going to make sure you do. We promise."

CHAPTER EIGHTEEN

ROSE STARED AT herself in the mirror.

Several minutes ago Anne had finished helping her into her wedding dress and Phoebe had put the finishing touches on her makeup. So many months of working toward this moment, and now she and Donovan were about to be married the way they'd planned.

The wedding dress Anne had made for her was perfect, probably the best work Rose had ever seen her do, and Phoebe had done a fantastic job with her hair and makeup.

"If you're ready," Phoebe said in a gentle voice, "everything's all set to go."

Amazingly it had all come together. Julie had stayed up most of the night putting last-minute touches on the cake decoration, and the finished product was astonishingly beautiful. The flowers were in place, covering so much of the interior that it seemed like a rose garden. Tyce's musicians had sounded fantastic during their rehearsal earlier. The guests were waiting in their seats. The officiant was there.

All they needed for the wedding to begin was for the bride to actually walk outside.

Anne put a hand on her arm. "Rose—"

"I just need another minute, okay?"

Phoebe and Anne gave each other a look before Rose's best friend said, "We'll be right outside."

But Rose didn't hear anything her friends said as she stared at the total stranger standing in front of the mirror. Her stomach was roiling, her heart was racing and her fingertips were numb as she pressed them hard into her palms.

A knock sounded on the door, and even though Rose didn't call out for the person to come in, her mother stepped inside. Susie Martin was wearing a deep rose-colored dress that Anne had made for her. She looked beautiful, and was suddenly the only person in the world Rose wanted with her.

Her mother moved beside her in front of the mirror. "Your friends told me that something wasn't right." Their eyes met in the mirror, her mother's warm, Rose's full of deep-seated panic.

"I just need a few more minutes to wrap my head around all of this."

"Oh, honey," her mom said with a smile, "you know you can tell me anything, don't you? Just like when you were a little girl."

Rose remembered coming to the bowling alley after school on days when some boy had made her cry, or when one of the mean girls had made awful comments about her being a poor girl who couldn't afford the right clothes. She'd always tried to hide things like that from her mom, because her mom had been doing the best she could for both of them. But her mother had always known exactly what Rose was going through, without her having to say a word. That was when her floodgates would open up and she would tell her mother everything, until she felt better.

But today Rose didn't know what she could say. She simply didn't know how to explain the way she felt, or what good it would possibly do if she did.

She'd made up her mind, and now there were hundreds of people out there waiting for her. Her friends. Donovan's friends. Their families.

"Don't cry, sweetheart."

Her mother's arms came around her just as Rose whispered, "I feel like all this isn't real. Like *I'm* not real. I look in that mirror, and I see a beautiful bride. But it isn't *me*."

"Do you know what I see when I look in the mirror?" her mom asked. "I see the little girl who used to have to come to the bowling alley after school because I couldn't be at home. I see the girl who managed to make a good life for herself even when I couldn't give her everything I wanted her to have. I see a beautiful woman who has worked hard to get into a position where she can do anything she wants. I'm so proud of you, Rose."

Rose reached up to wipe away the tears before they could streak her makeup. "Then why don't I know what to do right now?"

"I've made some bad decisions in my life, so maybe I'm not the best person to give advice, but I'll say one thing. There have been times when I thought your father was one of those mistakes, but if I hadn't met him, then you would never have been born, and you are the one thing I'll never regret. I love you, and I don't think you ever can go wrong trusting in what you love. And it also occurs to me," her mother continued, "that if there's one person in this room qualified to give advice to a bride on her wedding day, it isn't me. It's you, Rose. If there was another bride standing in your place and she told you that she felt the way you do now, what would you say to her?"

Rose was stunned at the simplicity of her mother's advice. Advice she suddenly had no choice but to heed now that it had been given.

Yes, she was a nervous bride, but not because she was excited at the prospect of spending the rest of her life with Donovan, not out of anticipation of seeing him at the end of the aisle waiting to take her hand in marriage.

No, the truth was that she was almost broken with nerves because she could see the sheer scale of the mistake that she was about to make, and she had let herself be trapped by all the expectations around her. She was about to go through with the wedding because Donovan wasn't a bad guy, and because she didn't want to be a woman who upset people.

And yet, if a bride had come to her and said any of that, she knew exactly what she would have told the woman. *Don't go through with the wedding unless you're sure you're marrying the one you really love.*

Rose knew whom she really loved.

And it wasn't Donovan.

"People are going to be so angry with me."

Her mother squeezed her tighter. "Let them be angry. They can take it up with me if they want to be angry. You think Vanessa McIntyre is going to be any nastier than some of the people we get in the bowling alley on a Friday night? So long as you're happy, I don't care if the whole world is angry."

Rose had underestimated her mother so much. What did it matter if Susie Martin still worked at the bowl-

ing alley, or if she didn't have the same social graces
as Donovan's family?

Her mother would do anything for the people she
loved, and that was what really mattered.

Rose had been trying to deny that she loved RJ. She'd
been trying to tell herself that Donovan was the one she
wanted, but as much as she liked him, she didn't love
him. Not the way she loved RJ. Liking someone wasn't
a good-enough reason to marry them, even with two
hundred and fifty people waiting for her to make her
way down the aisle.

Rose turned fully into her mother's arms. "I love
you, Mom."

"I love you, too, honey." Her mother pulled back to
grin at her. "Everything's going to be all right."

People had been saying that to her all week. Finally,
Rose believed it might be true.

Rose went to the door and found Anne just outside.

"I need you to bring Donovan in here."

"But it's not good luck for the groom to see the bride
before the wedding."

"That's okay," Rose said. She took a deep breath and
explained, "There isn't going to be a wedding."

Anne's eyes widened. "Seriously?"

Rose nodded. "Seriously."

Anne reached out a hand for one of Rose's. "Oh.
That's…that's *incredible*."

"I'm sorry you went to such trouble with the dress."

"Forget the dress," Anne said. "I'll go get Donovan."

Less than sixty seconds later, her mother was gone
and Donovan was walking through the door to her dress-
ing room.

"Rose, what's going on?"

God, she hated hurting him. He didn't deserve it. But she knew it would only be worse if she drew things out any longer.

"I'm sorry. I know this is the worst possible timing, and you're a wonderful man, but the wedding's off."

"Off?" Donovan repeated the word as if he didn't know what it meant.

"I'm sorry," Rose repeated, "but I just can't go through with it."

"Oh, is that all this is," Donovan said, sounding relieved. "Rose, you're suffering from wedding-day jitters. I'm sure every bride goes through them, but once you start walking down the aisle, you'll be fine."

"Donovan," Rose said, stepping back from him as he tried to move forward to comfort her, "trust me, I know far more about wedding-day jitters than you do, and this has nothing to do with them. I just can't marry you."

"And you've just decided that now?" Donovan didn't raise his voice. He never raised his voice. It was just one of the things about him Rose wouldn't miss. "On the day of our wedding, with everyone we know out there to see me humiliated? And after we've finished building a home together?"

"I know the timing is horrible and I'm sorry. I really am. But the truth is, I care about you, and I like you very much, but I don't love you. Not the way I should to be able to marry you."

"Doesn't the fact that I love you count for anything?" Donovan shot back.

Guilt nearly took Rose over completely. "I'm sorry, Donovan. I don't want to hurt you, but you deserve to have someone who loves you with all her heart."

And she already knew whom she loved with *all* of her heart.

She had to find him. Right away. Before he thought she'd gone and married another man.

Rose hitched up her dress, and started to run.

CHAPTER NINETEEN

ORGANIZING A LITTLE LEAGUE practice at such short notice hadn't been easy, but it had been worth the effort, and not just because the kids were obviously enjoying themselves. With them to keep an eye on, he was committed to staying here, even when he was desperate to know what Rose looked like on her wedding day. RJ could almost see her now, in her dress, looking so beautiful and perfect in the middle of all those roses....

"Coach RJ? Are you going to throw the ball?"

Finally realizing that a baseball had landed at his feet, he picked it up and threw it back. Unfortunately, even working with his baseball team wasn't keeping away thoughts of Rose. The best it could do was force him to stay here, away from her wedding, so that he wouldn't be able to torture himself watching her marry another man. Just the thought of that made everything tighten painfully inside him.

He couldn't do it. He couldn't stay away. He had to at least see her.

"Sorry, guys," he said. "It looks like I'm going to have to cut out of practice a little early today."

"But, Coach—"

RJ was already moving. Thankfully, a couple of the kids' parents who were sitting in the stands were happy to take over for him.

He knew he couldn't go on giving up everything for her. Except, even as he thought that, RJ knew he'd go on giving up everything for Rose whenever she needed him. He couldn't do anything else.

She was the love of his life, and she would *stay* the love of his life, even if he could never be the love of hers.

He headed for his truck and was almost there when he saw the figure running across the baseball field.

Rose was wearing her wedding dress. It was rumpled and dirty, and her hair had come loose from the elaborate style it had obviously been in. When she saw him, her entire face lit up with the biggest smile he'd ever seen. She kicked off her heels and ran even faster across the grass toward him.

What is she doing here?

Maybe, he thought wildly, the wedding setup had collapsed, or Vanessa McIntyre had choked on a crab cake, or the musicians had only been able to play death-metal interpretations of the wedding march. He didn't need to look down at his watch to know that Rose should be saying *I do* right about now. He'd been dreading that moment ever since she had announced her engagement.

But if she was here, then that meant she wasn't at her wedding with Donovan, which had to mean—

"I love you," Rose gasped out. She was almost completely out of breath from sprinting across the grass. "I love you. I've always loved you. And I—" She panted. "Oh, God, it's so much harder to run in a wedding dress than it looks…."

Kissing her probably wasn't the easiest way to let her get her breath back, but RJ couldn't help himself.

This moment was so perfect—so perfectly *Rose*. Just

slightly out of step with everyone else's idea of perfection, and all the more beautiful because of it.

And when he took her into his arms and he kissed her, she kissed him back so passionately that they ended up stumbling against his truck together.

Eventually, they drew back, just looking at one another. For the moment, nothing else was needed. They loved one another, and that was enough.

Even so, there was one thing RJ had to say. "I can't believe you ran all the way here in your wedding dress and heels."

"It was worth all the crazy looks people gave me. I don't care what other people think. I only care what *you* think."

"I think you're the most beautiful woman in the world, Rose. I love you so much."

"I've always loved you, too. I just… I thought I needed to pretend to be someone else. But you always saw exactly who I was."

"You're the most amazing woman I've ever known. You make people's lives better just by being near them. You make *my* life better, and I'm hoping you're planning to keep making my life even better."

"I'm definitely planning on that," Rose said with a smile that held every ounce of love she felt for him. "My mom was the one who helped show me what I knew was in my heart all along."

"I've always thought your mother was great," RJ said. "I'm looking forward to convincing her that I'm good enough for her daughter. Because if I were her, I'd be crazy protective of you."

"Can you bowl?" Rose asked.

"I'm never going to go pro, but I'm not bad."

"Then I'd say you're probably going to do just fine with my mom."

They held each other for a long while, not talking, not even kissing. Just simply being there with—and for— one another. Nothing had ever felt so right as holding Rose in his arms, and RJ knew deep in his heart that it was where she'd be for the rest of their lives.

CHAPTER TWENTY

FROM THE CHALET'S bridal suite, Rose could hear Tyce playing a simple, beautiful tune on that beat-up old guitar of his. It was hard to believe six months had rushed by so quickly. Dealing with selling the house she and Donovan had been building and unraveling all the other details of her almost-wedding and honeymoon hadn't been easy, but things were all finally resolved, with RJ helping her every step of the way.

"Are you ready?" Anne asked her.

Rose didn't even have to think about it. "Yes, I've never been so ready. And, Anne? If I forget to say it later, thank you for repairing my wedding dress so beautifully."

"It was my pleasure. Just don't go running down the street in it again, okay?" She grinned. "At least not until after you say *I do*."

Rose waited for her maid of honor to open the door and then she stepped out, heading through the elaborate set that RJ and his brother had spent so much time putting back together.

The roses were amazing. They were in full bloom thanks to careful preparations on Phoebe's part, creating a riot of color that was simply breathtaking. Rose had tried suggesting to RJ that he might want to use a different setup for their wedding, but he'd shaken his head.

"I dreamed it up for you," he'd said, "though I might make one change…."

Rose found out what that was as she walked outside and saw rose petals spilling down around her as family and friends stepped out, one by one, to exchange roses. Phoebe, Julie, Whitney and her mother were all there, along with the whole extended Knight clan, all of whom had been quick to embrace her from the moment they met her. Marge Banning and her husband were beaming at Rose as she made her way down the aisle.

Finally, she made it to where RJ was waiting for her along with the officiant and RJ's brother, Patrick.

God, how she loved him. And how lucky she was that he'd fought for her…and that she'd finally listened to her heart.

"We're gathered here," the officiant began, "for the marriage of Rose Martin and RJ Knight…"

Rose knew the words by heart, having heard them hundreds of times at other weddings. Yet this time was special.

Because it was *her* wedding.

All those months ago she'd pulled out of her own wedding knowing no bride should ever feel as awful as she had. Whereas today she hoped every last one of her future brides felt exactly the way she did as she placed her hand in RJ's, and gave her entire heart over to him. They had the perfect magical combination of happiness, fulfillment and contentment that only came from true love.

And then RJ said, "I do," and the officiant asked her if she would take him to be her husband.

They had chosen the simplest vows for their ceremony, without the complicated speeches other brides and grooms often wrote. And when Rose looked over at RJ, she knew they'd already said the most important thing they could to each other.

I love you. Forever.

Rose looked into RJ's eyes and said, "I do."

She kissed him, feeling as if it was for the first time. She melted in his arms and he pulled her closer and silently professed his love to her one more time.

No question about it, she was the luckiest woman in the entire world.

The ceremony was followed by the first dance and then cutting the cake, and the evening was a glorious blur of close friends and family wishing them every happiness. Finally, Patrick came by and told them, "Sorry to interrupt, but the limousine is outside ready to take you off on your honeymoon whenever you're ready."

They were going to head up to Canada to a little cabin out in the woods with nothing around for miles but each other.

"Thanks, Patrick," she said, just as Phoebe approached.

"Sorry, Rose," Phoebe said, "but you know how you said to keep your cousin Lyle away from the champagne?"

Rose's response was cut off by the sound of the cello in Tyce's string quartet breaking a string and going completely out of tune on a particularly loud note.

And then, a beat later, as if it had been choreographed into a three-part disaster sequence, one of their younger guests skidded face-first into what was left of the wedding cake.

So much for a perfect wedding day, thought Rose.

And yet as long as RJ was there beside her, holding

her in his arms and loving her with every breath, none of it made a difference.

She shot RJ a grin. "You ready?"

"You bet."

"We love you guys…and we'll see you in two weeks," Rose called out to her friends, just as RJ took her hand to run with him for the waiting limo.

The others would handle things for now. She was absolutely certain that there would be plenty of wedding-related disasters at The Rose Chalet for her and RJ to sort out when she got back from her honeymoon.

And, honestly, she wouldn't want it any other way.

* * * * *

SPARKS FLY, the final book in Lucy Kevin's
KISS THE BRIDE *anthology, is just over the page.*
Enjoy!

SPARKS FLY

CHAPTER ONE

"Wow," ANGELINA MORGAN said aloud as she got out of her car in front of the enormous mansion. "That is one seriously huge house." She'd seen pictures of places like this in magazines, but had never actually been inside one.

She'd set aside two hours for this feng shui consultation.

She'd need two weeks.

Feeling much as she imagined Maria must have felt in *The Sound of Music* when she saw the captain's house for the first time—*I need to have confidence,* she thought—Angelina took a deep breath and headed up the long front path.

She rang the doorbell and waited. No answer. She rang it again.

Finally, she heard footsteps approaching and the door opened. Angelina was about to introduce herself…but the words died on her lips.

The man standing before her was, in a word, *perfect.* Dirty-blond hair contrasted with blue eyes. Tanned skin highlighted bold cheekbones, a strong nose and gorgeous lips.

"Are you Angelina Morgan?"

Stunned by her unprofessional thoughts about her client, she barely managed a yes. She hadn't had a sexual thought about a man in months and was alarmed that her dead libido should perk up at such an inappropriate time.

She was even more alarmed when her client said, "Will Scott," then shook her hand, causing a frisson of heat to surge through her.

Quickly pulling her hand back, she fumbled for one of her business cards and said, "I'm so sorry about being a few minutes late. I've rarely been to this neighborhood and I'm afraid I got a little lost. In any case, given that your house is larger than I anticipated, I want you to know that I'm happy to stay and work with you for as long as it takes."

"Actually, I've got some pressing work to take care of, so the quicker we can get this done, the better."

Angelina knew she should be accommodating. Not only was she late, but judging by the size of his mansion, he was probably counting every minute in her company as millions of dollars lost.

Intending to start again with a clean slate, she conjured up her most genuine smile. "First of all, Mr. Scott—"

"Call me Will."

Angelina gave a slight nod of her head in acquiescence. "Okay, Will, I'd like to find out how much you know about feng shui, particularly since this consultation was given to you as a gift from a friend."

"Not a friend, exactly." He paused slightly. "Susan is my ex-wife."

Angelina barely stopped herself from exclaiming, *Oh, really!* Clearing her throat, she said, "As I was saying, due to the fact that this feng shui consultation was given to you as a gift from your, uh, ex-wife…" She stopped to clear her throat again. "It's important for me to know how much I'll need to explain."

"Frankly, the only thing I'm worried about is the neighbors finding out I'm dabbling in magic and witchcraft." Stepping past her, he looked out at the street. "You don't have any signs on your car, do you?"

Silently reminding herself that she had always been able to convert staunch disbelievers into the ancient art's greatest proponents, she said, "Why don't we discuss the ideas behind feng shui for a few minutes before we jump into the consultation? That way you will understand why it has absolutely nothing to do with magic or witches."

"Just as long as we're done before my meeting."

Angelina felt a tension headache coming on. "Did Susan make it clear that we need at least two hours for the consultation?"

"Two hours? I don't have two hours." Will's cell phone rang and he lifted it up to look at the screen. "I need to take this call."

As he moved away from the door, a sudden breeze slammed it shut in her face, leaving Angelina standing alone on his front step.

Utterly shocked by how things were going, for the first time in her life Angelina actually wished she did know some witchcraft.

If this man thought she was going to wait around for him to get his act together, he was sorely mistaken. His ex-wife, Susan, must have been a very calm, forgiving person to have been married to him at all. Susan could have her money back. First thing Angelina was going to take care of when she got back to her office was getting rid of Mr. Scott as a client, once and for all.

And good riddance.

CHAPTER TWO

STILL MORE THAN a little irritated by the time she returned home, Angelina slammed her car door. She marched up to the front door of the cute house she was renting, and jammed the key into the lock.

Letting herself inside, she leaned against the back of the door and surveyed the clutter in her living room. She spent so much time helping other people deal with their messes that she rarely had time to deal with hers anymore.

"I really need to clean my house up soon," she muttered as she took in the stacks of magazines, books and papers.

Walking into her office, she sat down in front of her computer to check her emails. She found a message that had just come in from Rose at The Rose Chalet. Angelina had always wanted to work with Rose and she quickly scanned the message. Rose had just offered her the option of using the chalet as a location for Angelina's upcoming cover story in *Professional Woman* magazine.

The irony of her situation was not lost on Angelina. Her job was helping others find balance in all areas of their lives, but since her business had taken off, her personal life had been knocked completely out of balance by her professional success. Case in point: she couldn't remember the last time she'd been out on a date and actually enjoyed herself.

It figured, somehow, that the first man she'd been attracted to in years was not only an off-limits client, but arrogant and disrespectful, as well.

No. She wouldn't dwell on her lackluster personal life. She had more important business to take care of—like getting ready for the feature in *Professional Woman* magazine.

Flipping through her client book, she found Susan's number. She picked up the phone with firm purpose and dialed.

"Susan. It's Angelina Morgan."

Susan sounded thrilled to hear from her. "How was your consultation with Will?"

Best just to be honest, Angelina thought. "I'm going to have to refund your money. I'm afraid he is not at all interested in having a feng shui consultation."

"How can you say that?" Susan's tone was accusing.

"He left me standing on his front porch to go take a phone call…and he didn't come back." *Not to mention the fact that he was insufferably rude.*

"Oh, I see" was Susan's quiet response.

"I would rather not work with people who need to be really sold on the idea of feng shui. It just doesn't do either the client or myself a whole lot of good. So, really, I'm partially to blame. I didn't realize Mr. Scott was so resistant to the idea. I should never have accepted your money in the first place. I will arrange a full refund right away."

"But you've got to help him. Somebody has got to help him."

Angelina sighed. Why couldn't these things be easier? "Susan, I don't think—"

"Let me explain about Will. He's my ex-husband, and now you probably understand some of the reasons why I divorced him. But he didn't used to be that way. I mean, he always enjoyed working, but when I first met him he was fun, too. Unfortunately, as his company grew bigger, he hardly ever came home, and when he was around he was glued to the phone or the computer."

Suddenly, Angelina felt like a marriage counselor. But Susan was on a roll, and Angelina didn't have the heart to cut her off.

"The last year of our marriage was awful. I hardly saw him and I felt like I didn't even know who he was anymore." Susan paused and added in dark tones, "And he sure as hell had no idea who I was. So I filed for divorce and moved out. Then I read an article in the *Chronicle* about how you have a knack for fixing people's love lives."

A warning bell went off in Angelina's head. "Susan, that article was a bunch of hyperbole. I don't actually fix my clients' love lives."

"Angelina, don't be so modest! The woman in the interview said she met with you and followed your advice, and then she met a wonderful man and now they're engaged."

Angelina wanted to interrupt Susan to inject some reason into the conversation, but Susan was too excited for her to get a word in edgewise.

"She said how one of her friends was going to get a divorce, but after you worked with her, she and her husband worked through their problems and stayed together. Don't you remember the story? They called you the Feng Shui Cupid."

Angelina tried not to groan out loud. That article had been dogging her for weeks now. It seemed the entire lovelorn population of the Bay Area read the *San Francisco Chronicle,* because she'd received dozens of calls from people asking if they could meet with the Feng Shui Cupid.

She hated that moniker. Her clients also got better jobs and felt healthier after working with her, but no one was calling her a Feng Shui Recruiter or a Feng Shui Doctor.

"Susan, I agree with you. Maybe Will could use some help, but I…" *Actually, Will could use a lot of help.*

Susan heard her weakness and jumped in for the kill. "Please help him, Angelina. You're my last hope for reconciliation."

Angelina was caught between self-preservation and guilt. She had to hand it to Susan—there was nothing quite like having a stranger make you completely responsible for the fate of their love life.

Against her better judgment, Angelina said, "I can't make the changes for him. It all depends on what he wants."

"So you'll try again?"

Angelina was dismayed by how easily she had been roped into taking Will on as a client. Again. "I'll give it one more shot. But don't expect a miracle."

WILL SAT IN his home office, staring intently at the computer screen, typing furiously.

He couldn't believe the new CFO had countered another one of his ideas. Will sent one final email and then leaned back in his chair to take a thirty-second break. He was going to get on the phone with the guy and chew him out for blatantly undermining his authority.

He ran his hands through his hair and shook his head. Lately, running Personal Technology Inc. was one headache after another. Whether it was the shareholders, the board members, the employees or the customers, the troubles seemed endless. Who knew, he found himself thinking, maybe this whole feng shui thing could really help. He had heard that Donald Trump used it, and look how well he was doing.

Oh, no! He had left the consultant standing on his front doorstep.

Will rushed down the hallway to the front door, but she was long gone.

When his ex-wife, Susan, had told him what she was giving him for his thirty-third birthday, his first question had been "Fung what?" And then he'd told her he had no intention of meeting a consultant of any kind at 2:00 p.m. today.

Unfortunately, Susan could talk anyone, including him, into a corner.

Against his better judgment, and not wanting to hurt her feelings, he had agreed to set aside two precious hours of his workday to spend it learning about some kind of mystical hocus-pocus. But that had been before the new executive staff at his company, PTI, had ambushed him with their radical plans, none of which, as CEO, he agreed with. After putting in several eighteen-hour workdays to keep things from blowing up in his face, he was utterly exhausted and in no mood for anything that wasn't marked *Urgent!*

Still, even though he thought Angelina's profession was ridiculous—he'd take science over fantasy any day—he owed her an apology. Not to mention the fact that Susan would probably send over one feng shui consultant after another until he let one of them in to look through his house.

He grabbed his cell phone and punched in the number listed on her business card. He was surprisingly glad to hear the consultant pick up and say, "Angelina Morgan speaking."

"Angelina. It's Will Scott."

Even across the phone lines he felt how much effort it cost her to sound polite and professional. She offered a cool "Hello." Susan always said he could charm the knickers off a nun. He had a feeling he was going to have to call on all his powers of persuasion to get back into Angelina's good graces.

"I want to say how sorry I am about abandoning you this afternoon."

Again, he heard the awful sound of silence across the line. Angelina was definitely angry with him.

"I don't know what to say other than my work has been very busy and it's got me doing crazy things like leaving a beautiful woman standing all alone on my doorstep."

Too late, Will realized he had just admitted he thought she was beautiful. Even now he could remember the way the sunlight had played off her dark brown hair, the way it had lit up her pretty hazel eyes. And the fact that her mouth had looked so soft.

So kissable.

In a very brisk and professional voice she finally said, "Thank you for the apology. I appreciate it."

Will released the breath he hadn't known he was holding.

"Actually, I'm glad you called," she said.

"You are?"

"I just got off the phone with Susan. I have a policy of not working with people who aren't interested in my services. I tried to arrange a refund for the consultation."

As disappointment moved through him, he realized he'd been lying to himself about his reasons for calling Angelina. Yes, Susan was like a dog with a bone and it would be faster and simpler to acquiesce to her plans. Yes, he owed Angelina an apology for leaving her standing on his front step while he took a phone call.

But the truth was he wanted to see her again.

"I'm sorry that I gave you that impression, Angelina."

He thought he heard her sigh before saying, "Susan was adamant, however, about rescheduling our consultation."

"She was?"

He sounded like a complete moron. The man who could convince investors to give him millions armed with nothing but a speech and PowerPoint presentation now appeared to have a vocabulary of about twelve words. *Way to make up for a really bad first impression, pal.*

"I agreed to try again. One more time." Angelina deliberately enunciated each word. "And this time, you'll need to guarantee me two uninterrupted hours of your time."

Will's phone beeped in his ear. It was his CFO. "Angelina, I need to get this call. Could I call you back?"

"No."

Will had almost switched over to the incoming call when he realized what she'd said. "No?"

"No," she repeated. "And I need your agreement to not answer the phone at any point during our next consultation."

The call from the CFO went through to voice mail.

It had been a long time since anyone had challenged Will in such a direct manner. But instead of being irritated, he felt a grudging respect for how she'd stood her ground. "Could you come back tomorrow afternoon?"

"I'm booked solid until next Thursday morning."

"Great," he replied without checking his schedule. He'd simply rearrange that day to accommodate her. He did own the company, after all. Time to use some of the perks that came with the title.

ANGELINA HUNG UP the phone and stretched out her neck, rubbing it with her hands. Will Scott was giving her a serious headache.

Unfortunately, he gave her something else, too. Something hot and steamy in a region of her body not used to much action.

Immediately her phone rang again. "Daddy!" Angelina's face lit up. "I'm so glad you called!"

"I have some big news for you."

"You're not sick, are you?"

"No." Her father laughed off her concern. "I met someone. Her name is Louise."

Angelina relaxed back into her chair. "Oh, Daddy, that's wonderful!"

"And we got engaged this morning."

She almost dropped the phone. "You what?" But as shocked as she was, she wanted to sound supportive. "I'm so happy for you."

"No one will ever replace your mother...." His voice trailed off.

Wanting to voice what was in her heart, Angelina said, "Mom has been gone for twenty-five years. You deserve love and happiness. You always have." Striving for an excited tone, she said, "Tell me how it all happened."

"Do you remember the last time you came home for a visit, and I asked you for some advice? I did everything you said. I put two pink roses in the vase in the living room, I put up paintings of happy couples and I got rid of everything from underneath my bed. The next day I met Louise at the local garden show."

"Dad, that's great. I'm so happy for you."

"Yep, we're pretty excited and we don't want a long engagement. I'm hoping you might be able to help us with wedding plans. Don't you know someone who does wedding stuff?"

"I'd love to help you and Louise. I'll call Rose over at The Rose Chalet and we can set up a meeting."

As her father continued to talk about his new love and their engagement, for the first time, Angelina really did feel like the Feng Shui Cupid.

A cupid with an arrow for everyone but herself.

After hanging up the phone, Angelina couldn't stop herself from thinking about the fact that she not only hadn't been on a date in over a year, but she sure as heck had never found anything even close to the true love her father had been describing.

"Have I been spending too much time working on my clients' love lives and not enough on my own?" she asked herself.

Blinking hard, she tried to think about whether she'd been hiding behind her hectic business.

But painful memories came at her instead.

His name was Bryce, and they'd met the summer she'd turned twenty-one when she was helping out with her father's housecleaning business in her hometown of Coeur d'Alene, Idaho. She'd been sure she'd met "the one" and freely gave him her heart and body. But in the end, she was just a plaything for a beautiful rich boy. He thought sex with the cleaning staff was a perk that went hand in hand with having an inflated bank account.

She'd learned a powerful lesson that summer. Rich people were fine to work with as clients, but she would never again make the mistake of trusting one with her heart.

She rubbed her temples with her index fingers as she thought about the handful of men she'd dated in the past five years. They all worked hard and were attractive, but they had bored her senseless.

And now she was fighting her attraction to a totally unsuitable man, a man who would no doubt stomp her heart to pieces were she foolish enough to give it to him.

CHAPTER THREE

THE FOLLOWING THURSDAY, Angelina was halfway up the path to Will's front door when he came around the side yard and called out her name. He saw surprise flash across her pretty face a split second before she tripped on the edge of a brick that was sticking up a half inch too high.

Will was able to catch her before she hit the ground, glad of the excuse to find out what it felt like to hold her.

It felt good.

Really good.

Angelina pulled away to stand on her own two feet. "Thanks for catching me. I'm not usually this clumsy."

Will had to fight the urge to pull her close to him again. Frankly, he was still more than a little perplexed by his attraction to a woman who was the polar opposite of his usual Barbie dolls.

Angelina asked, "Are you ready to get started?" snapping Will out of his fog.

"Sure."

They went inside and she said, "Why don't you take me through your house and tell me what you like and what you don't like about each room. Let's start with your foyer. How do you feel about it?"

The first totally inappropriate thought that popped

into his head was *I love it when you're in it,* but he settled for "It's okay, I guess."

Scanning the room, Angelina moved to stand in front of a painting. "Does this make you happy?"

The truth was, Will couldn't have cared less if the painting made him happy. But when he really looked at it, he saw for the first time that the artist had used acrylic on canvas to depict a sad man who stood in the middle of a wet, deserted street.

The painting sucked. "I don't like it."

"Why don't you like it?"

"It's depressing, and besides, even I could do a better job than—" Realizing he was saying too much, Will cut himself off.

Angelina pinned him with a questioning look.

Inwardly cursing himself for divulging any information at all about his personal life, Will said, "Seems like anyone could do a better job than this artist did."

"Feng shui is all about living with what you love. When we get rid of the things that bring us down and replace them with things that make us happy, we open ourselves up for good things to happen in our lives." Grinning, she added, "Don't be surprised if taking this painting down gets you the woman of your dreams."

"If that's the case," Will said as he reached for the painting, "let's get this pathetic loser off my walls ASAP."

Angelina could barely keep from laughing as she helped Will lift the heavy frame. Men were so predictable.

Will surveyed the new look of his foyer. "It looks better already."

Angelina was pleased that she could finally grace

him with a genuine smile, and right then and there she decided she was going to maintain a nice, agreeable banter with him throughout the rest of the consultation. No matter what.

Getting back to business, Angelina did a quick scan of the kitchen/family room. "You've got an awful lot of the fire element in here."

"The fire element?"

"There are five elements in feng shui. Fire, water, metal, earth and wood. The fire element is in your red rug, your fireplace and your electronics."

"And that's bad?"

"Well, not bad, exactly. Just not balanced."

"Maybe I should just take all of this to the dump and start over."

Angelina was surprised by her own chuckle. She'd barely replied with "Not unless you hate everything in here" when she made the mistake of looking into his incredible blue eyes.

Her mouth went completely dry. Again.

Oh, God, what was she doing? She knew better than to look at a wealthy, good-looking man like Will Scott with stars in her eyes. She was a twenty-six-year-old woman who had never gotten over her broken heart or her deep sense of shame from being so easily used.

And Will definitely had heartbreak written all over him.

WILL WAS ENJOYING watching the play of emotions run across Angelina's expressive face, when she abruptly turned away from him and began to study his living room with renewed zeal.

She pointed to a watercolor hanging in a dimly lit

corner. "Will, this is an incredible oceanscape. It would be the perfect water element to hang over your fireplace."

Will was tempted to tell her he had painted it in college. What would it be like, he wondered, to have Angelina's eyes light up with admiration? But he squashed the thought as quickly as it had come. He was CEO of a Fortune 500 company, and if anyone found out he had been serious about his hobby at one time, he'd become a laughingstock.

She reached into her briefcase and pulled out a sheet of paper. "This should help with explaining some of the hows and whys of what I do. It's called a *feng shui map.*"

Will scanned the page. "For some reason these charts remind me of computer programming." It also reminded him of what it was like to balance out all of the colors on a canvas.

Disturbed that he was thinking about painting again for the first time in years, he pushed his fruitless thoughts back into the recesses of his mind, where they belonged.

"Are you a programmer?"

Will was stunned. "You don't know what I do for a living?"

"We didn't exactly have time for you to tell me the first time we met, did we?"

More than a little surprised that she didn't know who he was, he said, "Again, I apologize for that."

Giving him a small smile that made his heart beat a little faster, she said, "So, you don't program computers?"

Feeling relieved, thinking that maybe for once he

wouldn't have to be on guard against another woman who only wanted to be with him for the notoriety of dating one of America's richest, most eligible bachelors, he leaned back against the kitchen counter, perfectly happy to let her think he was just an average rich guy.

"When I was first out of college, I used to program. But I haven't done any serious coding in years." He looked pensive and admitted, "Lately I've been missing the old days."

"Why?"

"I used to solve puzzles and create things. Now I spend all day dealing with problems."

His inner voice taunted him. *Hey, buddy, it's pretty hard to be wealthy enough to buy a small island, isn't it? Boo-hoo for you.*

He didn't know why he was telling Angelina any of this. Usually, he was either focused on expansion and profits, or occasionally hanging out with his business-school buddies, talking sports. Even with his ex-wife he had maintained an emotional distance.

Giving Angelina a sheepish look, he said, "I don't mean to be standing here complaining. Not when I have—" he gestured to his home "—all this."

"Feng shui is about finding a place where your heart can be happy and at peace. You can do that in a big home like this one or in a small apartment." Looking charmingly self-conscious, she added, "I have a tendency to get on a soapbox from time to time."

"No worries. I don't see any suds on the floor."

Angelina gave Will a crooked half smile that knocked his socks off. "How about you show me your home office next?"

As Angelina followed Will out of the living room, she tried to reconcile his admission about missing computer programming with her initial picture of him as a spoiled rich boy.

Get a grip, Angelina, she repeated over and over in her head, training her eyes on the oak flooring instead of the walking, talking temptation before her.

Caught up in controlling her raging hormones, Angelina plowed into him, hugging him like a spoon, her front to his back, her arms wrapped around his rippling six-pack as she tried to steady herself. And then he turned around in her arms and his mouth was mere inches from hers.

She was about to meet him halfway when her inner voice cried, *Stop throwing yourself at your client!*

Just go away, she told it, but then her critical inner voice turned things up another notch.

Don't forget, his ex-wife wants him back!

It was a supreme effort to pull away. Trying to put some distance between them, Angelina stumbled into the stair rail in the foyer.

No longer seared by the heat of Will's body, she quickly cooled down.

Will looked just as stunned as she felt.

On one level, she wished she could leap back into his arms, but she knew that was professionally impossible, not to mention inappropriate.

There was only one way for both of them to proceed: they both needed to behave as if the almost-kiss had never happened.

"My office is right around the corner," Will said in a slightly husky voice before disappearing into a room down the hall.

His telephone had been ringing constantly since her arrival but, true to his word, he had ignored it. Until now.

When she walked into his office she was so shocked by the utter chaos of the room that she temporarily forgot about her no-phone-calls rule.

It was one of the messiest rooms she had ever seen.

She quickly figured out that, according to feng shui, Will's just-been-hit-by-a-cyclone office sat smack-dab in the *reputation* area of his house. Odds were he was having trouble getting respect from customers and staff alike. The snippets of conversation that she overheard as she carefully picked her way through the piles of papers and boxes confirmed her suspicions.

Will spoke authoritatively into the phone. "I'm only going to say this one more time. We are going forward with our plans. I don't care what Albert is telling the board about competitive repercussions." Hanging up, he turned to face Angelina. "Welcome to my home office," he said grimly.

In her line of business, there were times to be gentle and times for tough love.

This was tough love all the way.

She gestured to the papers and boxes scattered throughout the large room. "It must be hard to work well surrounded by so much clutter."

He slumped into a leather chair. "Even my executive assistant refused to help clean it up."

"I don't blame her," Angelina said, surprised to see the powerful executive suddenly look so lost and forlorn. "Let's talk about clutter."

Will grimaced. "Haven't we already gone over that? My office is a dump."

Angelina leaned in closer, as if she was about to divulge an important secret. Will found that he was leaning toward her in anticipation.

"In feng shui there is no place to hide. You can't clear one area of your life by stuffing everything into another area."

"You're losing me."

"Pretend you took all of this stuff and moved it into your garage."

"Why didn't I think of that?"

Angelina gave Will a mock frown. "All that does is move the congestion to your garage. It blocks the flow of your energy in your life no matter where it is."

"But I need everything in here."

Angelina nodded. "Maybe. But then, maybe not. Tell me, when was the last time you went through every single book and paper and file and asked yourself, 'Do I really need this?'"

"You can't be serious."

Angelina stared at him, unblinking. "I am. When was the last time?"

"Never. Who has the time for that?"

"Actually, it can be kind of fun."

Will laughed out loud at that.

Angelina protested, "I'm serious!" but a smile was stealing across her face. "Well, maybe *fun* is overstating it, but there can be amazing benefits to putting the work in."

"Name one."

"Easy. Once you get rid of everything you don't need or love, you will have finally made room for all of the good things you do want."

He looked around the room contemplatively. Now

that she had pointed it out, he couldn't escape the heavy sense of chaos that pervaded his office. "Hmm. What you're saying is actually making sense."

Angelina grinned. "I'm so glad to hear you say that." She tried to move one of his boxes with her foot, but it was so heavy it hardly budged. "What have you got in here? Your rock collection?"

"Open it up."

Cautiously, Angelina peeled back the top of the box and grabbed a heavy rectangular slab of green metal, chock-full of silver wires. "What's this?"

"It's a test interface board. I used to design them." He walked over and picked one up. "I haven't seen one up close in a long time." Years fell away as Will reverently ran his fingers over the board.

At twenty-one he had dutifully plunged into engineering, giving up his far-fetched dream of being a painter. Designing circuitry was never as powerful a satisfaction as creating art, but at least he made good money.

"I can't believe you even know what one of these things does, let alone designed it. I do have one question for you, though."

"Ask away." Will hoped that he could impress her again.

"Do you really need so many of them?" Angelina peered into the box. "There are probably twenty in here."

So much for impressing her with his profound knowledge of circuitry.

"In any case, before I go," she said, looking at her watch and realizing that their two-hour appointment had flown by, "I should tell you that your cluttered office sits smack-dab in your reputation area. It's probably affecting your relationships with your staff and customers."

"How the heck do you know about the problems I've been having with my company? Did Susan tell you?"

Angelina looked surprised by his outburst. "No, we didn't speak about your work at all."

"Are you psychic or something?"

"Trust me, I'm not the least bit psychic." He could see her scanning the room for a semiclear pathway so she could escape. "So, how about you tackle your office and give me a call in about a month, and I'll come back to see how things are going?"

"A month?" He couldn't go a whole month without seeing her. "I don't think a month will work."

"I could give you two if that would be easier to fit into your schedule." Angelina pulled her organizer out of her briefcase to make note of the appointment.

"What I'm trying to say is that I'd like to take you out. On a date."

"A date?" She looked horrified.

"Yes, Angelina. A date."

"No, thank you."

The words were barely out of her mouth before she fled the room, ran down the hall and out his front door, and drove away.

CHAPTER FOUR

"So we almost kissed in his foyer. Big deal."

Angelina's friend Krista plopped her full coffee cup back into the saucer. "Big deal? You show up at this guy's house to do a consultation and he almost starts making out with you. That is definitely a big deal." Krista raised an eyebrow and gave Angelina a knowing look. "You wish he had, though, don't you?"

Angelina shook her head, saying *no* even as *yes* galloped across her brain.

"Liar."

Angelina sipped her mint tea, affectionately watching Krista over the rim of her cup. They had been best friends for ten years, two totally different women who complemented each other perfectly.

"Besides, it doesn't matter, because I'm not going out with him."

Krista clanked her cup down again. "Go out with him? Are you saying he asked you out? I swear, you always leave the good stuff out of your stories." She frowned. "So, why aren't you going out with him? He's cute, right?"

Cute didn't even begin to cover it, Angelina thought as she said, "Yes, but he's my client. I don't date clients."

Krista waved her hand in the air as if that reason

were completely irrelevant. "What exactly did you say when he asked you out?"

Angelina grimaced at the memory. "I said 'no, thank you.'"

And then she'd run.

Krista rolled her eyes. "I can't believe it. A hot guy, who I'm assuming probably has a good job and a nice house, asks you out and you act like he just offered you a refill."

Angelina defended herself. "It seemed like the right thing to do at the time." Plus, she'd been freaking out. Big-time.

"I'm not gonna let you off the hook this time. You need someone to tell it to you like it is, whether you want to hear it or not. First rule of romance—when a gorgeous, eligible guy asks you out, the answer is 'yes,' not 'no, thank you.'"

Angelina opened her mouth to protest.

"No buts," Krista said firmly. Still, she softened her tone as she reached out to take Angelina's hand. "I'm just telling you this because you're my best friend in the whole world and I want you to be happy."

"I know that. It's just…" She wished she could read her fortune in the tea leaves in the bottom of her cup. "I know change is good, but remember what a fool I made of myself when I was twenty-one?"

"Of course I remember. I was mopping up your tears for months. But it's been years since that jerk used you. If you ask me, you've completely forgotten how to have fun, Ang."

"I'm too busy to have fun."

"Exactly my point, honey. Look at me. I work sixty

hours a week on billion-dollar cases, but I know how to have fun."

Angelina retorted, "Sleeping around indiscriminately isn't my idea of fun."

"Look, one night of sex is no big deal. And it'll even fit into your schedule," Krista added with a grin. "Your hunky client sounds like the perfect guy to break you out of your rut."

"No way."

"Okay, then, how about at least kissing him?"

Angelina felt herself flush at the thought of kissing Will. "I don't—"

Krista cut her off. "Give me one good reason why not."

Angelina lowered her voice. "First of all, his ex-wife hired me to get him back."

"Oh," Krista murmured, obviously titillated by this new bit of information.

"Second, as I said before, I don't mix business with pleasure."

"You never know. It could be fun."

"And third, CEOs are not my type."

Krista held her hands up in defeat. "Fine. You and your never-ending logic have defeated me. Just think about it, Ang. You need to have some fun before you forget how. Speaking of fun, what are you doing tomorrow afternoon? There's a shoe sale at Nordstrom that can't be missed."

Glad for the change of subject, Angelina reached into her briefcase for her organizer to check her calendar. She knew she should start using the calendar on her cell phone, but she liked her old-fashioned pen-and-paper system.

"Oh, no. I left my Day-Timer at Will's house."

"Looks like you're going to have to go back to his house to get it, huh?" Krista folded her hands under her chin and fluttered her lashes. "Or wait for him to bring it to you," she added with a naughty undertone.

WILL COULDN'T CONCENTRATE. He'd finally come outside to look at his oversized and underused resort-type back garden. But no matter what he was doing, his mind kept going back to his greatest failure to date.

Never before had a woman turned and run from him. In all his previous experience with the opposite sex, he'd hardly had to expend any effort at all to get women to go out with him. The women he usually dated didn't look much further than his bank account, but Angelina clearly couldn't have cared less how many diamonds or houses he could buy her.

Maybe if I clean up the mess in my office, she'll come knocking on my door.

It was a ridiculous thought, but it kept playing like a broken record in his head, so he gave up and called his assistant and asked her to reschedule his meetings for the rest of the day.

He headed for the side door of his house before remembering that Angelina had told him to use the front door for better energy...or something like that.

He groaned. One visit from a feng shui consultant and he needed to see a good therapist.

Nonetheless, he walked around to his front door. Once inside, he headed down the hall to his office. Picking his way into the middle of the room, he reached into the box directly in front of him and got down to business.

Amazingly, as he threw away clutter that had been piling up for years, the voices clogging his brain shut up for the first time all day.

HOPING TO GET this over and done with as quickly as possible, Angelina marched up to Will's front door and rang the bell.

When Will opened the door, he let out a low whistle. "I can't believe feng shui works this fast."

Not having a clue what he was talking about, Angelina got straight to the point. "I left my organizer in your office. I just need to grab it and then I'll get out of your hair."

Will looked taken aback by her slightly frosty tone. She felt a little bad, but she had her heart to protect.

"I'm glad you're here, Angelina. I've got something to show you."

Following Will to his office, hating how much she liked to hear her name on his lips, she stopped dead in her tracks in the doorway.

"Wow." The room was spotless and the changed energy was impossible to ignore.

"You like?" Will asked, grinning from ear to ear.

"What an amazing transformation. How did you do it all so fast?"

He shrugged. "I couldn't concentrate on anything else with the mess in this room hanging over me. The shredder got one heck of a workout today. It's odd, but I almost feel as if I can breathe better in here now."

Angelina leaned against the doorway. "That's exactly how I explain feng shui to people who have never heard about it. If you follow the principles, you will feel like you can breathe better everywhere in your entire house."

Will rubbed his chin with his left hand. "I really get that now."

Angelina gave him a soft smile. "I'm glad." Knowing she had to break the spell Will had over her—and fast!—Angelina picked up her organizer and said, "I should really get going now."

"Why don't you join me for a cup of coffee in the kitchen?"

Angelina shook her head. "Sorry, I don't do caffeine. It makes me weird." Will raised an eyebrow and she laughed. "Okay, so it makes me weirder. Anyway, thanks, but no."

"How about decaf?"

For some crazy reason, Angelina couldn't resist the look in his eyes. "Just one cup." Wagging her finger at him, she warned, "And don't you try anything funny like mixing caffeine in. I won't be responsible for the consequences."

He held his right hand over his heart and said with mock solemnity, "You have my word. No funny business."

Angelina pulled up one of the stools to his kitchen island while Will reached in the cupboard next to the sink for the coffee beans.

She had always had a thing for tall, well-built men, which seemed particularly unfortunate right now, considering Will was off-limits in every way.

FROM THE MOMENT Angelina walked through his front door, Will had been struck not just by her beauty, but by her spirit and intelligence, as well.

The truth was, he had never felt this way about Susan. Marrying her had been, quite simply, the right thing to do. Get an MBA, start a successful company, marry a good-looking blonde.

"Angelina," he said, "do you feng shui boats?"

She looked surprised by his request, but she nodded.

"I'd like you to take a look at my boat in San Francisco this Saturday."

"I already have plans with my friend on Saturday."

"Bring her with you," Will insisted, his palms sweating as if he was a thirteen-year-old boy asking out the most popular girl in class. "We'll cruise out to Angel Island and then maybe drop the kayaks in and row around. While we're at it, we'll get some feng shui done."

He held his breath until—finally!—she said, "Yes."

CHAPTER FIVE

SATURDAY MORNING, Angelina woke up early and did her usual four-mile walk, hoping to work off some of her nervous energy.

She never should have agreed to this consultation on Will's boat. But Krista's words—*You need to have some fun before you forget how*—had been playing in her head like a broken record.

After her shower, she stood in her closet, wondering what the heck she should wear. Nothing seemed appropriate. Frustrated, as the clock ticked closer to 9:00 a.m., she put on her favorite jeans and a white scoop-neck T-shirt. Figuring it might be cold or windy out on the bay, she also pulled out a red sweatshirt and a jacket. Topping off the whole outfit with red tennis shoes, she looked in the mirror and declared herself ready to sail.

She was midway through plaiting her hair into a French braid when her doorbell rang. Quickly finishing the braid and slipping a covered rubber band around the end, she yelled, "Coming."

When she opened the door, she had to steady herself. Will looked more gorgeous than ever in his khaki shorts, Giants T-shirt and baseball cap.

"Good morning," she said as she locked the door behind her. *Don't drool all over him,* she chided herself.

But when she saw his car, she blurted out, "Mustang convertibles are my favorite car."

"You'd be surprised how many women complain that it's not a BMW or a Jaguar."

"What kind of women have you been driving around?" she said, cocking her head slightly to one side.

"The wrong ones, I guess."

She directed him to Krista's condo, which was a couple of blocks away. They knocked on the door and heard her friend call out, "It's open. Come in and I'll be ready in just a second."

As far as Angelina was concerned, Krista's place rode a very fine line between feng shui greatness and disaster. Her decorating style consisted of sharp lines and ultramodern furniture in varying shades of cream and gray. Angelina had often told Krista that if she ever felt ready to settle down with the man of her dreams, she should soften the sharpness inside her house. But since Krista didn't seem interested in limiting herself to only one man, Angelina let it be.

Krista flounced out through the doorway and made a Madonna-esque pose for them. "Am I gorgeous or what?" She pirouetted in a slow circle in white capri pants and a white crop top, an orange scarf tied flamboyantly in her wild mass of curly red hair.

"As always," Angelina agreed.

Before she could introduce them, Krista enveloped Will in a hug. All in one breath she said, "Hi, Will. I feel like I know you already. You're just gorgeous. I can't wait to see your boat. Isn't Angelina absolutely scrumptious?"

Will just laughed in response. "It's a pleasure to meet you, too, Krista." Stepping back out of her embrace, he looked at his watch. "We'd better get going or my friends may just sail off without us. Either that or they'll drink all of the beer on board," he added with a wink.

They flew up Highway 101, past the suburbs dotted along the bay, chatting about nothing in particular, relaxing into the freedom of a Saturday off—top down, blue skies and the ocean waiting to be explored.

Will took the Fourth Street exit and pulled into the pier next to the baseball stadium. He parked in his reserved spot and directed each of the women to grab a light cooler from the trunk. Unlocking the gate, he led them down Dock C to his boat, which was easy to locate because his friends were waving at them from the bow, drinks already in hand.

"Oh, my God, only a tycoon could own a boat like that." Krista looked more closely at Will and a flicker of recognition caught in her eyes. "Wait a second. You're the guy who—"

Will cut her off. "All aboard," he said as he tried to gauge Angelina's reaction to his boat. The last thing he needed was for Angelina to find out just how famous he was. He was truly enjoying the way she treated him just like anyone else.

Maybe he had done the wrong thing by inviting her on his boat. She was bound to ask some questions about his net worth, just like her friend was doing right now.

Adding to his problems, Krista was saying, "Damn, Will. The only time I've ever seen a boat this big was when I used to watch reruns of *The Love Boat* on TV as a kid. Is this really yours?"

Angelina elbowed Krista and changed the subject. "I'd love to meet your friends."

Will breathed a sigh of relief. Was it possible that
Angelina really didn't care about his wealth at all? His
inner voice mocked him instantly, saying, *Yeah, right.*
You think you've found a woman who doesn't want a
piece of your fame and fortune. If you believe that, I've
got a used car I'd like to sell you.

Will shook the voice out of his head. Leaving Krista
to gape in amazement at the opulent surroundings, he
placed Angelina's arm in his and walked with her down
the length of the boat.

Angelina leaned close and whispered, "Sorry about
that. Krista can be a little exuberant sometimes."

Will shrugged and then introduced her to his friends.
When Krista finally joined them, he had to make the
introductions all over again, which gave Angelina a
moment to settle back into her surroundings.

Frankly, she was floored by the size of Will's boat.
It was moored at the longest spot on the dock, equiva-
lent in size to two of the bigger slips.

Angelina wondered if he had actually earned it all
or if it had been handed to him on a silver platter. Not
that it mattered all that much, she reminded herself.
He was just a client.

She looked up from her musings just in time to wit-
ness sparks flying between Krista and Derek, one of
Will's friends, who was dressed very conservatively in
khaki Dockers and a white button-down short-sleeved
shirt with a pencil in the front pocket.

How interesting, Angelina thought to herself. Krista
usually had more chemistry with guys like James,
Will's other friend on board, who was flashier—a
quintessential playboy.

When Krista perched next to James, Angelina

thought disappointment flared in Derek's eyes. For
once, she hoped that the underdog would get the girl.
She didn't know why, but she had a feeling that this
gentle man might be the missing link in her friend's life.

Was Will her missing link?

The thought shocked her deeply and she sank down
numbly into the deck chair behind her. *He can't be
the one!*

Her one special man would not be the type to own a
fifty-foot yacht. She had always pictured herself with
someone undemanding and serene, a man with far less
presence than Will. Plus, how could she forget that his
ex-wife had hired her to help get him back? For the
hundredth time, Angelina rued the day she'd agreed
to take on this consultation.

"Right, Ang?" Krista said, and Angelina blinked
in confusion. Fortunately, before she had to fess up to
daydreaming, Krista said, "Oh, look, we're moving."

Will was getting ready to motor out of the marina,
so Angelina jumped up out of her seat and tracked him
down in the wheelhouse. "Do you need any help?"

"Help me pull up the rubber fenders and we'll be
off."

Angelina scampered onto the dock to unhook the
long white bumpers. Handing all ten up to Will, she
mounted the steps back onto the open deck.

"Keep an eye on the harbor traffic while I maneuver out, would you?"

"Aye-aye, captain," she said as she saluted him.

They made their way out of the marina with no problems, and then Will cranked up the speed, jetting them
under the Bay Bridge and out toward Angel Island.

The water worked its magic—the delicious sensation of wind whipping past, the sun warming her skin made Angelina relax and simply enjoy the day.

Will, who was steering from the flybridge up top, called down for her to join him. She carefully walked up the short metal ladder and came to stand beside him at the wheel.

Keeping a watchful eye on the boat traffic surrounding them, he asked, "Are you having a good time?"

"Oh, yes. This is so much fun."

Nonetheless, she knew she should keep her manner as professional as possible. "When we drop anchor, why don't we do some feng shui?"

Will shook his head. "No way. It's a beautiful day. Let's have a little off-the-clock fun first."

What the heck. A little fun wouldn't kill her.

Grinning impishly at Will, she said, "All right, you win."

Pulling her hair out of the French braid, she let it blow in the breeze. She was intent on letting herself go with the flow for once.

"Sailing past Fisherman's Wharf, going under the Bay Bridge, then looking out toward the Golden Gate. It's amazing. Have you always loved being out on the water?"

Slipping on his sunglasses to fight the glare from the water, he replied, "I guess so. I grew up spending every summer in the Adirondack Mountains of New York with my grandparents. There weren't many fancy things in that small cottage, but we had sailboats."

"Did your parents come out to the lake, too?"

"My mom did, when she could." He paused. "My dad skipped out on us when I was five. I haven't seen him since."

WILL KNEW HE'D already said too much. But he felt so comfortable talking with Angelina that the words kept coming.

"The thing is, it wasn't so bad that he left me. But my mom was on her way to becoming a truly amazing painter. After he left, she had to work two jobs to keep us flush, and by the time she got home she was usually too tired to paint. I used to set out her easels for her, hoping she would paint for even a few minutes, but she never did. By the time I was about to graduate from college, and I saw just how tired she had become from all her years of hard work, I vowed that one day I would make so much money she could paint all day, every day. I wanted to give her everything."

"I'll bet you did just that, didn't you?"

"I wanted to build her a mansion and fill it with clothes and jewelry, but the only thing she wanted was the summer house my grandparents rented all those years ago. I'll never be able to make up for what she had to sacrifice for me."

"It sounds to me like she has everything she needs. It sounds like she's happy."

Maybe so. But he would never be able to do enough to make up for the way his deadbeat dad had treated her.

Everyone clambered up onto the flybridge to join them, and Will hoped Angelina would forget his foolish babbling.

Rounding the corner into a calm bay off Angel Island, he announced, "Let's drop anchor and head ashore." A cheer went up from the crowd.

Turning off the engine, Will grabbed the two guys to help him lift and dump the huge anchor off the bow,

leaving Angelina and Krista alone up top on the flybridge.

Krista wasted no time. "Can you believe this yacht?"
Without waiting for an answer, she said, "And his
gorgeous friend James? Oh, my God, I could lounge
around on this boat forever! Your boyfriend is the most
delicious, wealthy catch in the entire world. In fact, he's
on this month's—"

Angelina glared at her friend. "Shh!"

"What? It's not like his big bucks are a huge secret
or anything."

Angelina rolled her eyes and thought, not for the
first time, how amazing it was that her best friend
could be so incredibly intelligent about some things,
but so clueless about others.

"First of all, he's not my boyfriend. And second,
every time you bring up how rich he is, you really embarrass him." When Krista opened her mouth to protest, Angelina smacked her on the arm. "What if every
person who met you commented on your big breasts?"

Krista grinned wickedly. "They usually do."

Angelina was more than a little exasperated by this
point. "You know what I mean. And by the way, I think
you should know you've got it all wrong. You're making your moves on the wrong guy."

Krista looked confused. "What? You don't think
James and I are perfect for each other? Our kids would
be absolutely adorable, you know."

"Try your look-how-shallow-I-am act on someone
else. I'm not saying he wouldn't be fine for a night—"

"Or two. Or three."

"Fine, give the guy a whole week. That's not the

point. All I'm saying is that I think you should consider Derek."

"He's not my type."

"He could be."

Before her friend could reply, Will called up to them from the deck below. "Anyone up for a ride to the beach in the dinghy, or in a kayak?"

Krista hopped up with a defiant look stamped across her features.

Leaning over the rail just enough to give everyone below a clear view of her ample cleavage, she said, "James, what were you planning on doing?"

"The double kayak," he replied in a bored tone.

"That sounds perfect," she said, pretending not to hear Angelina's snort of disapproval as she climbed back down to the lower deck and disappeared to help untie the kayak.

Angelina followed her down the ladder and joined Will and Derek by the dinghy. Derek offered, "Why don't the two of you take the dinghy to the island? I'll just hang out on the boat and get some sun."

"I've got a better idea," replied Angelina. "Let's all three of us hike the Island Loop Trail."

Within a few minutes they had rowed the small boat to shore and were on the trail, laughing and talking. Derek was a great companion, just as Angelina had suspected. He was funny, smart and athletic.

It was too bad Krista was going to miss out on a great guy just because she was too stubborn to open her eyes.

And if the thought crept into her mind that she herself was being a tad stubborn about a certain client of hers, she steadfastly ignored it.

As Angelina led the way on the trail, Will couldn't help but notice, yet again, what a beautiful figure she had. He checked to make sure that his friend Derek wasn't also admiring it—not that he would blame him if he was—but frankly, he was feeling increasingly proprietary about Angelina.

"Krista is focused on getting attention. Trust me, if you don't give her any, she'll be begging for it."

Will tuned back in to the conversation Angelina and his friend were having. "What are you two talking about?"

She turned toward Will with a devilish gleam in her eyes. "We're working out a plan so that Derek can make Krista crazy for him."

Derek looked momentarily uncomfortable before he shrugged and said, "Seems like a good idea to me."

Will laughed. "Okay, let's hear the rest of the plan. First you ignore her until she's— How did you put it, Angelina? 'Begging for it'?"

Angelina chuckled. "Exactly. Now, don't get me wrong. I love Krista dearly, but this time she has definitely gotten in the kayak with the wrong man."

"They looked pretty perfect together to me," muttered Derek.

Angelina patted his arm. "Appearances can be deceiving. Trust me, they're all wrong for each other. So, like I was saying, all you need to do is make it clear that you're not interested in her."

Derek stopped dead in his tracks and Will slammed into him, which almost knocked the three of them over like dominoes. "But I am interested."

"Look, if you just want to sleep with her once and never see her again, then do things your way." Angelina started hitting the trail with renewed vigor. "But my bets are on her falling madly in love with you if you take my advice. From that point forward, it will be up to you to keep her on her toes."

"How's he supposed to do that?" Will asked.

"Easy. Make her play by your rules at first. And then only give in to her in little ways. Women like Krista, who get everything they want all the time, can only fall in love with a man who is difficult to conquer."

Derek was nodding his head with new understanding. "How do you know so much about this?"

Angelina looked wistful. "Human Nature 101. We all want what we can't have."

WHEN THEY RETURNED to the beach where they'd left the dinghy, Angelina was surprised to see Krista waiting for them. Evidently she'd been waiting for them for some time, because she practically threw herself at them.

"What are you doing here?" Angelina asked. "I thought you'd still be out in the kayak with James."

Krista snorted. "Not a chance. He got an important call right after you guys left on your hike." She nodded back toward James, who was sitting on the side of the kayak, cell phone pressed up to his ear. "I've been here, all by myself, the whole time."

Angelina felt no sympathy for her friend. She simply gave her a look that said, *Maybe you should consider my advice next time.*

Derek, Angelina noted, was playing his new role to the hilt, seemingly more interested in the rocks on the beach than anything Krista had to say. In fact, after getting only monosyllabic grunts from Derek for several minutes, Krista started to pout.

Will was pulling the dinghy back out toward the water when a soccer ball knocked against his legs and two little boys came running up to get it.

"I'll kick it back to you," he said, and quickly got roped into an impromptu soccer match on the beach with a whole horde of little boys.

A few minutes later, slightly out of breath, Will rejoined them. "Sorry about that," he said with a grin. "Soccer's always been a weakness."

Angelina grinned back, amazed by this new side of him. "You're great with kids."

Abruptly, Will turned back to the dinghy and pushed it. "Not really."

Angelina was confused by his behavior. "Those kids loved playing with you."

But it was clear that the conversation was over, along with the afternoon outing. They all got back in the kayak and dinghy and headed to the yacht. Will started the engine and headed straight back for the marina. "Looks like the wind is picking up, and I don't want a rough ride on the way back."

Angelina looked at the sailboats on either side of them as they motored through the water. The sails were barely fluttering and the water looked remarkably like glass. *He must really want to get this consultation over and done with,* she thought to herself. But, she decided, she wasn't going to let her feelings be hurt.

Instead, she was going to milk every last ounce of enjoyment out of floating across the water and sitting under blue skies. She was completely fine maintaining a purely professional relationship with Will.

No matter what her heart said to the contrary.

ANGELINA ATTEMPTED to get involved in a conversation with someone else on board, but between the five of them, they were hopeless. Krista was alternately pouting and then trying to get Derek's attention. Derek was working so hard at ignoring Krista's advances that he wasn't much of a conversationalist. And James's phone kept ringing with hot stock tips.

By the time Will maneuvered his yacht back into the marina, Angelina was hugely relieved the outing was over. She was going to do a quick feng shui consultation and then she and Krista would get the heck out of there.

But Will seemed to have other plans. "Derek, would you mind taking Krista home?"

Panic crept up Angelina's spine at the thought of being alone on the boat with Will. "Krista doesn't mind waiting for me to finish the consultation, do you?"

But Krista looked thrilled by the turn of events. "I'd love to go home with you, Derek," she said, her invitation clear to everyone on the boat.

Angelina tried to catch Krista's eye to let her know she was needed as backup, but her friend had already kissed Will on the cheek and said, "Thank you for a great day and for introducing me to Derek."

Derek and Krista left, with James not far behind. James shook hands with Will before he headed down the dock, cell phone still pressed to his ear.

"I'm really glad you came today." All of the earlier awkwardness disappeared as Will closed the distance between them and every cell in her body went on high alert.

He was going to kiss her.

And she was going to let him.

In the end, she wasn't sure who made the first move. All she knew was that his mouth was on hers and hers was on his.

And it was the best kiss of her life.

She didn't know how long they stood on his boat kissing. She was barely aware of anything other than how good he was making her feel, until suddenly, she felt him pulling back.

Finally, she realized his cell phone was ringing. It was an odd-sounding ringtone and hard to miss.

Muttering a soft curse, he said, "I need to take this."

"Sure. Of course. Go ahead."

"Angelina, please, just wait a second. I'll hang up as soon as I can."

But she could see that his focus was already on his important phone call.

She waited for a few minutes for him, but then she finally realized he'd forgotten all about her.

Oh, God, she was such an idiot. She was just the hired help, conveniently there for whatever he wanted. Just like she'd been with Bryce.

She grabbed her bag, already calling a cab as she jumped off his boat and hurried up the dock.

WILL CUT HIS CALL short with his corporate lawyer and walked out to the stern to find Angelina…and pick up where they'd left off.

But she was gone.

He'd blown it again.

Susan had always been on him about his knee-jerk tendency to put business first, but he'd ignored her because business always *had* come first.

Now his ex-wife's words were coming back to haunt him.

CHAPTER SIX

"So you were kissing, and then when his phone rang, he forgot all about you?"

Angelina squeezed her eyes shut and considered hanging up on Krista. She had spent the entire night trying to forget the kiss with Will.

Trying to forget about being forgotten.

"Don't make such a big deal out of it. I'm already over it," she lied.

"Good riddance. He probably wasn't any good. Rich guys never are."

Irrationally, Angelina felt compelled to jump to Will's defense. "His kisses were amazing."

"Look," Krista said stubbornly, "all I'm saying is, once I saw that boat I knew something was up."

"You did?"

"Oh, yeah," replied Krista. "I'd definitely be suspicious of someone as rich as he is. Besides, it doesn't matter who he is, 'cause he has lousy taste in friends. The good-looking one never turned off his phone, and the *other* one," Krista said as though referring to something she had stepped on, "seemed to think he was too good for me. The loser doesn't know what he's missing!"

"I'll say," muttered Angelina under her breath.

"Anyway, I've decided to take pity on the nerd and go out with him next month."

"He asked you out?"

Krista humphed on her end of the phone and fessed up. "I sort of talked him into taking me to his company dinner. But we were talking about Will, weren't we?"

"Could we just forget about Will, Kris?"

Krista snorted. "Too bad he has to be so cute, with such a big yacht. But you know what? There's nothing that a little shopping can't fix. I'll be right over."

Krista hung up the phone before Angelina could refuse the invitation. Which was just as well, she thought sourly.

Suddenly, she had an urge to buy something blue.

WILL HAD PLANNED on calling Angelina all day Sunday. It wasn't that he was a wuss, he reasoned. It was simply that he never went into any kind of negotiation without a surefire plan of action, a backup plan and a last-ditch plan. And he knew he was going to need the plan of all plans to make things right with Angelina.

The problem was, he couldn't seem to think straight when it came to Angelina. He kept getting sidetracked thinking about her soft skin and her silky, shiny hair.

And how luscious her mouth was.

He grabbed a beer, turned on the football game and tried to settle into his usual Sunday routine. But thirty minutes later, he had absolutely no idea who was winning the game.

He couldn't take his mind off Angelina.

The doorbell rang. Will jumped up and spilled beer all over the carpet on his way to the door.

His ex-wife, Susan, opened her arms to him. "Surprise!" She hugged him, then stepped past him into the house. "I was just visiting a friend who lives nearby. I'm dying to see the changes you've made since Angelina came by to work with you."

She surveyed the living room and the kitchen expectantly and then turned to him with her hands on her hips. "You haven't changed anything. Did you scare her off again?"

The irony of the moment was not lost on Will. "Yes. No. I don't know. Do you want a beer?"

Susan made a face.

"Sorry, forgot you hate beer. I'll get you a glass of wine." He stepped into the kitchen and uncorked a bottle of merlot. Handing Susan the glass of wine, he said, "I did make one big change." He led her down the hall to his office, opened the door and moved out of the way so that she could step inside the room.

"How did she get you to do this?" She turned to him with an amazed look on her flawless face. "I could never get you to clean up your office. I was even afraid to go into it most of the time."

He shrugged.

She put her hand on his arm. "You have to tell me what she said."

He moved out of touching range and stuffed his hands into his pockets. "Something about stagnant energy."

Susan threw her head back and laughed. Will knew he should have kept the changes to himself and headed back into the kitchen. He had a spilled beer to clean up.

"I never thought I'd live to hear you talking about energy."

"Forget it, will you?" He knelt on the carpet with a wad of paper towels to sop up the spilled beer.

Susan was clearly on a roll, though, he noted with increasing dismay. Sitting on the edge of his coffee table in what he assumed was supposed to be a sexy way, she asked, "Have you worked on your love corner yet?"

Will kept mopping up the carpet and tried to pretend this wasn't happening. He said, "No," and then got up to throw away the paper towels.

Susan stood up. "You really should, you know, because she's famous for being the Feng Shui Cupid."

"The Feng Shui what?"

"The Feng Shui Cupid. She can get anyone to fall in love."

Will tried to mask his horror. *She can make anyone fall in love?*

He forcefully took control of his thoughts, telling himself that the idea of a Feng Shui Cupid was just as ridiculous as the idea that rearranging his home could change his life.

Then again, hadn't he felt better after cleaning up his office?

Deftly changing the subject, his ex said, "Let's go get something to eat at that cute French bistro on the corner."

Will couldn't think of anything he'd less like to do, but he'd always hated to hurt Susan's feelings. Resigned to his fate, he agreed. "Sure."

He liked Susan. She had always been a good friend. But why had he married her? Had he really been so obsessed with finding the perfect corporate-wife accessory?

The only thing he knew for sure was that he much preferred long dark hair, olive skin and hazel eyes over anything else.

AFTER AN EXHAUSTING TREK through every store in the mall, Krista insisted on taking Angelina to dinner before dropping her off at home. Having learned early on that it was usually easier to give in to Krista than to fight her, Angelina agreed. The bistro Krista picked was a little too close to Will's house for Angelina's peace of mind, but odds were a million to one that she would run into Will there. Besides, she couldn't go through the rest of her life trying to avoid him.

Their server had just delivered their wine when a breathtaking blonde walked through the door. Angelina tried not to stare, but the woman was so remarkable— perfectly dressed, coiffed, made up, even her shoes were perfect—that Angelina felt a senseless urge to pull out her sunglasses and put them on even though the sun was long gone.

Krista turned to see what had caught Angelina's attention. "Now, there's a piece of work. Think any of that's real?"

But before Angelina could reply, she saw Will walk into the restaurant right behind the goddess.

At least, she noted grimly, he had the grace to look chagrined when he saw her. Her prayer that he would ignore her so she could sneak out was not granted as he headed over to her table.

Angelina whispered to Krista in a shaky voice, "My worst nightmare has just come true."

Krista called out to a nearby waiter. "My friend and I need another couple of glasses of wine here. Pronto.

Unless you're thinking of switching to something a little more potent, Ang?"

Heck, yeah, I'm ready for something a whole lot more potent, like this gorgeous man standing in front of me, she thought hysterically. And then she remembered whom he was with—Ms. I'm Too Perfect to Be Real—and the fact that he had clearly found her completely forgettable.

Angelina tried to convince herself that it didn't hurt, but it did. There was no way she could ever compete with a woman like that.

In lieu of any better ideas, she fortified herself with a big gulp of white wine. Unfortunately, when she looked up, not only was Will still standing there, but the perfect woman had joined him.

Will cleared his throat and made the introductions. "Angelina, Krista, this is my ex-wife, Susan."

Angelina's heart sank even further as she looked at the woman who had hired her. This perfect vision was the woman who hoped Angelina's Feng Shui Cupid powers would win back the affections of her ex-husband? Couldn't she have just flicked her glossy hair over her shoulder and given him a come-hither glance to get the job done?

Worse still, Angelina was hit between the eyes with a sick dose of guilt for betraying the woman who had hired her in good faith by kissing her ex-husband. She wanted nothing more than to run out of the restaurant. At this point, fleeing the country seemed like a good idea.

"You're the feng shui consultant, aren't you?"

Angelina mustered up all of her I-am-a-seasoned-professional reserves. She stood up to shake Susan's hand. "It's nice to meet you."

The stunning woman caught her totally unawares by giving her a hug. "It is so incredibly fabulous to meet you in person. I just cannot believe what you've done with Will's office. Believe me, I tried for years to get him to clean it up, but nothing worked. You're a miracle worker. May we join you for dinner?"

Angelina noted Susan didn't wait for an answer as she gracefully lowered herself into a nearby chair. Susan seemed totally oblivious to any tension as she made herself comfortable. She ordered a salad and glass of wine from the hovering waiter, who practically fainted when she spoke to him.

Angelina desperately searched her brain trying to find a way out of this awful dinner. She sent a potent look across the table to Krista, silently imploring her to help think of an excuse to bolt. But Krista was sitting back, enjoying the show.

And some show it was. As Susan talked on and on about meeting the Feng Shui Cupid in person, and all of the miraculous things she had done for her clients, Angelina could only wish that she'd taken more time with her appearance that morning.

Jeans and a T-shirt really weren't cutting it. But the sad truth was that she could do a full makeover, top to bottom, and she still wouldn't be anywhere near being able to play in Susan's league.

If Susan was a Victoria's Secret model, Angelina was one of the Fruit of the Loom gang.

"Now, where was I?" Susan said much later. "Oh, yes, Will and I were having such a good time at his house tonight when he invited me to have dinner with him."

Will barely managed to keep from spewing his wine all over the table when he heard that flagrant misrepresentation of the few minutes they had spent in his house.

Susan immediately exclaimed, "Oh, honey, are you all right?"

Honey? "I'm fine."

Susan explained, "It's so hard to remember we're not married anymore. Sometimes a *honey* or two just slips out, doesn't it?" She gave Will a positively adoring look.

Will couldn't believe his luck. Here he was in a bistro he didn't want to be in, having a dinner he didn't want to eat, with a woman he didn't want to be with, staring into the eyes of the woman he *did* want to be with, but who clearly didn't want to be with him.

Not to mention the fact that being around Angelina had the oddest effect on him, causing his usually razor-sharp mind to turn to mush. He just couldn't stop staring at her.

Krista kicked him under the table. "Try not to be so obvious."

Oh, yeah, he had almost forgotten. His ex had some crazy notion that they were going to get back together. How the heck was he going to make it clear that he wasn't the slightest bit interested in her anymore?

Most men—okay, pretty much every man alive—would have jumped at the chance to be with Susan. She was good-looking and sweet. But she didn't have even an ounce of what the woman beside her had—a magical, sensual allure.

If his brain kept this up, he would have to resign from his company and turn to writing sappy love songs. He was glad for Krista's advice, though, and made haste to act accordingly. There was no point in letting Susan know she had competition.

Snapping out of his reverie, he noticed his ex had scooted even closer to Angelina and was sketching something on a napkin. She beamed at him across the small table, looking like a kid in a candy store. "Angelina is giving me a few tips right now. I'm drawing my floor plan for her. Isn't it exciting?"

Will grunted noncommittally.

"Tell me again," his ex-wife said, "where the love area of my house is and what I need to do. I can't wait to get home and try this out."

IF SUSAN GOT any perkier—or nicer—Angelina was going to be sick. Of course, she supposed if she looked like Susan and had the world lining up to kiss her feet, she'd probably be annoyingly cheerful, too.

Circling the love-and-marriage corner of Susan's floor plan, Angelina gave the woman a few tips on displaying things in pairs, using red and pink, and hanging romantic art. A few minutes later, when the waiter delivered their food, she forced down a couple of bites so that no one would see how out of sorts she was. Too bad her twenty-dollar salad suddenly tasted as if it was made entirely of bitter lettuce leaves.

Finally Susan patted her perfect lips with her napkin. "If you will all excuse me, I'm going to go powder my nose."

After she left, Krista leaned in to Angelina and said, "I thought people only said that kind of stuff in the movies."

Angelina fought back the frantic giggle that was bubbling up in her throat.

"Krista," Will said, "would you mind leaving Angelina and me alone for a minute?"

Her friend sat back in her chair and crossed her arms over her chest. "Whatever you have to say to Angelina, you can say in front of me."

Angelina turned to Krista with a smile, appreciating her show of solidarity, but the truth was, she wanted to get the whole thing over and done with Will as quickly as possible.

"It's okay, Kris. Would you mind getting the car from valet parking? I'll be out in just a sec."

Krista reluctantly stood up. "I'm right outside," she said, pointing her finger at Will, "so don't try any funny stuff or I'll sic your ex-wife on you."

"What do you want now?" Angelina wasn't wasting any time on pleasantries. Although she was nervous and guilty, she was also angry, which helped steel her nerves.

"Did Susan ever tell you why she hired you to work with me?"

So, he must have finally figured out that Susan wanted to reconcile, Angelina thought with perverse satisfaction. She wanted to see him squirm, but she could never divulge her private conversation with Susan. Trying to act detached and professional, she replied, "She is obviously concerned about you."

She could tell Will had more questions about Susan's motivations, but instead he switched tactics, reaching across the table for her hand. "I want to apologize about what happened last night on the boat. About taking that call. And I need to explain about why I'm here with Susan."

Angelina's mouth turned into what might have resembled a smile before she stopped herself. "That kiss was a mistake. A really big mistake. It won't happen again. And you don't need to explain anything about you and Susan. I hope you'll be very happy together."

And with that, she swept out of the restaurant in as grand an exit as she could pull off, desperately hoping that Krista already had the car running, ready for a quick getaway.

"I THOUGHT THE TORTURE would never end," Angelina said as she slid into Krista's car.

"No kidding. That woman couldn't get enough of you. She was practically sitting in your lap. Your lover boy looked like he was going to punch her."

"He's *not* my lover boy."

"So," Krista said in a knowing voice, "now you're bitter because she wants him back."

"I am not," Angelina protested, much too loudly.

"You are so falling for him."

Angelina glared at her best friend. "I am not."

Krista rolled her eyes. "Whatever. Anyway, now that I've given it some thought and have seen you two together again, I've decided it's a good thing."

Angelina snorted. "Name one way it could possibly be good."

"How about four? One, he is so hot for you I was practically getting singed at the restaurant."

"Stop making things up."

"Shush, I'm not done yet. Two, he's filthy, stinking rich."

"Excuse me?"

"Hello? Am I done with my list yet? Let's see, where was I? Three, according to you, his kisses light you up like the Fourth of July. Are you ready for number four?"

"I don't think so."

"Too bad. Because number four is the incontestable fact that the two of you are perfect for each other."

Angelina shook her head, refusing to believe it would ever work out between her and Will. "Try this instead," she said to Krista. "How about number one, his ex is perfect, number two, she's gorgeous, and number three, she's nice?"

"None of that matters," Krista replied confidently.

"How can you say that? You saw her."

Krista pulled up in front of Angelina's house. "He doesn't look at her the way he looks at you."

Angelina was afraid to hear anything else Krista had to say, so she got out of the car.

"Sparks, baby. They're flying." Krista started to pull away and then hit the brakes, yelling out the window. "By the way, I'd go pick up the latest copy of *People* if I were you."

Angelina stood on the curb and watched Krista's car round the corner, wondering about her friend's cryptic magazine comment. What could *People* magazine possibly have to do with the hole she had dug for herself?

She went inside her house, ignoring the mess in her living room again, and went through the motions of getting ready for bed. She hoped that once she crawled under the covers she would be able to dim the sight of Will and his vision-of-loveliness ex wrapped in each other's arms.

CHAPTER SEVEN

ANGELINA HAD BEEN tossing and turning for several hours. Her bed felt more like a torture rack with every passing minute. "I wouldn't be surprised if I have bruises all over," she muttered unhappily as she kicked off the sheets and sat up, sliding her feet onto the floor.

Unable to rein herself in, she sat down at her computer. Krista's comment about *People* magazine had put her brain on overdrive.

Feeling as if she were prying into a file marked *Private,* she typed *Will Scott* into Google. A few seconds later her screen was filled with listings for every kind of information imaginable—interviews, investor reports, gossip columns and picture galleries.

Angelina's head whirled. "He's this famous?" She scrolled through endless links about Will and the multibillion-dollar company he owned.

She let out a long breath. Suddenly she saw what a complete idiot she must have looked like to him, asking if he programmed computers for a living.

She was angry at herself and even angrier at Will for not letting her in on his little secret. Of course, she had to admit that if she kept up a little more with the news and current magazines, she would have recognized him immediately.

Against her better judgment, she clicked on the top link for a recent interview.

I met Will Scott, CEO of PTI, on a weekend after his morning run. As he walked up to me, hand outstretched, his muscles glistening in sweat, I found myself faltering as an objective journalist. I promise you this—one look in those blue eyes and the hardest soul would have been utterly lost, too.

Angelina snorted and looked for something more substantial. Finding a link for another interview, she read,

Rarely in my twenty years as a financial writer have I met a CEO more charming than Will Scott. Which begs the question—what is he hiding?

Angelina nearly laughed out loud at the preposterous statement. Still unable to control her wayward curiosity, she clicked on a link titled Will Scott: Fan Page and Photo Gallery.

Staring her in the face was page after page of pictures of Will with women who all looked the same: big breasts, long legs, blond hair, beautiful faces.

All of her old feelings of inadequacy bubbled to the surface. Suddenly she was twenty-one again and had just been told, *Did you actually think I'd be serious with a girl like you?*

Feeling hollow inside, she got up without turning off the computer, walked like a zombie back to her

bedroom, crawled under the covers and fell into a fit-
ful sleep.

Images of Will surrounded by a harem of supermod-
els danced through her head until daylight.

WILL WOKE UP EARLY, went for a jog, then came home
and reached into the refrigerator for some OJ. The digi-
tal clock on his microwave read 8:00 a.m., and he decided it was late enough to call Angelina.

He picked up his phone, but before he could press
the talk button, it rang. He checked the caller ID, hoping it was Angelina, but instead he was surprised to
read his mother's phone number on the small display.

"Mom?"

"Hi, honey. Did I call too early?"

"No, of course not. What's wrong?"

"First, promise me you won't get upset."

"Mom…" Will didn't like the sound of this one bit.

"Well, I was doing a little painting."

"At your easel?"

Joyce sighed. "No. I thought the window trim out
front needed a touch-up."

Will tried not to panic. He had a tendency to be
overprotective when it came to his mother, but he
couldn't help it. She was all the family he had.

"The ladder slipped and I had a teeny little fall."

"Where are you? On the ground? Is anything broken?"

"Honey, stop freaking out. Mary from next door
heard the fall and drove me to the hospital. It's just a
small fracture in my hip, so—"

"I'll be there this afternoon. I'll call you back as
soon as I've made the travel arrangements."

Will immediately arranged for his pilot to be at the airport in thirty minutes. He would call Angelina once his mother's situation was under control.

For the next several hours he was on the phone, either talking with the best doctors in the country about flying them out to the small hospital in New York, or dealing with urgent issues at PTI. By the time he got to the hospital, he was exhausted and frustrated.

His mother was propped up in bed sketching when he walked in. She looked up from her drawing and held her arms out, overjoyed to see him.

"Come give me a hug!" Joyce held him tight for a moment. "Well, if you aren't just as gorgeous as ever." Peering at him more closely, she added, "Definitely tired, though. Anything you want to talk about?"

He groaned. He had forgotten about her eagle eye. Hoping to distract her, he said, "I'm here to talk about you. I've called several specialists from New York City and—"

She held up a hand to halt him. "I know you want the best care for me, honey, and I appreciate it, but I'm just fine here with the local doctors." Will opened his mouth to protest. "I won't hear any more about it. The doctors have been wonderful and I've seen the X-rays. All I've got is a slight hip fracture."

"But, Mom—"

"My favorite son just flew all the way out here to see me, and I don't want to argue with him."

"I'm your *only* son."

Joyce grinned merrily. "That's right, isn't it? So then, let's talk about you."

He pulled up the nearest chair and plopped down into it, knowing he wasn't prepared to deal with Sergeant Mom in his current state of mind. Somewhat sarcastically, he said, "Would it help if I just gave you my diary?"

"I didn't know you kept a diary."

"I don't."

His mother's peals of laughter, which could be heard down the hall, brought in the troops. Half an hour later, Will was sure he had met every doctor, nurse and secretary who worked in the hospital. He was worn-out from all the handshaking and small talk, but it was a heck of a lot better than the maternal inquisition.

When the meet and greet had ended, Joyce said, "What do you bet every mother within fifty miles with an unmarried daughter is getting on the phone right about now?" Seeing his look of alarm, she said, "Sorry, honey. Word travels fast when an available, good-looking, successful man comes to town."

Taking pity on her son, certain that the troubled look on his handsome face had something to do with a woman—and that there would be plenty of time to get to the bottom of everything tomorrow—she said, "Why don't you head out to the cabin before the wannabe blushing brides show up? The guest room is all made up for you." Glancing out the window, she said, "I'd hurry to the house if I were you. I think I see the young ladies arriving already."

Will grabbed his car keys and gave her one last peck on the cheek. "I'll be back first thing in the morning." He raced out to his rental car, pretending he didn't hear any of the women calling after him.

ANGELINA BARELY MADE IT to the end of what had been an awful day. She'd had one problem after another and everything was made worse because she could not stop thinking about her encounter with Will in the restaurant last night.

Frankly, she was surprised by her own behavior. She had never been a bitter or jealous person. She was the one who had done Susan wrong, not the other way around.

But now the dam on her feelings for Will seemed to have broken and she couldn't figure out how to rebuild it.

Hoping to clear her heart and soul by working up a sweat in her garden, she stripped off her professional clothes, pulled on her comfortable, faded gardening duds, grabbed her clogs and gloves from the closet, and headed out to the backyard.

"Weeds. Perfect." She bent down and started yanking them out. With wild abandon, she weeded like never before.

Just as she was laying into another patch of dandelions, she heard the phone ring and ran inside, kicking off her clogs. She tried to convince herself she was anxious to get the call because it might be an important client, but she knew she was hoping it was Will on the line.

"Angelina?"

Hearing Susan's perky voice on the other end, Angelina stifled a groan and pulled off her gardening gloves. "Susan, it's so nice to hear from you," she lied.

"I wanted to call to thank you for working so closely with Will."

Angelina gulped in a mouthful of air and choked. She had never dreamed that her life could turn into such a ridiculous soap opera.

"His office looks better than I've ever seen it before. But that's not really why I'm calling. I hired you because of your reputation as the Feng Shui Cupid. I wanted you to reunite me with Will, as you well know, but I want to let you know that I've changed my mind."

"You've changed your mind?" Angelina echoed. "Why?"

"I've finally accepted the fact that I'm not the woman of Will's dreams. And he isn't the man of my dreams, either."

Angelina's mouth had fallen open and she was completely speechless. "I, uh…" she began, but thankfully, Susan was on one of her rolls.

"And, Angelina, it's okay. For the first time, I have a feeling that Will is going to be really happy. Even if it's not with me. In fact," Susan added, "I'd like to have you come over to my house for a consultation. It's time for me to finally get on with my own life."

Moments later, as Angelina hung up with a new consultation penciled into her calendar, all of her preconceived ideas about Susan had flown out the window. Susan certainly wasn't the fly-by-night, ditzy blonde that she looked to be. Hidden beneath her surface perfection was a deeply intuitive heart.

All this made Angelina wonder: If she'd been wrong about Susan, could she be wrong about Will, too?

CHAPTER EIGHT

WILL RELAXED the minute he entered his mother's house. Nearly every room in the small cabin looked out onto the lake, and there were memories of laughter and happiness all around him. After locking the front door to keep out any single women on the prowl, he picked up the phone and dialed Angelina's number, but he got her voice mail again.

Not comfortable with the idea of pouring his feelings out to her voice mail, Will vowed to call her again in the morning to set things straight. He just hoped she wouldn't hang up when she heard his voice.

He was used to getting what he wanted regardless of the obstacles in his way. But for some reason, dealing with Angelina was proving to be the most difficult test of his life.

None of his current worries, however, stopped him from having a romantic dream about her that night. He woke up at 5:00 a.m., images of her beauty, her smile, still vivid in his head. He went into the kitchen, plugged in his computer and got online, hoping work would ease the ache he felt inside.

It didn't.

Will was back at the hospital at 8:00 a.m. sharp. His mom was already sitting up in bed and drawing in her sketchbook.

"Good morning, honey. Didn't get much sleep last night, did you? Want to talk about it?" At Will's stunned look, she said with a twinkle of mischief in her eyes, "I have all-seeing-mother abilities."

Will rolled his eyes, although what she said was true.

"Besides," she added, "I've got nothing better to do until the doctor agrees to let me go home today, so you may as well eat some of this god-awful food on my tray and tell me everything."

Will laughed. He sometimes forgot how different his mother was from every other mother in the world. Spending time with her was more like hanging out with one of the guys. Well, sort of, anyway, if one of the guys was his mom.

He bit into the muffin she handed him and had to go spit it out in the bathroom sink. "I think they baked cement into it."

"There's gum in my purse." Not missing a beat, she asked pointedly, "So, who is she?"

Will looked up from digging in her bag for the gum.

"You have 'woman trouble' written all over you." Joyce folded her hands on her lap. "Why don't you start at the beginning?"

By the time Will made it to the end of his story, Joyce was worn-out from holding in her laughter. One day he would be able to see the humor in the situation, but right now he was too overwhelmed by what sounded to her like love at first sight.

Will's cell phone rang, and as he spent a few minutes dealing with a corporate issue, Joyce developed a plan.

Later that day, happily settled back at home with

her paints and canvas, she sent Will off to the grocery store and put her plan into action.

She picked up the phone and dialed Information. "I'd like the number for an Angelina Morgan in San Francisco, please."

Five minutes later, Joyce called the airline and charged one first-class plane ticket to her infrequently used credit card. She was happy that some of the money Will insisted on depositing into her savings account each month was finally being put to good use.

ANGELINA STILL WASN'T exactly sure what had happened. One minute she was being clearheaded and firm with Will's mother, explaining how it was impossible for her to rearrange her schedule to fly to New York for a consultation. Angelina told her that she'd be happy to give her the number of an excellent consultant in New York. She was also very clear about the fact that five thousand dollars was far too much money to pay for her services. But the next thing she knew she was in her bedroom packing an overnight bag, and an airport limo was parked in her driveway.

On the drive to the airport, she wondered what the real story was behind the out-of-the-blue phone call. She didn't believe for one minute that Will's mother desperately needed her expertise. But since it would be several more hours before she could get any real answers, she tried to relax and enjoy the new experience of flying first-class.

It really was very nice, she admitted as she chose *Breakfast at Tiffany's* to watch on the personal DVD player the flight attendant gave her. She couldn't help but enjoy the gourmet meal they offered a little while later.

Kicking out the footrest, she accepted the glass of champagne the stewardess offered her at the end of the movie, and closed her eyes. Later tonight would be soon enough to unravel everything connected with this last-minute trip. Right now she was going to concentrate on savoring this small taste of the good life.

JOYCE LOOKED UP at the clock. 9:00 p.m. "Honey, I'm going to turn in now."

Will looked up from his laptop. "Do you need help with anything?"

She wheeled over to him in her on-loan wheelchair. "Just give me a kiss on the cheek and I'll roll away."

Will chuckled. "You're pretty good with that thing. Where'd you learn to maneuver it so well?"

His mother winked at him. "I'd tell you, but then I'd have to run over your toes." She paused, her smile softening. "It really is nice to have you home for a few days."

"Next time, you don't have to throw yourself off a ladder to get me here."

Joyce was laughing as she wheeled off out of the living room, leaving Will alone with his thoughts. All day, he'd been calling Angelina, but every time, her voice mail picked up.

Whenever he had a problem, he'd always been able to find a good solution. But he was floored by his continuing ineptitude in dealing with Angelina. He wished he could find a way to make things right with her.

Just then, a knock sounded at the door. He prayed that it wasn't another young woman sent over by her parents to meet him. He opened the door slowly, expecting the worst.

He couldn't believe his eyes. "Angelina?"

"Will? What's going on?"

Angelina looked even better in real life than she had in his dreams. Her clothes were slightly rumpled, but rumpled looked amazing on her.

"I've just flown all the way across the country and all you can do is stand there gaping at me?"

Will wasn't sure what possessed him just then. He knew he should have better control over his baser urges, but he just didn't.

"You're right. I should have done this instead." He reached for the woman he hadn't been able to stop thinking about.

And kissed her.

ANGELINA WAS SO SURPRISED by Will's kiss that she kissed him back.

It should be illegal for anyone to kiss as well as he did, she thought. Will deepened the kiss, and Angelina whimpered in response. But when Will made a low sound of pleasure deep in his throat, Angelina immediately crashed back into the real world.

She broke off the kiss and stumbled away from him, hating the fact that he was too darn potent for her to be able to think rationally. "Stop trying to confuse me. Tell me what's going on right now," she insisted, congratulating herself on her fairly poised delivery, considering that she felt as put together as an unmade puzzle.

"I don't know. I have no idea why you're here. All I know is that I've been calling you every hour for two straight days. You have no idea how frustrating it is when all I get is your voice mail. But now you're here, standing right in front of me."

Angelina was stunned by his soliloquy. "You've been trying to contact me for two days?"

"Maybe I should have left a message, but I wanted to explain things in person."

He wanted to *explain things*. It was too close to what Bryce had said to her at the end of that fateful summer. Will had just kissed her as if he was dying of thirst and she was a glass of water. But when was she going to learn that passionate kisses didn't mean anything to men like them?

Trying for mature, hoping for calm, Angelina managed to say, "It's okay. You don't need to explain anything to me."

"I don't?"

She pasted a cheerful smile on her face. "I understand perfectly."

"You do?"

"Of course."

"But—"

Angelina cut him off before he could say anything more. Needing to take control of the situation, she faked a yawn. "I guess your mom didn't tell you that she asked me to come and meet with her. It's late, and if I'm going to have a good consultation with your mother tomorrow morning, I'd better get some rest."

"My mother called you?"

Angelina stared at him in disbelief.

CHAPTER NINE

JUDGING BY THE LOOK on Angelina's face, he knew she wouldn't believe him if he told her the truth. Frankly, he was having a hard time believing what his mother had done. She was worse than any of the other scheming mothers he'd encountered during the past twenty-four hours.

But was it wrong to be so pleased by her meddling?

"I hate to tell you this, but there's only one spare bedroom."

A look of utter disbelief and exhaustion settled over Angelina's face.

Will cleared his throat and jammed his hands in the pockets of his jeans. He wanted to reach out for Angelina to comfort her, but something told him his touch wouldn't be welcome. Not when she was so clearly upset with both him and his mother.

"I'm going to grab my stuff right now and clear out so you can have it."

He groaned inwardly, knowing that there was no way he was going to be able to get any sleep on the couch in the living room, with Angelina just a wall away. As it was, he was fighting the urge to pull her back into his arms.

How could it be that in weeks he had gone from

being perfectly sane and in charge of his life to losing control over everything?

Right now, his only chance at temporary sanity was to dunk himself in the cold lake.

IT TOOK WILL only five minutes to pack up his things, but Angelina swore it took an hour. He must know the effect he had on her. She was absolutely certain he was deliberately torturing her.

When he finally said, "Good night," without turning to face her, then shut the door behind him, Angelina fell onto the bed gasping for air. She had been holding her breath while Will was in the bedroom with her. Within seconds, a bone-deep exhaustion hit her, and she couldn't even muster up the energy to brush her teeth or take off her clothes.

She woke up at midnight, momentarily disoriented before she remembered where she was. In New York. At Will's mother's house.

His scent was all over the sheets and the pillowcase. It was self-torture lying there, breathing him in, having no choice but to relive the sweetness of his kisses.

She sat up in bed and brushed the hair away from her face. Maybe a walk in the brisk night air would help to clear her mind. Stripping off her horribly wrinkled clothes, she rummaged around in her luggage for a pair of jeans. She slipped them on, along with a hooded sweatshirt.

A door from her room led out to the lake. She stepped out onto the deck and the moonlit view took her breath away.

She would never grow tired of the vision of still

water at night with the moon's reflection upon it. For a moment, she felt a deep sense of peace.

Angelina stepped onto the sand, which was cool and damp beneath her toes, ready to feel the water lapping against her legs. But when she heard a splash she stopped dead in her tracks. She moved quickly to hide behind a large tree trunk.

What was Will doing swimming in the middle of the night?

Afraid to even breathe for fear he might discover her spying, she remained standing behind the tree, gaping as he rose up out of the lake. Even though she could see that he was wearing swim trunks, he was still so physically beautiful that just looking at him took her breath away.

When she inadvertently gasped, she clamped a hand over her mouth, praying he hadn't heard her.

No such luck. Will stopped his progression out of the water. "Is someone out there?"

Angelina forced herself not to act like a coward. Stepping around the tree trunk, she said, "I just came outside for some air. I'll go back in now so you can finish your swim in privacy."

He called out, "Come in the water. It feels great."

She had no idea her heart could race so fast. She was so tempted—more tempted than she should have been. "No, I can't do that."

"There's nothing like a midnight swim beneath a full moon," he told her in a gentle voice that resonated all the way through her.

The picture he painted was tempting. Incredibly tempting. She could see the scene play out in her head—she'd join him in the water and then they'd end up kissing again…or more.

And then she'd hate herself in the morning.

Still, she had to force herself to say, "Good night, Will," and turn back toward the cabin.

Back in the bedroom, Angelina stared at the four walls until she began to notice all of the cute touches in the cabin she hadn't seen earlier that night. The walls and the ceiling were done in a beautiful pickled pine. The room was bright and clean, yet warm and relaxed at the same time. Will's mother had a natural gift for balance and comfort.

And above the bed hung one of the most beautiful paintings Angelina had ever seen.

A man and a woman were entwined on the sand. Love radiated from them.

It was exactly the kind of love she longed for…and feared she'd never find.

CHAPTER TEN

THE NEXT MORNING, Will was up and staring blankly at his laptop when his mother came rolling into the kitchen, looking worlds better than she had the previous day. Joyce whirled around in her wheelchair and poured herself a cup of coffee.

"Angelina get here all right?"

"She certainly did." Will looked accusingly at his mother. "And what a surprise her arrival was."

"Don't you take that tone of voice with me, young man. If I want to hire a feng shui expert, I'll damn well do it."

Will had to work to fight back a grin. "If that's your version of the tough-mom routine, it needs a little work."

Joyce chuckled. "I thought the *damn* added a nice dramatic flair."

Right then, Angelina walked out of the guest bedroom, and Will momentarily forgot his mother was even in the room. Angelina looked more gorgeous than ever.

But while he couldn't take his eyes off her, she didn't even seem to know he was in the room as she rushed over and clasped his mother's hands in hers.

"Joyce, it is such a pleasure to meet you."

"Likewise, my dear. I hope your trip wasn't too tiring."

Angelina paused and then murmured something about it being fine. "How are you feeling this morning?" She regarded Joyce's wheelchair and cast sympathetically.

"Not too well, I'm afraid," Joyce responded, forcing her eyes away from Angelina's sharp gaze, lest she give away her game.

Will's eyes shot to his mother's face. He thought about calling her bluff, but she was having such a good time trying out her new acting skills, he let it go.

"Honey," Joyce said, turning to Will, "Margie is expecting you to go over right now to pick up some treats she made."

"But, Mom," he complained, sounding less like a full-grown CEO and more like a little boy who wasn't getting his way, "all of her daughters were over here yesterday dropping off food. What else could they possibly have made for us between now and then?"

Joyce shooed him out of the kitchen, deftly using her wheelchair to get him moving toward the front door. "And remember, dear, be nice to all of her lovely girls. I'm sure they'll want to have a good long chat with you since you were too busy to talk yesterday." After he closed the door behind him, Joyce wheeled back into the kitchen. "Sit down, dear, and I'll make you a cup of tea."

Angelina just wanted to get the consultation over and done with, but she knew when she was beaten, so she dutifully took a seat.

She sat quietly at the kitchen table while Joyce boiled the water. Even with Will's mother confined to a wheelchair, Angelina had a feeling she was barely going to be able to keep up with her.

Joyce handed her a steaming cup of chamomile tea. "I hope you don't mind how insistent I was about having you come out to New York to meet with me."

Angelina wasn't sure how to respond. The truth was, she did mind. Not because she had anything against Will's mother, but because she couldn't handle being this close to her son.

Joyce waved away any answer she might have come up with. "Frankly, it's not me I'm worried about—it's Will."

Angelina was thankful she'd just swallowed her mouthful of tea. Otherwise she would have spit it out.

"I think you need to know about his father."

"Joyce, I think we should be focusing on you if we're going to—" she began, but Will's mom cut her off.

"When Will was young, he idolized his father, Howard. You should have seen them—wherever Howard was, you were sure to find Will. If Howard was building something, Will had his toy hammer out and was pounding on blocks. He was five years old when his father left without saying goodbye.

"Before Howard left, Will was carefree, happy. He loved to paint with his fingers—anywhere and everywhere. I should know," she said, chuckling softly. "I spent hours cleaning finger paint off the walls and the furniture." Too quickly, the smile fell from her face. "Then, overnight, Will stopped being a child. He shouldered the burden that his father left behind. Even when he was a little boy he tried to be the man of the house. It was as if he felt that it was up to him to support us both. No matter how much I tried to let him know that I could take care of us, he always felt responsible for me." Joyce looked up at Angelina, her eyes glazed with unshed tears. "The worst thing, though, was when he told me he was never going to have children of his own."

"Why would he say a thing like that?" Angelina asked.

Joyce shook her head. "He has some crazy notion that he's going to be just like Howard. That he'll let down his own children."

"Will would never do that," Angelina protested hotly. "He's amazing with kids."

Joyce nodded in agreement. "I know that, and you know that, but he doesn't seem to." She cleared her throat. "I know I sound like a meddling mom, but yesterday I saw a joy in him I haven't seen in almost thirty years—when he was telling me about you." Angelina's mouth fell open, but no sound came out. "And now that we've met, I like you just as much as I thought I would."

Angelina didn't know what to say. "Joyce, I thought you wanted a feng shui consultation." She was barely able to get the words out with so many conflicting thoughts swirling inside her head.

Will's mother patted her hand. "Oh, honey, I do. But I truly am exhausted. Do you mind if we postpone the consultation until later this afternoon?"

Angelina had no choice but to nod helplessly.

Joyce grabbed her empty teacup and put it in the sink, but before she wheeled herself out of the kitchen and into her bedroom, she turned back with concern in her eyes. "Suddenly I feel terrible about all of this. I've never been a matchmaker before. I'm afraid I'm not very good at it. I hope one day you will forgive me."

Angelina smiled. "Joyce, there's nothing to forgive." She couldn't blame Will's mother for the state of her heart, or even for cajoling her into coming out to New

York. "I'm the one who decided to get on that plane. I could have said no."

With that, Joyce gave Angelina a wide smile, then wheeled out of the room.

Having said as much to Joyce, Angelina had to finally face the truth. No matter what she tried to tell herself to protect her heart, she had walked on that plane because she wanted to find out more about Will from the person closest to him.

She threw on a sweater to ward off the slight chill in the air and stepped through the sliding door and onto the back deck of the house, which overlooked the lake.

Angelina couldn't help but be delighted by the beauty all around her. The water was so perfectly blue she felt as if someone must have painted it. Poplar and birch trees blanketed the mountains surrounding the lake. She felt as if the mountains were wrapping their arms around her, whispering softly that everything was going to be okay.

Throughout her life, whenever Angelina was grappling with problems, she had found her answers by spending time in nature. It occurred to her now, as she walked through the incredible Adirondack Park, that living amid suburban sprawl in California had her on the verge of losing touch with the natural surroundings that were integral to her peace of mind and happiness. Yuppie heaven and high tech were hardly her style.

A voice in her heart told her she wasn't in the right place anymore. Suddenly, Angelina longed to be back in a quiet community where people were more concerned with who was throwing the weekend barbecue than who had the newest cell phone.

As she walked past the cute cottages, people of all

ages waved at her while they gardened or played with their kids on the beach. What would it be like to live on this lake? It was a crazy thought, but something about it felt so right. At the same time, Angelina didn't know if she could trust herself to make the right decisions about her life, considering that she seemed to make all the wrong decisions about men.

She sat down on the public dock and gazed out at the lake. A family of ducks swam under the dock, but she was so engrossed in her thoughts she hardly saw them. Will scared the daylights out of her when he plopped down beside her.

When her heart rate returned to normal, she asked, "How were things with Margie's daughters?"

He put his head in his hands. "Worse than you could ever imagine. They had actually put together a scrapbook of articles about me."

In a soft voice she said, "Why didn't you tell me the truth about who you are? Krista was the one to tell me to check out the latest copy of *People*."

"I know it might sound ridiculous, but when you get to be a public person, you become suspicious about why people want to be around you." He looked up at the blue sky, as if looking for assistance in what he was going to say next. "At first, when we met, I assumed you knew who I was. But when you didn't know what I did for a living, it was such a relief."

"I suppose," Angelina conceded, "it must be hard to be so well-known."

"The truth is, I can't remember the last time someone was interested in me, instead of what I could do for them. Until I met you. That's why I didn't want you to know too much about me."

"How could you think that something as stupid as how much money you have in the bank, or how many times your picture appears in magazines, matters to me?"

Will turned and held her heated gaze. "I've never met anyone like you."

All of her anger evaporated with that simple sentence. She was unable to drop her eyes, unable to break the fragile bond that they were building.

"Can you forgive me?" He grasped her hand tightly in his own.

She wondered, for a moment, what he wanted her forgiveness for. For lying to her? Or for being a better man than she had the grace to admit he was?

Suddenly, she forgave him everything. She had no choice. Her feelings for him were that strong. "Yes, I forgive you."

She thought he was going to lean in to kiss her and she could hardly wait to feel the sweet pressure of his lips on hers. Instead, he stood and reached out a hand to help her up.

"So, tell me, what were you thinking so hard about before I got here?"

Angelina reeled slightly from the change of subject. "I wasn't thinking about anything much," she lied, knowing she couldn't possibly admit that she'd been thinking about him. "Your mother said she was going to rest a little, but I'm sure she's waiting for me by now. I should be heading back."

Will, who hadn't let go of her hand, said, "Not so fast. Mom can wait. Right now, I want to take you with me to my favorite place."

Now that he was being straight with her, she didn't

even bother to protest. She wanted to be with him more than she wanted to leave, so she followed him willingly to his car. "Where are you taking me?"

He waggled his eyebrows at her. "The information on this trip is on a need-to-know basis. And you, sweet Angelina, don't need to know."

A few minutes later, they arrived at the site of a small carnival, complete with a Ferris wheel, a miniature roller coaster, an arcade and a booth selling cotton candy and toffee-covered popcorn.

He was out in a flash to open her car door. Her hand in his, he made a beeline for the Ferris wheel.

"Madam," he said as he paid for their tickets then helped her into the slightly battered seat on the vintage ride, "your carriage awaits."

Amazingly, Angelina really did feel like a princess. They inched closer and closer to the top as the rest of the passengers boarded. When they reached the very top, he said, "When I was a kid, I thought this was the top of the world. I would save all my paper-route money and come here with a fistful of nickels, over and over again, just to see what the world looked like from the sky."

Angelina followed his gaze out across the lake to the thick forest beyond. "It's incredibly beautiful."

"Every summer I'd memorize this picture, trying to keep it with me for the next nine months until I could come back."

She felt as if she was looking straight into his heart. "Couldn't you have taken a photograph to keep with you?"

"A picture could never do this justice. I tried to paint it once in college, but…" He stopped short.

Angelina was surprised to learn Will could paint, and for a moment she was utterly speechless. By the time she pulled herself together, all she could manage was a lame "I didn't know you painted." Realizing she sounded like an idiot, she added, "Except for finger paints, that is."

He gave her a confused look, so she explained, "Your mother told me how you used to smear finger paints all over the house when you were a little boy."

He was quiet for a long moment. "Funny. I don't remember that."

She laughed. "She definitely does." Will grinned and Angelina fit the puzzle pieces together. "You really take after her, don't you?"

"I wish. I used to fiddle with painting in college, but eventually I accepted that the only way I was ever going to make a living was out in the real world, working in an office like everyone else."

Even as she listened to Will's flippant remarks about his artistic talent, or lack thereof, Angelina guessed he was being far harder on himself than any art critic or teacher could have been. Not only was he discounting all of his special talents that made it possible for him to start a Fortune 500 company, but she could hear the passion and longing in his voice when he talked about painting, no matter how he tried to disguise it.

Their ride was soon over and she lost her chance to probe deeper into Will's artistic past. He grabbed her hand and directed them across the park to the mini roller coaster. After they were seated, Angelina said, "You should know, I'm not very good on roller coasters."

Will gestured to the pint-size ride. "Even ones with butterflies and sunflowers painted on the side?"

"Even those." At his look of disbelief, she explained, "When I was about five, a fair came to our town in Idaho. It had a roller coaster like this one and I begged my father to let me ride it, even though he said I was too small."

Will gave Angelina a slow smile. "Let me guess. You didn't give up until you got your way."

She lightly punched him on the arm before continuing her story. "I still remember that ride. It was the scariest thing I had ever done. I screamed 'Let me off!' the entire time."

He was obviously trying to hold in his laughter. "Go ahead," she said, poking a finger in his chest, "laugh at me. But just wait until this thing gets going and I scream so loud you go deaf."

He wrapped his arms around her and kissed her forehead. "You probably just needed someone to hold you tight."

She tensed as the ride started, but his body was so warm against hers, and his arms felt so safe around her, that she was surprised to find herself actually enjoying it.

A couple of minutes later when the coaster came to a stop, he helped her step safely back to the ground. "So, how was it?"

She smiled up at him. "I can't believe it," she marveled. "It was almost fun!"

"Now, that's almost a resounding endorsement for the hug-you-tight technique," he teased. Putting one arm around her, he steered them toward the cotton-candy booth. "Now that we've worked up an appetite, it's time for sustenance."

He bought them each a huge stick of cotton candy and an enormous bag of popcorn to share. They took their feast out to the end of the public pier and stuffed themselves.

Mouth full of sticky spun sugar, Angelina said, "I don't normally eat this kind of stuff."

Will gave her a wolfish glance. "It shows."

She blushed and stuffed a hunk of cotton candy into his mouth so he couldn't say anything else to embarrass her. *"Mmph, mmph, mmph,"* he grunted.

"Don't you know you're not supposed to talk with your mouth full?" she scolded, her eyes twinkling.

Finally, after another couple of sticky bites, Angelina's aching stomach got her attention. "Ugh," she said, sitting back with her hands holding her flat stomach. "I just had one too many mouthfuls of sugar."

"Me, too," he said, tossing the rest of his cotton candy into a nearby garbage can.

As they sat next to each other, feet dangling over the end of the pier, Angelina thought about how good it felt to be with Will. Just hanging out and having fun, Angelina felt at this moment that she had everything in the world she would ever need.

Could it be? Had she finally been able to work her Feng Shui Cupid magic on herself?

CHAPTER ELEVEN

BY THE TIME they made it back to Will's mother's house, Joyce was up and painting at her easel in the living room. "How was the carnival?"

Angelina opened her mouth to ask how Joyce could possibly have known that they were at the fair, but Will reached for one of her hands and held it up. "Pink hands. This stuff is impossible to wash off. Mom always caught me when I tried to sneak junk food."

"Which was, if I recall correctly, every single day," Joyce added, trying to assume a repressive motherly look and failing badly.

Angelina laughed, enjoying the interaction between Will and his mother. Still, she couldn't help but think that she should have been working with her client all this time. "I'm sure you didn't fly me all the way out here to ride roller coasters and eat cotton candy with your son, so if you will just give me a moment to wash up, we can get started. If you're up to it, of course."

"Go ahead and take your time washing up. I need to clean out my brushes anyway."

When Angelina had left the room and closed the guest bedroom door firmly behind her, Will muttered, "If she only knew how wrong she is."

"Speak up, sonny boy, old ladies are present."

Will barked out a laugh. "Playing that old-lady card

again, are you? As if you won't be able to outrun me the day you get out of that wheelchair." Noting the smug look on his mother's face, he turned the tables. "All I was saying was that you did, in fact, fly her all the way out here to ride roller coasters and eat cotton candy with your son."

Joyce tried to affect a bewildered look, but when Will said, "Just admit it," she let it fall away. He would have said more, but his cell phone rang and he excused himself to answer it, taking the call outside on the front porch.

Joyce breathed a sigh of relief that she had been saved by the bell. Not that she had anything to apologize for, of course. From everything she had seen so far between her son and Angelina, it seemed that her matchmaking plan was working quite well indeed.

ANGELINA WASHED HER HANDS with soap and hot water in the guest bathroom and wondered about the glowing woman staring back at her in the mirror. Her eyes were bright from something stronger than sugar or carnival rides.

She looked like a woman who was falling in love.

She loved the way Will cared for his mother. She loved how hard he'd tried to be the man of the house when his father had left them. She loved the way he made her laugh and how he'd held her tight when she was frightened on the roller coaster.

And, oh, did she love his kisses.

Alarmed by the strength of her feelings, Angelina splashed her face with cool water, then let it run over her hands until they were practically numb.

She hoped she could mask her feelings from his

mother, even though she was pretty sure it was a pointless endeavor. Joyce noticed everything around her—so
there was no way she could be blind to the way Angelina felt about her son.

Joyce was just laying her last brush down to dry
in the kitchen when Angelina stepped into the living
room. "Where should we start?"

Angelina quickly scanned the room and noted that
Will was gone. "The kitchen is just fine."

Angelina hoped they could get through the open
kitchen, dining and living room before Will reappeared.
She had a terrible hunch that if he was in the room,
she wouldn't be able to concentrate on anything at all.

Working on the main rooms in the cottage ended
up being a quick affair, just as Angelina had thought
it might be. They moved a rocking chair to a different corner of the living room so that people wouldn't
trip over it. Then they put up a small mirror behind
the stove so that Joyce would be able to see what was
going on behind her while she was cooking.

When they moved into the guest bedroom, Angelina
said, "Joyce, this watercolor above the bed is one of the
most beautiful paintings I have ever seen."

"I agree. Will has more innate talent than any painter
I have ever known."

Angelina's mouth fell open. "Will created this mas-
terpiece?" Quickly, she put two and two together. "He
did the watercolor oceanscape in his house, too, didn't
he?"

"He certainly did," Joyce replied, full of pride. "He
was only twenty-one when he painted it."

Before Angelina could remind herself to keep a professional distance, she said, "But, Joyce, Will told me

today he wasn't good enough. How he had to accept his lack of talent and get a normal job to earn a paycheck. But you know what? I didn't believe him. I couldn't. Not when I heard the passion for art in his voice. I saw his love of painting in his eyes."

She looked up finally, realizing she had just aired all of her private thoughts—and feelings—to Will's mother. "Forgive me," she said, feeling horribly embarrassed. "I don't mean to be babbling like this. I'm just so surprised."

Joyce patted her hand. "No need to apologize to me. I know exactly how you feel. The day he came home with all of his brushes and canvases packed up in a crate, telling me he was finished painting, saying he was done fooling around—it broke my heart."

As they made their way through the rest of the house, Angelina couldn't help but wonder what had happened to the boy who had wanted to be a painter, but gave it up to carry the weight of the world on his shoulders instead.

THEY HAD JUST walked back into the kitchen when Will stepped inside, stuffing his cell phone into his pocket. It was clear to both women that something was very wrong.

He ran his right hand through his hair. "I've got to get back to California right away." In answer to both women's perplexed stares, he said, "Looks like the new CFO is trying to convince the board to have me removed." Turning to his mother, he asked, "Will you be all right without me?"

Joyce patted his hand. "I'll be fine. I'm just glad

you were able to come at all. Soon you can come back out for a vacation."

"How would you like a ride back in my private jet?" Will asked Angelina. "It's waiting for us at the airstrip."

Angelina looked back and forth from Will to Joyce, trying to make up her mind. "Your mother already purchased a first-class ticket for me, and I don't want to waste her money."

"Don't worry," Joyce said, a grin on her lips. "I used Will's money to pay for your ticket. It's the only time I've ever used that ridiculous credit card he set up for me. I should really get rid of it. Go with him. His private plane is really fun."

As soon as Angelina left the room, Will spoke softly. "Thanks, Mom, for bringing Angelina here." He couldn't say anything more. Not until he and Angelina talked about their future—a future he wanted more than anything.

Joyce wheeled up to Will. He bent down and she kissed him softly on the cheek. "You're welcome."

Angelina hugged Joyce goodbye and ten minutes later she was walking up the small flight of steps that led to the interior of Will's private plane. It was more sumptuous than anything she could have imagined. He gave her a tour and she was amazed to find that the jet even had a bedroom on board.

Moving back into the seating area, she remarked, "This is even better than first class."

Will laughed. "It's not bad."

"Take it for granted, do you?"

He looked around at the thick leather seats, the huge entertainment center on the wall behind the cockpit, the decked-out bar, and the bookshelf full of current magazines and his favorite books. "No, I don't. It's more like I don't always feel that I deserve it. Does that make sense?"

Angelina cocked her head to the side. "Do you really feel that way?"

Instead of answering, Will helped her get seated and then popped his head into the cockpit to give the pilot the go-ahead.

"What can I get you to drink?"

"Whatever you've got," Angelina said, intent on their conversation. "You haven't answered my question yet."

He poured each of them a glass of merlot, then sat down and buckled in. "Sometimes it feels like the life I've built for myself isn't the one I'm supposed to be living. It's funny, isn't it," he said, "how one day we wake up and wonder why we're doing the things we are doing?"

Angelina nodded and took a sip of red wine for courage. Throwing caution to the wind, she said, "Your painting in the guest room is absolutely stunning."

Myriad expressions crossed Will's face—surprise mixed with pride, finally ending with a shuttering of his eyes, which had been so open to her just moments before. "My mother told you."

Angelina knew she had hit a tender spot, but she refused to back down so easily. "During our consultation, I couldn't help but let her know how much I loved her work, especially the painting in the guest bedroom. She told me you were the painter. Your art is so wonderful, Will. How could you have stopped painting?"

"I never stood a chance out there in the art world."

"And just what evidence do you have for that?"

"What was I supposed to do? Get some galleries to hang up my paintings in the unlikely chance that someone would want to buy them, while my mother worked day and night to support me?"

Angelina swallowed hard, but held his gaze. "Yes. I think that was exactly what you were supposed to do."

ANGELINA COULD SEE that Will was uncomfortable with the way their conversation was going. She felt bad for pushing him, knew that was one of her greatest faults. A feng shui consultant was simply supposed to observe and make suggestions. She'd always been far too invested in what her clients wanted to hold back on any kind of judgment.

But more than anything, she wanted to see Will happy.

"I'm sorry," she said in a soft voice. "I shouldn't have said that."

He was silent for a long moment. Finally, he said, "You surprise me at every turn, Angelina. It's not a bad thing. Not at all."

She reached out for his hands, but holding them wasn't enough. The kiss that came next wasn't enough, either.

Since the moment she'd met this man, she'd been fighting her attraction to him. But now it was more than pure desire that drove her. She was falling in love with him.

And she wanted more.

She stood up. Holding out her hands to him again, she waited until he was standing in front of her.

"I'm so glad I saw your lake. Your paintings. That I was able to meet your mother."

"I am, too, Angelina."

Slowly, she led him away from their seats, toward the back of the plane.

"Now I'd like to take a closer look at your onboard bedroom."

THEY SPENT THE NEXT several hours in the small bedroom kissing, touching, giving and getting pleasure from one another. There were no words of love between them, but Angelina tried to convince herself that they didn't need to speak them aloud.

Not when they were saying everything they needed to say with their bodies.

When the pilot's voice came over the intercom, telling them they would be landing in twenty minutes, they dressed quietly and buckled themselves back into their seats without a word.

"Just in case I get too wrapped up in dealing with the mess at the office, I want you to know I'm thinking of you. Always."

Angelina nodded. "Me, too," she said, too caught up in emotion to say anything more.

"My legal counsel is already here," he said apologetically as he helped her down the steps to the tarmac. "Do you mind if I have my driver take you home?"

Angelina regretted that their idyll had come to an end. The real world had intruded much too soon. "That's fine."

Will bent down to give her a kiss filled with promise, then walked her over to his limo. And as he watched her drive away, more than anything he wished he could go home with her instead of going straight onto a corporate battlefield.

CHAPTER TWELVE

FOR THE NEXT two weeks, Angelina thought of little else but Will. Again and again she replayed their sweet and sensual lovemaking, their wonderful conversations, their spin on the Ferris wheel.

Krista tried to pick up the slack in Angelina's life, getting into the habit of just "dropping by" for coffee or a walk, or the inevitable shopping trip. What great irony it was, Angelina thought later, that the bomb should fall on her while she was in the mall.

In the middle of trying on some designer shoes at Bloomingdale's, Krista suddenly dropped the pair she was trying on. "I need to go to the bathroom. Now."

She dragged Angelina up the escalator and around the formal-wear section into the ladies' room.

"Quick. Give me a tampon," Krista said, holding her hands out to Angelina expectantly.

Angelina frowned. "I don't have any on me."

"You always get your period two days before me."

Angelina did some quick calculating. "I don't have my period, Kris."

"No way. You're regular as clockwork."

Slumping down onto the beaten leather seat in the lounge outside the stall, Angelina felt her world shatter.

"I didn't exactly tell you the whole story about what happened in New York. On the plane, actually." Angelina put her head in her hands for a few moments and then looked up, staring blankly at the wall behind her friend. She whispered, "We had sex."

"On the plane? You slept with Will on his private jet?"

"Yes. It was my idea. I just couldn't wait anymore." She looked up at her friend. "Happy now that you know everything?"

"Only if it was great sex," Krista said, managing to prompt a laugh out of Angelina.

"The best." Angelina slumped deeper into her chair. "What if I'm pregnant?"

Minutes later, they were standing in front of the row of pregnancy tests at the nearby pharmacy. Angelina felt faint. "Kris, what am I doing here?"

"Don't worry, sweetie. I'll be here with you every step of the way." Krista pointed to a bright pink-and-blue-striped box. "This is the one I've seen advertised."

"The one where the perfect couple is deliriously happy and can't wait to add a perfect baby to their perfect life?"

"That's the one." Krista swiped it off the counter and walked up to the checkout line.

Mutely, she followed her best friend out onto the sidewalk. "Thanks for buying that for me."

"No problem, Ang. You shouldn't have to buy this for yourself. It's even worse than buying your first condoms when you're still in high school."

Angelina raised an eyebrow. "I was in college before I did that."

"Speak for yourself. I was in junior high."

Angelina laughed. "You were not, you big bragger."

But when they got in Krista's car, with the ominous

package sitting on her lap, Angelina was far too scared
to smile any more.

What if the line is blue?

ANGELINA PEED on the strip and prayed for pink. After
all, she reasoned, she'd been under a lot of stress, and
that could have made her a few days late.

"I can't take it anymore," Krista said, pushing the door
open and grabbing the indicator strip off the counter, but
Angelina had already seen the results for herself and
slipped down the cold tiles onto her bathroom floor.
Tears spilled down her cheeks. Krista squatted down to
rock Angelina gently back and forth, murmuring that
everything was going to be okay.

"No," Angelina said, wiping the tears from her face
with the backs of her hands. "Everything isn't going
to be okay."

Krista refused to listen. "Once you tell Will, he'll
be thrilled, and—"

"He never wants to have kids," Angelina sobbed,
wiping at her nose with the back of her hand. "People
are always using him because he's rich and famous.
He'll think I got pregnant to get at his money."

"Scoot over," Krista said, sitting next to Angelina
on the floor. "So maybe he said he didn't want kids,
but he's crazy about you and he'd never think something like that."

In an instant, Angelina knew what she had to do.
"I'm not going to tell him. Not yet. Not until I get my
life in order."

"You have to tell him, Ang."

"I will eventually, I promise. I'm going to have this

baby and I'm going to love it so much, but I'm not going to force Will to be a part of it."

"What are you doing?" Krista said as Angelina stood up, walked to her office and turned on her computer.

"I'm finding a house to rent on Wishing Lake and then I'm leaving. As soon as possible."

Krista stood staring at Angelina. "Wait a minute. You don't want to tell Will about the baby yet, but you're going to move to the lake his mother lives on? Won't she know something's up when your belly turns into a beach ball?"

"It's not Joyce's fault that Will doesn't want children. I know she'll be the best grandmother in the world. And, besides, we both know it's time for me to leave suburbia. I need to be a part of nature again." Angelina finished explaining and glanced up at her friend. "Are you going to help me or just stand there looking confused?"

"Give me the phone," Krista said. "I've got some Realtors to call."

WILL FELT AS IF his world had turned upside down. He was knee-deep in the most complex financial and legal negotiations of his career and all he could think about was Angelina. He was sure at least one of the twenty people crammed into the airless boardroom must have picked up on his unusual inattention by now.

Worse still, he had started doodling on his yellow notepad during the endless discussions. Will hadn't even noticed he was drawing until Jerry, his lead counsel who was seated next to him at the head of the large oval table, leaned over and said with a chuckle, "Hey, that's a pretty good likeness of Bob you've drawn there."

Will snapped out of his fog and looked down at his notepad. He had drawn a comical yet accurate caricature of the offending orator, complete with bulging nose, bushy eyebrows and a waistline that had expanded from one too many power lunches.

Hastily, he turned to a fresh page and silently chewed himself out for not keeping closer tabs on the meeting. The fate of his company was at stake, he reminded himself sternly. Couldn't he put up with a few days of stale air and lifeless discussions in order to get things back on track?

Shaking the muddled thoughts and pictures from his head, he struggled to focus on the business at hand. But he found the only way he could hold on to his sanity was by keeping his pen busy on the paper, capturing his version of the events as they unfolded.

Will thought he had completely squashed all remaining urges to create art when he'd packed up his brushes that last year of college. He was amazed to find that suddenly, in the most unlikely of circumstances, his hands and mind wanted to create with a vengeance. After more than ten years away from art, he was increasingly drawn to seeing what he could come up with next, with only a pen and paper as his tools.

While he drew and listened with one ear, he thought about how much he missed Angelina. During the past two weeks, he had barely found the time to call her each evening to check in for a minute or two. It was selfish of him, but he desperately needed to hear her voice each day. When things got really crazy behind closed doors, when voices were raised with threats, and brows were being mopped at the end of the latest round, Will found that just thinking of Angelina and the short time they had spent together made it feel like less of a do-or-die situation.

Interestingly, Will's detachment was throwing his detractors off course. Instead of being the admitted corporate shark he had been for the past decade, he was letting his opponents flail about helplessly by not going up against them. It was yet another thing that he had to thank Angelina for.

Just as this thought crossed his mind, the negotiations escalated to a fever pitch. Excusing himself, he left the room and walked down the hallway until he was outside breathing in fresh air in the parking lot. Moving to lean against the trunk of a tree, he pulled out his cell phone and dialed Angelina's number.

Damn it, he thought when he got her voice mail. He needed to talk to her; he needed to hear her voice.

He didn't know when exactly she had become so important to him. Just that she was.

"Angelina," he said, knowing better than to hang up without leaving a message this time, "I'm calling to let you know that I may be out of touch for another few days." He paused, trying to gather his thoughts. "Things here are at the breaking point and I've got to head deep into the trenches until the war is won." He laughed softly into the phone, his only smile in days. "Sorry about the war metaphors. I guess they don't call it 'corporate warfare' for nothing." He was getting way off track, so he cleared his throat and said, "What I'm trying to say is, I miss you. And even if I don't call you for a while, I'm thinking about you every moment. And I—"

Midsentence, he stopped speaking, realizing he was just about to say, "I love you." Overwhelmed by the force of his emotions, he fumbled out, "And I can't wait to see you again."

He clicked his phone shut and leaned against the tree trunk, wondering when he had become such a bumbling fool. But because it had been a while since he'd slept for more than a few hours at a time, he cut himself some slack. He needed a long hot shower and to sleep for twenty-four hours straight.

He went back inside to face his opponents, and as the corporate battle raged on, he found solace and strength only by drawing Angelina again and again on his yellow notepad. He drew her from every well of memory he could mine—sitting on the dock at the lake, standing on his front porch the day they met, hiking on Angel Island. He even drew her sitting on top of the Ferris wheel with the lake and trees behind her, a place he thought he would never have been able to get right.

But with Angelina smiling up at him from the sketch he had drawn, he suddenly realized that she had been the missing link all along.

ANGELINA HEARD the phone ring and instinctively knew it was Will. She stopped packing up her office and stood still as a statue, afraid to even breathe for some absurd fear that he would hear her and know she was avoiding him.

When the red light on her phone started to blink with a message waiting, she hesitantly picked up the receiver and dialed her mailbox number. At the sound of Will's voice, she wanted nothing more than to weep. But she had promised herself when she woke up that morning, after a long night of tears, that she was going to face her new life—the life she had manifested through her own actions—with a positive outlook. If not for herself, then for her baby.

All day she had been working diligently to get her affairs in order for her big move across country. She had contacted each of her clients with referrals to other consultants, deflecting their questions regarding her sudden change of plans by mustering up a cheerful tone of voice and speaking vaguely about "the wisdom of change."

Angelina, however, wasn't sure that there was anything wise at all about the changes she was making. But she did know she could no longer live fifteen minutes away from the man she loved, with his baby on her hip. Both of their lives, she acknowledged with a further sinking of her heart, would become a media spectacle if and when anyone ever found out.

At the very least, she felt a small measure of peace knowing that Krista had found her a cozy cottage on Wishing Lake in New York and that her child would grow up with a loving grandmother close by. Krista had negotiated a deal with the owner whereby Angelina could lease for six months, and then if she wanted to stay, she would be able to buy it at a fair price.

Joyce was going to be surprised by her sudden return to the lake, and frankly, Angelina wasn't sure when or how she was going to tell Joyce that she was pregnant with Will's baby. No matter how she looked at the situation, it wasn't fair to make Joyce pay for their sins.

The situation with Will, on the other hand, was far less clear. She would have to come clean with him at some point in the future. But first she needed some time to sort things out for herself.

Including how to get over a broken heart, particularly when she'd been instrumental in breaking it herself.

By noon Angelina was utterly exhausted from packing and thinking and worrying. She had just plopped down on the couch in her living room to take a five-minute nap when Krista came barreling through her front door already midsentence.

"...heading out for my lunch break and I thought I'd drop by to see if you wanted anything to... Ang, you look terrible."

Angelina nodded sleepily in agreement. "I'm just so darn tired," she said, yawning halfway through her sentence. "But I still have so much packing to do."

"Nonsense. I'm hiring you a packing company." Angelina started to protest, so Krista said, "It'll be my going-away present to you, even though you know I don't want you to go away."

Angelina kicked her feet up on the ottoman in front of her and closed her eyes. She was just dozing off by the time Krista had completed her call to the moving company. Her best friend shook her awake.

"The movers will be here ASAP. Take the keys to my apartment and go get some sleep. I'll stay here and tell them what to do."

Angelina felt tears spring up in her eyes. She gave Krista a fierce hug. "You're the best."

Krista returned her hug, saying affectionately, "You pregnant women are all so emotional."

"Don't remind me." She took Krista's keys and shoved

them in her pocket. "Are you sure you don't mind taking care of this for me?"

Krista, who had already made herself perfectly comfortable on the couch, waved her out the door. "Go already. Who knows, maybe one of the moving boys will be a cutie."

"What about Derek?"

Krista waved her hand in the air. "His company party isn't until next month. And besides, just because I said I'd go out with him doesn't mean I've got a chastity belt on until then."

Angelina laughed and groaned at the same time. "Thanks, Kris."

"I know you'd do the same for me."

Angelina nodded and walked out the front door. It was true. If Krista ever got in a predicament like the one she was in, she would help her best friend in any way she could.

Who is the one leading a seemingly unblemished life now?

Angelina admitted regretfully that while Krista's life was outwardly wild and reckless, at least she had more sense than to lose her heart to a completely unavailable man and get pregnant all at the same time.

ANGELINA SLEPT like the dead in Krista's apartment. By the time she returned to her house, it was empty except for a suitcase in the foyer with an envelope on it.

Angelina walked through the rooms in disbelief. "How could anyone have possibly packed up my house so quickly?" Her words reverberated off the bare wood floors and empty stucco walls. She went back into the foyer and opened up the envelope.

"What the heck?" A first-class ticket to New York fell out and onto the floor. She picked it up. She was booked on a direct flight to Albany from San Francisco, leaving at 8:00 p.m.

Unfolding the note, she read Krista's flowing handwriting.

Ang,
In case you were wondering, the movers were all cute and I promised that if they got you packed up on the double, I would take them out for a drink. Looks like my little scheme did the trick. (Although I hope they're at least twenty-one… and did I mention how cute they are?) I know you wanted to get out of here as soon as possible, so I booked you a ticket to New York for tonight. No moving gift is complete without first class. The Realtor is expecting you at 8:00 a.m. tomorrow, with the key to your new house. You know I'm no good at goodbyes, so I arranged an airport limo to come and get you. Whatever you need, call me. And keep the sheets clean on your guest bed. You never know when I'll be at your door.
Love, Kris

Angelina leaned heavily against the inside of the front door and held Krista's letter to her chest. She wondered what she had ever done to deserve such an amazing friend. Someday she hoped she could repay her for all of the support she had given her during this impossible time.

The airport limo was already parked in her driveway. She popped her head out the front door, signaling to the driver that she needed a couple more minutes. She picked up her cell phone and made a call.

"Hi, Dad, it's me."

"Hi yourself. Louise and I were just talking about you. We just got back…."

Angelina interrupted. "Listen, Dad, I've got some news for you." Not having the words to tell him the whole truth, she simply said, "I'm going to be out of town for a while and I just wanted you to know." She rushed on before he could ask any questions. "But I haven't forgotten about my promise to help out with your wedding…."

Her dad interjected, sounding a bit sheepish, "Actually, honey, I have some more exciting news for you."

In a rush, he explained, "Louise and I just couldn't wait. We're in Las Vegas and we literally just got married! I was about to call you with the news when I reached for my phone and saw that you were calling me."

Angelina took delight in hearing the excitement in her father's voice. His newfound happiness was so evident. She listened as he gave her all the details and told her about the hotel and the ceremony.

Looking at her watch, Angelina said, "Dad, I hate to interrupt again, but I've got to get to the airport. I'd love to hear more about the wedding and I really want to meet Louise. She sounds perfect for you. How about I call you in the next day or two?"

"Oh, sure thing, sweetie. I can hardly wait for my two best girls to meet each other."

Disconnecting the call and turning to look one last time at what had been a wonderful home, Angelina picked up her suitcase, opened the front door, and walked out toward the limo without a backward glance.

ANGELINA WAS STARING blankly ahead in the waiting area for Gate 15 at SFO when a young couple with a baby sat down next to her. She watched them kiss and cuddle their child and something inside her tore apart. When the mother passed the sweet baby girl to the father, and Angelina saw the look of utter delight on his face as he cooed nonsense words to his daughter, Angelina jumped up out of her seat and ran to the nearest pay phone.

She called Will's house and cell, but wasn't surprised when he didn't pick up. He'd told her in his message that he was going to be on lockdown at his company. She dialed the number for PTI. An operator picked up. "PTI headquarters. How may I direct your call?"

Angelina caught her breath. "I need to speak to Will Scott, please."

The operator sent Angelina's call through. "Will Scott's office."

"This is Angelina Morgan and I need to speak to Will Scott immediately."

"I'm afraid that isn't possible. Mr. Scott is in a meeting right now."

"Please," Angelina begged as the gate attendants began boarding her airplane. "I need to speak with him right away."

"I will direct you to his voice mail—"

"If you would only tell him he has a urgent phone call from Angelina, I know he'll take the call and—"

"I'm sorry, ma'am. Mr. Scott is in closed session with the board. You will have to call back later."

Tears bubbled up again in her eyes as she put down the phone. Ignoring the looks from nearby passengers, she hastily wiped her eyes with the back of her hand and boarded the plane.

CHAPTER THIRTEEN

OVER THE PAST forty-eight hours, Will hadn't slept, shaved, or eaten more than a fistful of pretzels. It might have been delirium kicking in, but for the first time in his career, he couldn't see how any of the crap he was going through to keep control of his company was worth this kind of stress.

More than one person that he had considered a friend had turned on him. Apart from Jerry, there was no one he could trust. Not one of them had proved that they would stick by him when the chips were down, nor trust him to make the best decision for their employees and stockholders.

During the past ten years he had looked forward to what every new day at the helm of his company would bring. But today, everything was different.

No, it wasn't just today, he admitted. Over the past couple of years, as PTI had become bigger and bigger, he rarely—if ever—had a chance to even get close to hands-on with the electronics side of the business. Instead, he was always in boardrooms like this one.

Right now he didn't care about corporate profits. He just wanted to hold Angelina close to him again, laugh with her. He wanted her to remind him, in her straightforward yet captivating way, just how much more there was to life than running a company.

But more than anything, he wanted to tell Angelina how much he loved her.

Will heard one of the lawyers bark out his name. Blinking up at the group of men and women, he felt as if he was seeing them all for the first time. They looked like a bunch of hostages sitting, pacing and even slumped against the floor of the artificially lit board-room. In that moment, something inside him clicked into place.

Standing, a wry smile on his face, he said, "Gentle-men, ladies, this meeting is now adjourned. I will let you know when I make my decision as to the next step in resolving this conflict."

He confidently strode out of the room, a new spring in his step, deaf not only to the cries of outrage from many of the room's occupants, but also to the hallelu-jahs from the older board members who were barely holding on from lack of rest, food and fresh air.

Will quickly debated whether or not to go home and shower before heading to Angelina's house to surprise her, and opted for a quick shower and shave. "Better not go in there smelling like a garbage dump." He laughed aloud as he slid into his car and started the ignition.

For the first time since he'd left Angelina at the air-port, Will felt alive. He rolled the top down and turned on the radio to his favorite classic-rock station. Quickly covering the short distance from his office to his house, he left his car in the driveway and dashed through his front door, stripping off his clothes on the way to the best shower of his entire life.

After drying himself off with a plush towel, he decided his wisest plan of action was to catch a couple of hours of sleep. After all, he thought to himself as he slipped between his sheets, Angelina deserved a coherent declaration of love and a proper marriage proposal. In his slightly delirious, sleep-deprived state he was sure to fumble things and end up sounding like an ass.

Will slept soundly for several hours. Upon waking, he felt better than ever and got ready to go. He dressed quickly and drove the short distance to the mall, heading straight for Tiffany. Nodding in greeting to the many salespeople on the floor who said, "Welcome, Mr. Scott," as he passed by their display cases, he crossed the store and proceeded straight to the back room, which was reserved for regular customers.

Jim, the head salesperson, said, "Mr. Scott, it is my pleasure to see you back in the store again."

"Likewise, Jim," Will replied, a ready smile on his lips. Leaning forward, he lowered his voice in a confidential manner. "I was hoping you could help me with something very important."

"Of course, sir."

"I need you to find me the most exquisite engagement ring you have on the premises."

Jim inclined his head in understanding and prepared to bring back a selection of rings for Will to consider.

"Oh, and, Jim? Could you make sure it has something red in it?"

With a smile and a nod, Jim disappeared into the back room, leaving Will temporarily alone with his thoughts. He couldn't wait for the moment when Angelina became his.

He already knew just what he wanted: a short engagement, a long honeymoon and a family of little girls with Angelina's good looks and quick mind.

FLYING FIRST-CLASS for the second time in her life should have been exciting, but all Angelina did was sleep. "What a waste. If Krista asks, I'm going to tell her that I kept the flight attendants busy the whole time," she whispered to herself after being awoken by the pilot announcing their impending arrival.

An efficient flight attendant must have seen her lips move. "Ms. Morgan, would you like some juice or coffee?"

Angelina mustered up a smile. "I would love a glass of orange juice," she said with a dry tongue, appreciating the perks of flying first-class, knowing full well that the customers behind the thick blue curtain were not having their every whim catered to.

As she took a fortifying gulp of her orange juice, she tried to imagine her new life in a cottage on Wishing Lake. But, instead, all she could think about was Will.

And how much she already missed him.

She put her glass down with a shaky hand, and the flight attendant gave her a quick pat on the shoulder. "All of us have a bad day every now and then, honey. Don't beat yourself up over it. Everything is going to be all right."

Angelina blinked back the tears that sprang into her eyes from such a heartfelt expression of empathy from a total stranger. Leaning back against the soft leather seat, she tried to make believe that everything actually was going to be all right.

WILL DROVE STRAIGHT from the jewelry store to Angelina's house. He wasn't going to let one more thing get between him and the woman he was meant to be with for the rest of his life.

He pulled up to the curb in front of her house and noted that her red VW Bug was not parked in the driveway. "Probably parked in the garage," he said cheerfully to himself.

Tapping his right pocket with the palm of his hand, making sure the engagement ring was still there, he walked confidently up the front path and rang the doorbell. When Angelina didn't answer, he tried the doorknob to see if she had left it unlocked by accident.

It twisted easily in his hand. He rang the doorbell and started to walk inside, a huge smile on his face. He was looking forward to surprising Angelina with his unexpected presence.

He stepped into a completely empty house, unable to believe his eyes.

She was gone.

WILL SPENT THE NIGHT with a bottle of Jack Daniel's, and woke up on his living room floor with a pounding head and a mouth that tasted like old socks. When the doorbell rang, he didn't even realize it was the doorbell. Instead, it sounded like one hundred cannons all firing in his head.

He rolled over into a sitting position, not quite sure what had happened. As he heard a key turn in the lock, he suddenly remembered everything and wished the bottle of whiskey wasn't empty. He badly needed another drink.

The sound of high heels clicking on the wood floor was as painful as someone playing the drums right next to his head. He looked up, bleary-eyed. His ex-wife was standing with her hands on her hips, looking down at him.

"What happened to you?" she said in a strangely serious voice.

"Not so loud. You're killing me with that racket."

"How about this?" she said, as she picked up a large hardcover book from the coffee table and threw it down on the floor.

Will covered his ears with his hands a millisecond too late. "This is what death must feel like," he groaned, squeezing his eyes tightly shut, hoping that when he opened them his nightmare would have ended.

"Not even close," his ex-wife said smoothly as she slid neatly onto the couch and crossed her legs.

"Why are you here?"

"I have spent the past twenty-four hours fielding angry phone calls from the wives of your board members who are worried that they aren't going to be able to make the payments on their vacation homes anymore."

"Oh," Will said, his voice flat.

"Do you mind telling me why you walked out of the most important meeting of your career? I swear," she said, throwing her hands up in the air, "I had no idea what to tell these women. You've always been so incredibly *responsible*."

Will was trying to figure out what the hell he should say, when she spotted the engagement ring lying on the carpet next to the fireplace.

Susan picked up the ring and examined it with a knowledgeable eye. "Wow. What an incredible ring."

Will stared blankly at it.

Susan plopped herself in an uncharacteristically sloppy heap next to him on the carpet. "You bought this for Angelina, didn't you?"

Will snapped out of his drunken stupor in an instant. "How could you possibly have guessed that?"

"I would have had to be completely blind, deaf *and* dumb to have missed the sparks flying between you and Angelina that night at the restaurant. You probably realized pretty quickly that I sent her to work with you because I wanted to try to get back together. But once I saw the kind of chemistry the two of you had, I knew I needed to give you up for good. You never once looked at me the way you were devouring her."

"Susan, I need to apologize to you for being such a jerk for so long," he began awkwardly. "I can't believe I never took the time to find out who you really are on the inside. I was so selfish from the start."

Susan's eyes glistened slightly. "We tried our best to make things work, but we were never right for each other, were we?" Seeming to catch herself before she got all mushy on him, she cleared her throat and held up the ring. "So, now that we've got all of that cleared up, why don't you tell me why this ring was lying over there on the floor?" When he didn't answer right away, she added, "I know I wasn't much of a wife, but I hope I can be your friend."

Will felt tears well up in his eyes, but he couldn't chalk it up to being drunk. For all he'd drunk the night before, he was now stone-cold sober. He reached out for Susan's hand and gave it a quick squeeze. "Thanks, Suze."

His ex gave him a small smile and waited patiently for him to talk.

"Angelina doesn't love me," he said, feeling like a pathetic, wet, shivering dog. "I thought she did, but she doesn't."

"What could she have done to make you believe that?"

"I left those stupid negotiations to go and propose to her, and when I got to her house it was empty. She left—she's gone."

He had opened himself up to Angelina, and she had left with his heart and given no forwarding address.

"Like your father?" Susan asked softly.

His head whipped up. "Excuse me?"

"Will," Susan began, "you've been living your whole life with a wall around your heart because of what your father did to you and your mom when he left. You've been carrying around this misguided sense of responsibility for so long that you haven't even noticed how it's wrecked your life." Before Will could say one single thing in his own defense, Susan hammered him with "Has it even occurred to you for one single second that there may be another reason why Angelina left that has nothing to do with her not loving you?"

When he didn't say anything, she said sternly, "Maybe you should stop wallowing in your own self-pity long enough to give it some thought."

"Don't bother mincing words. It's just my entire life we're talking about here."

"I know that. And that's why I'm trying to help you get things straight." She stood up and brushed the wrinkles out of her linen slacks. "You know what you need to do now, don't you?"

"Find Angelina."

"And?" Susan prompted.

"And love her forever."

His ex-wife leaned over and gave him a gentle kiss

on the cheek. "Although I'd suggest you take a quick shower first. You wouldn't want her to run away screaming when she smells you from across the room."

CHAPTER FOURTEEN

"WHAT TOOK YOU so long?" Krista said when Will barged into her Banks & Bidley law office in downtown Palo Alto.

"I take it you're not surprised to see me?"

"I take it you had a really important business meeting you couldn't get out of?"

It would have been impossible for Will to miss the sarcasm lacing her every word. "I was an idiot. But I'm here now."

His admission seemed to make Krista happy. "She's in New York."

"New York? Why?"

Krista shook her head. "You're going to have to figure that one out for yourself," she said, but she wrote *Wishing Lake* on a piece of paper and held it out to him.

"You're going to look great as the maid of honor," he said as he leaned across the table to give her a quick hug, then hightailed it out the door.

Krista swiveled in her chair to watch Will run out to his car and speed off. She sighed and thought about Derek, whom she hadn't been able to get out of her mind for the past few weeks. Even though he was a total nerd.

"Why can't I find my own CEO?" she muttered as she turned back to her latest case. "Heck, I'll even take a VP at this point." She smiled as she thought about her best friend and the man who obviously couldn't live without her. "He's right about one thing, at least. I'm gonna look *damn* good at their wedding."

THE FIVE-HOUR FLIGHT to New York gave Will plenty of time to think about his life. Way too much time, in fact, considering he was still trying to stay clear of anything too deep or painful. Hoping to keep himself occupied with some light reading during the flight, he reached for the stack of newspapers next to his seat.

Will soon comprehended his tactical error. His picture was on the front page of the *Wall Street Journal,* the *New York Times* and the *Financial Post.*

Playboy CEO Walks Out on Takeover Negotiations. Shareholders Are Outraged as PTI Stock Takes Its Biggest Dip Ever.

Tech Tycoon Leaves Company in Jeopardy.

CFO Alleges Illegal Activity at PTI. Will Scott, CEO, Implicated in Dirty Dealings.

"You've got to be kidding me." Will was hardly able to believe the headlines in the newsprint spread across the table before him. He waited for his brain to get into gear. He needed to work on a game plan for getting his company back on track.

"Come on," he urged himself when no inspiration was forthcoming. "There's got to be a good idea in that thick skull of yours."

He paced the small confines of his private plane, figuring that some movement was all he needed to get the blood going to his brain again. The only reason he had walked out on the negotiations in his boardroom was so that he could see Angelina. After that was taken care of, he was going to head right back into his office and throw himself wholeheartedly into running PTI again.

Will heard the little voice in his head taunting him. *Hey, buddy, you know you don't ever want to go back into that place. So why are you fighting it? You're too much of a sissy to be a painter, aren't you? You always loved the excuse that you couldn't be a painter because you needed the money. But now that you've got money, you're petrified to start painting.*

Will wondered if he was going crazy from lack of sleep.

If you go back into that office and keep playing CEO, you know what's going to happen to you, don't you?

He was responsible to his shareholders and…

You'd get that damn word responsible *gilded in gold if you could. That way you could run from ever having to feel anything again. You could just say, Oh, look at me. I'm so important and responsible for everyone.*

No. He didn't do that. Did he?

Why do you think your wife left you? Now you've got another chance at being happy, but you're gonna blow it, aren't you?

No. He was going to ask Angelina to marry him.

Now, isn't that sweet, the voice mocked. *Won't she be ever so happy playing the cute little wife to the big, fancy lady-killer CEO?*

Will finally saw the truth. She was going to hate it.

That's right, Einstein. So why don't you admit that you hate it, too?

But he didn't hate it. At least, he didn't hate everything about it.

Fine. Let me just ask you this. Would you rather be

*standing behind a canvas right now painting, or back
in the boardroom locked in for forty-eight hours?*

Will punched the backrest of the seat beside him.

"Sir?" The pilot opened the cockpit door and leaned
out, looking at him with concern. "Are you all right
back there?"

Will quickly composed himself and nodded. "Everything's fine, Charlie. Thanks for the smooth flight."
The pilot gave him a thumbs-up and closed the door
again, leaving Will alone with his thoughts.

He poured himself a glass of neat whiskey from the
bar. It was time to stop focusing on doing the "right"
thing all the time. Maybe all these years of being responsible simply for the sake of responsibility had been
a fool's game.

Will reached for the air phone and called Jerry, his
lead counsel, the only man he could trust to carry out
his extraordinary decision in a fair, objective fashion.

It took nearly thirty minutes to outline his plan for
stepping down as CEO of PTI and disbursing the bulk
of his owner's shares equitably among the coworkers
who had stuck with him through good times and bad.

He was about to hang up when Jerry said, "I'm proud
of you, kid. It's about time you learned that there's more
to life than running this company. I almost lost my
family about ten years back before I finally figured
out that they came first. Mind if I ask you what you're
going to do now that you're free?"

Will cleared his throat. "I'm going to win back the
woman I love and convince her to marry me, even
though I'm an idiot and don't deserve her."

"Ah," Jerry said, his voice full of memories. "Sounds
like true love to me. Beg if you have to, you hear?"

"I'll try and remember that."

"And one more thing," Jerry said.

"What's that?" Will asked, looking forward to any additional advice the wise older man had to give him.

"I've been thinking about those drawings you were doing. Boy, did they make me laugh. You should let more people see your talent."

ANGELINA DROPPED HER BAGS onto the knotty-pine floor of her new home. She breathed a sigh of relief that this lakefront cottage had a clear sense of comfort and well-being. Just being inside the house, she felt a small bit of contentment seep into her system.

In fact, as she walked around admiring the furniture and the artwork, she was reminded to a great degree of being in Will's mother's house. Needing to make the cottage seem like hers, even before the truck came with all of her belongings in the next couple of days, she wheeled her suitcase into the master bedroom to unpack a few pictures of her family and friends.

As she walked through the doorway into the large suite, she was stunned by the phenomenal view of the water before her...and she saw Will everywhere she looked.

"Give it some time, Ang," she told herself as she bent down to unzip her bag. "One day you'll be able to make it a whole five minutes without thinking about him."

She finished unpacking and decided to go for a walk along the lake. Maybe she'd even get up the nerve to go and see Joyce, even though she was still unsure about how she was going to explain her sudden move.

"Oh, well," she said as she laced up her tennis shoes. "I'll cross that bridge when I come to it."

Before she left the house, however, she did the one thing she should have done so many months ago. She went to the love-and-marriage corner of her new rental home and placed a small porcelain statue of a man and woman, entwined in their love for each other.

Feeling much more centered with just that small feng shui touch, she headed off the porch onto the white sandy beach that stretched all around the freshwater lake. She wasn't too surprised when her feet took her to the left, away from Joyce's cottage.

"It seems that my feet are cowards, too," she said, making fun of herself.

She didn't know how long she'd been walking before she found herself standing in front of the Ferris wheel. Several families and a lot of kids were at the amusement park, enjoying the rides. Angelina sat down on the same bench she had shared with Will to watch them play and have fun.

She held her hand over her still-flat stomach and whispered to the life growing inside her, "One day, you're going to be riding that roller coaster and coming home with pink hands."

Upon landing at the small airstrip by Wishing Lake, Will headed straight to his mother's house. He strolled in the front door without knocking, knowing it would be unlocked.

"Guess who?" he said, hoping to surprise his mother with his presence.

"So, you're finally here for her, huh?" Joyce replied

unceremoniously, not even bothering to pause as she added brushstrokes to her latest canvas.

The whole thing was so damn preposterous, he felt as if he was on the roller coaster at the carnival. "I stepped down as CEO this morning. It'll hit the news by tonight."

"And?" his mother prodded.

"And I'm going to start painting again."

Joyce pumped her fist by her side, like a pro basketball player after swishing a three-pointer. "Yes!"

Will grinned crookedly. "Glad to have your support, Mom."

Joyce pointed a finger at him. "Do you have some other good news to tell me, young man?"

"First you need to tell me where Angelina is."

"She's renting a cottage on the lake with an option to buy."

"You can't be serious." Will couldn't figure out why Angelina would have picked up, left California and rented a house on Wishing Lake within a span of just a few days.

"But she, uh…" Joyce said, stopping to clear her throat. "She doesn't exactly know that I was the person who leased it to her." At Will's confused look, she added, "Her friend Krista arranged all the details with me directly."

Standing in his grandparents' summer home, where he had spent so many perfect summers as a kid, he was more excited and nervous about seeing Angelina than he had ever been about anything else his whole life. He patted the box in his pocket and took a deep breath.

"Everything is going to be just fine, honey," his mother said, adding, "Now get out of here. You've done enough worrying and thinking already. It's time to win over a very important woman."

TAKING OFF at a blazing clip down the beach, Will headed toward the Ferris wheel that was just barely poking up through the trees on the other side of the lake. He was sure he'd find her there, in the special place where his heart had always been.

Winding past the food booths and the roller coaster, he caught sight of her silky hair blowing in the breeze as she handed her ticket to the man running the Ferris wheel. Increasing his pace to a run, he pushed past the teenagers in line and handed the man a twenty.

He barely had time to slide in next to Angelina before the gate for her seat shut.

"Will?" She put a hand over her heart in surprise. "What are you doing here?"

"Angelina. You're beautiful." He brushed his hand over her cheek. "I'm sorry I let my work take me away from you. But that won't ever happen again. I'm officially unemployed."

"What do you mean?"

"I stepped down from my company this morning."

"Are you joking?"

Will made a lightning-quick move and managed to catch both of her cold hands between his warm ones. "I've never been more serious about anything in my whole life."

Angelina closed her eyes and shook her head. "This can't be happening."

Will felt as if a piece of him had just died. "I want to be with you. I thought you wanted to be with me, too."

"I do, but once I tell you my secret you're going to

hate me forever and then you won't even have a company to go back to and then you're going to hate me even more."

Tucking his hand gently under her chin, he lifted her face to his. "Nothing you could say would ever make me hate you. I love you, Angelina. Don't you know that?"

Whatever impact Will thought his words of love would have on Angelina, it wasn't the new explosion of tears that slipped down her cheeks and onto their hands. He had no idea what to say to her, sensing somehow that it would be wiser to wait for her to tell him about the horrible thing that was eating her up inside.

She looked at him, her beautiful hazel eyes full of emotion. "I'm pregnant."

"Say that again?" He was unable to comprehend her words.

"I'm pregnant and I know you don't want to have a baby and I'm not asking you to act like a father, but I'm going to keep it and love it, and I hope you know I don't ever want any of your money."

"We're going to have a baby," Will whispered reverently, gazing at Angelina with sincere love in his eyes.

"You're not mad?"

"How could I be mad about the best news I've ever heard?"

"But Joyce said you had decided never to have—" she began, only to be cut off by an earth-shattering kiss.

Will captured Angelina's mouth in his and drank his fill of her. When they came up for air, he said, "I love you, Angelina, and I want to marry you and have lots and lots of babies together."

Angelina gaped at him, her mouth a tiny circle. "But what about your father?"

"It's taken me nearly thirty years to put that pain to rest. But with your love, I think I'm most of the way there." She was still staring at him as if she could hardly believe what she was hearing, and he said, "I'm not doing this right, am I?"

Still on the ride, he couldn't get down on one knee. But he didn't care. He needed to ask her now.

Right now.

"Angelina, will you marry me?"

Angelina was trying to catch her breath, which was impossible with everything spinning so fast. "What are you going to do without your company?"

"You know, we could probably discuss this later," he said, grinning at Angelina, falling more in love with her every second that passed, "but to answer your question, I'm going to paint."

Her eyes lit up for a moment, but then dimmed again. "I'm thrilled that you're going to paint, but you can't give up something you're passionate about. I saw how reverently you held those circuit boards in your office."

"You're right. I did have a dream to build a company, and it was great for a long time, but—"

Angelina cut him off. "I love you with all of my heart, Will. If you need me to be a corporate wife, I can do that. Please don't give up your dream for me."

Will rubbed his thumb over her lips. "You're the reason I'm daring to dream again. I'd rather play around doing chip design on the side than sit in boardrooms making executive decisions. But most of all, I'd rather take all that faith you have in me and try to paint again. Now it's your turn to promise me something."

"Anything," she whispered.

"I know how hard you work, honey, and how good you are at what you do. But I want you to promise me you'll take care of yourself. That you'll let me take care of you. For our baby, but mostly for yourself."

This time Angelina gave Will a loving kiss. "As soon as I found out I was pregnant, I realized that I needed to do what I'd been telling my clients to do. I promise you, I'm going to figure out how to balance my work with the rest of my life. With you. With our baby."

Will stole one more kiss. "Now that we've got all that figured out, I'd really like to hear your answer."

Angelina looked deep into Will's eyes. No matter how much she had tried to fight it, no matter how far she ran to escape it, she would love Will with all of her heart until the day she died.

"I love you, Will."

"And?" Will prompted her, his heart pounding wildly in his chest.

"Yes. I would love to marry you."

He finally remembered to pull the little box out of his pocket. "I almost forgot to give you this."

Angelina didn't want to leave his warm embrace, but the light blue box beckoned. Still safely ensconced in his arms, she took it from him and opened it up.

"Oh, my God, Will," she said, staring openmouthed at the incredible ring he had bought for her.

"Do you like it?" he asked, hope ringing in his voice.

She looked at him and laughed. "It's absolutely beautiful."

He slipped the four-carat ruby surrounded by six half-carat diamonds arranged on a simple gold band onto her left ring finger. "A jewel of fire, for a woman whose fire outshines everything else."

"Come here, my darling ex-tycoon," she whispered as she pulled his head down toward hers, "and you just might feel my flames licking at your skin."

And with that, Will let his entire soul be consumed by the woman he loved.

EPILOGUE

THE MEDIA WENT into overdrive once word about Will's resignation became public. They couldn't get enough information about his new painting career and the whirlwind engagement. To top it off, the article about Angelina in *Professional Woman* magazine hit the stands and the phones never stopped ringing. It was crazy for a few weeks, and Will and Angelina even considered following in her father's footsteps and eloping at city hall. Instead, with advice from Rose at The Rose Chalet, they managed to pull off a beautiful, romantic wedding surrounded by family and close friends. They were married on the beach, in front of his summer cottage in New York State. It was now their permanent home and it would always symbolize the place where they first fell in love.

Will's ex-wife, Susan, was overjoyed by their nuptials, and if anyone at the wedding was surprised by how well she got along with both the bride and groom, they didn't show it.

Angelina's father walked his daughter down the aisle, and he had tears in his eyes as he placed her hand in Will's. He and his new wife, Louise, watched his daughter with pride, overjoyed that, like themselves, she had finally found true love. Joyce, standing beside them, was constantly wiping away tears throughout the ceremony and reception. She was so proud of her son and she had so much to be happy about.

And Krista did, indeed, look fabulous as the maid of honor. Whether it had to do with the gorgeous dress she wore, or the glow she had from standing beside the handsome best man, Derek—who was looking at her in very meaningful ways—it was hard to tell.

* * * * *

**A no-nonsense female cop reluctantly
teams up with the one man who makes her
lose control in a deliciously sensual new novel
from *New York Times* bestselling author**

LORI FOSTER

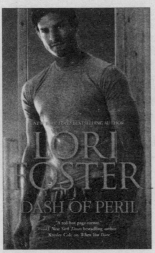

To bring down a sleazy
abduction ring, Lieutenant
Margaret "Margo" Peterson has
set herself up as bait. But recruiting
Dashiel Riske as her unofficial
partner is a whole other kind of
danger. Dash is 6'4" of laid-back
masculine charm, a man who loves
life—and women—to the limit.
Until Margo is threatened, and he
reveals a dark side that may just
match her own....

Beneath Margo's tough facade is a
slow-burning sexiness that drives
Dash crazy. The only way to finish
this case is to work together side
by side...skin to skin. And as their
mission takes a lethal turn, he'll have
to prove he's all the man she needs—in all the ways that matter....

Be sure to connect with us at:

Harlequin.com/Newsletters
Facebook.com/HarlequinBooks
Twitter.com/HarlequinBooks

www.Harlequin.com

PHLF857

Desire and loyalty collide in the riveting conclusion to *USA TODAY* bestselling author

KASEY MICHAELS's

series about the Redgraves—four siblings united by their legacy of scandal and seduction...

Punished for his father's crimes and scorned by society, fearless soldier Maximillien Redgrave fights to protect England. But his quest to restore his family's reputation is his own private battle. Trusting the irresistible young Zoe Charbonneau, whose betrayal destroyed his closest comrades and nearly unraveled his covert mission, is a mistake he intends never to repeat. So when the discovery of a smuggling ring compels him to embark on a voyage straight into danger, he's prepared for anything—except to find Zoe on his ship.

Believed to be a double agent for England and France, Zoe must clear her name in order to save her life. Convincing Max of her innocence seems impossible, until inescapable desire tempts them both to trust—and love—again. But a circle of enemies is closing in, and their time together might run out before they outrun danger....

Available wherever books are sold!

Be sure to connect with us at:
Harlequin.com/Newsletters
Facebook.com/HarlequinBooks
Twitter.com/HarlequinBooks

H HARLEQUIN® HQN™

™ www.Harlequin.com

PHKM860

Two classic stories from the *New York Times*
bestselling queen of romantic suspense

LISA JACKSON

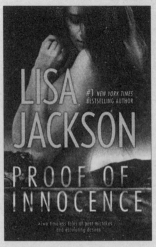

Yesterday's Lies

It's been five years since
Trask McFadden betrayed Tory's
trust, landing her father behind bars.
She'd hoped Trask was out of her
life forever, but now he's returned to
the Lazy W Ranch, claiming to have
discovered a clue that might prove
her father's innocence. For the sake
of her family, Tory's trying to forgive,
but she's finding it much harder to
forget when Trask's presence begins
to stir up feelings she'd thought
were long gone….

Devil's Gambit

Tiffany Rhodes's horse farm was
in trouble long before she met
Zane Sheridan, a breeder with a
shady reputation. Yet she can't help but feel relieved when Zane
offers to buy her out. Though Tiffany doesn't trust him, she's drawn
to him like a magnet. What does this mysterious man want from
her…and can she contain her desire long enough to find out?

Available wherever books are sold!

Be sure to connect with us at:

Harlequin.com/Newsletters

Facebook.com/HarlequinBooks

Twitter.com/HarlequinBooks

www.Harlequin.com

PHLJ877

From #1 *New York Times* bestselling author

NORA ROBERTS

come two classics about not letting your best-laid
plans get in the way of life *or* love.

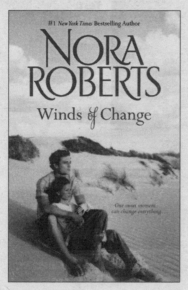

One sweet moment can change everything…

Be sure to connect with us at:

Harlequin.com/Newsletters
Facebook.com/HarlequinBooks
Twitter.com/HarlequinBooks

REQUEST YOUR
FREE BOOKS!

2 FREE NOVELS
FROM THE ROMANCE COLLECTION
PLUS 2 FREE GIFTS!

YES! Please send me 2 FREE novels from the Romance Collection and my 2 FREE gifts (gifts are worth about $10). After receiving them, if I don't wish to receive any more books, I can return the shipping statement marked "cancel." If I don't cancel, I will receive 4 brand-new novels every month and be billed just $6.24 per book in the U.S. or $6.74 per book in Canada. That's a savings of at least 22% off the cover price. It's quite a bargain! Shipping and handling is just 50¢ per book in the U.S. and 75¢ per book in Canada.* I understand that accepting the 2 free books and gifts places me under no obligation to buy anything. I can always return a shipment and cancel at any time. Even if I never buy another book, the two free books and gifts are mine to keep forever.

194/394 MDN F4XY

Name   (PLEASE PRINT)

Address   Apt. #

City   State/Prov.   Zip/Postal Code

Signature (if under 18, a parent or guardian must sign)

Mail to the Harlequin® Reader Service:
IN U.S.A.: P.O. Box 1867, Buffalo, NY 14240-1867
IN CANADA: P.O. Box 609, Fort Erie, Ontario L2A 5X3

Want to try two free books from another line?
Call 1-800-873-8635 or visit www.ReaderService.com.

* Terms and prices subject to change without notice. Prices do not include applicable taxes. Sales tax applicable in N.Y. Canadian residents will be charged applicable taxes. Offer not valid in Quebec. This offer is limited to one order per household. Not valid for current subscribers to the Romance Collection or the Romance/Suspense Collection. All orders subject to credit approval. Credit or debit balances in a customer's account(s) may be offset by any other outstanding balance owed by or to the customer. Please allow 4 to 6 weeks for delivery. Offer available while quantities last.

Your Privacy—The Harlequin® Reader Service is committed to protecting your privacy. Our Privacy Policy is available online at www.ReaderService.com or upon request from the Harlequin Reader Service.

We make a portion of our mailing list available to reputable third parties that offer products we believe may interest you. If you prefer that we not exchange your name with third parties, or if you wish to clarify or modify your communication preferences, please visit us at www.ReaderService.com/consumerschoice or write to us at Harlequin Reader Service Preference Service, P.O. Box 9062, Buffalo, NY 14269. Include your complete name and address.

ROM13R

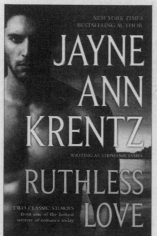

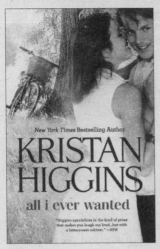